A Touch
of Autumn Gold

BY THE SAME AUTHOR

"Julie"
A captivating novel

With Rucksack and Bus Pass
Walking the Thames Path

Roots in Three Counties
Family history

A Touch
of Autumn Gold

Beverley Hansford

Matador
9 Priory Business Park
Kibworth Beauchamp
Leicestershire LE8 0RX, UK
Tel: (+44) 116 279 2299
Fax: (+44) 116 279 2277
Email: books@troubador.co.uk
Web: www.troubador.co.uk/matador

ISBN 978 1783060 702

British Library Cataloguing in Publication Data.
A catalogue record for this book is available from the British Library.

Edited by Helen Banks

Typeset in Bembo by Troubador Publishing Ltd
Printed and bound in the UK by TJ International, Padstow, Cornwall

Matador is an imprint of Troubador Publishing Ltd

This book is dedicated
to all those people in their later years
who are young in heart
and live their lives to the full.

Chapter 1

Old Bill Bellows leaned on his stick and gazed at the scene in front of him. It was a routine he carried out every morning. After buying his daily newspaper he would take a stroll along the short seafront before returning home, occasionally stopping to chat to anybody he met on the way who might be inclined to linger with him.

On this particular morning the beach in front of him was almost deserted. Just after breakfast and in mid-May, it was too early in the season for many beach-lovers to appear. Not that the little West Country town of Brillport received many visitors; not like when he had been a lad and the town had enjoyed its own railway station. In those days, crowds of holidaymakers from the Midlands had descended on the town each week. Now there was a supermarket where the station had once stood, and the crowds went to Spain for their holidays. Even the Grand Hotel relied on past glories. Business conferences and pensioners staying overnight on coach trips provided its main income these days.

He looked up at the sky. The clouds that had brought the overnight rain were quickly disappearing and the sun was beginning to dry things up. It was going to be a good day, he thought; perhaps he would do some gardening later on, his main interest since retirement.

As he pondered the idea, his attention was once again drawn to the beach. It was the woman walking alone who interested him. Not a young woman, he thought, but still quite sprightly. She walked with a moderate pace as if enjoying the feel of the sand beneath her bare feet. He guessed that she had joined the beach from one of the houses away to his right, once stately Victorian family homes, but now converted into holiday flats. He had observed her taking careful steps across the strip of shingle and stones to reach the firm sand left by the receding tide and then starting to walk towards the rocks at the far end of the beach. He assumed she was a holidaymaker going for an early morning stroll. He watched her stop and hesitate for an instant. He guessed the sand must be cold to walk on so early in the morning. Strange, he thought, the notions visitors had. See a beach, and they had to walk on it, never thinking of the temperature beneath their feet. But the woman obviously decided to continue with the punishment, because she immediately resumed walking.

Next, a man appeared who also intrigued Bill. He assumed from the man's sudden arrival that he had come from the Grand Hotel, which was just behind them. He passed quite close by. He's hardly dressed for the beach, thought Bill. The stranger's outfit consisted of a pair of crumpled cord trousers, an old tweed jacket and sturdy boots, making him look more like a walker than a beach-lover. Bill eyed him up. Like the woman, he was not a youngster: certainly retired, but a few years younger, Bill reckoned, than his own ripe age of eighty-four.

The stranger looked at Bill and issued a brisk but pleasant 'Good morning.'

'Good morning.' The reply was polite and cautious, but optimistic that there might be a chat in the making.

The man glanced at the brightening sky. 'It's going to be a good day,' he observed as he continued walking. Clearly he was not one to stop and chat.

'I reckon so,' said Bill.

The stranger passed beyond a comfortable talking distance and Bill watched as he walked across the sand in the same direction as the woman. Although she was a little distance in front, with his quicker pace the man would soon be overtaking her. Each of them left a clear set of footprints in the wet sand. Then he saw the space between the lines of prints begin to widen. The woman was now walking towards the sea, while the man was making for the steps in the rocky outcrop that led to the cliff footpath. Bill decided he had been correct. The woman was out for a morning stroll, while the man was a walker. Satisfied with his conclusions, Bill turned to continue on his way. As he took one last look at the beach, he saw the woman appear to stumble and then do a kind of hop to a nearby rock and sit down. The man abruptly changed his direction and went over to her.

'I say, are you all right?' The words were spoken with a tone of concern.

The woman looked up, slightly startled. She gave a small smile of reassurance.

'Oh yes, quite all right, thank you. It's just that I trod on something sharp.'

The man looked down at her foot, to which she was holding a tissue, and then turned his attention to where she had come from. He traced her steps for a few yards. It was easy to see where the pattern of footprints changed. He examined the sand for a few seconds.

'Ah, that's the culprit: a broken bottle almost hidden in the sand. Fortunately quite clean,' he announced, as he pulled the offending object loose and held it up.

She made a face. 'Oh dear. I never saw it. I just felt it. It was quite sharp and it's made my foot bleed a little.' She removed the tissue from her heel. It was stained red in places.

The man put his rucksack down on the rock beside her. 'Hold on a minute, I've got a first aid kit here somewhere.' He undid the straps of his rucksack and rummaged in its depths. 'Ah, got it. There are some plasters in there and some antiseptic wipes as well.' He placed the small green wallet on the rock beside her.

She smiled at him appreciatively. 'You're very well prepared. Were you in the Boy Scouts?' she asked.

He laughed. 'No. I learned my first aid in the army.'

'The army?'

'Yes, the Medical Corps… National Service… You know.' He grinned.

She smiled again. 'Oh yes, of course. My husband was in the Service Corps.'

He opened the first aid kit. 'There we are,' he announced.

The woman scanned the contents and then looked again at her foot. 'Well, if I could beg a plaster off you, I would very much appreciate that.'

He nodded in agreement. 'Help yourself to anything you want.' He glanced at her foot again. 'I think I would wash off any sand that might be around the wound first,' he advised.

'Do you think this water is clean?' she asked, looking at the pool of water at the base of the rock she was sitting on.

'Oh yes, it's only seawater left by the tide a few hours ago. This part of the beach will be covered at high tide.'

She dipped her foot in the water and splashed the sole. 'Ow! It's cold!' she exclaimed.

The task she was engaged in gave the man a few moments to study her. She was, he guessed, somewhere around his own age of sixty-nine – perhaps a bit younger. Her blonde hair was tinged with grey, but it rather suited her, he thought. Though casually dressed, she had an air of elegance about her, and her toenails were painted a delicate shade of pink. He liked to see an older woman well groomed.

'A good thing I had a tetanus injection quite recently,' she remarked thoughtfully as she swung herself back into a more comfortable position and started to dry her foot with another tissue. She glanced up at him. 'I do a bit of gardening, and I cut myself a few months back,' she explained.

'It's always a good idea to have a tetanus injection after a garden cut,' he said.

She turned her attention to the first aid kit. 'Now, perhaps a wipe and a plaster. It looks worse than it is, I think.'

'Of course. Here we are.' He sorted out the two required items and held them out. 'Can I help?'

'Oh, I think I can manage.' She looked up at him and smiled again, a rather pleasant little smile, as she took the wipe and the plaster. It only took a few minutes for her to dress her foot, and she did so in silence, intent on the job in hand. As she smoothed the plaster, she spoke again. 'That's it, almost as good as new, thanks to your help.' She stood up, carefully testing her weight on the damaged foot.

'I'd put my shoes on again if I were you,' he suggested, 'just in case the plaster tries to come off.'

She made a wry face. 'I didn't bring any. The flat we're renting has an access directly onto the beach. There didn't seem to be any point in carrying my sandals.'

'Perhaps I can give you a hand back,' he offered.

'Oh, that's very kind of you, but I'll manage fine. It's not very far.'

She held out her hand and once again she smiled pleasantly. 'Thank you very much for your help. If I hadn't seen you I would have had to hop back to the flat.' She laughed.

He grasped her hand. 'Glad I was able to help. I'm John Hammond.'

'I'm Debbie Patterson.' She held his hand lightly, looking at him with that little smile. As she released her grip she asked: 'Are you on holiday, John?'

'Yes, that's right. I came down yesterday for a week, just to do some walking and hopefully take some photos. Photography is my hobby,' he added.

'Oh, how interesting! There's plenty of scope round here for taking pictures.' She enhanced her statement with a nod towards the nearby cliffs.

He nodded in agreement. 'Yes, I thought I would try the cliff path this morning. The weather forecast is good for today.'

'I've not been that way. I must try it sometime.' She followed his gaze to the steps cut into the cliff leading up to the coastal path.

He prepared to leave, but hesitated as if a bit reluctant; as if he wished to extend their brief meeting.

'Are you on holiday as well, Debbie?' he asked, scrutinising her a little.

She smiled and glanced quickly at her blouse and slacks. 'Yes, I came down here a week ago with a friend, but unfortunately yesterday she had to return home. A sudden death in the family.'

'That's sad, and also unfortunate for you.'

'Yes, it is, but these things do happen.'

'What's the weather been like?' he asked, perhaps to change the subject.

'Hmm, a bit unreliable. Yesterday was the best day so far.' The reply was accompanied by a quick look at the sky, and a grimace.

He hesitated a few seconds as if trying to think of something else to say.

She broke the brief silence between them. 'Well, I mustn't keep you from your walk. Once again, thank you for your medical care.' She smiled at him as she prepared to leave, carefully testing her foot on the sand.

'Perhaps I'll bump into you again during the week.' He returned her smile.

'Oh, I expect that's quite likely. Brillport isn't a very large place,' she replied breezily.

'Goodbye for now, then.' He picked up his rucksack and prepared to sling it over his shoulders.

'Goodbye. And thank you again for your help.' And with that she was gone.

He watched her for a few seconds as she made her way back in the direction of the town, walking slowly and carefully, attempting not to put her injured foot completely on the sand. Then he continued his walk, turning his attention to the steps a short distance away, and the notice 'TO THE CLIFF PATH'.

He concentrated on climbing the steep and uneven steps until he was halfway to the top of the high cliffs that dominated the coastline at that point. Then he decided it was time to take a breather and admire the view. With a photographer's eye he surveyed the scene, searching for that elusive shot. Then he turned his attention to the beach. He could see Debbie making her way slowly back to the town. He saw her stop and turn to look in his direction. He wondered if she would see him if he waved. He decided to try. She waved back and then carried on walking.

Chapter 2

Debbie woke to the sound of rain beating on the window panes. It was one of those mornings when initially sleep patterns dominate, and at first she was unable to recollect where she was. Then her memory quickly returned.

She was in the bedroom of the holiday flat she had rented for two weeks with Madge. It was the second night she had spent there alone, since her holiday companion had departed for home so suddenly.

She lay there listening to the wind driving the rain against the window. She could see the outline of the window quite clearly, but the rain and heavy clouds made daylight slow to establish itself. She turned the bedside light on and looked at her watch. The hands showed that it was nearly seven o'clock. It was around her normal rising hour, but today she was happy to linger in the rare indulgence of just lying back and doing nothing, letting her thoughts wander where they would.

Her musing brought back the memories and events of the previous day. When she had decided to walk on the beach, it had been a desire perhaps stimulated by childhood memories and stirred into action by the simple fact that while she was with Madge it was something she would not do. Madge had little interest in the beach other than the view it provided.

The steps leading down from the patio had provided easy access to the beach. It was one of the advertised features of the ground-floor flat that the beach could be reached via a locked gate and a dozen or so steps. Once she was on the beach, there had been a strip of shingle and sharp stones to navigate, but with the expectation of firm sand beyond. The awaited pleasure had been short-lived. So early in the morning and still wet from the receding tide, the sand had not been all that comfortable to walk on. Within a couple of minutes her feet had been cold. She had toyed with the idea of returning to the flat and securing the comfort of a pair of sandals, but had changed her mind. No, she would persevere and fulfil her original intention to walk to the outcrop of rocks and back. It wasn't that far. She had been conscious of an old man standing on the short bit of promenade away to her left, watching her.

She had almost reached her goal when she felt a sharp stab on the heel of her right foot. At the sight of the blood seeping from the wound she had been alarmed that the cut might be a deep one.

The sound of a voice had startled her. She had been unaware that anybody else was on the beach. She had looked up to see a man of about her own age standing a few yards away, dressed in a rather shabby jacket and cord trousers. He had a pleasant face and the mop of grey hair suited him. It was his look of concern that had prompted Debbie to accept his offer of help. Normally she might have hurriedly refused assistance in such a situation, but there was something calm and caring about him.

Looking back, she had rather enjoyed their brief meeting. She would have liked to chat longer with him, but courtesy had pushed her into ending the interlude.

She had hobbled back to the flat before venturing into the town to purchase a few first aid supplies, just in case. The afternoon had been spent sitting in one of the chairs on the patio, enjoying the sunshine and reading her book, her injured foot propped up on a chair. She had ended the day completely bored with her own company, particularly since she was away from her home surroundings.

The light coming in through the window stirred Debbie from her musing. She decided to get up and have a cup of tea. That turned into breakfast as she made some toast and ate it sitting in one of the easy chairs in the sparely furnished sitting room, watching the clouds scudding across the sky. The grey sea was now topped by a mass of white-capped waves, and the rain beat down on the patio, whipped about by the unyielding wind. It was a dismal prospect for any early morning walk. Debbie had hoped to try out her injured foot to see how it felt, but that prospect was completely out.

It was after ten when she managed to venture out. The rain had eased a little but the wind was still blowing quite strongly. Desperation to escape from the claustrophobic flat and the desire to have some fresh air made the decision for her. She would brave the weather. She would wear her plastic hooded mackintosh. An umbrella would be useless in that wind.

Before setting off on the five-minute walk to Brillport's short high street, she was concerned that her injured heel might still be painful to walk on, but she was pleasantly surprised to find that things were not too bad. She could still feel it, but walking wasn't too much of a problem.

She was unsure whether any shops would be open on a Sunday morning, but in the high street she found the post office open with newspapers for sale. She went in and purchased the *Sunday Telegraph* and a bottle of badly needed milk. She had used the last in her breakfast tea.

Once outside the shop again, she found herself in a quandary. The weather frowned on a proper walk, yet a return to the flat with even the newspaper for company was not immediately appealing. She decided to walk along the narrow promenade that faced the sea immediately behind and parallel to the high street. It was reached by a short alleyway between two shops. Once there, she questioned the wisdom of her decision. In the high street there had been some shelter from the breeze, but out on the promenade she received the full buffeting of the wind blowing in from the sea. She was about to consider turning back to the comparative comfort of the high street when she noticed a welcoming sign: 'Beach Café'. The premises appeared to be open and the prospect of a coffee and a chance to get out of the wind was inviting.

As soon as she opened the door she saw him. John Hammond was sitting at one of the tables engrossed in a newspaper spread out in front of him. He was the only occupant of the small café. The breeze from the door as Debbie entered the room made him look up. Recognition immediately lit up his face.

'Good morning, Debbie,' he said. His greeting was accompanied by a friendly smile.

'Good morning, John.' Debbie lifted her mackintosh hood from her head. 'Whew! What a day!'

John nodded. 'Not very encouraging weather, is it? But it's due to fine up this afternoon.'

'Well, that's good news.' Debbie smiled politely at him and then glanced at the counter at the end of the room. There was the smell of coffee in the air. 'I must get myself a hot drink,' she said. He watched her walk to the counter.

A young girl emerged from the kitchen behind. She gave Debbie a disinterested look. 'Can I help you?' The tone of the voice was as enthusiastic as her expression.

'Yes. I'd like a coffee, please.' Debbie smiled at her.

'Espresso?' the girl asked, reaching for a mug.

'No, just plain filter, please,' replied Debbie.

The girl filled the mug and placed it on the counter. 'Anything else?'

Debbie shook her head. 'No, that will do nicely, thank you.'

'One pound fifty. There's milk and sugar on the table.'

Debbie paid for her coffee and the girl immediately disappeared into the kitchen. Pop music could be heard in the background. Debbie picked up the mug and looked around for a desirable table to sit at. John had been watching her. He quickly collected his newspaper together and called across to her.

'I say, do come and join me,' he invited.

'Thank you.' Debbie walked towards him and placed her mug of coffee on the table. She glanced around the café again as she took off her mackintosh and hung it on the back of a chair. Then she gave John her full attention as she sat down at the table.

John grinned at her and spoke in a low voice. 'Our hostess isn't very friendly, is she?'

Debbie looked towards the counter and kitchen. 'I suppose it must be a pretty dull job for a young girl,' she said thoughtfully.

John nodded in agreement, and then asked: 'How's the damaged foot this morning?'

Debbie smiled at him. 'It's beginning to heal up beautifully thanks to your prompt medical care. I didn't do much after I got back yesterday – just rested and read my book. I was afraid it might be painful to walk on this morning, but it isn't too bad really.' She poured a little milk into her coffee. 'I just had to get out for a walk this morning. The flat is rather small and it can get a bit claustrophobic after a while.'

'Yes, I know the feeling. If you're an active person, you just have to get out and about after a while.'

'How did your day go yesterday?' asked Debbie.

'Oh, I had a great time. I walked about three miles along the cliffs, took some interesting photographs as well and in the afternoon I went to a cricket match here in the town.'

Debbie tested her coffee. 'My husband used to like watching cricket,' she remarked thoughtfully.

John was about to reply, but she spoke again suddenly.

'Where are you staying, John?' It didn't seem to be a casual enquiry. She looked genuinely interested.

'The Grand Hotel.'

Debbie's eyes lit up in recognition. 'Oh yes, I know it. We had dinner there one evening last week. It looked a nice place to stay.'

'Yes, it's got quite an old-fashioned air about it.'

Debbie sipped her coffee again. John took the opportunity to ask another question. 'Have you stayed in Brillport before?'

Debbie shook her head. 'No, this is my first visit, but my friend Madge, who I came down with, has been here several times. I think I mentioned yesterday that unfortunately, last Friday she had to return home. Her brother died suddenly.'

'Yes, that must have been a shock.' He looked at Debbie intently.

'It was, actually. He was only sixty. And he hadn't been ill or anything.' She glanced down at her coffee and then looked up again,

11

speaking more softly. 'He was her younger brother and I think they were quite close. The only other relative is an aged aunt. That's why Madge had to rush away. We'd booked the flat for a fortnight, so I said I'd stay on for the rest of the holiday. I spend quite a bit of time on my own, so it doesn't matter.'

'I know what you mean,' replied John. Her comment had partly answered the question that had been on his mind. Clearly she was either a widow or divorced.

It was Debbie who spoke next. 'How about you, John? Have you been to Brillport before?'

He thought for a second. 'Gosh, it must be over twenty-five years since I was here last. We came down a couple of times for a holiday when my son was small. It's changed quite a bit in that time.'

Debbie returned to her coffee. For a couple of seconds she seemed to be deep in thought. Then she spoke again. 'Since my husband died, I haven't gone in for holidays to any great extent. I think it's partly because being on your own makes you a bit of an outsider in a crowd.' She looked at him, as if searching for confirmation.

John nodded enthusiastically. 'I know exactly what you mean. Being on your own on holiday can be a lonely experience. Just after my wife died, I went on several coach tours, thinking at least I would be part of a group, but I found the same thing. It would be mostly couples and even if you got on well with one of them, you felt a bit of a third party.'

Then Debbie asked: 'Where do you live?'

Again he could tell that her question was one of interest rather than curiosity. 'Reading.'

Her eyes lit up again. 'That's not so far from me. I live in Oxford.'

'We moved to Reading from Croydon when my son was quite small, and we stayed there, partly because it was convenient for Rob's education. I commuted to London to work.'

'What was your job?'

'I was an accountant, for my sins. Rob has followed my example. Must run in the family.' He laughed.

12

'My husband was an accountant when I met him,' she remarked thoughtfully. 'Then he became financial director of Brightstone. Do you know it?'

John nodded. 'I know of it.' Brightstone was a pretty big civil engineering outfit, he remembered.

'Have you always lived in Oxford?' He wanted to know more about her.

Debbie shook her head immediately. 'No. I was brought up in London. We moved to Oxford when our daughters were quite small, and we stayed. A bit like you in Reading really.' She looked at him knowingly.

'How many daughters do you have, Debbie?'

She smiled. 'Two. The eldest, Jan, is married with a small son, and the youngest, Trish, well, she doesn't seem to be in any hurry to get married.'

'I would have liked to have a daughter,' John remarked thoughtfully.

'Have you just the one son?' Debbie enquired tactfully.

John nodded. 'Yes. After Mary had Rob, we were advised by the doctors not to have any more children.'

Debbie detected a shade of sadness in his reply. 'You would have enjoyed having a daughter,' she said sympathetically.

After a pause, she asked: 'Do you live on your own, John?'

He nodded again. 'Yes. I lost my Mary seven years ago.'

'Oh. I'm sorry.' Debbie would have commiserated further, but she could see that he wanted to continue.

He looked down at the table. 'It all happened quite quickly. She started to feel unwell and had a check-up and they diagnosed cancer. She died two months later.' He glanced up at Debbie as he finished speaking.

'So sudden. That's very sad,' replied Debbie. 'Just at the time when a married couple can be looking forward to spending more time together.'

'Absolutely. We had been making plans for our retirement.'

13

There were a couple of seconds of silence between them, John taking a sip of coffee and Debbie wondering whether she should relate her experience of losing a partner. It was something she didn't talk about a lot, but somehow it seemed the right thing to do now. 'Ron, my husband, died suddenly, too,' she said, looking at John. 'He went off to work one morning. He gave me a goodbye kiss and waved to me from the car as he drove away. He always did that.' She gave a little sigh. 'A couple of hours later I got a telephone call. He had collapsed at work. I rushed to the hospital, but it was too late. He died before I could get to him. He'd had a massive heart attack, the doctors told me.'

John had been listening intently. His sympathetic reply reflected his recognition of her experience. 'It's an awful shock when it happens like that.'

Debbie gave a brief nod of agreement. 'Yes, it is. I had to appear strong for the girls' sake, but it took me a long time to get over it.'

John drank the last of his coffee. 'How did they cope with the loss of their father?' he asked.

Debbie thought for a moment. 'Jan seemed to cope quite well, but Trish was extremely upset. She was very much a Daddy's girl.'

John studied her for a few moments. She was quite a cheerful person, he had noticed – almost bubbly at times, in fact. But he had detected a tiny degree of sadness when she related the death of her husband. He decided to change the subject and bring their conversation back to lighter matters. 'So what made you choose Brillport for your holiday?' he enquired.

'It was Madge's suggestion really. She asked me to join her, so I thought, oh well, why not?' Debbie's cheerful countenance had reappeared.

John was about to ask her another question, when a sudden ray of sunshine briefly shone into the café. While they had been chatting the weather had changed.

Debbie reacted immediately. 'I do believe it's stopped raining!' she exclaimed.

John smiled. 'The weather forecast was right,' he observed.

14

Debbie pushed her mug away from her, indicating that her coffee break was over. She didn't want to appear rude, but at the same time she didn't want to hinder John. 'Well, I'd better be making a move,' she said, rising from her chair and taking hold of her mackintosh. 'Thank you for the chat,' she said, giving John a pleasant smile.

'It was a pleasure. I enjoyed talking to you.' He meant it.

They moved to leave the café together. The girl behind the counter watched them go, but said nothing. Once they were outside Debbie noticed her go over to their table to collect the dirty mugs.

Though it had stopped raining, it was still blowing hard and the isolated ray of sunshine had already disappeared behind the clouds. Debbie glanced up at the sky. 'Well, I hope that bit of sunshine was a promise of better things to come. At least it's stopped raining,' she said, laughing.

John looked at her enquiringly. 'I was wondering...' he began nervously. He regained his courage. 'I was wondering if you were doing anything this afternoon. There's a manor house not far from here. It's quite interesting – they even have a minstrels' gallery and a... and a tea room,' he added quickly. 'I've got my car here. I was thinking of having a look at it. I was wondering if you'd like to join me,' he suggested hopefully.

Debbie hesitated for a few seconds and then gave him a rather coy smile. 'I'd love to,' she replied.

'Can I pick you up somewhere?' John asked enthusiastically

Debbie smiled at him. 'I can walk round to your hotel. It's not far from where I'm staying. About what time?'

'How about quarter past two?'

'Quarter past two it is. I'll see you then. Goodbye for now, John.' She gave him a brief smile before turning to leave.

Chapter 3

Debbie hurried back to the flat. For one thing she didn't want to walk too long on her injured foot, and it also occurred to her that she would have to make some sort of meal for herself before meeting John for their afternoon outing. On top of that the thought of spending ten minutes with the newspaper she had purchased and catching up on the news if she had time was also appealing.

Back in the flat she quickly changed into her dressing gown. She was surprised how damp her slacks had got during her morning excursion in the rain, and her sandals were decidedly wet. She put both items in the kitchen to dry off and then decided to have a quick look at the newspaper before lunch.

She sat down in the chair beside the French window looking out onto the patio. From here she could observe the changing weather. Though it was not perfect it had vastly improved since the early morning. Now patches of blue sky intermingled with the clouds allowed frequent bursts of sunshine. It looked promising. She glanced at the newspaper on her lap but scarcely absorbed its contents. Instead she allowed her eyes to wander round the room. A three-piece suite long past its prime, together with a dining table and four chairs, completed the main furnishing. The shabby sparsity was reflected in the bedroom. Two beds, a wardrobe and a dressing table were all that was considered necessary. Debbie had been disappointed in the flat immediately she had entered it. She had found its drab functionality a bit depressing after the cosy comfort of her own home. It was Madge who had booked the accommodation and Madge appeared to be happy with her holiday surroundings. Out of politeness Debbie had kept her feelings to herself.

It had been much the same with the holiday. She had made the mistake of going away with someone of a completely different outlook. In fact, on reflection she knew very little about her companion. Madge had been the older sister of Debbie's school friend Amy. Debbie had kept in touch with Amy with the odd letter and Christmas cards. Then a few years previously Amy had died. Debbie had encountered Madge again at the funeral and had been surprised to learn that she lived fairly close to Oxford. Since then Madge had made a point of dropping in unexpectedly to see Debbie when she was in town for something or other.

When Madge had suggested that Debbie accompany her on holiday, Debbie had had reservations. Instinct had told her that she had very little in common with Madge. It was Jan who had persuaded her. 'Mum, why don't you?' she had said. 'You know, after that bout of flu you really need a restful break somewhere.' In the end Debbie had agreed to go.

Within the first few days she realised it had been a mistake. Madge wanted to tear around everywhere in her 4x4, scarcely spending any time looking at things. Meals were generally snacks in a pub or café, and any kind of dressing up was out. Madge preferred to drape her muscular frame in baggy trousers and tops, with the result that Debbie had felt overdressed even wearing a skirt. The menial tasks such as food preparation and washing up had usually fallen on Debbie's shoulders, and at times Madge had exhibited a tendency to be bossy, perhaps a legacy from her career in the army.

A sudden burst of sunshine flooding the room with light roused Debbie from her meandering thoughts. She glanced at her watch. Time and the morning had slipped by. If she was to be ready by two o'clock, there was hardly time to make a meal for herself. Oh well. She would make do with the tin of soup she had bought the previous day.

She made her way to the tiny kitchen. This necessitated going through the hall corridor, which also served the two flats upstairs. Both she and Madge had quickly realised that it was necessary to be respectably dressed before leaving the bedroom to visit the bathroom or any of the flat's other rooms.

17

As Debbie emerged from the living room, the front door opened and one of the guests from upstairs entered the hall. She was carrying two bulging plastic bags, one of which looked as if it might collapse at any minute. She looked at Debbie for a second and then greeted her. 'Good morning, dear. Phew! It's such long way to the town. I should have taken the car.'

'Good morning, Betty.' Debbie did not respond to her neighbour's other comment. She found the five-minute walk to the high street quite a pleasant one, but perhaps Betty's overweight accounted for her opinion.

'I just had to go out to get Henry's newspaper and something for our dinner,' Betty remarked, moving towards the stairs. She glanced at Debbie's dressing gown and continued her chat. 'Just got up, dear? I expect you miss your friend.' She smiled knowingly.

'No, I went out earlier and got wet,' explained Debbie.

'We had a lie-in today,' said Betty. 'Henry likes to take things easy on Sundays.' She leaned over the banisters in Debbie's direction and then almost whispered: 'I think we'll go home tomorrow morning. Henry has an important meeting on Tuesday and I don't like it here. It's too quiet for me.'

Debbie smiled sympathetically. 'Enjoy the rest of your day.'

Betty continued climbing the stairs. Her reply was a bit stifled by the effort of carrying her bags. 'Oh, I will, dear. And you too.'

Debbie continued to the kitchen. She smiled to herself. Her neighbours were an odd couple. From the brief encounters she had had with them over the last week they appeared to be ill suited to each other. Both were middle-aged. Henry appeared to be well educated and a quiet studious man. Betty on the other hand was extremely extrovert, tended to overdress and made no secret of her humble background. It occurred to Debbie that with them leaving she would be on her own in the house, as the top flat was unoccupied. She dismissed the thought. She lived in a house on her own when she was at home. Now where had she seen that tin-opener?

John must have been looking out for Debbie, because as soon as she came through the swing doors he emerged from the lounge. He had changed into a pullover and slacks and carried a camera bag over his shoulder. He walked towards her, hand outstretched.

'Hello again.' His greeting was accompanied by a cheery smile.

'Hello.' Debbie shook his hand. 'I'm not late, am I?' she asked, a bit anxiously. 'I wasn't quite sure how long it would take me to walk here.'

He smiled at her again. 'Absolutely bang on time.'

'I'm all ready.' Debbie indicated the handbag draped over her shoulder. 'I've got my camera, a plastic mac in case it rains, and a spare plaster – just in case.' She looked at John and laughed. She had changed into a neat pair of red slacks complemented by a white blouse under a short jacket, and a pair of white slip-on shoes. The outfit suited her, he thought.

'How's the foot? Will you be able to walk OK?' he enquired. There would be a fair bit of walking and standing that afternoon.

Debbie considered the question. 'Well,' she replied cautiously, 'I can still feel it when I put weight on that area, but I'm sure it's all right really.'

'Great. Let's go, then.' John turned to the entrance and allowed his free arm to encircle Debbie without actually touching her, as if to lead her.

Debbie allowed herself to be guided. She thanked him as he held the door open for her. Once outside, they were bathed in sunshine. John glanced up at the blue sky. 'Ah!' he exclaimed. 'Sunshine as promised.'

'It's lovely now,' Debbie remarked. 'But it's a bit breezy,' she added, patting her hair and looking up at the puffy clouds now racing across the sky.

John chuckled. 'March winds in May,' he suggested. 'But at least the rain has gone.'

They quickly reached his car. He used the remote sensor to unlock the doors as they approached it.

'I have a little car, but mine still has to be locked with a key,' Debbie commented, watching his action and hearing the thud of the locks being released.

John laughed. 'It takes a bit of getting used to. When I first got this car, I kept wanting to use the key to unlock or lock it,' he admitted.

Debbie slipped into the front seat and clicked the seat belt into place. 'You're very brave driving all this way on your own,' she said. 'I don't think I'd have the courage to do it.'

John started the engine and reversed the Ford Focus out of the parking space. 'I took it steady and stopped a couple of times for a break. I don't really drive enough since I retired. Sometimes I think it's a waste of money having a car, but it does come in handy at times.'

'I only use mine for shopping and that sort of thing,' remarked Debbie.

'My flat is only a few minutes' walk from the shops,' said John, 'so it's quite convenient for me to walk and get some exercise at the same time.'

'Have you always lived there on your own?' Debbie asked, eager to know a little bit more about her companion.

John nodded. 'Yes. After Mary died, I found the house a bit too large for me. Rob was already married with a home of his own, so I sold up and moved into the flat.' He paused as he turned off the main road, and then continued. 'I was extremely lucky. It really is a very nice flat in what the estate agents describe as a sought-after area. And all the residents are retired people,' he concluded.

Debbie paused for an instant before making a reply, as if in thought. 'I still live in the family home,' she commented, adding after another pause: 'I expect one of these days it will become too big for me to manage. The girls keep on to me to sell up and move, but I don't see why I should while I can still deal with everything.'

Their conversation was brought to a brief halt. They were suddenly confronted by a sheet of storm water across the road. It was single-line traffic through the water, and they had to wait for two other cars to make their way through the obstruction.

'It's all the rain we've had since yesterday,' commented John.

'I know,' said Debbie. 'It rained heavily during the night. I woke up several times and heard it.'

They negotiated the water and drove on for a few more miles, and then the entrance to their destination appeared: a wide, sweeping drive with a lodge and iron gates that stood wide open. A signboard informed visitors that this was Pellworth Manor, open every day 2–5.30pm. They bumped over a cattle grid and made their way along the tree-lined drive. It took no more than two minutes or so before the manor itself appeared, an imposing Elizabethan-style building surrounded by a moat.

'Oh, isn't it picturesque? I shall have to get a photograph of it!' exclaimed Debbie.

'It's such a long time since I was last here that I'd almost forgotten how impressive it was,' remarked John.

They followed the directions to the car park. It was already half full.

'It seems quite popular,' observed Debbie.

'I think it is. There's even a glossy brochure now. I picked one up at the hotel.' John parked the car neatly between two others and pulled on the handbrake.

Once out of the car, they followed the footpath with its sign 'To the House'. At the front door a notice indicated 'House and Garden: Adults £5.00, Children £2.00, Concessions £4.00'. John was already reaching for his wallet.

'Oh no, please let me pay,' protested Debbie, frantically delving into her bag for her purse. Oh, why did it always have to go right to the bottom, underneath everything else? John beat her to it. By the time she had retrieved her purse, he was already at the small table in the entrance hall where a pleasant-looking woman sat with a cash box.

'Two concessions, please,' requested John, placing a ten-pound note on the table.

'I pay for the tea then,' said Debbie.

'Excellent compromise,' announced John with a grin as he pocketed the change.

They joined the little group of people waiting for a guided tour of the house. They were in an impressive hall with panelled walls and a graceful staircase leading upwards. After a few minutes a middle-aged woman joined them and then led the way round the house, explaining that the manor dated back to the fifteenth century and that during the Civil War the owner had sided with the King and the house had been burnt down by Cromwell's army. Later on, the family fortunes had revived and the mansion had been rebuilt in the present grand style. Works of art had been acquired by subsequent generations of the family. One of the bedrooms had a gigantic four-poster bed.

'Have you ever slept in one?' John whispered to Debbie.

'Just once, a long time ago, on my honeymoon,' Debbie replied softly, as if remembering something. 'Have you?'

John shook his head. 'No,' he said simply.

His brief answer made Debbie wish she hadn't been so insensitive in her reply, but it was too late now. Everybody was moving on and leaving the room.

It was almost four o'clock when the tour of the house ended in the huge dining area with its minstrels' gallery. From here visitors were let out from the house by a side door.

'Shall we have tea, or shall we have a look at the garden first?' John asked.

Debbie thought for a moment. 'Let's look at the garden first and then we can sit down and enjoy our tea,' she proposed.

'Good idea.'

The obvious enthusiasm in his reply made Debbie glad she had suggested it. That way they would have more time to chat. She was eager to learn more about her companion.

They walked around the well-laid-out garden. Debbie clearly knew more about flowers than John did. At one point he asked her: 'Do you do a lot of gardening?'

'A fair amount,' she replied. 'I've got quite a sizeable garden, but I have a man come in to do the heavy work like digging and mowing the lawn.'

'Do you grow any vegetables?' John enquired, thinking it would be a subject he knew more about.

'Oh yes, I've got some runner beans in the greenhouse ready to go out, and some tomatoes as well.' Debbie's reply was brimming with enthusiasm.

John glanced at her. He found it hard to imagine her petite frame in gardening gear, but clearly there was another side to her.

'How about things like potatoes? Do you grow those?' he asked.

'Tom, the man who helps me in the garden, gives me a hand with those, and we share the harvest,' she replied, adding as an afterthought: 'Last year we had a bumper crop. I'm still eating them.'

'Fantastic!' he enthused. Then he announced: 'I've got an allotment.'

Debbie's surprised reply was tinged with amusement and reproach. 'Hey, I've been bumbling on about gardening, and you're doing it big time. I bet you're an expert.'

John laughed. 'Not really,' he replied. 'You should have heard what Mary used to say about my gardening efforts. I never used to be able to tell whether something was a weed or whether it was meant to be there.'

Debbie was about to say that sometimes it was difficult to tell the difference, but before she could John spoke again.

'I do like my allotment,' he remarked thoughtfully. 'It gets me out in the fresh air and there is a bit of a social side to it as well.'

'And the produce to enjoy,' Debbie interjected.

He grinned. 'Of course,' he agreed. 'And last year I won the best marrow competition.'

'There you are!' Debbie exclaimed. 'You are an expert.'

They continued to wander round, finding a common interest in the walled vegetable garden. On their way to the tea room, Debbie stopped to take a photograph of the house. When she had finished, she rejoined John, who stood a few feet away also busily engaged with photography. She waited until he had taken a picture and then was intrigued to see him looking at the back of the camera.

'It's digital, isn't it?' she asked.

John glanced up. 'That's right. I haven't had it that long, but this trip I wanted to try and take some unusual photographs for the next competition in the camera club I belong to. The pattern of the timberwork on the house is rather interesting. Have a look.' He held the camera towards her.

Debbie stared at the tiny screen. 'That's really good!' she exclaimed.

'And the best bit, of course,' remarked John, 'is that if you don't like the result, you can delete the photograph and start again.'

'But what about the film?' Debbie asked, somewhat mystified.

John smiled. 'There is no film,' he explained. 'You have a memory card. Look, I'll show you.' He opened a little door in the camera and carefully slid out a tiny card.

Debbie was intrigued. She looked at the card and then enquiringly at John. 'How long do they last?'

'Ages, if they're looked after.' John replied, still smiling slightly at her puzzlement.

'And how many pictures can you take with a card?'

John was quite eager to enlighten her. 'It depends on a lot of things,' he explained. 'How the camera is set up, the type of picture you take – and the cards have various capacities. This one will take about seventy shots,' he added, replacing the card in the camera.

'Phew.' Debbie was still trying to get her head round the technology. 'But don't you need a computer?'

John shook his head. 'It's not essential. You can have the photos printed out from the card in a photographic shop, or these days you can get a little machine that will do the job for you.'

Debbie appeared to be speaking her thoughts as she replied. 'I know my son-in-law Paul has a digital camera, but he's also a wizard with computers. That's his job.' She pondered for a few seconds as she walked alongside John to the tea room. 'Are they difficult to use?' she asked, turning to him.

John was reassuring. 'Not a bit. No more difficult than film cameras. You would have no problems.'

Debbie laughed. 'You don't know me and new technology. It was a major breakthrough for me learning to use a mobile phone.'

By this time they had reached the tea room. Debbie pushed open the door and entered, John immediately behind her. The room was quite full, but Debbie spied a couple about ready to leave a corner table. She turned to John. 'This is on me. You grab that table in the corner.'

John hesitated for an instant and then, remembering their earlier agreement, nodded assent and quickly headed for the empty table. He sat down to establish possession and waited for Debbie to return.

Chapter 4

It was close to six o'clock when Debbie returned to the flat. She entered the hall just as her neighbours were coming down the stairs, clearly on their way out for the evening. Both were dressed up, Betty to the extreme in a low-cut dress that showed her ample bosom and probably more of her legs than was advisable.

They both greeted Debbie, but it was Betty who initiated the brief conversation. 'Have you had a nice afternoon, dear?' The question was accompanied with a rather condescending smile.

Debbie had hardly time to answer 'Yes, thank you' before Betty made an excited announcement.

'It's our last night. Henry's taking me out. We're going to live it up.' She beamed at her husband and then smiled and winked at Debbie.

Debbie wished them an enjoyable evening and watched them disappear through the front door, Betty struggling in a pair of ridiculously high-heeled shoes. She smiled to herself as she went into the sitting room. What was it, she wondered, that prompted some women to dress in a fashion that was absolutely unsuitable for them and achieved the opposite of what they intended? To quote the old saying, mutton dressed as lamb. And why did somebody, perhaps their husbands, not tell them how they looked? It was odd.

As soon as she was in the sitting room, Debbie slipped off her shoes and dropped into the easy chair in front of the French windows. The gusty wind of earlier in the day had disappeared and the sea now looked calm and blue in the evening sun. It was a pleasant view.

Sitting there observing the scene, she went over the events of the day. In just a few hours her holiday had altered dramatically. Instead of spending the whole day alone, as she had since Madge left, she had enjoyed the company of another human being. After meeting John that morning in the café, her whole outlook had changed. Normally if a man she had only just met had suggested that they go out together, she would have refused, erring on the side of caution – the proper thing to do. But there was something about John that had made her cast aside her normal reserve. Perhaps it was his obvious shyness or even the plain fact that they were two people who were lonely. Whatever it was, she knew she liked his company – and what harm could there be in sharing pleasure, as long as she kept her feet on the ground? After all, she was on holiday.

The visit to Pellworth Manor had been a major highlight of the day. She had enjoyed going there with John. His calm, reserved manner appealed to her – he was a bit like Ron in that respect. She abhorred brash, over-confident males.

When they had gone for afternoon tea, she had arrived at the table where John sat patiently, a laden tray in her hands.

'I had to wait a bit for these to arrive. I hope you don't mind.'

She had observed John's almost boyish delight at the appearance of the freshly baked scones with jam and cream. 'I don't normally indulge,' she had remarked, 'but once in a while it's rather nice.'

'Rather. Worth waiting for,' John had replied with enthusiasm, adding for good measure, 'and I didn't have much at lunchtime.'

'Nor did I,' she had laughed, remembering her skimpy meal.

They had chatted over tea, finding out a bit more about each other, and had been among the last to leave the tea room.

On the way back to Brillport the conversation had tended to die away. She had been wondering whether John was actually enjoying himself as much as he appeared to, but even when she protested that she could walk back to her flat from the hotel, he had insisted on delivering her to the door. After pulling up outside the flat, he had switched off the engine. Clutching her bag, she had turned to him. 'Thank you for a lovely afternoon. I really enjoyed it. It's been really nice.'

'I was thinking…' John had started, and then stopped. He had tried again. 'That is… I was wondering if you would like to join me for dinner tonight at the hotel… No strings attached,' he had added, watching her face for her reaction.

She had almost smiled at the last bit. She could understand now why he had been a bit quiet. He had been figuring out the best way to ask her. She had hesitated for an instant. After the pleasant afternoon the thought of another evening on her own in a strange flat was not appealing. At the same time, she had felt the need to lay down boundaries. She had smiled at him. 'I'd love to – provided I can share the bill.'

Beaming, he had replied: 'That will be fine.'

She had given him one of her coy smiles. 'What time?'

'Dinner is between seven and ten.' Then, glancing at his watch, 'Half past seven?'

'That will be good. It gives me a nice bit of time,' she had agreed, getting out of the car.

'I'll pick you up.'

'Oh no, I'll walk. It's not far. I need the exercise after those scones and cream.' She had been quite emphatic.

John had nodded. 'See you later, then.'

'Look forward to it.' With a wave of her hand, she had closed the car door.

As she sat there recalling the events of the afternoon, Debbie's thoughts turned to John's invitation. Though she had accepted readily, her decision had been prompted by the thought of spending another evening on her own in the gloomy flat. Now she began to wonder if she should have agreed to go. This was the first time she had done anything like this since Ron had died. All of her socialising had been with her family or her female friends. She wondered what her daughters would think of her decision to spend the evening with a man! She could almost hear their disapproval.

She dismissed the thought. She was allowing her imagination to run wild. She had had a pleasant afternoon and now she was joining somebody she had met for dinner, and that was all there was to it. John had already said: 'No strings attached.' It was up to her as well to keep things in proportion and maintain boundaries.

Thinking of her two daughters suddenly jerked Debbie into the present. She had promised both of them that she would switch her mobile phone on every day so that they could contact her if necessary. While she was out with John she had kept it turned off. She retrieved it from her handbag and switched it on before placing it on the arm of the chair. She leaned back and closed her eyes. It was nice just to take five minutes before having to get ready for her evening out.

Within a few moments her calm was interrupted by the familiar bleep of a text message. Quickly she pressed the button to read it.

'Mum. Give me a ring. Urgent.' It was from Jan.

Slightly concerned, Debbie keyed in the number she knew by heart. She held the mobile to her ear. It seemed a long time before anybody answered.

'Hello, Mum.' Debbie recognised her daughter's voice.

'Jan, what's happened? I got your message.'

'Mum, I left that message ages ago.' There was a bit of indignation in the voice.

'Oh, I'm sorry, dear. I've been out and my mobile has been switched off.'

'Oh, MUM.' Debbie could hear the exasperation. Jan was always telling her off for not keeping her mobile on all the time. She took no notice of her daughter's tone of voice. Instead she spoke before Jan could give her the usual lecture on mobile operation.

'But what's wrong?' Debbie insisted.

'Oh, nothing serious. I was wondering if you could look after Jamie Tuesday after next.' Jan's voice was quite normal again now.

Debbie took a deep breath. So why the urgent bit...? Jamie was her three-year-old grandson. She did not allow her thoughts to creep into her reply. 'That'll be all right, dear. About what time?'

'Hmm, in the afternoon – about two-ish.'

'Two o'clock Tuesday week. I'll put it in my diary.' Debbie made a mental note to do it as soon as she was off the phone.

'Is Madge back yet?'

'No, not yet. I haven't heard from her since she left. I expect she's busy.'

'What are you doing on your own down there? You must be bored to tears.'

'No, I'm fine. I'm quite happy.' Debbie was amused at Jan's concern. She spent the greater part of her time on her own.

'What's the weather like?'

'A bit changeable. It rained this morning, but this afternoon was sunny.'

'It's the same here.'

'How's Paul's back?' asked Debbie. Her son-in-law had recently damaged it playing squash.

'Oh, it's OK now.' Jan's reply was non-committal.

Debbie looked at her watch. Jan's long mobile calls were legendary. 'I'd better go, dear. I don't think I have much talking time left on my mobile.'

'OK, Mum. Talk to you soon.'

'Goodbye, dear. Love to Jamie and Paul.'

'Bye, Mum.'

Debbie switched off her mobile again. At least she had escaped the usual lecture from her daughter on the advantages of changing her mobile to monthly payments, and in turn she had escaped the usual task of explaining to Jan that her mobile was an emergency telephone and a pay-as-you-go method suited her just fine.

She stirred into action. Glancing at her watch during her chat to Jan had reminded her that if she was going to be on time for her appointment with John, then she had better start getting ready. Panic almost set in as she realised that she needed time to have a shower and she simply had to do something with her hair, after its adventures in the wind.

Half an hour later she was in the bedroom deciding what to wear. A survey of the wardrobe quickly solved the problem. She had a slightly longer navy blue skirt she had popped into her suitcase at the last minute, just in case there was something on one evening, and she had a white blouse that went with it. Thanks to Madge's disinterest in such matters, she had not yet considered wearing either. Likewise the new pair of tights she had purchased remained unopened. Closer examination of the blouse indicated problems. It had become slightly creased in the suitcase. Confident that she was on her own in the house, she flew out of the bedroom in her underwear and into the kitchen – she had seen an iron and board somewhere… In one of the cupboards? Somehow she managed to coax the iron into doing what she wanted in spite of its obvious age. She felt rather pleased with her efforts when she returned to the bedroom.

She dressed hurriedly, conscious that time was running out. When it came to footwear, another minor problem loomed. The shoes she had packed to go with the outfit had high heels. Not a ridiculous height, but nevertheless higher than normal. Would she be able to walk in them with her damaged foot? She decided to risk it. She was not invited out by a member of the opposite sex every day and she wanted to look smart. She could hardly wear her sandals with tights, and the only other shoes she had brought with her, which she had worn that afternoon, would be a pretty awful match for the outfit she had chosen.

She was conscious that she had only just enough time to walk to the Grand Hotel when at last she slipped her jacket on and grabbed her handbag. At the front door, she dropped into her usual habit of checking that she had the key to open it again. Then she slammed the heavy door behind her.

It was a pleasant sunny evening. She walked slowly, taking careful steps in shoes she didn't normally do serious walking in. These days, unless it was a special indoor occasion, she confined her footwear to more comfortable choices. After a few minutes, she was relieved to find that the cut on her foot didn't bother her too much. True, she could still feel it just a bit, but perhaps that was due to the different angle of her foot in the shoe. It would only take about seven minutes to reach the Grand Hotel.

John had made his plans carefully. The idea of inviting Debbie to dinner had come to him during the afternoon. Driving home he had debated whether it would be the right thing to do at this stage. One half of him wanted to enjoy her company; the other half counselled him not to appear too demanding. He didn't want to come across as a womaniser. In the end his desire for Debbie's company had won the day. He had been delighted when she readily accepted his suggestion. It was then that his planning had commenced. Once back at the hotel, he had made a point of looking into the dining room. Luck had been on his side. The friendliest of the three waitresses had been setting the tables for dinner. She had looked up, surprised at being interrupted by one of the hotel guests. It had only taken him a few words to explain his mission, and his request had been carried out with a cheerful smile and a reassuring 'No problem.' There and then the waitress had placed a 'Reserved' notice on the table of his choice: a nice table for two in an alcove with a window overlooking the sea. That bit of the planning over, he had retreated to his room to shower and change.

He arrived back in the foyer with five minutes to spare. He hadn't arranged to meet Debbie in any particular part of the hotel, and he didn't want her to arrive and have to search for him. He wandered into the bar. A few people were there enjoying pre-dinner drinks. He ordered a half-pint of lager, exchanged a few pleasantries with the barman and then carried his drink to a seat from which he could watch the foyer and see Debbie arrive. Oddly, for some reason he felt a bit nervous. He hadn't felt like that for years. It reminded him of his youth and dates with girlfriends. The first date had always been accompanied by a feeling of apprehension, and concern that things would not work out. He wondered why he experienced such a feeling now. After all, he reasoned, he had already spent the best part of the day with Debbie, and he found her easy to get on with. Someone he felt in tune with. He concluded that his concerns stemmed partly from the fact that he was doing something that for him was highly unusual:

entertaining a woman without others present. It was something he hadn't done for a long time.

He didn't have long to wait. He had hardly taken more than a couple of sips of his drink when she emerged from the hotel entrance door. She had changed again, he noticed. The two-piece outfit she now wore suited her well. He was glad he had made a bit of an effort with his own clothes and was wearing his blazer and the old striped tie that went with it.

He hurriedly got up and went into the foyer to meet Debbie. Her face broke into a cheerful smile as she spotted him walking towards her.

'Good evening. Fancy meeting you!' he said.

'And so soon!' she responded, following his humorous lead.

John laughed. 'How about a drink? I've just set one up for myself.'

Debbie smiled approvingly. 'I'd love one,' she replied.

John led the way into the bar. Once inside he turned to her. 'What can I get you?'

'I'll have a small sherry. A sweet one,' Debbie whispered, looking round the bar with an interested eye.

John went to get her drink and Debbie sought out a free table in a corner. He stood at the bar and watched her go, secretly enjoying the first sight of her walking in higher heels. She moved with a certain confidence as if she was not unused to the exercise. Funny how high heels immediately gave a woman a certain elegance. For her age, Debbie had quite a good pair of legs, he observed. It was the barman needing his attention that jerked him out of his thinking.

He paid for Debbie's drink and then collected his own on the way to the table where she was sitting.

Debbie watched his movements. As he arrived at the table she had chosen, she exclaimed apologetically: 'Oh, I'm so sorry, John. I didn't realise you were sitting over there.'

John looked at her and gave a brief grin. 'It's not a problem,' he replied. 'I only sat there to see you coming.'

Debbie made a bit of a face. 'I thought I was going to be late. First I had to ring my daughter Jan, and then when I started to get ready I discovered this blouse needed ironing.' She glanced down at it as she spoke.

John followed her gaze and smiled politely. 'It looks fine,' he said.

They took a long time over dinner, instinctively savouring the leisurely time to chat. In the end they were one of the last couples to leave. Debbie had noticed their waitress giving the occasional glance in their direction while she was clearing up. She leaned across the table to John and whispered: 'I think they'd like us to go.'

John glanced at his watch and nodded. A signal to the waitress brought her hurrying over with the bill. Debbie was pleased to see this happen. Clearly John was paying for evening meals at the hotel on an individual basis; it gave her the opportunity to exercise her earlier request to share the bill. John attempted to protest, but she was adamant.

Once outside the dining room, they both paused. John turned to her.

'I'll see you back to your apartment,' he said.

Debbie protested. 'I can manage. Really, it's not far.'

John persisted. 'I want to see you back safe and sound.'

Debbie conceded defeat. Her protest had been a bit half-hearted. She hadn't really fancied the walk back to the flat on her own in the dark.

They walked at a leisurely pace, which suited her, although she knew John was certainly slowing down out of consideration for her. She had already discovered that he had a tendency to stride out, with his slightly longer legs. He was in fact several inches taller than she was, even though she was wearing higher heels.

It was a pleasant evening, with stars popping up here and there and the hint of a moon somewhere hidden away. Debbie felt happy and contented. John's company today had added a fresh dimension to a so far rather dull holiday. In a lull in the conversation she turned to him. 'I've really enjoyed today.' The tone of her voice conveyed her feelings.

'I've really enjoyed having your company.' His reply was brief, but she knew he meant it.

It was John who spoke again first. 'Would you like to join me tomorrow?' He paused for an instant, but before she had a chance to reply, he continued. 'The weather forecast is good and I was thinking of driving out somewhere in the car again. There's a National Trust property I'd like to visit… We could have lunch there as well,' he added hopefully.

Debbie threw caution and logic to the wind. 'I'd love to. I've got my National Trust card with me.' Her reply was enthusiastic.

John was pleased. 'It's settled, then,' he replied confidently. 'I'll pick you up at ten o'clock, if that's all right with you.'

'That's fine. I'll be ready.'

When they reached the flat, Debbie hesitated. She didn't want to invite John in, at least not just yet. She need not have worried. It was John who solved her minor problem. As they stopped outside, he took her hand.

'Can I leave you abruptly?' he asked. 'I'd like to look at the map and sort out a route for tomorrow before going to bed.'

Debbie placed her free hand on his arm. 'Thank you for a lovely day, John. Goodnight.'

'Goodnight, Debbie. Sleep well.' Then he released her hand.

She watched him walk away, and returned his brief wave before opening the front door.

The house was in darkness and it was several seconds before she found the hall light switch. It was comforting to have everything bathed in light. She went into the sitting room and turned the light on there. It seemed an age since she had left it earlier in the evening. The newspaper she had purchased that morning lay on the chair unread. She sat in the armchair and casually picked it up to scan its pages. Something made her reach into her handbag and take out her mobile phone. Just as well to check whether anybody wanted her. Her perusal of the newspaper was abruptly halted by a bleep announcing the arrival of a text message. It could only be Jan or Trish. Concerned, she pressed the button and read the text. 'COMING BACK TUESDAY. CAN WE RETURN WEDNESDAY? FUNERAL THURSDAY – MADGE'.

Debbie sat with the phone in her hand. She had forgotten that she had given her mobile number to Madge. Suddenly a feeling of sadness crept over her. She hadn't envisaged Madge returning to pick her up until the following weekend. It meant that she had only one more day with John Hammond and then their brief holiday friendship would be over.

Chapter 5

It was the brightness of the room that woke Debbie up. She lifted her head from the pillow quickly, thinking she had overslept, but the hands of the bedside clock only showed half past six. The sun shining through the window curtains had alerted her, illuminating the familiar surroundings of her own bedroom. Reassured, she lay back for a few minutes, thinking.

Five weeks had passed since she had returned from her holiday, five weeks in which she had gradually been drawn back into her normal routine. She would have been the first to admit that in the first few days of her return home she had felt it difficult to pick up the threads and carry on as usual. The few days she had spent with John had renewed in her the almost forgotten pleasure of sharing pleasant times with a person of the opposite sex, and it had been an interlude that had made her acutely aware of the dullness of her everyday life. It had required all her dedication and logical thinking to put her time with John into the realms of a holiday friendship.

The 'plop' of the daily newspaper being delivered through the letter box and landing on the hall floor halted her reminiscing and brought the new day into focus. She threw back the duvet and went over to the window, swishing the curtains aside. For a few seconds she gazed down at the garden, parts of which were already bathed in the early morning sunshine. She watched a thrush with amusement as it struggled to extract a worm from the lawn. Eventually it succeeded and flew off in the direction of the vegetable patch further down the garden. It was looking at this that made Debbie revise her plans for the day. There was work to do in the garden. Today was

Tuesday, and Tom would be arriving promptly at eight o'clock. The side gate would need to be unlocked so that he could wheel his bicycle down the side of the house and gain access to the garden without disturbing her. She would ask him to dig over the plot next to the runner beans and then she could plant out the lettuces that were waiting in the greenhouse for transplanting. She would do the shopping tomorrow.

The decision made, Debbie put her plan into action. A quick shower, and soon she was downstairs and in the kitchen. Clicking the kettle switch, she went into the hall to collect the *Daily Telegraph* from the hall floor. She scrutinised the headlines as she wandered slowly back into the kitchen.

By the time Tom arrived, she had partaken of a light breakfast and was dressed in her 'working gear', as she termed her old jeans and a shirt. She opened the back door to greet him as he carefully leaned his bicycle against the wall of the house.

'Good morning, Tom.'

Tom looked up from taking off his bicycle clips. 'Good morning, Mrs Patterson,' he replied in his usual slow and respectful voice. He looked at the lawn at the back of the house and this clearly prompted his next remark. 'I'd best cut the lawns this morning. I reckon it will rain again tomorrow.' He glanced up at the sky.

'It would be great if you could. Oh, and...' Debbie suddenly remembered. 'Can you dig that patch next to the beans? I need to transplant those lettuces in the greenhouse.'

'I'll do that,' Tom replied agreeably, turning to walk in the direction of the garden shed.

Debbie watched him go. Tom never indulged in a lot of conversation, though over the years she had got him to respond to her, usually over his mid-morning cup of tea or coffee with her in the kitchen. He had worked in a local engineering company all his life, and he had come to work for her every week when he retired, shortly after Ron had died. She knew she would be lost without him. He did all the hard jobs in the garden and kept the front and back lawns immaculate. She had only to ask him to do something and in his quiet methodical way it was carried out.

Five minutes later, just as she was about to join him in the garden, she heard the familiar sound of the motor mower. If anybody could coax that ancient and temperamental machine into life, it was Tom. But the noise of the mower was diminished by a sound closer to her. The phone was ringing. She sighed as she kicked off her gardening shoes and hurried into the lounge. A familiar voice greeted her as she picked up the phone on the desk.

'Mum, it's Jan.'

'Hello, dear. You're early.'

'Mum, can you do me a favour?'

'What is it, dear?' Debbie had a good idea what the answer would be.

'Can you look after Jamie this afternoon? Paul has come up with some dinner dance on Saturday he wants me to go to and I'll have to get a pair of shoes to go with the dress I've bought. This afternoon is the best time for me to do any serious shopping.'

Debbie sighed to herself. Bang went her planned long day in the garden. Her grandson demanded her full attention when she looked after him. Still, hopefully she still had the rest of the morning before Jan arrived.

'All right, dear. What time will you bring him over?'

'About half past one – will that be OK?'

'That'll be fine.'

'Thanks a lot, Mum. I've got to dash. We'll see you later, then.'

'OK, dear.'

'Bye Mum, and thanks again.'

'Goodbye, dear.'

Debbie replaced the receiver and sat at the desk for a few moments. The last five minutes had made a mess of her plans for the day. She quite liked looking after her grandson, but recently Jan did have a habit of asking her to have him at short notice. It was the second time that month.

She joined Tom in the garden, busying herself doing odd jobs until he was available to dig over the ground she had allocated for the lettuces. She was just about to start tying some of the bean plants to their sticks when he arrived beside her with his fork and started to dig with strong, mechanical strokes.

Debbie slipped off her gardening gloves to deal with the ties.

'It's not too wet to dig, is it?' she asked, glancing at the ground Tom was working on. There had been heavy rain the previous day.

'Nay, it's a bit moist, but I'll manage it,' Tom replied between forkfuls.

'Oh good. I'll be able to get those lettuces in later.' She almost added: 'If I get time.' Everything she wanted to do in the garden was going to be a rush now.

Both of them worked away, mainly in silence, broken occasionally by Debbie asking Tom how his wife's health was now, or enquiring about his daughter, who lived in Margate. Tom would from time to time make such comments as 'Slugs are bad this year. Watch your lettuces,' or 'You need to get those tomatoes in the greenhouse out now.'

Debbie was about to ask him to transplant the tomatoes for her, when in the distance the ringing of a phone could be heard.

'That's your phone,' Tom announced.

Debbie sped away, fully expecting the phone to stop ringing before she reached it. She kicked off her garden shoes with abandon at the kitchen door and rushed into the lounge. One of these days she would start using the cordless phone Jan and Paul had given her for Christmas. She crossed the lounge carpet to her desk. The phone was still shrilling.

She grabbed hold of it, a bit breathless from her run from the vegetable patch. 'Hello.'

'Ah, Debbie, I thought you were out. It's Alice.'

'Hello, Alice. I was in the garden.' With that Debbie waited. Alice was Mrs Martin-Smith, a prominent member of the Women's Institute committee. A phone call from her could only mean one thing – she wanted Debbie to do something.

Alice continued, unaware of Debbie's apprehension. 'Yes, it's a marvellous day, isn't it?' There was a few seconds' pause, and then she continued. 'I'm glad I caught you, Debbie. I wanted to talk to you before the next meeting.'

Alarm bells rang in Debbie's ears. She tried her best not to allow her concern to appear in her response. 'What do you want to talk to me about?' she asked, as cheerfully as possible.

'Well, you know there's a vacancy on the committee now that Gladys Spencer has stepped down.' Alice waited for her comment to register before continuing.

'Yes...' Debbie's reply was slow and cautious. She knew what was coming next.

Alice continued, seemingly oblivious of Debbie's hesitation. 'I've been talking with a few members of the committee. We would like to propose you for the vacancy.'

Debbie was overcome with panic. 'Oh, I couldn't do anything like that. It... It really isn't my thing,' she stuttered.

Alice was undeterred. 'You underestimate yourself, Debbie. You would be perfect for the job. Just think about it.'

Debbie did not want to think about it. She shook her head, even though Alice could not see her. 'No, no – not really. It just isn't for me. I couldn't get up and speak in public and do that sort of thing.'

Rather than deter Alice, her answer seemed to have the opposite effect. 'Nobody can until they try,' she replied immediately, adding for good measure, 'and the whole point is that we need somebody like you on the committee – somebody who is down to earth and who can keep the rest of us in order.'

Debbie could not help smiling. The thought of keeping some of the committee members she knew in order was really quite amusing. She realised that she wasn't being firm enough in her refusal.

'No. Thank you very much for asking me, but I would just not be any good at committee work.' She said it as positively and as firmly as she could.

There was a slight pause before Alice responded. 'You don't have to decide right at this minute. The next meeting isn't until next month. I'll phone you again just before that, and if you decide to go ahead I can propose you,' she chipped in before Debbie could say anything else. 'I won't say any more now. Just think about it.'

Debbie laughed. 'Thinking about it won't change my mind,' she replied, wishing Alice would take no for an answer.

Alice did not respond to her remark. 'I'll say goodbye now, Debbie. Have a wonderful day. It is glorious, isn't it, after all the rain we've been having?'

'Yes it is. I'm busy gardening.'

'I'm sorry if I disturbed you. I'll let you get back to it. Bye-bye, Debbie. Think about what I've said.'

'Goodbye, Alice.'

Debbie replaced the handset. She felt a bit irritated with herself for not being more forceful in her refusal. Now Alice Martin-Smith will no doubt talk to other people in the WI and they will try to persuade me, she reflected. In the early days of her widowhood she had found the outings to the WI a useful way of getting out of the house. Now she often found herself not so compatible with its atmosphere. Certainly the idea of her being on its committee was out of the question, if not ludicrous. No doubt over the next few weeks Alice Martin-Smith or another forceful member of the committee would return to the attack, but she would just have to deal with that when it happened. She reached into her desk to retrieve her desk diary from its cubbyhole to check when the next meeting was. As she did so, a business card fell out onto the desk. It was the card John had given her when they had parted.

Debbie sat looking at the card she now held. The tiny object stirred happy memories within her. It now seemed a long time since he had given it to her, but in fact it was no more than a few weeks. When Madge had announced that she was returning with the sole object of collecting her and returning to Oxford, a cloud of sadness had come over her. She had enjoyed the time spent in John's company and now it was to be abruptly wrenched from her. Secretly she had hoped that Madge would not return until the end of the week, when the rental on the flat ran out. But it was not to be.

When she had joined John the following morning for their day out, she had related her news quite soon after getting into the car. John, with his usual calm approach to things, had simply smiled at her and remarked casually: 'So it's back to routine in Oxford.'

She had smiled politely and replied briefly: 'Yes, I'm afraid so.' And that had been that. From there on she had tried to put the matter out of her thoughts. She did not want the thought of this being their last day together spoiling her anticipated pleasure.

The day had proved to be even more pleasant than she had envisaged. The weather had turned out to be warm and sunny, just as John had predicted. They had toured around, visited a National Trust property and stayed there for lunch, which she had insisted on paying for. They had taken lots of photographs, John with his sophisticated digital camera, and she with her little compact until her film ran out. Then she had watched him, intrigued by the digital process. In the afternoon they had returned to Brillport via the coast. At one point the road ran right beside the sea. John had stopped the car at a convenient lay-by to admire the stretch of sandy beach and weigh the scene up for photographic possibilities.

She had watched for a few seconds and then exclaimed: 'Let's paddle.' She had slipped off her shoes in an instant and was already out of the car before John had started to fumble with laces and socks. Two minutes later he had hurried after her as she scampered towards the sea. Her head was thrown back, enjoying the smell and the feel of the salty air.

'Don't tread on anything,' John had called out, laughing at her exuberance. The warning had curbed her enthusiasm. Her cut foot was healing fast, but she did not want to repeat the incident.

'It's quite mad, isn't it? Doing this, I mean. I suddenly felt sixteen again,' she had exclaimed as John joined her and took her hand.

'Mad, but nice. Gosh, I haven't done this for years,' had been his reply.

Hand in hand they had walked along in the sea, enjoying the feel of the tiny waves lapping over their feet. They had walked a long way like that, until John had remarked that if they were to get back to Brillport at a reasonable time they had better return.

Once again he had invited her to join him at the Grand Hotel for dinner, and she had been a willing partner, only lamenting that she didn't have a different outfit to wear. John had just laughed at her concerns and replied that he was going to wear the same again.

It was at the end of dinner that John had suggested that as Madge would not be returning until at least midday the following day, they could meet somewhere for a goodbye coffee in the morning, and she had readily agreed. The next day it had rained and they had met in the Beach Café again. They had chatted, neither of them wanting to acknowledge the fact that they were playing out the final moments of their brief friendship. Towards the end of the interlude she had suggested to John that they exchange addresses, so that she could add him to her 'Christmas card list', as she termed it. It was then that he had given her his card.

When it came to saying goodbye, she had had a lump in her throat. She had always hated goodbyes, but this one seemed to be worse than usual. She had immersed herself completely in the brief interlude with John, and now it was to end. She had fought back the tears. John, as always, had been beautifully in control. He had taken her hand and looked at her. 'Thank you for your company the last two days. I've really enjoyed it.'

'I have too, John. It's been marvellous sharing with you.'

It was she who had decided to take the initiative. She had reached forward and placed a kiss on his cheek. 'Goodbye, John.'

'Goodbye, Debbie. Take care of yourself.'

He had released her hand, but hers had lingered on his arm for a second. 'And you, John.'

And then she had broken free and quickly turned away before the tears enveloped her.

She had walked away briskly, but just once she had turned and looked back. John had been still standing where she had left him outside the café, watching her. She had waved, and he had waved back...

It was the clock chiming in the hall that roused Debbie from her bitter-sweet memories. She glanced at her watch. It was time to make Tom his drink. She placed John's card carefully back in her diary. She wondered what he was doing. No doubt he too was once more immersed in the routine of living, his holiday just a memory, and the time they had spent together relegated to the realms of a holiday friendship. That was how it was. You met people on holiday and enjoyed the time with them, but that was all. After the holiday you never saw them again.

As she thought about it, the same wave of sadness she had experienced when parting from him briefly swept over her once more. In all probability she would never see him again. Oh yes: she would send him a Christmas card as she had promised. He might even return the compliment, but nothing more. And in time everything, even people, just became a memory.

A second glance at her watch jerked Debbie out of her melancholia. Tom would wonder what had happened to his mid-morning drink. And what about her gardening plans? She hurried to the kitchen.

Chapter 6

That particular morning, Tom seemed to want to linger a little longer than usual over their chat. Debbie listened patiently, making a comment or asking a question here and there. She had not the heart to cut the conversation short, though she was aware that her precious gardening time was slipping away.

At last Tom disappeared back into the garden. Debbie collected the dirty mugs and dumped them in the sink. They could wait until later. Five minutes later she rejoined Tom in the garden. Tom was already transplanting the tomatoes she had raised from seed in the greenhouse.

'Good plants you've got here,' he remarked, as she walked past him on the way to the garden shed.

'Yes, they are good, aren't they? I'm rather proud of them.'

She groped in the interior of the shed and found her fork and trowel. Now for the lettuces, she thought. She collected the tray of tiny plants and surveyed the patch of ground Tom had just dug for her. Her pondering was rudely interrupted.

'I thought this was where I'd find you.'

Debbie recognised the voice immediately. Her heart sank. It was Madge. Of all the people to turn up now, she thought. But she made a big effort to appear sociable.

'Hello, Madge. I didn't expect to see you this morning.' They had not had any contact since Madge had driven Debbie back from Dorset in her 4x4 and dumped her unceremoniously outside her house.

'Had to go to the dentist again and thought I'd drop in to see you. Any chance of a coffee?'

That was one thing you could rely on with Madge. She did not beat about the bush. Debbie smothered her irritation. 'Of course,' she replied. 'Come into the kitchen.'

She tore off her gardening gloves and dropped them by her tools. That was the end of gardening for the morning. Madge was not known for her brief visits.

She led the way back to the kitchen.

'What do you keep this big place going for?' Madge gave a quick glance round the garden.

Debbie laughed, more to hide her irritation than anything else. 'You sound like Jan. She's always on about this house being too big for me.'

'You could get a nice little flat somewhere if you sold this place,' continued Madge. 'And have money in the bank,' she added.

Debbie smiled. 'And then what would I do with my time?'

They entered the kitchen. This broke the pattern of their conversation, which suited Debbie. It was bad enough having her daughters constantly berating her about the house being too large for her to manage. She could do without Madge joining in the discussion.

The reprieve was short-lived. Easing her ample frame into one of the kitchen chairs and casually picking up the newspaper Debbie had abandoned earlier, Madge returned to the conversation. 'That guy you have to help you in the garden, how much do you pay him?'

Debbie picked up the kettle. 'Six pounds an hour,' she replied. She felt annoyed with herself for answering Madge so obediently. Madge had an uncanny way of using her directness to extract information she wanted from people. Debbie was rather intimidated by her, a feeling that had increased with their proximity during the recent holiday.

'There you are then. You could save that money to start with,' Madge announced.

Debbie thought desperately for a suitable reply. As well as terminating her gardening, Madge seemed to be particularly irritating this morning.

'How was the dentist?' Debbie asked, ignoring Madge's last remark.

The ploy worked. It seemed that Madge was not feeling particularly well disposed towards her dentist. She launched into an expansive account of her last few visits. Debbie listened, glad that the conversation had been diverted away from her.

When the kettle boiled, she made a mug of coffee for Madge and half a mug for herself, which she did not want. She opened a packet of ginger biscuits and liberally filled a plate with them, remembering that they were one of Madge's favourites. Then she sat down opposite Madge and listened, pretending to be interested.

It was well over half an hour later that Madge, after drinking her coffee, consuming a large proportion of the biscuits and talking non-stop, announced that she would have to go. Debbie escorted her to the front door and watched her drive away. She closed the front door with a sigh. Gone was any hope of doing any more gardening now. She would just have time to get herself a bite to eat before Jan arrived with Jamie.

She wandered back into the kitchen just as Tom tapped at the door to tell her that he was leaving. She was just deciding what to eat when she heard a commotion outside the front door. She hurried to the source of the noise and flung the front door open wide. Jan stood there fumbling for her key, her arms full, holding on to Jamie at the same time.

'We thought we'd come a bit earlier. Is that all right, Mum?'

'Of course it is. Come on, Jamie, give your gran a kiss.'

Debbie took hold of her grandson. Jan deposited her belongings in the hall and returned to the car for the other necessities that accompanied her son's visits to his grandmother.

For the next few minutes pandemonium ruled as Jamie, anxious to show off his latest toy, clamoured for Debbie's attention, and Jan rushed in and out from the car. Eventually Debbie managed to herd them both into the kitchen.

'Have you eaten?' she asked, almost knowing the answer.

Jan shook her head. 'Not yet, Mum.'

'Some soup all right?' Debbie asked a little anxiously.

'Super.'

Debbie quickly put everything else out of her thoughts as she busied herself providing some sort of meal, mindful of Jamie, who continued to demand her attention. By this time, just like Madge, Jan had dropped into a chair and picked up the newspaper.

'Mum, do you think I'm getting varicose veins?'

Jan's question diverted Debbie's attention from heating up the soup. She glanced towards the chair where her daughter sat now intently scrutinising the backs of her legs.

'It's not noticeable, dear.'

'Paul thinks I am,' Jan retorted.

Debbie thought perhaps her son-in-law was better qualified to answer her daughter's question, but did not venture to say so. Instead, as she returned to the cooker and the soup, she remarked casually: 'Wearing high heels all the time may not help.'

Jan's indignation came over loud and clear. 'Well, I'm not going to slop around in flats, thank you very much. Besides, you wear high heels at your age and you haven't got any varicose veins.'

'I've got a few small ones,' Debbie replied quietly, still wincing over Jan's 'at your age' remark. As an afterthought she added: 'I don't wear high heels all the time – only on special occasions, and when I do they are a sensible height.'

'I don't see the point,' Jan retorted.

Debbie could recognise the signs. Jan was all set to have one of her arguments on the subject. Ever since Jan was a teenager Debbie had tried to advise her about the folly of wearing high heels all the time, particularly when she was pregnant with Jamie. Her efforts had always come to nought and ended in an argument. She decided that now was a good time to change the subject. 'How's Paul's job going?' she asked brightly.

Jan screwed up her face. 'He's fed up. He doesn't get on with his boss still and he thinks he should get more money. He keeps applying for jobs. He wrote off for one in Scotland last week.'

Jan's last few words left Debbie concerned. 'You wouldn't seriously consider moving to Scotland, would you?' she asked.

Jan shrugged her shoulders. 'I don't know. We might.'

Debbie brought the soup to the table. The thought of her immediate family moving some distance away was a bit depressing. Her younger daughter already lived in London and only made occasional visits. If Jan, Paul and little Jamie moved away... She hurriedly changed her thinking and consoled herself that similar suggestions had cropped up before and come to nothing. No point in crossing bridges before they were reached.

'What's the big event you're going to on Saturday?' she asked, recalling Jan's need to go shopping.

Jan supervised Jamie's eating as she answered. 'Oh, it's one of those business events mainly for the men – we women just have to hang around and look interested. Paul insisted I buy a new dress.'

'What's it like?'

'Blue, with rather a nice V-neck. He'd be mad if he knew how much I paid for it.' Jan made a face to round off her remark.

'But you want to look nice,' insisted Debbie.

'Hmm, if you listened to Paul you'd think we were paupers. I should have gone back to work after having Jamie.'

'Oh no – that's the worst thing you could have done. At least wait until he starts school.' Debbie was shocked at the suggestion.

Jan looked a bit glum. 'I just hope I'll get a job then.'

'Of course you will, with your experience,' Debbie insisted. Jan had had a job high up the ladder in publishing before Jamie came along.

Jan was not convinced. She shook her head. 'You don't know, Mum. I'll have been out of things for five years then. Employers think you're past it after that long – even a few months is bad enough.'

'But—' Debbie's sentence was cut short as Jan, looking at her watch, jumped up from her chair.

'Gosh, look at the time! I've got to go, or I'll be late. No, Jamie, you stay with Gran.' Jamie was already tagging along behind her.

The same pandemonium sprang up as on their arrival. As Jan dashed upstairs to the bathroom, Jamie's face puckered in preparation for a wail. By the time Jan returned and kissed her son goodbye, tears were already accompanying the wail.

Debbie held him close while Jan got into her car and gave a final wave. 'Come on, Jamie, let's find the toy box,' she suggested soothingly as she closed the front door.

The strategy worked. In the cupboard under the stairs Debbie kept a cardboard box full of old toys and bits and pieces to amuse her grandson during his visits. Jamie's attention immediately switched to something more interesting, and his tears ceased.

It had been a long afternoon. In the three hours Debbie had been looking after her grandson the floor of the lounge had become strewn with toys and other abandoned items of interest. Jamie demanded her almost constant attention, with the result that she found it difficult to concentrate on the simplest of tasks.

It was while she was sitting at her desk in the corner of the lounge, one eye on Jamie, whose focus was now on some building bricks he had found, that the phone on the desk rang.

She picked up the receiver. 'Hello.'

A male voice answered. 'Hello, Debbie.'

She did not recognise the voice. 'Who's speaking?'

'John, John Hammond.'

Debbie's reaction was immediate. 'John! How are you? It's lovely to hear from you.'

'I'm fine. I just thought I'd give you a ring. I was thinking…'

Debbie's attention was suddenly diverted elsewhere. 'Potty.'

John was still speaking. Debbie was attempting to listen to him with one ear and Jamie with the other.

'POTTY!' Jamie's cry was more urgent.

It was no good. 'Coming, Jamie,' Debbie called, jumping up from her chair. 'John, I'm dreadfully sorry. I've got my grandson wailing for the toilet. Can I ring you back?'

'Of course you can. I'll give you my number. It's—'

'Just a minute – let me get a pen.' Debbie panicked. Where was that pen she'd been using? Got it. Please hang on, Jamie, she prayed.

'OK, I've found it, What was that? 0118...' She frantically scribbled the number down, one eye still on Jamie. Quickly, she read it back to him. Then: 'Got it! I'll ring you back, John. Lovely to hear you. Bye for now.'

She hardly heard his reply. As she put the receiver down, all her attention was on her grandson. Fortunately she reached him before a disaster took place. She breathed a sigh of relief. Then, as he settled down again, the significance of what had just happened began to sink in. John had contacted her! Oh, why did it have to be on a day when everything was happening? And why did Jamie decide that he needed the toilet just at that moment? She longed to pick up the phone again to talk to John, but she knew that as soon as she did so something else would happen. She would just have to wait until Jan collected Jamie.

It was another hour before Jan returned. Then there was the process of getting them a drink before they departed. Jan wanted to chat and to ask her mother's opinion of the shoes she had bought. All the time Debbie fretted with the thought that she should be ringing John back. Would he think her delay meant she didn't want to talk to him? The thought nagged at her. It seemed an eternity before she stood at the door waving Jan and Jamie off.

When they had at last disappeared from view, she closed the door and made straight for her desk. Anxiously she dialled the number she had scribbled on a bit of paper. She glanced at her watch. It was almost two hours since John's call. She heard the phone ringing and ringing at the other end of the line, but there was no answer. She could have wept. The frustration of the situation overwhelmed her. Why, why, she asked herself, did this have to happen? John must think she had deliberately made an excuse to ring back because she didn't want to talk to him. Then a horrible thought struck her: suppose she had taken down his number incorrectly and was trying to ring the wrong one?

She took a deep breath and tried to think logically. It was quite possible that John had gone out. He couldn't be expected to just sit by the phone waiting for her to ring back. As to the number, well, she had checked it with him. Then a thought suddenly struck her, prompting her to mutter 'Silly me' under her breath. Of course: John's phone number would be on his card. She dug the card out from its cubbyhole and checked the number she had scribbled down against the printed one. It was correct. She would give it half an hour and then try again.

She busied herself tidying up the collection of toys she had amused Jamie with, deliberately taking as long as possible to gather them all up, put them in their box and return it to its home under the stairs. Next she tackled the pile of dirty dishes in the kitchen sink. At least it gave her something to do while she waited.

She was halfway through when the phone rang. Drying her hands as she went, she rushed to answer it. As she picked it up, she almost said 'John?' but the voice was female. It was Mrs Hudson, the woman who cleaned for her once a week. Could she come late tomorrow? She had to take her daughter to the dentist. Struggling with disappointment, Debbie would have agreed to almost anything. After commiserating with Mrs Hudson, she replaced the handset and, feeling deflated, went back to her washing up. Finishing that would bring her up to her self-imposed half-hour.

Ten minutes later she sat at the telephone again. She listened to the ringing tone begin. She waited, her heart thumping slightly. She remembered her previous try and the continuous uninterrupted ringing. This time a familiar voice answered.

'John Hammond.'

A surge of joy swept over Debbie. Her words came out in a rush. 'John, it's Debbie. I'm so sorry about what happened when you rang. I had my grandson here and I had to wait for his mother to pick him up. Then when I rang back you were out. I'm so dreadfully sorry. It's lovely to talk to you again.'

'Hello again. Sorry I was out. I ran out of milk and had to dash to the corner shop.' Debbie could hear a slight laugh at the other end of the phone. 'How are you?' he asked.

53

Debbie's voice could not mask her enthusiasm at talking to him again. 'I'm fine. How are you? What are you doing with yourself?'

'Oh, keeping myself amused. I spent this morning on the allotment. I thought I'd better take advantage of the glorious day.'

His reply reminded Debbie of her own efforts that morning. 'I tried to do some work in the garden today, but then my daughter Jan rang and asked me to look after Jamie,' she said, 'so that was the end of my gardening.'

'Ah, the trials of being a grandparent.' There was humour in his voice.

Debbie was going to respond, but John spoke again. This time he was serious. 'Debbie, my reason for phoning. Are you still interested in buying a digital camera?'

Debbie tried to collect her thoughts quickly. The question was completely unexpected. Oddly enough, after talking with John on holiday and observing his camera in use, she had thought about it several times, though her thinking had been a link to John rather than an intention of going out and buying one. Now she could sense something in the air.

'Yes, I am, but I've hesitated to go out and buy one on my own,' she replied, wondering what John had in mind.

She did not have to wait long. His reply was full of enthusiasm. 'Good! Now what I suggest is that I come over to Oxford and help you buy one.'

Debbie was immediately on cloud nine. If John had suggested they go out and buy an elephant she might have agreed. The point was that she would be seeing him again. The thought filled her with anticipation and pleasure. Her response was immediate. 'I'd love to. When can we make it?'

'How about Friday?'

Debbie already had her diary open in front of her. She could forgo her usual yoga session. 'Friday's fine. How do we meet up?'

'I thought I'd come over by train, but I haven't checked the time yet.'

Debbie thought quickly. 'What about making it in the morning and I'll buy you a lunch? I know a lovely restaurant we can go to.'

'Sounds a marvellous idea. It's a date. I'll nip down to the station tomorrow and check the times of the trains, or have a look on the internet.'

'Will you let me know, John? Then I can meet your train.'

'Of course. I'll give you a ring Thursday night.'

'That's marvellous. I'm looking forward to it.'

'Me too.'

A brief wave of anxiety came over Debbie. She had to voice the concern that was beginning to replace the euphoria of a few seconds earlier. 'John, you do think I'll be able to manage, don't you? Using a digital camera, I mean. I'm a bit of an idiot with modern technology.'

She heard him laugh. 'Ten minutes' instruction, and you'll be an expert.'

Debbie admired his confidence. 'I'll take your word for it,' she replied, chuckling at his assessment of her ability.

John was undeterred. 'I was looking at a marvellous little device yesterday,' he replied. 'You can print out your photographs at home with it. We could get you one of those as well.'

Debbie was still thinking of her skills. 'Oh, that sounds a bit complicated,' she said.

'Not at all. You could handle it OK.'

Debbie was not so sure. 'I'll need convincing,' she laughed.

'No problem at all. We'll sort you out on Friday. My son's just arrived, so I'd better ring off now. I'll talk to you again on Thursday.'

'OK then, John. Bye for now, and thank you for contacting me.'

'Thank *you*. Cheerio until Thursday, then.'

'Bye, John. Bye.'

Debbie replaced the receiver. The day was good after all. The excitement of talking to John again made everything take on a new and vibrant aspect. Memories of her few days on holiday with him floated into her thoughts as she wandered into the kitchen, vaguely contemplating preparing something for her supper. Almost automatically she filled the kettle with water and switched it on, her thoughts focused on the coming Friday. She looked out of the window at the garden, now bathed in the early evening sunshine, and her thoughts suddenly turned to more pressing matters. Without further ado she sprang into action. She clicked off the kettle and grabbed her gardening clothes from the cupboard. The sunny evening was beckoning. She would get those lettuces in after all.

Chapter 7

John was enjoying the train ride. It had been quite some time since he had travelled by train and he relished the rediscovered experience. He had purchased his usual copy of *The Times* at the station, intending to utilise the journey reading it, but somehow it had not worked out that way. Again and again thoughts of Debbie and the day ahead distracted him and filled him with pleasure.

He recalled their last day together in Dorset. When Debbie had announced that her friend was returning and that she would be leaving the following morning, he had been immediately saddened, but had been determined not to show it. It had brought back the feeling he used to get on the last day of the school holidays.

It had been even worse when they said goodbye to each other. He had been surprised when Debbie rushed away, but somehow he knew how she felt. Wandering back to the Grand Hotel for lunch, he had been overwhelmed by the thought that in all probability he would never see her again. She would go home to her life and he would go home to his. Ships that pass. He felt he knew the full meaning of that saying now.

The remainder of his holiday had been drab and barren. The weather had not helped. On more than one occasion he had found his activities marred by the persistent rain, which appeared with depressing regularity each day. He had been glad when it had been time to pack his bag and return home.

In the weeks since, Debbie had frequently appeared in his thoughts. The few days he had spent in her company were still vivid memories. He could still see her walking into the foyer of the Grand

Hotel, taking elegant steps towards him. He remembered her infectious smile, which seemed to come from the heart, while the thought of her impulsive chatter at times made him smile, even now. He had been surprised how much they had in common in their thinking and their interests, which they had talked about quite freely. Most of all, his brief interlude with Debbie had made him aware of the dullness of his lifestyle and his need to share with someone of the opposite sex. The realisation had come as a bit of a shock to him. Since Mary had passed away, he had ambled along, not even thinking about it. At first this had been out of loyalty to Mary and then very gradually it had become a way of life. Meeting Debbie had changed all that. He had suddenly rediscovered the joy and pleasure of sharing each day with another person.

The more he had thought about Debbie, the more his feeling of isolation had increased. The idea of contacting her had occurred to him on a few occasions. She had given him her address, just as he had given her his. However, he had argued with himself that possession of her address did not imply that she wished to continue their brief holiday friendship. What had she said? Something about adding him to her Christmas card list. That was probably how she viewed the situation. A fleeting holiday friendship. How many times did that happen to people, he wondered.

In spite of the logical arguments he had with himself, the thought of contacting her still appealed to him. The problem was that he had no valid reason to get in touch with her. What would he do? Just ask her how she was?

It was while working on his allotment one day that the idea came to him. He recalled her interest in his camera and his suggestion that he help her buy one. She had appeared quite enthusiastic at the time and then the conversation had moved to other matters. Now that conversation was the key to John's strategy. Why not offer to come to Oxford and help her buy a camera? That suggestion would always give her the opportunity of ending the contact by saying she had changed her mind. He decided to phone rather than write; that way the contact would be more personal. He didn't have her telephone number but hopefully he could obtain it if it wasn't ex-directory.

He had hardly been able to believe his good fortune when at last he heard her voice. Her enthusiastic response to his suggestion had immediately filled him with joy at the thought of meeting her again. His idea had turned out even better than he could ever have hoped. Now it had only remained for him to work out the details to make the meeting a pleasurable day for them both.

He took his time when the train reached his destination, letting the crowds disperse through the ticket barrier first. When he had spoken to Debbie the previous evening, they had arranged to meet in the station foyer. Now he anxiously scanned the people standing there, worried that he might miss her. Then he saw her, standing well back from the crowd, intensely watching the barrier from which he had just emerged. She gave him a little wave as soon as she spotted him, and he hurried over to her.

His holiday memories of her were reinforced immediately, only this time her petite elegance was portrayed in a slightly different way. Instead of the casual approach adopted during her holiday, Debbie had chosen a trim navy blue figure-hugging costume. John thought she could easily be mistaken for a mature businesswoman rather than a grandmother in her sixties. The outfit suited her, he thought, and he was glad he had taken a bit more care with his own appearance.

Their hands clasped and Debbie offered her cheek for a kiss. 'John, it's lovely to see you again,' she said.

'It's nice to see you, Debbie. I've looked forward to today.'

Debbie smiled at him warmly, still holding his hand. 'Me too. What would you like to do first? Shopping or coffee?'

'Coffee would be nice.' He grinned.

'Right.' Debbie hitched her bag a little further onto her shoulder. 'I know just the place. There's a church in town that has a lovely restaurant and they do a marvellous cup of coffee.'

'Lead on,' John enthused.

They walked out of the station. The grey clouds of earlier had rolled away, and suddenly everything was bathed in sunshine.

'I thought it was going to be dull and cool again,' Debbie remarked, with a quick glance at the sky and then at her costume. 'That's why I put this on.'

John nodded. 'It's been pretty damp lately. I've had quite a job to keep up with things on the allotment.'

'How is your allotment?' Debbie sounded as if she was really interested.

'It needs a bit of sunshine to help things along. Because of the weather I haven't managed to get there as often as I'd have liked.'

'And now you spend a sunny day helping me.' She gave him one of her little coy looks.

'All work and no play makes Jack a dull boy,' he quipped as a way of answering her tricky remark.

They set off, John remembering to shorten his steps to allow Debbie to keep pace. He noticed that she had on the same shoes he had seen her wearing on holiday. As they walked he became aware of their two hands close to each other. Without thinking, he took hold of her free hand. She responded immediately, gripping his firmly. In five minutes they were at their destination. They chatted over coffee like old friends, Debbie bubbling with seeing John again, relating anecdotes of life with Jamie, and asking him about his allotment and other aspects of his lifestyle that had not come up during their first few days together. Time flew past, and the original half-hour Debbie had mentally allocated for coffee stretched into an hour. John listened, responding with answers or asking a question from time to time.

Eventually Debbie glanced at her watch. 'Gosh, just look at the time! I think we should go, don't you?' She stood up and prepared to leave the restaurant.

John followed suit. He had been looking forward to helping her buy a camera. He had already done his research and had a pretty good idea of what would be suitable. The first shop they went to had in stock everything he had in mind, and as it was not busy, the young man serving them was able to be more attentive. Debbie tried her best to ask simple, sensible questions, leaving the technical ones to John.

Only when it came to choosing the colour did she allow her feminine intuition to rule, selecting the silver camera in preference to the black. John thought it would be a good choice for her and a decision was made. Debbie handed over her credit card, and a few minutes later they emerged from the shop, John carrying a large bag with the shop's name on it.

Immediately outside, Debbie stopped and turned to him. 'Thank you, John. I would never have dared to do it on my own.'

'You'd have been all right in that shop – they were very helpful,' he observed with a smile.

Debbie gave him one of her looks. 'There could be some debate about that. You just don't know me and modern inventions.'

John just chuckled. He was getting used to her condemnation of her own ability.

Debbie made a new suggestion. 'Now, can I buy you an early lunch?'

'It sounds a good idea, but really I should treat you,' John replied.

Debbie shook her head. 'No. It's on me. How about the place where we had coffee?'

'It sounds fine to me. Let's go.'

They took a long time over lunch, happy to be in each other's company. After a while, during one of the few lulls in their conversation, Debbie looked at her watch.

'It's lovely chatting like this, John, but I'm just thinking that if we want to give ourselves enough time to play with my new toys, do you think we should go?' She looked at him for confirmation.

It was John's turn to glance at his watch. 'Yes. Perhaps it would be a good idea, though I'm sure it won't take long to show you how everything works.'

As he finished speaking, he gave a fleeting look round the now crowded restaurant. He leaned across the table to Debbie and whispered: 'Besides, I think our table is badly needed.'

Debbie smiled. 'I've been conscious of it for a few minutes. Let's go.'

As they left the restaurant, she turned to him with a slightly anxious look on her face. 'You don't mind driving with me, do you, John?'

'Of course not. Why should I?'

'Oh, it's just that some men don't seem to like being driven by a woman. Ron used to do all the driving when we went out together.'

John smiled at her. 'I don't mind at all,' he replied.

'That's a relief.' She laughed.

Secretly she had been worried about using her car to meet him, at one point almost deciding to take a taxi instead. Memories of driving with Ron had surfaced and made her anxious about the minor ordeal ahead. In the end she had grasped the bull by the horns and taken the car. She was relieved by John's laid-back attitude.

She led the way through several back streets. After about five minutes she turned into a gap the width of a car between two buildings.

'Parking is quite difficult here,' she remarked as they emerged into the sunlight again and found themselves in a small car park. Seeing John's enquiring look, she added: 'I'm rather lucky. I know someone who has a business here – a friend of Ron's – and if there is space I can park here. It's quite convenient at times, but I don't abuse the privilege.'

'Lucky you.'

Debbie walked towards a small blue Ford. 'This is me,' she said, rummaging in her bag for the keys.

She unlocked the car door and slipped into the driver's seat, leaning over to lift the locking knob on the passenger side. John moved in beside her, placing their purchases on the back seat and pretending not to notice that her skirt had ridden well up over her knees as she sat down. By the time he turned round again, she had discreetly remedied her minor predicament and was feeling under her seat for a change of shoes. 'I never got used to driving in heels,' she said.

John smiled politely as he clicked his seat belt on and settled himself in his seat for the drive. Being driven by somebody else was a luxury he seldom experienced. Debbie placed the car in gear and started to move off. She was glad she had reversed into the parking space so that she could drive straight out. Manoeuvring in a tight space had never been one of her strong points, and the car park had filled up since she had parked earlier, so reversing out would have been difficult.

As they set off, she was still feeling apprehensive about driving with a man as passenger. She was glad it was John and not somebody else. As they emerged from the car park into the road she remarked: 'I don't really drive enough. I should use the car more.'

'You keep it in nice condition,' John observed, looking round the interior.

Debbie smiled. 'It's quite old, really. Ron bought it for me shortly before he died.'

For a few seconds she was silent. The arrival of the car and Ron's sudden death were closely interwoven. He had died just three weeks after buying the car as a surprise birthday present.

It was John who broke the brief silence. 'I bought mine when I retired. I treated it as a sort of celebration gift to myself.' He laughed.

Debbie laughed as well. 'What better way?' she agreed cheerfully.

They drove for what seemed to John to be only a short time and then Debbie turned off the main road into a pleasant, tree-lined avenue. After the busy road they had just left, the lack of traffic was quite noticeable. Solid detached houses lined the road on each side. Debbie turned the car into the driveway of one of these and drew to a halt in front of the detached garage.

'Here we are,' she announced, pulling on the handbrake and switching off the engine.

John looked around, interested. 'You have a very nice house,' he enthused.

'We bought it when my daughters were quite small. The girls were brought up here and I am still here,' Debbie replied breezily. She suddenly laughed as she locked the car. 'If you listened to my daughters, you'd think I was too old and decrepit to live here on my own.'

They moved towards the front door, Debbie carrying her high-heeled shoes, and John the bag from the camera shop. Debbie fitted the key into the lock and threw open the door.

'Come in, John. Welcome to my home,' she said, slipping off her driving shoes and picking up a pair of soft leather house shoes.

'How is your foot now?' John asked, his gaze focusing on Debbie's nylon-clad toes.

It's fine now. I've just got a teeny-weeny scar, which I'm sure will go soon,' she responded cheerfully. 'Make yourself at home,' she added.

As he waited for Debbie to finish changing her shoes, John surveyed his surroundings. The hall was square and made a rather pleasant entrance. The stairway was unusual in that instead of being right opposite the front door it started its ascent to the right and then climbed in three stages, with a small landing at each stage. 'I like your stairway,' he commented.

Debbie followed his gaze. 'It is rather unusual, isn't it? It was one of the things I liked about this house when we first looked at it. That and the garden.'

'Where shall I put these?' John asked, indicating the bag he was still holding.

'Let's put it all in the study. I don't want the girls to see it until I'm really proficient.' She crossed the hall and threw open a door. John followed her into a small room furnished with a desk and bookshelves. A sewing machine stood against one wall. John placed the bag on the desk.

Debbie turned to him. 'Work first, or refreshment?' she asked.

John grinned. 'Let's get you started on digital photography first.' He was already taking boxes out of the bag.

Debbie made a bit of a face, but she was happy to go along with his suggestion. Part of her was keen to learn the new skill, but another part was apprehensive and wanted to put off the time when she would have to concentrate on learning. Secretly she was glad John had been firm about it. Women, she thought, need a little control from men at times.

John was a good teacher. He carefully removed the camera and accessories from their packaging and showed her how everything worked. He got her to insert the batteries and the memory card in the camera and then directed her finger to the on/off switch.

'Hey! I've actually done it!' came her squeal of delight as the camera sprang into life.

'There's better to come,' announced John, glancing out of the window. 'We need to take some photographs now,' he added, smiling at Debbie's childlike wonderment.

They went out into the garden and John patiently took Debbie through the process of framing and recording a shot. Again and again he went through it with her until he was satisfied that she was confident.

It was when they returned to the study again and John set up the little printing machine that Debbie was completely taken over. John showed her how to put the memory card in the printer and operate the controls. Within a few minutes the picture she had taken in the garden was in her hand. She gasped in amazement.

'It's fantastic! I never imagined you could do this.'

'Now, you do it all,' John instructed.

'Do you think I can? Remind me what to do first.' Debbie was fired up with enthusiasm now.

John repeated his patient instructions, getting her to do everything until she had a good grasp of it all. The rest of the afternoon flew by. It was Debbie who wilted at last.

'Do you know, I think I've got it! I just hope I can remember everything. It really is fantastic. I can't wait to surprise the girls, but I'll practise a bit first. How about a cup of tea?' She looked at John expectantly.

'Great idea. I'm ready for one now.'

Debbie ushered him towards the lounge. He hesitated before entering, and on seeing the carpeted room he politely slipped off his shoes, just in case they were muddy from the garden. Debbie almost stopped him but quickly changed her mind. One of the things she had noticed about John was that he was always so polite and considerate. It seemed to be a rare quality these days. Instead she told him to make himself comfortable and hurried to the kitchen to sort out the goodies she had purchased earlier in the day for their tea. She kept up a kind of conversation with John from the kitchen as he relaxed in one of the armchairs. The lounge was pleasant and airy. The pale green carpet set off the cream leather sofa and chairs beautifully, and the oil paintings hanging on the white walls were of light and cheerful country scenes. It was one of these that caught John's eye. He got up to have a closer look at it and was still absorbed when Debbie came into the room carrying a tray. She discarded her own shoes to keep him company.

'My sister painted it,' she commented, putting down the tray. 'It's a Suffolk scene. She used to live there.'

'It's quite good. I like it,' replied John, coming back to his chair. 'Do you paint?' he asked.

Debbie laughed as she poured out the tea. 'I used to try, but I was nowhere near as good as Gwen. There are some daubings of mine around somewhere.'

'What about your daughters?' John asked, accepting the cup of tea she offered.

Debbie shook her head. 'They have no interest whatsoever. It's funny how children are different – but then again Ron never had any interest. He was more interested in sport than arts.'

'Do you just have one sister?'

Debbie nodded. 'Just the one. Gwen is a year older than me. She lives in Canada, somewhere near Vancouver. She keeps asking me to go and see her, but the thought of the long flight puts me off.'

John agreed enthusiastically. 'That's a bit like me. My brother lives in Australia. He keeps asking me to visit him. I suppose I should make the effort. There are nieces and nephews I've never seen.'

Debbie took a sip of her tea. 'Well I did manage to see mine when they visited England several years ago.'

They chatted on as Debbie plied John with sandwiches and cake. Just as he was refusing a third cup of tea, the telephone rang. It was one of the other women from the Women's Institute trying to persuade Debbie to accept the nomination for the committee. By the time she had extricated herself from the situation and politely ended the conversation, ten minutes had slipped by.

'I'm sorry about that,' she said, returning to her chair. She explained the reason for the call. 'It was bit tricky trying to decline gracefully. It's the second time somebody has rung me about it.'

'Why don't you? You'd be good at it.'

Debbie smiled and shook her head. 'Not really,' she said. 'It's not what I'm looking for in life.'

It was fast approaching seven o'clock when John at last looked at his watch and announced that he had better make a move. 'Can I get a bus or a taxi to the station from here?' he asked.

Debbie was horrified. 'Certainly not,' she replied. 'I'm going to run you there.'

They drove back to the station in the evening sunshine. The traffic was lighter now and it seemed no time at all before Debbie pulled onto the station forecourt. They both got out of the car under the watchful eyes of the taxi drivers, who were carefully guarding their territory.

'I won't come into the station. I don't think it would be a wise thing to do,' Debbie remarked, pulling a face and glancing towards the taxi drivers, who were eyeing her activities closely.

She came round to John's side of the car. He took her hand. 'Thank you for a lovely day, Debbie. Thank you for everything.'

'Better than the allotment?' she asked mischievously.

'Much better. I really enjoyed the day.'

Debbie was serious again. 'I hope you've enjoyed it as much as I have. It's really been fantastic, every bit of it. And thank you for showing me how to use the camera. I just hope I don't forget everything.'

John smiled at her. 'Well, I'm only a phone call away if you get stuck.'

Debbie looked up at him. She still held his hand. 'Thank you for everything, John. Will you come again sometime?'

John smiled at her. 'Of course. I'll be in touch.'

'I'll look forward to that. Now I'd better go before I get a ticket or something.' Debbie glanced anxiously at the watching taxi drivers. 'Goodbye, John. Thank you again.' She leaned towards him to offer her cheek.

He pulled her towards him. This time his arm was around her as he kissed the cheek she offered. 'Goodbye, Debbie.'

She watched him disappear into the station. With a wave of his hand he was gone. She decided to make a quick exit under the accusing eyes of her watchers.

Chapter 8

Debbie recognised the vehicle immediately. The trim black sports car parked on her drive belonged to Trish. Debbie was just returning from shopping and, having carried her bags of purchases the half-mile or so from the local shops, would be glad to get inside the house and put them down.

It was nearly a week since she had seen John, and for the last few days she had been feeling particularly good about everything. John had rung her two days after his visit to check how she was getting on with her new camera, and they had chatted for a long time; then she had called him to check on one minor point. She was pleased with how she had mastered the new technology. She had decided to wait until she had all the family together before showing off her new skill.

But on top of that she had been conscious of a new focus in her life. She often thought about John, and only that morning she had seen a notice for a concert in town and had already decided to ring him in the evening and invite him over for it. Now as she saw Trish's car on the drive, she wondered if she would be able to do so, particularly if Trish stayed the night, which she frequently did when she arrived late in the afternoon like this.

Debbie let herself into the house.

'Is that you, Mum?' a voice called from upstairs.

'Yes, dear, it's me.'

'I'm just coming down.'

As Debbie walked into the kitchen with her shopping there was the unmistakable clatter of her daughter running down the stairs. The next second she was in the kitchen.

'Hello, Mum.'

'Hello, dear. It's nice to see you. You really shouldn't run down the stairs like that in those shoes, though. If you catch your heel you'll have a nasty accident.' Debbie winced every time she heard Trish thundering down the stairs. The heels of her shoes seemed to grow higher with each visit.

'I always run up and down stairs,' Trish insisted. 'Mum, is it all right if I stay the night? I've got to go to Bristol tomorrow and I thought I'd drop in to see you on the way.'

'Yes, of course, dear. What would you like for supper?'

'Hmm, not fussy really. What have you got?' Trish sat down on a convenient chair.

'How about a salad?

'Fine. I'm not very hungry anyway.'

'Do you want it now or a little later?' Debbie asked, putting her shopping away.

'Oh, later. I'm going to change out of these clothes, and I want to try and find something in my room first.' Trish got up and hurried in the direction of the stairs. Debbie smiled. Her younger daughter's matter-of-fact approach to everything could be amusing at times.

'OK, dear. Let me know when you want supper.'

Trish dashed up the stairs, making Debbie wince again. It was a full twenty minutes before she reappeared again in the kitchen, this time noiselessly. She had exchanged her smart business suit for jeans and what looked like a man's shirt. Bare feet accounted for her silent entrance.

'Mum, I can't find my red sun top. Have you seen it?'

'No, dear. I haven't moved anything. If you left it in your room it must still be there.' Debbie was almost tempted to add that given the untidy state of Trish's room, it was no wonder she couldn't find anything. Instead she added as an afterthought: 'Perhaps you already took it up to London.'

Trish shook her head. 'No, I'd know if I had it at the flat.' There was almost a tone of indignation in her voice.

'Have a look for it again after supper,' suggested Debbie, thinking that might just give her a few minutes to telephone John. The box office had told her that the concert tickets were selling fast and she should book as soon as possible. Her original plan had been to ring John that evening and then go into town the following morning as soon as the box office opened.

Trish had already flopped into a chair again. 'I need it to take on holiday next month.'

'Where are you going?' Debbie asked, busy with the lettuce. It was the first time she had heard about Trish's holiday.

'Spain. I'm going with Don.'

'Don?'

'Oh, he's my new boyfriend. He moved in with me last week.' It was almost a casual remark.

Debbie hadn't heard of Don before. 'You never mentioned him, dear,' she said, trying to sound as casual as Trish.

'Oh, I only met him about a month ago.'

Debbie turned to her daughter. 'Is that wise?'

'What do you mean?'

Debbie could sense the defensive nature of the question. She tried to be as diplomatic as she could. 'Well, letting him move in when you've known him such a short time.'

'Oh, Don's all right.'

'Be careful, dear – that's all I mean.'

'You were young once yourself,' Trish retorted.

'Yes, but we didn't carry on the way you young people do today,' Debbie replied, rather hastily. She hadn't meant to say it quite like that.

'Well, what about you and Daddy?'

Debbie took the bait. 'We didn't sleep together until we were married,' she replied quietly.

'Oh well, this is the twenty-first century. Things are different now.'

Debbie sighed, almost to herself. 'So it would seem,' she replied.

She decided to leave matters there. At times she worried about her younger daughter. She admired the way Trish had secured for herself what appeared to be a good job in marketing and the smart appearance that went with it. It was her lifestyle that bothered Debbie. They had had a similar conversation about boyfriends on a number of occasions. Trish's free and easy manner with members of the opposite sex was a direct contrast to how her older sister had behaved.

'Can we eat now, Mum?' asked Trish. 'I've got masses of work to do this evening.'

'Of course. It's all ready. Is it all right if we have it here?' Debbie had already laid the kitchen table.

'No problem.' Trish was already sitting down. Over the meal they exchanged their news. Debbie only saw Trish on average about once a month, and they spoke occasionally on the phone. It was nice to have a bit of time to relax and talk about everything that was happening in the family, and Debbie was keen to learn more about Trish's current lifestyle. At last Trish said she wanted to get on with her work, and this was the cue for Debbie to start collecting the dishes. Five minutes later, when she popped into the lounge Trish was perched in one of the armchairs, mobile in hand and laptop close by, engrossed in her work. It was, thought Debbie, the ideal moment to ring John. She could do it on the telephone extension in her bedroom.

It only took a minute to go upstairs to her bedroom and dial the number. The phone at the other end rang for a long time before it was picked up.

'John Hammond.'

'John, it's Debbie. I thought you were out. I was just about to give up.'

'Oh, hello, Debbie. Sorry about that – I've been out and I was just coming back. I could hear the phone ringing as I came up the stairs.'

'Have I called at a bad time? I can ring back.'

'Not at all. I'm glad I caught you. How are you getting on?'

'Really well. I've exceeded my own expectations and I've nearly run out of paper for the printer. I'll need to buy some more soon. I can't wait to launch my expertise in front of the family.'

She heard a chuckle at the other end of the phone. 'Great! You can get the paper in the shop where we bought the camera.'

'I'll buy some tomorrow. But how are you, John?'

'Nothing to complain about, except this damp weather we're having. I even had to stop working on the allotment yesterday because of the rain.'

Debbie commiserated. 'I know, I just can't get into the garden.'

There was a two-second silence, and then Debbie dived in with her news before John could say anything else. 'John, I was in town today and there's a concert on next Thursday. It looks good. Schubert. Beethoven. Would you like to come?'

'I'd love to. What time is it?'

'Somewhere around seven, I think.'

'I could come over early. We could make a day of it.'

'That would be lovely. Will you be able to get back all right?'

'Should be able to. If not, I'll bring the car, or I'll stay overnight somewhere.'

'I'll get the tickets tomorrow. I'm so pleased you can come.'

'MUM, ARE YOU THERE?'

Their conversation was halted. The unmistakable sound of Trish's voice was coming up the stairs.

'I'm up here, Trish. I'll be down in a minute,' Debbie called out, her hand over the mouthpiece of the phone. She turned her attention to John again.

'I'm sorry, John. Did you hear that? I have my daughter staying with me tonight. She was just calling me.'

There was a laugh at the other end of the phone. 'Duty calls.'

'You could say that. I'll ring you tomorrow. Would about the same time be OK?'

'That would be fine. I'll look forward to it.'

'OK, then. Bye for now.'

'Bye, Debbie. Thanks for phoning. Until tomorrow, then.'

'MUM!' The voice was more urgent.

Debbie replaced the receiver. She was pleased with herself.

Tomorrow she would buy the tickets as soon as the box office opened and then she could plan the day with John. She went to meet Trish, who was now coming up the stairs.

It was the day before the concert. Just after lunch, when Debbie opened the fridge door to get milk for a drink, she noticed how little there was left. She had used more than usual with Trish staying overnight. There was enough for the rest of the day, and perhaps even for breakfast if she was careful, but certainly not much more for anything after that.

Since living on her own she had dispensed with the regular morning delivery of milk, finding that she often didn't get through a pint in a day. But it was rare for her to run so low. She was thankful that Jan or somebody else hadn't dropped in and required entertaining.

The weather was fine. She decided to walk to the mini-supermarket half a mile away to replenish supplies. While she was there she could top up on one or two other things.

It was a pleasant walk. She could cut through several leafy back roads and then come out on the main road only a few yards from the cluster of shops. Life felt good. Tomorrow she would see John again.

Just outside the shop she bumped into Grace Carrington, who lived at the end of her road. 'Hello, Debbie.' Grace stood to one side as she spoke, clearly indicating that she wanted to talk.

'Hello, Grace. I just dashed out to get some milk.' She met Grace quite frequently. She, too, was a member of the WI. She was a retired teacher who had never married and now lived with her brother, a retired headmaster.

'I'm glad I saw you,' said Grace. 'Have you heard the news?'

'No. What news?' Debbie was a bit puzzled. She wondered whether it was something to do with the suggestion that she should fill the vacant committee place at the WI. She was unprepared for Grace's next comment.

Grace lowered her voice as if she did not want to be overheard. 'Jill Foster's husband came home from work the other day and found her dead in the kitchen. She was only sixty-seven.'

'Oh, how awful!' Debbie's reaction was spontaneous. It was Jill Foster who had persuaded her to join the WI after Ron had died. Jill and Freddie Foster were a sociable couple who lived in the next road to Debbie. Freddie was still working even though he was well past retirement age.

'It must be awful for Freddie,' Grace went on. 'They were so close. I know there is a son who lives in the north of England, but I don't know about any other family members.'

A wave of sadness came over Debbie. She knew how Freddie Foster must be feeling. The memories of the sudden telephone call from Ron's office telling her he had been taken ill flooded back to her. 'We must do something. We must be able to help in some way,' she suggested.

'I think the neighbours next door are supporting as best they can,' replied Grace. 'It's so awful... I was shocked when I heard the news,' she added in the same concerned tone of voice.

'When did it happen?'

'The evening before last. I heard yesterday morning.'

Grace's words struck a sombre note with Debbie. How isolated our modern way of life is, she thought. A sad event like Jill's death had taken place over twenty-four hours ago, yet how many people in the immediate area would know? If she hadn't bumped into Grace, it might have been several days before she heard the news. The thought prompted her reply. 'As neighbours I feel we should do something. We can't just do nothing.'

'I'm sure you're right. But I don't know what one can do.' Grace's reply was not inspiring. Her tone irritated Debbie.

'Well at least we can telephone or something,' Debbie protested.

'Yes, perhaps we should do that,' Grace said, but without enthusiasm.

They talked for another few minutes, and then Grace turned the conversation to the WI. Debbie knew what was coming. She had little inclination to discuss yet again whether she should or should not fill the vacancy on the committee. She politely disengaged herself and went into the shop. It occurred to her that Grace might wait for her, as they would both have to walk the same way back, so she was relieved to find that she had already disappeared when she emerged from the shop five minutes later. She wanted to walk alone with her thoughts.

She made her way home in a subdued mood. Learning about Jill had cast a shadow over the day. The worst bit was that she was not entirely sure why the news had affected her so strongly. Perhaps the announcement of a sudden death had revived the loss of Ron years before. She knew that for Freddie Foster it would be almost as if things had come to a sudden halt. One moment everything was normal, and the next moment life had been completely changed forever. Of one thing she was certain: such tragic events were a reminder of the fragility of life.

Her melancholy ponderings were interrupted when she encountered Polly Wilkinson with her Pekinese dog, Ming. Polly was a well-known figure in the area and could usually be seen at some point in the day taking her faithful companion for a walk. Nobody seemed to know how old she was, but she had been around for a long time. Still fit and active, she lived on her own in her tiny bungalow, did her own shopping, and carried on her life quietly. Everybody stopped to talk to her and pat Ming, who always maintained a dignified indifference.

Debbie followed tradition and stopped to chat. They talked about the weather, and Polly commented on how Ming got upset if they couldn't get out for a walk on time. Debbie wondered whether she should tell her about Jill Foster, hesitating because relating the news so soon after hearing it made her feel like a bit of a gossip. She need not have worried. Polly's next remark was: 'Have you heard about poor Mrs Foster?' Debbie replied that she had heard a short time ago. At that point Ming decided he wanted to continue his walk, and their brief conversation came to a halt. Debbie said goodbye and went on her way.

By the time she reached her own street, Debbie was beginning to feel a bit better. In spite of Grace Carrington's slightly apathetic response to her suggestion, Debbie decided she would telephone Freddie Foster in the near future. It was the least she could do, she decided.

As she neared the house and glanced up at the sky, it became apparent that it was perhaps a good thing to be close to home. The earlier sun of the afternoon had now disappeared and grey clouds scudded across the sky, threatening more rain. A breeze had also sprung up, which had a chill feel to it.

Debbie turned into her drive. She stopped for a moment to glance at the rose bed at the side of the dividing hedge between her house and the neighbouring one. The roses needed some attention. She would ask Tom to look at them, or she could do it herself. Not tomorrow, though. Tomorrow was already completely taken care of. The thought of seeing John again was cheering. Then, conscious that the bags she carried were getting heavy, she made her way to the front door.

As soon as she opened it and stepped into the house, she was conscious that something was wrong. Something was different. There was a slight draught blowing through the hall. That never normally happened. She carried her bags into the kitchen and the sight that met her eyes brought forth a cry of anguish from her lips. 'Oh no!'

The back door was half open.

Debbie's first reaction was to scold herself. How could she have done anything so careless? She had never done that before. Then she saw the broken glass on the floor. Suddenly her heart was thumping. She looked around, anxious and fearful.

'Oh no,' she whispered again, almost to herself. 'I've been burgled.'

Chapter 9

Debbie was rooted to the spot. Her heart was pounding. The shock was beginning to register. And then a new fear gripped her. Suppose there was still somebody in the house...? She waited, wondering what to do. Should she run next door for help? Her thoughts were in turmoil. For a few seconds she remained motionless, just standing there, waiting.

Bit by bit her reasoning returned. If there was anybody in the house they were very quiet. Didn't burglars make a noise opening drawers and things? Gradually some semblance of courage returned. There was no sound anywhere in the house. She went into the hall and looked up the stairs. She called up: 'Who's there?' No answer came.

She looked in the lounge. Her desk was open. She went into the dining room and the study. Everything looked in order; even her new camera and printer were where she had left them.

She wandered back into the hall. Still she could not pluck up the courage to go upstairs. Again she called out: 'Anybody there?' She strained her ears for any sound, but everything was eerily quiet. She waited another few minutes, wondering again whether she should go next door and ask her neighbours for help.

Eventually she concluded that no burglar would have remained upstairs for this length of time. She remembered looking at her watch as she approached the front door, and a good twenty minutes had now elapsed. She had to go upstairs.

Fearfully she mounted the stairs, making as much noise as she could. Everything on the landing seemed to be in order. She threw open the door of the bathroom, then the toilet, then the bedrooms.

She hesitated when she came to her own bedroom, but she had left the door half open earlier. Relief crept over her. At least she was now alone in the house. She went back downstairs and into the kitchen. She closed the back door and locked it. Then she went back into the lounge. A few things had been pulled out of the desk, but nothing seemed to have been taken. She had had her purse and credit card with her. She picked up the phone and dialled.

'Hello, Jan. It's Mum.'

'Hello, Mum. I was going to phone you this evening.'

'Jan, I've been burgled.'

'What? How? When did this happen?'

'I just went out to the shops and when I came back the glass was broken in the back door.'

'Has anything been taken?'

'I'm not sure. I don't think so.'

Jan took control. 'Look, Mum, you must check. Have you phoned the police?'

'Not yet, dear.'

'You need to. I'll come over as soon as Paul comes home.'

'Oh, would you, dear? That would be welcome.'

'Don't worry, Mum, I'll be over in less than an hour. Check if anything has been taken and ring the police.'

'OK. I'll do that now.'

'I won't be long. See you soon, Mum.'

'All right, dear. Bye for now.'

'Bye, Mum.'

Debbie heard the phone click as Jan replaced the receiver. She was glad of her calm and practical approach to things. Of her two daughters Jan was the more down-to-earth.

She sat at her desk for a minute or two. She felt calmer now. She knew that she had to take control. She had to sort things out somehow.

She wandered back into the kitchen and cleared up the glass. The hole in the door worried her but there was nothing she could do about it for now. Guilt was already creeping into her thinking for leaving the key in the back door. Normally it was her habit to remove it and put it under the mat when she went out. Of all the days when she hadn't carried out her routine, this had to happen. Everybody would think she was becoming senile or something like that.

She carefully went through the rest of the house again, checking for anything out of place or missing. The odd thing was that, apart from the slight disturbance around her desk, nothing else appeared to have been touched.

She rang the police as Jan had suggested. It took her a minute or two to get through, and then a female voice answered. Debbie explained her dilemma and was advised that the crime had been logged and that somebody would visit her as soon as possible. Debbie thanked the woman, replaced the receiver and waited.

The first person to arrive was Jan, almost an hour later. 'Mum, I'm sorry I took so long. Paul was a bit late coming home,' was her greeting.

'Oh, that's all right, dear. Just thank you for coming.' Debbie felt a bit of relief now that a second person was around.

'Mum, are you all right?' Jan looked anxiously at her.

'Oh yes, I'm a bit calmer now. It was just the shock of coming back and finding everything. It's a horrible feeling knowing that an intruder has been in the house and has been everywhere.'

'Show me everything.' Jan still looked anxious.

Debbie showed her the broken glass in the door and together they went over the house. They had a cup of tea while they waited for the police to arrive. An hour went by, then two. Debbie could see Jan sneaking the occasional glance at the clock on the wall.

At last as it was nearing eight o'clock Debbie took charge. 'You really must get back to Paul and Jamie, dear,' she said firmly.

'Are you sure you're all right, Mum? Do you want me to stay the night?' Jan still looked worried.

Debbie knew she had to put on a show of strength. 'Oh, I'll be fine. It was just the initial shock. I'm not as shaky now.' She even managed a smile as she spoke.

Jan seemed to accept the pretence, saying that she would contact her mother the following day. Debbie watched her leave and then returned to wait.

It was almost an hour later that she saw a police car draw up on her drive. She hurried to the front door just as two police officers were about to ring the bell. Debbie's immediate reaction was to think how young they looked.

'Mrs Patterson?' one of them asked her.

'Yes.' Debbie's reply was uncharacteristically brief.

'You've had a burglary?'

'Yes. This afternoon, while I was out,' Debbie replied as she stood on one side to allow the two young women to enter the hall. Both looked around, observing everything.

'Can we see where they got in?' It was the same officer who spoke. Debbie took them into the kitchen and showed them the damaged door.

'Was the key in the door?' the police officer asked.

'Yes, it was. I usually remove it when I go out, but today I must have forgotten.' Relating her carelessness made Debbie feel bad. She knew what the next remark would be.

'You should always take it out. You can see how easy it is for somebody to gain entry.' The officer looked at Debbie, who didn't know what to say. Her careless moment weighed down on her.

'Do you live on your own?' For the first time the second officer spoke.

Debbie assured her that she did. Then the two police officers wanted to look over the rest of the house. Debbie obediently obliged. As she showed them her desk, the officer who did most of the talking commented that it was quite possible that Debbie had interrupted the intruder when she returned and that was the reason nothing was missing. It was something Debbie hadn't thought of. When they were back in the kitchen, the first police officer produced her notebook to take down all the details. What was her full name and address? Her age? The time of the crime? What had been taken? Had she seen

81

anybody? Question followed question, and by the time they had finished, Debbie was beginning to feel quite stressed again.

At last the police officers seemed satisfied. The notebook was put away and they made a move to leave. Once again the officer who had done most of the talking glanced at the back door with its broken glass.

'Do you normally use the bolt on the door?' she asked.

'If I go away for any length of time, but it is so stiff and difficult to move that I don't always use it if I just go to the local shops,' Debbie replied.

'You should get it replaced and you should also consider installing an alarm system on a house like this.'

The remark made Debbie feel even more helpless and inadequate. 'Perhaps I should look into it,' she replied, adding by way of justification for her hesitation: 'It's just that this is a very quiet neighbourhood. We never have any problems.'

'There was another incident in this area today, just before you reported yours.' It was the second police officer who spoke.

'Oh, where?'

'I'm afraid we can't tell you that, for security reasons.'

Debbie said nothing.

Then the second officer spoke again. 'I suggest you contact our Crime Prevention Officer. He will be able to offer you some advice on security.'

'Thank you. I might do that.' She didn't know what else to say.

The two police officers made their way towards the front door. Debbie opened it for them. On the step they paused and said they were sorry for her dilemma and that if there were any developments they would be in touch. In the meantime she should consider improving her security.

Debbie watched them go and then dropped into a chair in the lounge. Her legs felt like jelly and on top of that her feelings of inadequacy were now bubbling beneath the surface. The attitude of the two young police officers had been to treat her as if she were incapable of dealing with things, or at least were managing things badly. True, both Jan and Paul had urged her from time to time to make the house more secure, but it had always been one of those things she intended to look into and had never considered urgent. Now her carelessness weighed heavily on her. First it had been leaving the key in the door, and now it was her laid-back approach to things. Everybody would definitely think she was becoming unable to cope any longer.

It was the telephone that alerted her from her period of reflection. As she went to answer it a flash of panic struck her. She had said she would ring John that evening to confirm the arrangements. With everything going on, it had completely slipped her mind. Now he must be ringing her. She picked up the receiver.

It was a woman's voice. 'Hello.'

Debbie immediately thought it must be Jan, but it was someone else.

'Hello, Debbie. It's Rosemary Bilton. Is everything all right? We saw the police car outside.' The Biltons lived almost opposite.

'Hello, Rosemary. Actually I had a break-in while I was out at the shops this afternoon. That's why the police were here.' Debbie didn't know the Biltons all that well; they had only lived in the road a short time.

'How awful. Poor you. Was anything taken?' Rosemary sounded quite concerned.

'Not as far as I can see. The police think I disturbed the burglar when I came back.' She had now come to accept that idea.

'Thank goodness for that. Lucky for you. There was another break-in down the road today, at the Rawlingses'. Did you know?'

'The police did say something about another incident. But they wouldn't elaborate.'

'Mrs Rawlings actually saw the young man running away.' Rosemary's voice was lowered a tone as she related this bit of news.

Debbie only knew the Rawlingses by sight. 'Was very much taken?' she felt obliged to ask.

'Oh yes, I think so.'

'Do you know what time it happened?'

'About four, I think.'

'That was about the time of mine.' Debbie thought for a few seconds. Clearly whoever had broken in had made the rounds of several houses.

It was Rosemary who spoke first again. 'You know, we should really get a Neighbourhood Watch scheme going in the road. Patrick has always said so.' Patrick was her husband.

'It might be a good idea,' Debbie replied, adding as an afterthought: 'Perhaps we can ask a few other people if they would be interested.'

'I'll get Patrick onto it. He'll like doing something like that.'

Debbie smiled at Rosemary's enthusiasm to organise her husband. From what she observed Patrick Bilton looked a bit henpecked at times. Before she could answer, Rosemary chipped in again. 'Anyway, Debbie, I hope you didn't mind me phoning you. It's just that I was a bit worried seeing the police car.'

'It was quite sweet of you. I really appreciate it. Thank you very much.' Debbie really meant what she said.

'Not at all. I'll say goodbye now. I just wanted to make sure you were all right.'

'Thank you again. Goodbye, Rosemary.'

Debbie put down the receiver. It was nice that the Biltons had taken the trouble to enquire, particularly when she didn't know them all that well. They always seemed to be busy with their own affairs.

She suddenly thought of the two phone calls she must make. One to John, as she had promised, and she also ought to contact Trish and tell her what had happened. Heaven would have to protect her if Trish heard the news from her sister or somebody else and not directly from her mother. Debbie had learnt through experience to treat both her daughters exactly alike, otherwise she would have to endure the indignation of her younger offspring.

She dialled Trish's mobile number but there was no answer. She was about to ring off when an answering service cut in. Debbie hesitated about leaving a message. She hated talking to a machine, but in the end she left a short message: 'Hello, Trish. It's Mum. I just wanted to tell you something, but I'll ring you again tomorrow.'

There was method in her strategy. In saying she would phone the next day, she hoped Trish would not return her call at some unreasonable hour when she had gone to bed. It had happened before. She knew Trish would get her message without any delay. As Debbie had frequently observed, Trish, like many of the younger element of society, spent a considerable amount of time on her mobile. She had long since dispensed with a house phone and relied entirely on her mobile for verbal communication.

Debbie looked up John's number and dialled. It was far later than she had intended.

Chapter 10

John was having a good day. It was, however, a busy one. He had woken up early and this had prompted him to go to the allotment earlier than usual. He had even arrived before the regular early bird, Stephen, who usually turned up before seven. He had already been busy for half an hour or so when Stephen made an appearance. John called out a greeting to him. 'Morning, Stephen. Overslept?'

There was something like a grunt from Stephen, followed by a more audible reply. 'Morning. Car wouldn't start.'

'You'll have to spend some of your money and buy a new model,' John shouted back. Stephen's allotment was several plots away.

'Graham's going to give me his old car sometime – when he feels like it,' Stephen called back, already starting to open his shed.

John grinned to himself. Stephen's ancient and unreliable car was a bit of a joke on the allotment. Nobody could figure out how he got it through its MOT test every year. Like many of the regular allotment holders he was a pensioner. From what he said to his allotment neighbours, he appeared to have a complaining wife and a bit of a love/hate relationship with his only son, Graham. Every morning at the same time he arrived promptly at his patch and stayed there until one o'clock, silently working away. Rarely did he speak unless spoken to, and then the reply would be brief and to the point. If the weather was bad he fiddled around in his shed until it was time to go.

John started to busy himself. He had not been to his allotment since rain had stopped him working there a day or two before, and as usual the work had started to pile up. He worked steadily until around ten and then stopped for a mug of coffee, made using hot water from his flask. It was a bit of a routine he had, sitting in the doorway of his tiny shed and watching the world go by. By this time there were always other people working away and there would usually be somebody who had time to stop and chat. Stephen apart, it was a very sociable community.

John worked away until well after midday. Debbie popped into his thoughts on more than one occasion during the morning. He was looking forward to tomorrow and seeing her again. He was now conscious that she was playing a leading part in his thinking at the present time. Scarcely half an hour went by when his thoughts did not return to her. He had rediscovered the pleasure of having a member of the opposite sex to share with and he found he enjoyed the experience. True, he had only seen Debbie once since their holiday meeting, but by now he realised that he held her in great esteem. Being with her seemed to bring him alive again, jerk him out of the humdrum bachelor existence he had fallen into since Mary died. Of course, he reasoned, he had no idea how Debbie felt, but he felt confident enough to assume that she would scarcely have invited him over to see her again if she had not enjoyed the previous occasion. Like him she was no doubt enjoying the experience of similar company and appreciating the break from normal routine.

On his way home he decided to call in at the Dog and Duck. Often when he finished his allotment toil, particularly if it was around midday, he would stop by at his 'local', as he termed the establishment, for what he considered was a well-earned half-pint of lager.

As he entered the bar, he thought it seemed a bit crowded for a Wednesday. He could see the two regulars, Bob and Harry, seated in a corner, but around the bar counter a small group of young office workers lingered, the young men in their smart business suits trying to impress the young women perched on the bar stools who with stilettos hooked onto the bar stools and skirts riding high on their legs acted out their acquired sophistication.

John stood back for a moment while the landlord finished serving the group. The scene reminded him of his early days in business, and similar bar interludes. Not a lot had changed, he thought: boys and girls each playing out their role, though these days the girls allowed more of their legs to be seen. The wearing of tights had allowed women this freedom.

The landlord, Jonathan Hawkins, finished serving the group. He had seen John arrive.

'Good afternoon, John. The usual?' His hand was already on a glass.

John smiled and nodded. 'Good afternoon, Jon. Yes, please, and I think I'll sample a cottage pie as well.' He had had a quick look at the written menu behind the bar. Today he didn't fancy going home and cooking a meal.

Jonathan placed the full glass of lager on the counter and noted down John's order for the kitchen. He knew John quite well: he had been coming for a few years and often dropped in about this time to share a drink and chat with the other regulars. Normally he would have stayed with John for a few minutes, but a couple had come into the bar and were waiting behind John and needed his attention.

John paid for his drink and meal and ambled over to the table where Bob and Harry were sitting.

'Good afternoon, Bob. Good afternoon, Harry,' was his pleasant greeting to them as he placed his glass of beer on the table and prepared to sit down.

Bob replied with an equally cheerful greeting. Harry's was uttered with less enthusiasm. It would have been hard to imagine two characters less alike. Bob, though close to retirement, ran a small butcher's shop close by and popped into the Dog and Duck for a pint and something to eat at lunchtime. He was a cheerful individual who always seemed to be smiling behind the glasses he wore. Harry was the direct opposite. A retired postman, he wore a most doleful expression on his face most of the time and was rarely known to look on the bright side of things. Bob had once remarked that if he were to smile, his face would crack. The highlights of Harry's day appeared to be his pint at the Dog and Duck and then a few hours in the betting shop along the street.

'Heard the cricket score?' Bob asked as John settled down at the table and took a sip of his drink. A test match was being played.

John shook his head. 'No, I've been on the allotment all morning. Not heard a thing.'

'England ninety-eight for three,' announced Bob, always up to the minute with such information.'

'Hmm. Not so good, is it? I hope rain doesn't stop play again like yesterday,' replied John.

'Won't make any difference to the score,' remarked Harry gloomily. England, he was sure, were set to lose the current series.

'Ah, optimism is a great thing,' John chipped in, amused at Harry's gloomy outlook.

The arrival of John's dinner provided a brief interruption in their conversation. Afterwards the chatting resumed, mostly generated by Bob and John. After a while Bob said he had to get back to his shop, jokingly remarking that, unlike some people, he wasn't retired and he had to earn a living. John drained the last of his drink and Harry stuffed his newspaper into his pocket. It was a general signal for the party to break up. The trio left together, with a nod in the direction of Jonathan. Outside Bob hurried off to his shop and John walked with Harry as far as the betting shop and, with a brief 'Cheerio. Good luck,' watched him disappear into its depths.

John walked at a steady pace the half-mile or so to his flat. It was well after two o'clock when he turned down the side road where he lived. It was in a neighbourhood that was often described as being 'sought-after'. John considered himself extremely lucky to have been able to purchase it. When he had started to collect himself together after Mary died, it had become increasingly apparent to him that it was not practical to go on living alone in a big house. He had spent some time looking at various flats, none of which had inspired him to any great extent. Then he had discovered the small block where he now lived. Unfortunately, it was one of those places where people tended to stay put, and there were few opportunities to purchase. Estate agents had shaken their heads when he had enquired about a possible purchase coming up. Then, through a friend who knew he was looking for a flat, he heard about an elderly couple who were planning to sell up and move into sheltered accommodation. To his amazement and obvious joy, it turned out to be a top-floor flat in the very block he had his eye on. Immediately after viewing it he had made an offer, much to the appreciation of the owners, who had been dreading an extended process of selling. The flat was light and airy, catching the morning sun on one side and the evening sun on the other. It was spacious and well designed, consisting of a fairly large sitting room, one good-sized bedroom, a second, smaller one, a kitchen and a bathroom. Divided from the road by pleasant lawns and trees, it was quiet and peaceful, as John had found to his satisfaction.

He whittled away the rest of the afternoon shopping, paying a couple of bills and then driving his car round the corner to the filling station to top up on fuel for the journey to Oxford. He had scarcely used the car since returning from holiday and he checked the tyre pressures and the oil level at the same time. Walking the short distance from the garage block to the front entrance, he encountered one of his neighbours, who was inclined to chat. Once indoors again, he made himself a cup of tea and had a look at the newspaper. It was close on seven when he put it down and turned his thoughts to Debbie again. Must ring her, he thought, just to confirm the arrangements for tomorrow. He raised himself from his comfortable armchair and gazed out of the window at the scene. As he did so he thought he recognised the car that had just turned into the parking area off the road. A minute or so later, his outside doorbell rang. He pressed the button on the intercom.

'Hello. Who's there?'

'Dad, it's Rob.' The unmistakable voice of his son came over loud and clear.

'Come in, come in.' John released the outside door.

He opened the door to the flat just as Rob arrived at the top of the stairs. There was a lift, but Rob, like his father, scorned its use and usually walked up the three flights.

'Hello, old chap. What brings you round?'

Rob dropped into the chair his father had vacated five minutes previously. 'Finished work early today. I came home and then went to the gym. Thought I'd drop in to see you on the way back.'

'Great to see you. Want a drink or something?' John asked. Rob usually partook of some form of refreshment on his visits.

'Some tea would go down well.' Rob grinned up at his father.

'I'll make us a cuppa.'

John headed for the kitchen. Rob idly picked up the newspaper, which John had abandoned on the floor next to the armchair.

'How's work?' John called from the kitchen.

'Same old rubbish,' Rob called back. 'They cut the staff and expect more production.'

'Glad I got out of it when I did.'

The kettle started to sing. 'How's Cathy?' John called out. He was fond of his daughter-in-law.

'She says her back's a bit better, but she's still going to see the specialist next week,' Rob replied after a second's interval, diverting his interest from the paper.

John returned from the kitchen with two mugs of tea. He placed one on the table near Rob. He didn't really want any more tea himself, but to be sociable he put the second cup down on the table next to him as he sat down on the sofa opposite Rob. Rob dropped the newspaper on the floor.

'I see the rail fares are going up again,' remarked John. Rob commuted to London by train every day.

'Yes. I heard that too. Same old thing, every year an increase.'

'It was bad enough when I used to go up to town all those years ago,' John reflected.

Rob sipped his tea. 'What have you been up to, Dad?'

'Oh, keeping busy – allotment and so on. I'm going to Oxford tomorrow.'

'What's on there then?' Rob enquired in an interested tone of voice.

John took a sociable sip of tea. His answer required a bit of thought and discretion. 'Actually, I'm going to a concert with a woman I met on holiday. I may stay overnight if it finishes very late.' He made his reply sound as casual as possible.

Rob seemed to accept the information without undue concern. 'What's she like?' he asked, smiling at his father.

'Debbie? She's very nice. You'd like her.' At this stage John hoped the topic might end. He had not, however, bargained with Rob's curiosity.

'Where will you stay if you stop overnight, Dad?' asked Rob, taking a big swig of tea, at the same time looking at his father intently.

John's response was quick. 'Oh, hotel or B&B. There are plenty of places around.'

Rob was still looking at him, and there was a trace of a grin on his face. John got the message and added quickly: 'I know what you're thinking, old chap, but it's not that kind of relationship. We haven't got that far yet. Debbie and I are just good friends.'

Rob appeared to accept the statement and to John's relief his next question changed the subject. 'Cathy wants to know if you'd like to spend the day with us on Sunday – come over in time for lunch.'

'I'd love to. I haven't seen her for weeks. I'll bring a bottle of wine.' John tended to view Cathy as the daughter he had never had. Her cooking was excellent. He always enjoyed the meals she prepared for him.

They chatted on for an hour or so, catching up on various bits of news and making observations and comments on this and that. Eventually Rob looked at his watch and said he'd better be going. John got up and walked to the door with him. Rob paused at the door, one hand on the catch.

'We'll see you on Sunday then, Dad,' he said.

'Looking forward to it. Thank Cathy for the invitation.'

Rob opened the door and walked through. 'Cheerio then, Dad.'

'Cheerio, old chap. Thanks for dropping in.'

John watched as he started to descend the stairs. He put up his hand as a final goodbye, and Rob disappeared from view.

John closed the door and went back into his sitting room. He looked out of the window. The sun was already casting late evening shadows. He watched Rob drive out into the road, and then he was gone. He picked up the mugs and returned them to the kitchen. His own was still a quarter full, but it had long since gone cold. He walked back into the lounge. He must ring Debbie soon. Before that, though, he would spend another ten minutes with *The Times*. One of these days he would manage to read it all the way through. It was funny how you never seemed to have time for some things. He dropped into the chair vacated by Rob, picked up the paper and started to peruse its pages. He lifted his eyes for a moment as his concentration was diverted by a thought. He pondered how Rob had immediately hinted that he would be spending the night with Debbie tomorrow. People always tended to think in that direction, even your own family. Such an idea had never entered his thoughts. Debbie was an attractive woman, but that was as far as it went. Damn it. After all, he was close approaching seventy and Debbie wasn't so far off. A sudden panic struck him. Suppose Debbie had thought the same when he had mentioned staying over in Oxford? The thought was disturbing to him. He closed his eyes for a minute and pondered it.

The sound of the telephone woke him with a start. The sun had almost set and was casting orange shadows around the room. Damn. He must have dropped off in the chair. How long had he been asleep? He jumped up. It must be Debbie ringing him. Slightly annoyed with himself, he made a grab for the phone. It almost slipped out of his hand, but he managed to hold on to it.

'Hello, John Hammond.'

'John, it's Debbie. I'm so sorry I'm so late.'

Embarrassment flooded over him. 'Debbie, I'm dreadfully sorry about this. I intended to ring you ages ago and stupidly I dropped off in the chair.'

'Don't worry, John. In a way I'm glad you didn't phone me earlier.'

He could detect a trace of distress in her voice. There was not the same vibrancy he was used to. It prompted a quick response from him. 'You sound a bit under the weather. Anything wrong?'

There was a little laugh at the other end of the phone. 'Oh, I'm sorry, John. I didn't mean to come over that way. It's just that I've had an awful day. I came back from the shops this afternoon to find I'd been burgled and then I had to wait for the police to come round and that sort of thing. It's all made me feel quite stressed, but I didn't mean to unload it all on you.'

A wave of sympathy swept over John. 'How awful. Tell me about it. Did you lose a great deal?'

'No, that's the odd thing. I can't see that anything was taken. The police seem to think I disturbed whoever it was when I came back. I was only gone about half an hour, but now I've got a broken pane of glass in the back door.'

John could sense Debbie's distress. He felt a bit helpless being so far away. 'What did the police say?'

'Well, two policewomen came round. I think they thought I was a bit past it. I don't know why, but I'd left the key in the back door. I usually remove it when I go out, but – I don't know – perhaps being in a rush I didn't today. I don't think they thought very highly of that. Perhaps they thought I was going a little senile.'

He heard her laugh again, but he knew it was forced. He could imagine how she must be feeling. 'Look, don't worry about that. It can happen to anybody. I've done it. Everybody does it at some time or another.'

There was a slight pause before Debbie answered him. It was clear she was digesting his comment. 'I suppose you're right. It's just that I felt so awful talking to the police. They must have thought what a stupid woman I was to leave a key in the door. I can see them looking at me now.'

'What did they say?'

'I think they thought my security was a bit lacking. Oh, and apparently there was another burglary just down the road round about the same time.'

'Hmm. Opportunists, I expect. Doing the rounds.'

'I expect so,' Debbie replied sadly.

'So what happens now?'

'I'm not really sure… Nothing, I think. They did say they would contact me if there were any developments, but I don't expect they will. Oh, and they thought I should get an alarm fitted. I haven't got a clue how one does that. I shall have to get my son-in-law onto it.'

'It might be a good idea.'

'I suppose so,' Debbie replied gloomily, and then, as more immediate problems entered her thinking, she added: 'And in the meantime I've got this broken glass in my back door and the police suggested I get some new bolts fitted.'

John had been thinking as she spoke. 'Look, Debbie. About tomorrow: do you want to cancel out? You seem to have so much on your plate.'

Debbie's reply was instant. 'Heavens, no, John. I'm looking forward to it. DO PLEASE come.' There was an anxious note in her voice.

John thought quickly. A glimmer of an idea was beginning to germinate. Before he could reply, Debbie pleaded: 'You must come, John. What time shall I expect you?'

John's idea was beginning to blossom. He still had that bag of tools in the spare bedroom. They had been useful when he had helped Rob on various DIY projects from time to time. They could come in handy again tomorrow. He launched his plan.

'How would it be if I came over early? I could have a look at the broken glass. I'm sure I could fix that.'

'Oh, John, would you? I'd be so grateful. But it seems such a cheek when it's supposed to be a day of pleasure.'

He laughed. 'You don't know me. I'm a real little DIY fiend.'

'It would be a relief to get that glass fixed.' Debbie's reply showed her anxiety. He knew he had done the right thing in offering his services.

'I'll come over early,' he announced firmly, and then, thinking his plan out, he added: 'I'll be in my working gear. Can I change at your house before we go to the concert?'

'Of course you can.'

'OK, then – I'd better get myself sorted out. Expect me in the morning. That will give me a bit of time to see what's what.'

'That's great, John. I really appreciate your help.'

'That's settled. Until tomorrow, then.'

'OK, John. Goodbye. See you tomorrow. Safe journey.'

'Goodbye, Debbie. I hope you have a good night.'

John put the phone down. He was glad he had offered to go to Oxford earlier than planned. He had noticed the change in Debbie as soon as he mentioned it. When she had first spoken he could tell she was stressed, but by the time they said goodbye she had brightened up considerably. Poor Debbie. What a thing to happen. The least he could do was to put a bit of glass in the door for her.

He went into the spare bedroom, which served as his workroom. His desk was in there, and his computer. It also served as a depository for all the items he didn't use regularly. He found the old leather bag that now held his collection of tools. He rummaged among its contents for a few minutes. Yes, with a bit of luck he had everything he needed. He was looking forward to a bit of DIY. Now, where was that suit cover he used to have? He would need it for transporting the clothes he would wear for the concert in the evening. After a bit of a search he found it tucked away in a corner of the wardrobe. After collecting all the items he could think of that he might need, he deposited them in the sitting room. All he had to do now was to remember to set the alarm clock as a safeguard against oversleeping.

Chapter 11

Debbie had just wandered into the lounge for something or other when she saw the car turn into her forecourt. It was instantly recognisable as John's. The sight of it immediately flung her into a panic. She was still in her dressing gown. Of all the things to happen! Why had she not foreseen this? John had said he would arrive early. She had not, however, expected this to be before nine o'clock.

She knew there was no time to get dressed. Then desperation forced a glimmer of an idea through. She hurried to the front door and opened it. Letting the door shield most of her, she looked out. John was opening the boot of his car.

She called out: 'Good morning, John.'

John looked up. 'Good morning, Debbie,' he called out. 'I hope I'm not too early for you.'

'No, of course not. I'm going to leave the door on the latch for you.'

With that she clicked the latch into place and hurried upstairs. She had to act quickly. Thank goodness she had already showered before having a light breakfast half an hour previously. Her dressing gown was hurriedly abandoned, and slippers kicked underneath the bed. She slipped into a pair of slacks and a shirt. She heard the front door thud as John closed it. This prompted her to walk out onto the landing to call out: 'I'll be with you in a jiffy.'

She thought she heard an 'OK' in the distance, but she was already back in her bedroom, running a comb through her hair and adding a touch of lipstick. A pair of comfortable shoes, and that was the best she could do in the time available. She hurried downstairs again. She found John in the kitchen looking at the gaping hole in the back door.

He turned to greet her as she entered. 'Hi. Sorry if I'm a bit early.'

Debbie could feel herself blushing. It was no use: she might as well be honest. 'Don't apologise. I'm a bit behind. I intended to be ready early.' She hesitated for an instant. 'I was in my dressing gown when you arrived.'

John smiled politely. 'I had a good run up. No hold-ups on the road. I thought it would take me longer at this time of day.'

He was a bit annoyed with himself for not letting Debbie know what time he would arrive. It was embarrassing for her to be caught out like that. He diverted the conversation away from the subject by turning his attention back to the door. 'I can see how they got in.'

'Will you be able to do anything with it?' Debbie asked hopefully.

'Of course I will. Measure up, buy some glass, and we're well on our way,' he replied cheerfully.

'Oh, thank goodness. I'm so pleased you offered. If Tom had been here I expect he would have had some suggestions, but he isn't due again for a few days.' She already felt the relief of John being around and taking control.

John opened his tool bag to extract a rule. He grinned at her. 'No problem,' he said cheerfully.

Suddenly a thought struck Debbie. It produced an exclamation of near anguish. 'John! You've got up early, driven here, and I haven't even offered you so much as a cup of tea. I must be crazy. Have you had breakfast?'

Her outburst just produced a little laugh from John. 'I had breakfast before I left, but a cup of tea or coffee would be great – oh, and a piece of paper so that I can jot down these measurements.'

Debbie handed him her kitchen pad and filled the kettle. She was feeling better already.

After she had phoned John the previous evening, the thought of the long night ahead of her had been daunting. She had put off going to bed until quite late, and then she had made an anxious round of the house, checking that windows were closed and doors locked. Then she had retired to her bedroom, anticipating a restless night. For the first time ever she had locked her bedroom door and put her mobile phone on the bedside table. She had read for a bit but had put the book down when she found herself reading the same sentence over and over again. The next thing she knew was that it was two hours later and the bedside light was still on. She had switched it off and dropped off to sleep again. In spite of waking up several times, she had spent a reasonably restful night, relieved eventually that her worries had come to naught. She had taken her time over showering and starting to get dressed and then, undecided as to what to wear, she had slipped her dressing gown on to have her breakfast. That decision had resulted in her being caught out when John arrived.

She clicked the kettle to boil and turned to face John again. He was still busy with the door. 'Would you like a piece of apple cake with your tea?' she asked.

John's reply radiated enthusiasm. 'Rather! I haven't had any for ages.'

'I made it the day before yesterday. Jamie loves it.' Debbie was already taking the cake tin out of the cupboard.

She poured the water into the teapot and set it on the table. There was the soft thud of the post arriving. She went into the hall to collect the three letters that were lying on the mat. She studied the envelopes as she returned to the kitchen. 'Two bills, and a letter from my sister,' she commented, placing them on the table. Almost in the same breath she announced: 'Tea's ready.'

'Great!' John turned his attention to the kitchen table.

'You can wash your hands upstairs. And you've cut yourself.' Debbie had noticed the blood on his hand. 'There are some plasters in the bathroom cabinet. Can I get you one?'

John flashed her one of his grins. 'No problem. I'll find them.'

Debbie made a little face at him as he passed her to go upstairs. That was one of the things she liked about John: he always seemed so self-reliant. She busied herself getting out the mugs and plates. It was several minutes before he returned, brandishing a plaster on his finger.

Debbie had taken the time to glance at the letter from her sister. She put it down as John appeared, and picked up the teapot. 'My sister is always on to me to correspond by email,' she said, pushing a mug of tea towards John, who had seated himself at the table.

'Why don't you treat yourself to a computer?' he suggested, helping himself to milk.

'That's what she keeps saying,' said Debbie, as she cut two slices of apple cake. She placed a plate in front of John. 'The problem is I haven't a clue about computers. I wouldn't know where to start.'

'I could show you what I know,' John offered.

'I expect you're an expert,' Debbie replied. There was a tone of enquiry in her voice.

John took a sip of his tea. 'Well, I know enough to turn them on and off,' he said. His reply brought forth a spontaneous laugh from Debbie. John's understatements were quite comical at times.

She thought for a moment. 'I suppose it's possible to go somewhere and receive some sort of education in using computers,' she said.

'It is, but if you ever thought about getting a computer, I could always help you.'

'Would you really?' Debbie was almost enthusiastic, and then as her logic took over, she added: 'The problem is that I don't know if I would be able to pick it up. It all looks so complicated.'

John swallowed a mouthful of cake. He shook his head. 'The problem is that the younger generation grew up with computers. Our generation didn't, but that doesn't stop us having a go and catching up,' he said with conviction.

'I suppose you're right,' Debbie replied thoughtfully.

They chatted for ten minutes or so and then John drank the last of his tea and got up from his chair, announcing that he was off to buy some glass. Debbie thought there was probably a place not too far away and gave the best directions she could. When John had gone she busied herself in the kitchen washing up the dirty dishes that had collected from their tea break and her breakfast. Then she sat down to read the letter from her sister. It once again included the suggestion that Debbie visit them sometime. As she finished reading the letter, it suddenly struck her that she had still not phoned Trish. Sometimes it was easier to reach her daughter at work. She went into the sitting room and dialled Trish's workplace. Trish was in a meeting, but the friendly receptionist, who knew Debbie, told her she would let Trish know as soon as the meeting finished that her mother had phoned.

It was over an hour before John returned. The shop Debbie had directed him to had been able to cut and supply the glass, together with a tub of putty, but did not stock the other items he had in mind to buy. The man in the shop had directed him to a DIY store, where he had completed his purchases: two brass bolts for the top and bottom of Debbie's back door.

Debbie was in the kitchen when he rang the doorbell. She hurried to let him in. He stood there holding several packages. 'Got everything,' he said cheerfully in reply to Debbie's 'Hi'.

He set to work immediately. The glass was a shade too large, so he had to shave a millimetre of wood away to make it fit. He was clearly enjoying himself. Debbie pottered about, occasionally stopping for a few minutes to watch him and say a few words.

The telephone rang. It was Trish.

'Hello, Mum. Did you want me?'

'Hello, dear. I hope I'm not disturbing you when you're busy.'

'No, it's all right. I've just had a lousy meeting and there's another one this afternoon.'

Debbie could feel Trish's frustration. She seemed to have to attend an awful lot of meetings. 'Oh dear. I hope it wasn't too bad,' she said.

'Oh, it's OK, but it's just that these meetings get me down sometimes. What did you want me for, Mum?'

'I just wanted to tell you that I had a burglary yesterday.'

'What? How did it happen?' Trish was fully alert to the situation and concerned.

Debbie had not intended to alarm her daughter. She explained in detail, trying to make light of the incident. She knew from old that Trish could overreact in situations like this. She didn't share Jan's calm, placid temperament. In the end it appeared that Trish had accepted her mother's explanation, so Debbie wasn't quite prepared for her next remark.

'Mum, don't you think that house is too big for you to live in?'

Debbie sighed to herself. This topic reared its head at frequent intervals from both her daughters. Her reaction was the usual one. 'Well, I'm not ready to go into a home just yet. Besides I enjoy living here, with the garden and everything.'

Trish was not convinced. 'Yes, I know, Mum, but there will come a stage when you can't manage everything.'

Debbie was becoming annoyed. 'Well, when that time comes, I'll do something about it.'

She could almost hear the sigh at the other end of the phone. There was a slight pause before Trish replied. 'I'm sorry, Mum. I'm just thinking of you, that's all.'

Debbie responded as best she could. She didn't want to upset Trish in any way. 'I know you do, dear, and I appreciate your concern, but I'm just not ready at the moment to make a move. Besides, even if I had a flat as you suggest, it could still be burgled.'

'I know, Mum. I'm sorry if I upset you.'

Debbie responded quickly. 'You haven't, dear.' She thought it diplomatic to change the subject. 'How's life with you?' she asked.

'Fine. Mum, I have to go now. I'll try and contact you later.'

'OK, dear. Bye for now.'

'Bye, Mum.'

Debbie put the phone down and sighed gently. At times her younger daughter could be quite forceful. She returned to the kitchen, where John was working away, whistling softly to himself. He glanced up as she came in.

'That was my daughter Trish on the phone. I'd been trying to contact her to tell her about yesterday,' she said casually.

'What did she say?'

'Oh, she keeps on about this house being too big for me. Sometimes I get a bit fed up with it. You'd think I was old and decrepit.'

'Generation gap, I suppose,' John replied.

'Yes....' Debbie was about to respond, when she suddenly thought about her hospitality. 'John, I'm letting you work away here. Can I get you a coffee or something?'

'Good idea. Coffee, please.'

Debbie filled the kettle again and happily set it to boil. It was nice having a man about the house working again. It made her recall the times when Ron had busied himself doing jobs and she had been called upon to hold this or that and keep him supplied with endless cups of tea. She had just made the coffee when the front doorbell rang.

'Oh, who can that be?' Her question was almost to herself.

She placed the full mugs carefully on the table and went to answer the door. Before she got there the bell rang again. She opened the door to see Jan and Jamie standing on the doorstep.

'Hello, Mum,' was Jan's greeting, and then, turning to Jamie: 'We were out shopping and we thought we'd call round and see Gran, didn't we, Jamie?'

Jamie had already pushed past Debbie into the hall. Debbie quickly recovered from the shock of the unexpected arrivals.

'Right. Come on in, then,' she responded breezily. 'We're just having some coffee. John's replacing the glass in the back door.'

They went into the kitchen, Jamie first. He halted abruptly on seeing John working and was unsure whether he should respond to John's 'Hello, young fellow.' John had already guessed that he was Debbie's grandson.

Debbie introduced them all. So far she hadn't mentioned John to either of her daughters. 'Jan, this is John. John, this is my daughter Jan... and this is Jamie.'

Brief introductions over, some semblance of order returned. Debbie made a cup of coffee for Jan and found some orange juice for Jamie. John and Jan sat down at the table. Debbie produced the apple cake again. Polite but free-flowing chat ensued. John made his break brief and returned to work on the door, watched intently by Jamie, who was now getting used to all this activity going on in his gran's normally quiet house. From time to time he responded to John's questions and comments as he became more comfortable with his presence.

Jan helped her mother wash up the mugs and plates and then she and Jamie got ready to leave. Debbie waved them goodbye, then returned to the kitchen. A new pane of glass was now fitted to the door.

Debbie regarded John's handiwork. 'John, that looks great. I'm ever so grateful.'

John smiled politely. 'It wasn't a big job,' he remarked.

'I think it's fabulous, you being able to do jobs like that. You're so versatile.'

'Many talents. Master of none,' responded John drily.

'Oh no, don't say that,' Debbie protested. 'Anyway, you seem to have made quite an impression on Jamie. He couldn't take his eyes off you.'

John continued his work on the door while Debbie pottered about in the house. It was past one o'clock when it suddenly struck her that it was time to have a proper meal. She returned to the kitchen. John had removed the old door bolts after a long struggle with rusted screws. Now it was only necessary to fit the gleaming new ones he had purchased.

'Are you ready for some food?' Debbie asked.

John looked up. He hadn't given a lot of thought to eating, but now he was beginning to be aware that he had had breakfast early and nothing since apart from the apple cake mid-morning.

'That's a good idea,' he replied simply.

Debbie looked at him questioningly. 'What shall we do? Shall I cook us a meal?' She hadn't given a great deal of thought to her catering arrangements for the day.

John appeared to think for a second, but his idea was already in place. 'How about a snack now, and then a meal out before the concert?' he suggested.

'Oh, that would be nice.' Debbie wished she had thought of that. She opened one of the kitchen cupboards, seeking inspiration. 'How about a toasted cheese sandwich?'

'Great.' John's reply was brief, but Debbie had got used to his way of speaking and his tendency to make understatements.

They took their time over the simple meal, discussing a range of subjects from holidays to burglaries. At length John returned to his struggle with the door bolts and Debbie cleared up the dishes, still chatting to him as she worked.

It was well on the way to mid-afternoon when John stood back, surveyed his work and announced: 'That's it. Finished.'

Debbie was close by and responded to his remark immediately. 'It's a fantastic job! I do really appreciate it, John. I'm not sure how I'd have got it done without your help.'

John demonstrated the new door bolts. 'They'll be a bit easier to use than the old one,' he said proudly.

Debbie tried them out. 'That's marvellous, John. It's made me feel much more secure now. I don't know how to thank you.'

John just grinned at her.

Debbie took control. 'Right. You need to clean up and relax a bit after your hard work, and I'm going to make us a cup of tea.'

John didn't protest. He collected his tools together and took them out to the car. When he came back Debbie was sweeping up the debris from the floor.

'Hey, I'd have done that,' he protested.

Debbie shook her head. 'I need to make some contribution. All I've done so far is watch you,' she said firmly, but her remark was accompanied with a smile.

John found himself shepherded in the direction of the spare bedroom. He had already taken everything he needed for the evening out of the car. When he came back downstairs ten minutes later, Debbie was in the sitting room. She looked up as he appeared.

'I thought we'd have our tea in a bit of comfort and then afterwards you can relax while I get ready. Is that all right?'

'It's fine with me,' John replied agreeably, easing himself into a chair.

'Good.' Debbie settled herself into a chair opposite him and commenced to pour out the tea. 'I thought we could leave about five-ish. That would give us plenty of time. Would that be OK?' She thought of something else, and added: 'There's just one thing, though. Would you mind if we used my car? We can leave it in my friend's office car park.'

'It's no problem at all. I'm lazy about driving these days, anyway. I'm quite content if somebody else wants to drive,' John replied, helping himself to milk.

His reply pleased Debbie. She had been a bit nervous about mentioning the situation, because she was still anxious about being the driver. They chatted away over tea and then at last Debbie looked at her watch and decided it was time for her to get ready. Reminding John to make himself at home, she disappeared upstairs.

When it came to deciding what to wear for the evening, she hesitated. Several garments were taken out of her wardrobe and then replaced before she finally chose a rather nice slim-fitting dress in a delicate shade of green. She had bought it for a wedding several years ago and it had hung in her wardrobe ever since. Would it still fit? She was pleased to find that it did. Well, that settled that. She also had a light coat she could wear. As for the shoes she had bought to go with it, when she took them out of the box she was alarmed to see that they had higher heels than she remembered. Could she still wear them? Even trying them on didn't answer the question. They seemed all right, but she wasn't walking in them. That was when the difficulty might arise. In the end she opted for the heeled pair she had worn on holiday. It was too big a risk to try out the others.

While she had been away, John had been amusing himself. He had cleared the crockery into the kitchen, hesitated about washing everything up and then spent some time reading Debbie's newspaper.

When Debbie appeared he was surprised at the effort she had made. Her outfit suited her well and he felt a bit shabby in his trusty blazer. Seeing her looking so elegant made him wish he had brought his suit instead, but there was nothing he could do about the situation now. He looked approvingly at her. 'You look very elegant this evening,' he said as she returned to her seat.

Debbie smiled. It was nice to receive a compliment sometimes, particularly from a man. 'Thank you. I thought I'd give this outfit an airing. I haven't worn it for ages.' She glanced down at her feet. 'The problem is that I don't think I dare wear the shoes that go with it for walking outside. They've got rather high heels. Do you think this pair goes OK with the dress?'

John gave her one of his grins. 'I think they look great.'

Debbie was content with his answer. She had never quite fathomed out the attraction high heels had for so many men, but she felt she would get an honest answer from John. One thing was certain: she would have to change shoes to drive.

Debbie enjoyed the concert. For the first time in over twenty-four hours her mind was taken off the burglary. It was a good night out all round. She drove carefully, if a bit nervously, into the city centre through the evening traffic and found a space in her friend's office car park. She took John's arm as they left the car and walked in search of a suitable restaurant. In the end they enjoyed a meal in a steak house. It was early evening and they had the place almost to themselves. Afterwards they took a leisurely walk to the hall where the concert was to be held. She bumped into several people she knew, and they looked with curiosity at John, but she simply introduced him as a friend and left it at that.

It was as they left the concert hall that the evening was slightly marred. The weather had been grey and sultry all day and as they walked back to the car the first drops of rain started to fall. 'Oh no – it's raining and we haven't got an umbrella,' wailed Debbie.

John, practical as ever, summed it up. 'We'll have to hurry.'

He quickened his pace and Debbie struggled to keep up with him. Even so, by the time they reached the car, now on its own in the office car park, the rain was falling steadily and they were getting quite wet. Debbie fumbled in her bag for the car key. Where was it? Things always got right to the bottom of her bag just when she was in a hurry. At last she found it, and with an apology to John, who was waiting patiently with one hand on the door handle, she unlocked the driver's door and climbed into the car. It took only a second to flick up the door catch to let John in. 'I hope I didn't get you soaked through, keeping you waiting in the rain like that,' she said, inserting the key in the ignition.

'It'll dry off. How about you?' John replied, running his hand over his hair.

Debbie made a face as she dived under the driving seat for the flat-heeled shoes she used for driving. 'I'd have worn something else if I'd known it was going to rain.'

She disliked both driving in the dark and driving in rain. The combination of the two required all her concentration. She was pleased when their journey of ten minutes or so was over. The rain was now falling heavily. They made a dash for the front porch. The brightness of the hall light made them aware of how wet they were.

'Phew. What a night.' Debbie looked down at her outfit. It hadn't fared very well. She could feel her tights wet and clammy against her legs. 'I'll have to change out of these clothes,' she remarked.

'I think I will as well, for the drive back.' John was looking at himself in the hall mirror.

Debbie led the way upstairs. John made for the spare bedroom he had used for changing earlier and Debbie darted silently into her own. It only took her a few minutes to strip off the wet outfit, change her tights and put on the clothes she had worn during the day. There was little she could do with the wet garments other than hang them up to dry. She was downstairs a good three minutes before John came down the stairs carrying his overnight bag and suit cover. He too had changed back into his daytime garb.

Debbie looked down at herself and laughed. 'The ball is over and Cinderella's rags return,' she said brightly.

'And Prince Charming's,' responded John.

Debbie was moving towards the kitchen door. 'I'll make us a drink,' she said. 'What would you like?'

'It had better be a coffee to keep me awake in this lot,' replied John, nodding towards the front door. The rain was now beating down noisily.

Debbie was just feeling for the kitchen light switch when the whole room was lit up by a flash of lightning. 'Goodness!' she exclaimed.

John did not respond immediately. His thoughts were elsewhere. A gigantic clap of thunder prompted him to voice them. 'I think I'd better wait for a while until this has passed over,' he remarked glumly. 'Or perhaps there's a hotel or pub near here where I can stay.'

Debbie had noticed how quiet he had been since their return to the house, and now realised what he was thinking about. Driving the short distance home in the rain had been enough for her. She knew what to do.

'You're not going anywhere in this weather, John. You're going to stay here. I can quickly get the spare room ready,' she said firmly.

John wasn't so sure. 'I don't want to put you to such trouble. I can easily go to a hotel. Besides, there's your reputation to think of.'

Debbie adopted an even firmer tone. 'No, John. You're staying here. I insist. You can't drive home on a night like this.' Then she added cheerfully: 'So, no more arguments. I'm going to make us that drink.'

Chapter 12

Asking John to stay overnight had not been an impulsive on-the-spot idea. Debbie had already given some thought to the matter earlier in the day. When the weather took a bad turn and John was talking about driving home, she decided to take charge of the situation.

As she went into the kitchen to put the kettle on, the summer storm was still raging outside. Flashes of lightning lit up the garden every few minutes and the rain was falling heavily. She knew she had made the right decision: even to venture out to find a hotel room would be difficult. On top of that it was getting late: it was already well past eleven. As the kettle boiled she called out to John, who had remained in the sitting room. 'Are you sure you want coffee so late at night? I'm going to make myself a mug of cocoa.'

There was no immediate answer. Then John appeared in the doorway. 'I'll have cocoa as well,' he said simply.

It didn't take long for Debbie to make two mugs of milky cocoa. John watched her, occasionally glancing out of the window at the storm. Debbie thought he seemed quieter than usual. Then it suddenly struck her. Suppose John had got the wrong idea? Suppose he thought she had some other motive in inviting him to stay at her house? At first the idea seemed too ridiculous to even think about. Goodness gracious, they were both nearly seventy, not two kids of twenty. Yet the thought would not go away. It had lurked in the background ever since she had first thought of inviting John to stay over, and now it had surfaced and would not go away. It dominated her thinking as she made their cocoa, even though she kept the chatter up with John. By the time she carried the drinks into the sitting room, she had made her decision. She waited for a lull in the conversation, and then she implemented her strategy.

She spoke softly and as sincerely as she could. 'John, may I just say something?'

'Of course.'

She paused, choosing her words carefully. 'John, what I wanted to say was just this: when I invited you to stay the night, there were no strings attached.'

John smiled at her. 'I didn't think there were,' he said.

Debbie continued. 'It's just that I value your friendship very much. I don't want it to turn into something cheap and sordid.' She studied his face but he was beautifully in control. It prompted her to add: 'Besides, I don't know if I'm still up to that kind of relationship.'

That was it. She had said it. John was still smiling at her, as if in agreement. 'I feel exactly the same about our friendship. I enjoy your company very much, Debbie. I don't want to spoil things.' He couldn't help adding shyly: 'I'm not sure if I could make it these days.'

Debbie had risen from her seat to collect their empty mugs. As she walked past him she touched his arm briefly. 'I'm sure you could, but I'm going to get your room ready now.' It was a deft way of finishing a tricky conversation.

It didn't take long for her to prepare the room. She grabbed the sheets and duvet from the cupboard where they were stored and in five minutes she had the job completed. She pulled the curtains and left the bedside light on to make things look cosy, and then returned to the sitting room. John was busy reading the newspaper. He put it down and got up as she entered the room. The lightning and thunder had decreased and could just be heard still. Debbie glanced at the clock on the wall. It was close to midnight.

John took the hint. 'I think I'll turn in,' he said, following her glance.

Debbie moved towards him. She took his hand. 'Thank you for all your hard work today, John, and for a lovely evening.'

John grasped her hand firmly. 'I enjoyed it.' He held her hand for a moment, and then he gently placed a kiss on her cheek. 'Goodnight, Debbie.'

Debbie returned his kiss. 'Goodnight, John. Thank you for everything.'

She watched him collect his overnight bag from the hall and climb the stairs. On the second landing he looked back. 'See you in the morning,' he said, and then he was gone.

Debbie collected the dirty mugs and took them into the kitchen. She busied herself for ten minutes or so, waiting for everything to go quiet upstairs. Then she heard the sound of the spare bedroom door closing, and that was the signal for her to make her own move.

It seemed strange having a man sleeping in the house after so many years. It meant remembering to do the little things like wearing a dressing gown to go to the bathroom and locking the door while she was in there. It was a good ten minutes before she at last nestled into the softness of her bed. Away in the distance she could still hear the thunder occasionally. The rain had now settled into a steady downpour. With the window slightly open, the sound lulled her to sleep.

The next morning Debbie woke up slowly. For a few moments her memory was a blank. She lay there quietly, confident that it would return. Recollection of the previous evening made her glance first at the brightness of the early morning sun shining through the curtains, and then quickly at her watch. Was it late? The hands of her watch showed nearly seven. She lay there for a minute, thinking about the day ahead; then suddenly she remembered that John had said something about having to get back home during the morning for a dental appointment. Might he want to get up early? The thought propelled her into action; throwing back the duvet, she leapt out of bed. She was about to open the bedroom door when she suddenly remembered she had a male guest in the house. This prodded her into grabbing her dressing gown from its hook and slipping into it for the few yards to the bathroom. The last thing she wanted to do was embarrass John.

Twenty minutes later she was down in the kitchen pottering about. Already she had filled the kettle and it had started to sing. There was the familiar sound of the newspaper arriving through the letter box. She went into the hall to retrieve it and then sat at the kitchen table reading the headlines. The kettle came to the boil and clicked itself off. Debbie wondered whether she should take John a cup of tea in his room. She was still pondering this when she heard sounds of activity in the bathroom. He was already up. Debbie turned on the kitchen radio, partly to announce that there was activity downstairs and partly through habit.

Ten minutes later, as she was laying the kitchen table, John appeared in the doorway and greeted her with a cheerful 'Good morning!'

Debbie looked up and smiled. 'Good morning, John. Did you sleep well?'

'Absolutely. I never heard a thing until half an hour ago.' He was already pulling out a chair to sit at the table.

Debbie immediately became the hostess. 'What would you like for breakfast? Muesli and toast?'

'Marvellous. Home from home,' he laughed.

Debbie gave him one of her coy little grins. 'Ah. I remembered you said you had muesli for breakfast.'

The tea was now brewed. She filled two mugs and placed them on the table. She looked at the clock. 'What time do you have to leave?' she asked.

'I need to be back for eleven. I'll disappear about nine, if I may.'

'That's fine. Then I must go and do some shopping,' she replied, filling a bowl with muesli and placing it in front of him.

They had a leisurely breakfast. It was pleasant sitting there with the sun streaming through the window. All traces of the storm had disappeared and it looked set to be a fine summer's day.

They had almost finished and were thinking of making a move, when the front doorbell rang, followed by a loud knocking.

Debbie jumped up. 'Goodness! Who can that be? Perhaps it's the postman with a package.'

She hurried to the door, unlocked it and slid back the bolts. She peered round it to find Trish standing there.

'Trish! I wondered who it was. Gosh, you're here early.' Debbie opened the door wide. Trish was in her business suit. Her car was parked alongside John's.

'Sorry, Mum. Did I alarm you? I'm going to Birmingham. It was all arranged quickly after I spoke to you yesterday and I thought I'd drop in to see you on the way and find out how you are.' She walked past her mother into the hall.

Debbie closed the door. 'That's nice of you dear. I'm fine.' She added: 'I've been up a long time. It's just that I hadn't unlocked the door yet.'

'I guessed that when I tried my key.' Trish grinned.

Debbie led the way into the kitchen. Both her daughters had keys to her house. 'I'm sorry about that, dear,' she said over her shoulder.

John jumped up as they entered the kitchen. Debbie introduced him to a clearly surprised Trish. 'Trish, this is a friend of mine, John. John, this is my daughter Trish.'

John held out his hand. 'Hello, Trish,' he said smiling.

'Hi.' Trish took his hand limply and then sat down at the table.

'Cup of tea, Trish?' Debbie asked. 'I can brew another pot.'

Trish thought for a second. 'A cup of coffee would go down better. It will keep me awake. I was up at the crack of dawn.'

'What time did you get up?' Debbie asked over her shoulder as she refilled the kettle.

'Five o'clock. I've got to be in Birmingham at ten-thirty.' Trish was ignoring John, who was sitting opposite her. Her eyes focused on the newspaper, which was lying on her side of the table.

'Gosh. You'll have to rush.' Debbie returned to the table for a minute while she waited for the kettle to boil.

Trish shrugged off the remark. 'Oh, I'll make it OK. That thing of mine can move when it wants to. Trouble is, I got flashed by a speed camera coming out of London. I just hope there was no film in it. Otherwise that would be more points on my licence. I've already got six.'

'Oh, do be careful, dear,' responded Debbie.

John joined in the debate. 'I got caught last year for the first time ever,' he observed. 'Thirty-five miles an hour in a thirty zone on a Sunday morning. Problem was it was one of those roads that didn't even look as if it would be a thirty zone. Anyway, it landed me with three points.'

'It's just a money-making racket now,' grumbled Trish.

John felt a bit in the way. He guessed Debbie wanted to have a chat with her daughter. He made an excuse to get his things together and disappeared.

As soon as he had left the room, Trish leaned over to her mother and whispered: 'Who's he?'

Debbie was determined to appear casual. 'Oh, he's someone I met on holiday.'

Trish's eyes opened a bit wider. 'Did he stay here last night?' she asked.

'Yes, dear.' Debbie replied simply. She was determined to leave it at that for the present.

'Oh.' Trish looked at her mother. Debbie knew what she was thinking. She did not elaborate.

Trish changed the subject. 'Have you heard any more from the police?'

Debbie shook her head. 'No. I doubt somehow if I will,' she answered.

Trish went on to relate how one of her colleagues at work had recently had a burglary and went into vivid details, which Debbie could have done without but listened to patiently. John returned to the kitchen. It was a signal for Trish to gulp down the last of her coffee and announce that she had to go. She disappeared upstairs to the bathroom.

Two minutes later there was the sound of her tripping back down the stairs, a sound that made Debbie wince and pull a face. 'I'm terrified she'll fall down the stairs in those shoes,' she said.

John grinned. He had observed the extremely high-heeled black shoes Trish was wearing to match her business suit.

Trish burst into the kitchen. She grabbed John's hand. 'Goodbye. Nice meeting you.'

'Goodbye,' replied John.

'Bye, Mum.' She planted a kiss on Debbie's cheek and made for the front door.

As Trish drove out onto the road, Debbie turned to John and smiled knowingly. 'And that', she said, 'was my younger daughter.'

'Quite different from Jan,' observed John thoughtfully.

'Absolutely,' Debbie agreed. 'Jan takes after me a bit, but I don't quite know who Trish takes after.'

John looked at his watch. 'Time for me to make a move,' he said.

Debbie watched as he collected his belongings together and carried them to the car. He returned to the hall and took her hand.

'Thank you for everything,' he said.

'Thank you, John. I really appreciate all you've done for me.'

She still had hold of his hand. She kissed his cheek. 'Goodbye, John.'

John put his arm round her and kissed her cheek. 'Goodbye. See you soon,' he said.

Debbie watched him get into his car. She waved as he drove off, and then she went back into the house and quietly closed the door.

All of a sudden the house seemed strangely quiet. Now to clear up and head for the shops, she thought. Tidying up took a great deal longer than she had envisaged. By the time she had finished the morning was well advanced. She was just about to have a coffee and get ready to go out, when the front doorbell rang. She sighed softly and hurried into the hall.

Jan stood on the doorstep. She was alone, which was unusual. There was no sign of Jamie. 'Hi, Mum,' was her greeting.

'Hello, dear. I didn't expect to see you this morning.'

Jan stepped past her and waited for her to close the door. 'I've got some news for you and also I wanted to see you about something else.'

'Oh, that sounds ominous,' Debbie replied, leading the way into the kitchen.

Jan's only response was a rather vague 'No…'

Debbie wondered what had brought Jan to see her without Jamie. Clearly there was something important she wanted to discuss with her. Her immediate thought was that in view of what Jan had conveyed in the past, she was going to announce that she and Paul were going to move. It was the only thing Debbie could think of, and the thought saddened her. No doubt she would find out when Jan was ready.

'Would you like a drink?' Debbie was already filling the kettle, and Jan had sank into one of the kitchen chairs.

Jan thought for a second. 'I'll have a coffee,' she said.

It took Debbie a few minutes to make two mugs of coffee. Her plans to go shopping were sadly in disarray.

'Where's Jamie?' she asked, placing a mug of coffee in front of Jan.

'Oh, I've left him with Violet and Joshua.' Violet was one of Jan's friends. She had a little boy called Joshua who was about the same age as Jamie.

Debbie made no comment. Leaving Jamie with Violet was part of the plan, she guessed. She took a sip of her coffee and waited.

Jan held her mug in both hands, elbows on the table. She looked across the table at her mother. 'First of all, I've got some good news for you,' she announced.

Debbie hesitated. What could it be? 'That sounds interesting.' She gave a little laugh.

'Paul knows this guy who runs a business installing burglar alarms. He's going to have a word with him about coming to have a look at your house and putting in an alarm system.'

'Oh, that would be helpful, after what the police said. When will that be?'

'One weekend, I think. Paul will contact you to arrange a convenient time.'

'That's very kind of him. I do appreciate the thought. I wouldn't know where to start looking for someone.' Debbie had always got on well with her son-in-law.

'Most likely he'll do the installation a bit cheaper as well,' Jan said thoughtfully.

The other reason for Jan's visit was now uppermost in Debbie's mind. 'What was it you wanted to see me about?' she asked at last.

Jan was clearly thinking deeply before putting into words what she wanted to say. It was a few seconds before she spoke. 'Well, first of all Paul's been promoted and that means we won't be moving away.'

Debbie was about to comment how pleased she was, but Jan continued. 'The other thing is that we still want to move house, and… Paul and I have been talking.' She looked at her mother as if for inspiration. 'You know, Mum, this house is really beginning to be too big for you.'

Jan would have continued, but her words had irritated Debbie. Here we go again, she thought, same old theme. I've heard it before. Her irritation showed in her response. 'Well, everybody else seems to say so. I've never complained. I seem to manage everything quite well. The house is clean, the garden is maintained. I don't see the problem for other people as long as I can manage. I'm not ready for an old people's home yet.'

Jan knew she had said the wrong thing. She rushed in to repair the damage. 'Oh, Mum, don't get me wrong. I'm not saying anything like that. I'm just trying to help.'

Debbie immediately regretted her outburst. Jan and Paul were very good to her. She knew that. She quickly tried to smooth things over. 'I'm sorry, dear. It's just that I get a bit edgy when people keep on to me about selling up and moving into a flat. Trish was going on about it the other day.'

Jan looked at her. Her mother's last remark was going to make her next proposal difficult unless she trod carefully. She spoke slowly, thinking each word out carefully as she went. 'I'm sorry, Mum. I really didn't mean to upset you, it's just that Paul and I have been discussing the situation.' She hesitated, pausing to see how her mother was reacting.

Debbie waited. She wondered what was coming next.

Jan continued. 'Well, Paul's promotion will mean that we can afford to move to a bigger house.' She paused again. 'We wondered whether, if you did consider selling this house, we might be able to buy it from you.' She looked at Debbie, trying to assess how her proposal had been received. She added quickly: 'We would pay the market value.'

Debbie's brain was working overtime. This was the last thing she expected Jan to ask her. She struggled to take it in. She didn't want to upset Jan, and she needed time to think about it all. She didn't consider herself ready to make a move anyway. And there was Trish to think about. When she replied, she too chose her words carefully. 'Well, all I can say is that I'll think about it, but I don't really consider myself ready to move anywhere. I like living here and I would miss the space and the garden for a start. If there comes a time when I can't manage any more, then that's a different story.'

Jan rushed in with an afterthought. 'Oh, but we're not in any hurry,' she said.

To break the slightly tense atmosphere, Debbie gave a small laugh. 'I'm glad of that,' she replied.

Jan tactfully changed the subject. She knew her mother of old. She knew it would take time for her proposal to really register. She had told Paul it would be a long process. In the meantime it was best to drop the subject, and return to it later when the dust had settled.

They chatted for another twenty minutes or so. Jan was curious about John and wanted to know more about him, but Debbie was guarded in her answers. Just for the present, she was not inclined to share him with anybody. Anyway, she didn't want to give her daughters the wrong idea. It was better to keep everything casual.

At last Jan looked at the clock and said she had to go and pick up Jamie. 'Paul will be in contact with you over the alarm survey,' she reminded her mother as she walked to the front door.

'OK, dear. Thank him very much for his efforts.' Debbie was pleased about the idea; it lifted a burden off her shoulders.

She watched Jan get into her estate car and drive off. She went back into the house and into the kitchen again. The clock showed that it was past midday. Oh well, she thought: so much for my plan to go out. She hated going shopping late in the day, when it was crowded. Her routine was to go and do her big shop early in the morning while it was still quiet. She deposited the mugs in the sink, at the same time looking out of the window into the garden. The day was now bright and sunny. An idea suddenly struck her: why not abandon the idea of doing the shopping and go tomorrow instead? That way she could go straight out into the garden. The more she thought about it, the more the idea appealed to her. It prompted her to go outside and have a look at things. The first thing she saw elicited an exclamation of concern. 'Oh no!' The storm had pushed the bean sticks over at an alarming angle. That needed urgent attention, and with Tom not due for a few days she was the only person available to remedy the situation. Her mind made up, she strode back into the house to change into her gardening gear.

Chapter 13

John sat in the doorway of his shed. The day was cool for early October, grey and overcast, and to add to the dismal display occasionally a few spots of rain would fall but never develop into anything serious. It made the mug of coffee he was slowly drinking even more acceptable. There were few people on the allotment this morning. Stephen worked away silently as usual, and away in a far corner somebody had a bonfire going; the smell occasionally wafted over and tantalised John's nostrils. He had spent most of the morning taking down his runner bean canes. Each year at that time it was a kind of ritual. In a way it marked the change of seasons, from the growing one to the next phase of putting the allotment to sleep for the winter. There was always a bit of sadness about it, but also an air of satisfaction of a job well done; and then would come the planning for the next year.

This year things were slightly different for John. He had another interest in life: Debbie. He mused over this as he sat quietly drinking his coffee and surveying the scene before him. In the past, his allotment had been one of his main preoccupations in retirement, together with photography and his computer, but since meeting Debbie he had found that scarcely a day went by when he didn't think about her. Getting to know her had added a new dimension to his life and had made him realise how dull and lonely things had become over the years since Mary died. Apart from his interests, meeting a few people on the allotment and in the Dog and Duck, he had few opportunities to socialise. Of course, there had been a few holidays here and there, but they had only afforded a brief interlude from his daily routine.

His regular contact with Debbie had changed all that. During the summer months, they had phoned each other at regular intervals and had enjoyed several days out together. John would drive over in his car and they would make their way to a place of interest and enjoy each other's company. They were now relaxed with each other; there was no longer the restrained politeness that had characterised the beginning of their relationship.

For John, what had come with their deepening friendship was the confirmation that Debbie was an attractive woman for her age. He found himself looking at her as a desirable woman as well as a valued friend. At times he could hardly believe she was within a year or two of his own age, and a grandmother into the bargain. Perhaps it was because she was one of those women who present themselves as smartly dressed without going over the top and appearing ridiculous. It made him conscious that in the later years of their marriage Mary had tended to not bother so much with how she looked. She had devoted her energy to running their home and looking after him and Rob, and she had never liked socialising to any great extent. He had always had to almost drag her to his company's annual dinner dance. In a way, this had led to his own shyness and reserve, and had prompted him to choose solitary leisure interests that did not require any participation from Mary.

He had been amazed to discover that Debbie managed to do all the things she did and still appear as an attractive woman. She seemed to combine the roles of housekeeper, gardener and grandmother with comparative ease, yet still have time to appear well groomed. It was surprising, he pondered, how women differed in their approach to things.

His involvement with Debbie had shaken him out of his dull routine. It had even prodded him into buying a new sports jacket and consigning his old one to his allotment gear. He enjoyed doing little jobs for Debbie, like helping her buy a digital camera, and now she was considering buying a computer. He had thoroughly enjoyed repairing her back door after the burglary.

There had been odd moments in their brief friendship when he had allowed his fantasising to venture into the realm of considering Debbie as a permanent partner. His logic had swiftly ended such thinking. He realised that Debbie with her well-organised lifestyle was not inclined to seek a new partner. She had once conveyed this to him in the early days of their friendship.

As for him, the thought was too ridiculous to even consider. He hadn't slept with a woman for over eight years, and as far as physical intimacy went it was even longer than that. He could hardly imagine a staid old widower like himself sharing a bed with an attractive and desirable woman like Debbie.

There had been one moment in their friendship when he had been forced to think hard about the situation, and that was on the night of the storm, when Debbie had invited him to stay over in her house. For a horrible few moments he had wondered if he was going to be forced into a situation where he would have to back gracefully out of an awkward or even embarrassing situation. He had been relieved to hear Debbie's view of things and to understand that she felt exactly as he did about their relationship. In a way, that evening had cemented their friendship firmly, because each knew how the other felt.

He finished his coffee, packed the flask away in his rucksack, and then returned to pottering on his plot. He would telephone Debbie later in the day and enquire how she was getting on. It was close on a week since they had had any contact with each other. Perhaps he would suggest another outing before the weather changed and the darker evenings arrived. There was no reason why they couldn't have a day out in London. He would ask her how she felt about that.

He worked on for a while and was surprised when he looked at his watch to find that it was well past eleven o'clock. He would finish up now and on the way back call in at the Dog and Duck for a well-earned half-pint of lager.

It was just after midday when he walked into the bar. It was empty except for Bob Roberts. As John entered Bob looked up and called out: 'Morning, John. You're just in time.' He looked from John to his almost empty glass.

John took the hint. He called out cheerily. 'Good morning, Bob! Half a bitter?'

Bob gave a thumbs-up sign.

John turned his attention to the bar. A stranger stood behind it: a young man with ginger hair, who greeted John with a courteous 'Good morning'.

'Good morning. Half a pint of bitter, please, and a half of lager.' He rummaged in his pocket for the money. 'Where's Jonathan?' he asked, as the barman pumped up Bob's beer.

'Day off.'

'Ah, I see.'

'I'm Andy. I'm looking after the place for the day.'

'What are Jonathan and Meg up to, then?' John asked, more to keep the conversation going than anything else.

Andy laughed. 'Maybe looking for somewhere to live,' he said.

Jonathan and Meg had already announced that they were giving up the tenancy of the Dog and Duck. The news had cast a kind of gloom over the regulars.

'Are you thinking of taking over?' asked John.

Andy shook his head. 'No way,' he replied, taking John's money and going to the till. 'I think the brewery have plans for the place. I've heard it's going to be a steak house,' he added, giving John his change.

'Gosh, I hope not. I would miss the old place,' John observed, picking up the two glasses of beer.

'Sign of the times,' Andy replied. Then he turned to another customer, who had just come into the bar.

John carried the brimming glasses of beer to the corner table where Bob sat waiting for him.

'Did you hear that?' John asked, putting the glasses carefully down on the table.

'About this place becoming a steak house? I did hear rumours. Cheers!' Bob concluded his reply by taking a swig of his beer.

'Bit of a blow for the regulars. We'll have to find another hostelry.' John took a sip of lager.

'Good for business, though,' Bob laughed. He still had his butcher's shop.

'Where's Harry today?' John enquired.

Bob's face took on a more sombre expression. 'Taking his wife to see a specialist at the hospital. The old chap's quite worried about her.'

'What's the problem?' John asked, concerned at Bob's sudden change of demeanour.

Bob almost whispered his reply. 'Don't know for sure, but it looks as if it might be the big C.'

'Oh, I do hope not.' John's response was immediate. Then, as an afterthought, he added: 'Still, it's marvellous what can be done these days. Cancer is no longer an automatic death sentence.'

'I suppose not,' Bob replied thoughtfully.

John suddenly remembered that Bob had lost his own wife to breast cancer two years previously. He wondered whether it had been a good idea to make the last remark.

He was considering a follow-up comment to rectify the situation, when Bob piped up and changed the subject. 'How's the allotment?'

'Basically, just putting it to bed for the winter now and clearing up mainly. There are still a few winter crops growing – leeks, Brussels sprouts, things like that.'

'My son-in-law wants to go halves in an allotment with me,' Bob said thoughtfully.

'Well, there you are. Have a go,' John responded cheerfully.

Bob laughed. 'You don't know my son-in-law. He hasn't got the time. I'd be doing most of the work.'

John nodded. 'It can be time-consuming,' he agreed. Over the years he had seen plenty of people take a plot over with a great deal of enthusiasm that was of short duration once they realised how much time it required.

They continued chatting while they finished their drinks. Then Bob announced that he had to get back to the shop, and John agreed that he, too, needed to go. They parted at the door and went their separate ways.

John walked at a brisk pace. He wanted to shake off the slight gloom that the atmosphere of his half-hour in the pub had enveloped him in. The news from Andy about the future of the pub and Bob's information about Harry's wife had not been uplifting. He needed cheering up, he thought. Yes, most certainly he would phone Debbie that evening.

Debbie was not having a very good day. It had started well enough: she had intended doing the shopping early then spending a little time in the garden tidying up. But it had not worked out that way. Her car had simply refused to start. She had tried and tried and in the end had had to admit defeat and call the AA. She had then had to wait until an engineer got to her. His diagnosis had been quick and direct. The car needed a new battery. The engineer had started the engine for her and then suggested that she go straight away to have a new battery fitted. Debbie knew the place he suggested. It wasn't far away. She had used it to replace tyres. She had driven there terrified that she would stall the car and not be able to start it again, but she had made it to the garage without mishap. It had only taken a few minutes to fit a new battery and from there she had gone straight to the shops, conscious that it was Tom's gardening morning and that she needed to be back to unlock the side gate and let him through into the garden. Although she knew that he would be arriving later now that the days were shorter, he was already waiting on the drive when she got back. He accepted her explanation and apology with a smile, but said nothing. She had seen at once that all was not well. Instead of going straight to the garden shed as usual, he hesitated by the back door as if deep in thought.

Debbie decided to help things along. 'Did you want me for something, Tom?' she asked.

He hesitated for an instant. 'I was wondering if I could have a word with you, Mrs Patterson.' He sounded very serious.

'Of course you can, Tom. Come into the kitchen a minute.' Debbie knew she had to encourage him to say what was on his mind.

He followed her in, cap in hand. As soon as they were inside she turned to him. 'What's the problem, Tom?' she asked, as kindly as she could. It was obviously something important. Tom never normally acted like this.

Again he hesitated, clutching his cap for comfort. He cleared his throat. 'Well, it's just that Ada thinks we should go and live near our daughter.' He looked at Debbie.

Debbie did her best to appear normal in spite of the sudden shock. She hadn't expected this. She had imagined that perhaps Tom was after more money. He hadn't raised his hourly rate for several years. She struggled to hide her shock but managed to smile at him as she replied to his bombshell. 'Well, Tom, that's something for you to look forward to. Have you been thinking about it for some time? I shall miss you very much.'

Tom still looked a bit uncomfortable. 'I'm not so keen, but a house has just come up not far from our Betty, and with Ada not being so good and that, we thought it would be best for us.' He looked at Debbie for sympathy.

Debbie felt a bit sorry for him. Clearly he was in the hands of his wife and daughter. However, she could see the sense of making a move. Tom and Ada had no other relatives except their married daughter. In spite of the shock his announcement had brought, Debbie did her best to reassure him. 'It'll be all right once you've made the move and settled in, Tom, and Ada will enjoy being close to Betty. And Betty can help her as well.' She tried hard to sound positive.

Tom nodded, as if in partial agreement, but said nothing.

'When are you thinking of moving?' Debbie asked. It was important for her to know.

Tom looked a bit more cheerful. 'We've got to sell our place here. We were thinking of early next year,' he said.

This came as a relief to Debbie. At least she had a little time to think about getting someone else in. 'Oh,' she said, 'I thought you would be going straight away. So there's a bit of time before I lose you.'

'I'll be here till we go,' said Tom, looking at her for approval.

'Oh, that will be marvellous if you can. Then I'll have time to look for somebody else to help me. Do you know anybody who might be interested, Tom?' She strove to sound cheerful, but the thought of looking for a replacement was daunting.

Tom thought for a moment. 'I'll see if anybody at the Liberal Club's interested,' he said. Then, signalling the end of the conversation, he jerked into action. 'I'd best be getting started with something,' he said, and turned to make for the door.

Debbie followed him out. 'Thank you for telling me so early, Tom. I do appreciate it.'

He turned to her and nodded by way of a reply.

'I'll give you a call when I've made our drink,' Debbie called out as he headed for the garden.

Tom put his hand up in acknowledgment and disappeared from her view.

Debbie returned to the kitchen. Tom's announcement had come as a blow. Suddenly she realised how much she relied on him to do all the heavy work in the garden. It was odd, but in a way he had almost become part of her life. Now she would have to try and find somebody else. The thought was not appealing. Where would she start? Above all, she needed someone she could get on with and trust. Well, Tom had said he would try and find somebody, but he hadn't appeared very optimistic.

Suddenly she remembered that her shopping was still in the car. And the car needed to be put away. Routine snapped her out of her brief melancholy. She retrieved the shopping from the boot and drove the car into the garage. As she closed the garage doors, she paused and looked at the car. Quite apart from the battery failure, it was now advanced in years. Perhaps she should consider getting a new one that had all the modern attachments. The idea appealed to her, after this morning's problem. She would think about it; perhaps ask John what he thought. Thinking of John prompted her to make a mental note to perhaps give him a ring later. It was days since they'd spoken.

By the time Debbie had made Tom and herself a drink, chatted to him for fifteen minutes or so and then done one or two jobs, the morning had disappeared. When Tom popped his head into the kitchen to say he was going, Debbie realised that her original plan to spend some time in the garden in his company had gone sadly awry. She said goodbye to him and told him not to worry about the move, and he disappeared, looking less worried than when he had arrived.

She made herself something to eat. There was a WI meeting that afternoon and she had promised to go. She hadn't originally intended to do so, but then Amy, who lived in the next road and was an active member, had phoned her to ask for a lift, as her car was being repaired. Debbie had quickly changed her mind and readily agreed to Amy's request. She had only a limited interest in WI matters these days; she usually put in an appearance and that was it. She had been relieved that the attempts to bludgeon her onto the committee had died a natural death after her repeated refusals.

It was almost half past one when she set the alarm and locked her front door. She felt a bit more secure now when leaving the house. Paul had been as good as his word and on the weekend following the burglary had come over with his friend to survey the house. Three days later a quotation had arrived in the post. Debbie had immediately contacted Jan, who had then come over to collect it and discuss it with Paul. After an assurance from Paul that everything was in order, Debbie had given the go-ahead, and three weeks later two men had spent nearly two days in the house carrying out the installation. When they announced that they had finished and would show her how to use the system, Debbie's anxiety had set in. They had gone through everything very carefully with her until she seemed to have grasped the procedure. Even then she had made some notes and for her own comfort had insisted on trying everything while they were still there. After that, she was on her own.

In spite of the assurances from the installers, there had been some problems. Once, Debbie had come back from shopping to find the alarm blaring, and on another occasion it had woken her up at three in the morning. On each occasion she had rung the helpline and somebody had come to make adjustments. Both incidents had made her extremely anxious over the whole thing, and when it happened a third time, albeit this time at seven in the morning, she had almost reached the point of announcing that she wasn't going to use it. Then to her surprise and relief, things had settled down, and for two months all had gone smoothly. The main thing was to remember to set the alarm every time she went out. Even that morning, in her haste to get the car repaired, she had forgotten to do so and had scolded herself afterwards for her carelessness. Of course, another issue had been to instruct Jan and Trish in the art of alarm operation.

It was nearly six in the evening by the time she returned from the meeting. In spite of chatting to everybody, she had found it all a bit boring. Again and again she had found herself returning to Tom's announcement. She knew that without a pair of stronger hands available she would be unable to manage the garden on her own. It was another problem to sort out. In the meantime she had developed a headache. She felt glad that she was now home and could spend a relaxing evening.

As she turned onto the drive she found Trish's car pulled up against the garage. It looked as if her plans were going to go awry again. When Trish arrived at this time, she usually stayed the night. She let herself into the house.

'Is that you, Mum?' Trish called from upstairs.

'Yes, it's only me,' Debbie called back, as she went into the kitchen.

'I'll be down in a jiffy.' Trish seemed to be in the bathroom.

Debbie busied herself for a few minutes. It was nice to see Trish again; she hadn't had a visit from her for over a month. Certainly her quiet evening had most likely gone by the board. The most pressing thing now was deciding what to cook for supper. She supposed Trish would require something.

Suddenly there was the noise of footsteps on the stairs, announcing Trish's imminent arrival. Debbie automatically winced, but she did not need to worry. Trish was in her shirt and jeans, and barefoot.

'Hello, Mum.' She planted a kiss on her mother's cheek.

'Hello, dear. This is a surprise. It seems ages since you were here. Going to stay the night?'

'Yes, please. I'm on my way back from Birmingham and I thought I'd pop in to see you.'

'That's marvellous. You managed the alarm all right?' Debbie enquired.

Trish nodded and flopped into a chair. 'No problem. I'd forgotten about it until it started to buzz,' she said casually.

'Oh, that's good.' Debbie replied, relieved that she hadn't returned to the alarm blaring out. 'Now, what would you like for supper?'

Trish screwed up her face. 'Hmm, I'm not really hungry – just something.'

'How about some soup and an egg on toast?'

'Super.'

'Would you like it now, or later?'

'Could we have it later? I've got some work to do first and then we can eat and talk.'

Debbie readily agreed. It sounded as if Trish had already made up her mind anyway. It was almost two hours before they finally sat down to eat. It was during the meal that Trish dropped her bombshell. She paused halfway through lifting a spoonful of soup to her mouth. 'Mum, I'm getting married.'

Debbie struggled to hide her astonishment. 'Gosh, dear, that is a surprise. Who to, and when?'

Trish remained unperturbed and matter-of-fact. 'Don. We've decided to make it the twenty-third of December.'

Debbie tried to assimilate what she was hearing. 'So soon? That's only a few weeks away. Where are you planning to get married? There will be quite a lot to do.'

'In London, at a register office. It's the only time that's convenient for both Don's and my work. On Christmas Eve we're flying out to Bali for two weeks.' Trish seemed quite unaware of the shock she had given her mother. After a slight pause while she took another spoonful of soup, she added: 'Don wants me to have a white wedding.'

Debbie did her best to hide her shock and her disappointment. She knew that she could always rely on her younger daughter to be unconventional in what she did. Nevertheless, she had always hoped that Trish would be married in their local church, like her sister Jan. She tried to put some enthusiasm into her reply. 'That will be nice. You could have Jamie as a pageboy, and Jan as matron of honour.'

Trish's reaction was immediate. 'Not likely. I'm not having any screaming brats at my wedding, thank you very much.'

Debbie smiled sadly but said nothing. She knew Trish too well to argue. As she got up to cook the eggs, she remarked gently: 'Jan will be disappointed.'

'Too bad.' Trish shrugged off the suggestion.

Debbie did not reply. She concentrated on the work in hand. Eventually, noticing the lack of conversation, Trish suddenly got up from her chair and walked over and stood close to her mother. 'Mum, you are pleased I'm getting married, aren't you?'

Debbie stopped what she was doing. Swiftly she hugged her daughter. 'Darling, of course I am. It's just so sudden, that's all. And you know I haven't even met Don.' Debbie usually called her younger daughter 'darling' at special times. It was something that dated back to when Trish was a little girl.

'Oh, Mum, I'm sorry. Look, I'll bring him round soon, I promise.'

'That will be nice. I want to get to know him. Can you pass the plates?'

Debbie had released her daughter from the hug and returned to the cooking. Trish stood close by, watching her. Suddenly she asked: 'Mum, you will help me buy a dress, won't you?'

'Of course I will,' Debbie replied as enthusiastically and cheerfully as she could, at the same time rescuing the toast from the grill. She finished the cooking and handed Trish a plate. 'This is yours.'

For the rest of the meal, their conversation consisted of Debbie asking questions and Trish providing answers. Debbie was anxious to learn more about her future son-in-law. It seemed that Don was something in London's financial world and enjoyed a generous salary. From Debbie's questioning, it appeared that Trish did not know as much about him as Debbie would have liked; but she felt unable to say very much at this stage.

When they had finished eating, Debbie declined Trish's offer to help with the washing up. Trish immediately said that she still had some work to do but it would only take an hour and then she would be free to enjoy the rest of the evening. Debbie knew that in all probability it would work out to be longer. She welcomed the short period on her own. Somehow she needed a bit of time to absorb Trish's announcement. She was just about to start on the washing up, when she remembered John. With Trish holed up in her room upstairs, she had a window of opportunity to ring him. She left the kitchen and went into the lounge. All was quiet upstairs. Trish was out of sight and earshot. Now was the time.

John answered the phone almost straight away.

'John, it's Debbie. I just felt I had to give you a ring.'

'Hello there. I was going to ring you tonight. How are you?' He sounded elated at hearing her voice.

Speaking to him felt good. 'Oh, I'm fine. That is...' Debbie hesitated. No point in bothering John with her doubts and anxieties. Instead she altered her sentence. 'No. I'm fine, really. How are you?'

'Great. But you don't sound too sure. Anything I can help with?' He sensed that she was concerned about something.

Debbie hesitated again. She had not meant to unload her troubles onto John, but she knew his would be a sympathetic ear. Oh, why not, she thought. 'Oh, it's just that I've had one of those days. In fact everything seems to have given me a headache.' She stopped short of going into detail.

John detected her stress. 'So, what actually happened?' he asked.

Debbie thought for a few moments before answering. 'Well, first of all my car wouldn't start this morning. I had to call the AA out and then go and have a new battery fitted. Then as soon as I got back my gardener told me he was leaving. He's going away to live.'

'That's a bit of a rough deal.'

Debbie shielded her voice with her hand, just in case Trish might hear. 'And then on top of that Trish arrived at teatime and announced she's getting married. At Christmas, no less – and I haven't even met her future husband yet.'

'Phew. That is a bit of a load all at once.'

Debbie tried to give a little laugh. 'I know. But I expect I'll survive it all.'

'How's the alarm now?' John asked. He knew about the difficulties Debbie had experienced.

'Oh, no problems since I spoke to you last. It does seem to have settled down now. That's one good thing.' Debbie strove to appear more cheerful. It wasn't fair to bother John with all her anxieties. As an afterthought she added in a lower voice: 'The problem is remembering to set it each time I go out. I forgot it this morning when I had to get the car fixed.'

'Is the car all right now?' John asked.

'Yes. It was only the battery. You know, I suppose I should think about replacing my car sometime. It's getting quite old now. What do you think?' It was the first time Debbie had voiced her thoughts on the subject to anybody.

John thought for a few seconds before answering. 'I suppose it might be a good idea if you can afford to do it.'

'Perhaps I should get the wedding over first and then think about it early next year.' She had come to that decision while talking to him.

'I can always help you buy one,' John suggested helpfully.

'That would be very comforting,' replied Debbie.

'I think we should have another day out soon, and then we can talk about everything,' John said suddenly.

Debbie took up the idea immediately. Something to perk her up was just the tonic she needed. 'Oh, that would be heavenly. When and where?'

'I'll think of something. We'll choose a nice day for weather. It might have to be a short-notice decision.' John was thinking everything out as he spoke.

'That would be fine. We can always work it out somehow. I can't wait.' Debbie thrilled at the thought of a day out with John. Now the days were cooler she could wear the autumn suit she had bought last year.

They chatted on for almost half an hour, until John reminded her that she was running up an expensive telephone call. Debbie didn't mind; just talking to him felt good after the day's events. It was the sound of Trish coming downstairs that in the end made her decide to finish the call. She had just replaced the receiver when Trish arrived in the room.

'Have you finished now, dear? Would you like a drink of something?'

Debbie made two mugs of tea and settled down for another chat with Trish. She was anxious to glean as much information as possible about the forthcoming event. It was late when at last Trish announced that she was going to bed. After she had left, Debbie busied herself with washing the mugs and tidying everything up. After a while she heard Trish leave the bathroom and go into her own room.

Ten minutes later she at last lay in bed going over the events of the day. Quite a lot had happened; quite a lot of changes were on the way. First Tom going, then Trish's wedding. While she was pleased for her daughter, and even a tiny bit excited, she was still anxious about the suddenness of everything. But then that was Trish: she had never been any different. Debbie just hoped everything would work out all right. It had been nice talking to John again. It was thinking of him that gave her an idea. In fact, the more she thought about it, the more it appealed to her. It was a pleasant thought to fall asleep with.

Chapter 14

'Trish, you can't possibly wear a dress like that in winter. You'll freeze to death.' Debbie's voice echoed not only her disapproval but also her tiredness. Trish stood in front of her in the full array of a white off-the-shoulder wedding dress, watched by Debbie and the owner of the shop.

It was a cold November Saturday. Debbie had travelled up to London early, meeting Trish for coffee, and had then embarked with her daughter on a mission to purchase the desired wedding dress. They were already three hours into the quest and this was the third shop they had ventured into.

'But I think it's nice. Don will love it,' protested Trish.

Debbie strove to be as diplomatic as possible. 'It is a nice dress, Trish, but you have to remember that it's winter and the last thing you want to do on your wedding day is to look frozen to death. I would try and have something a bit more covered up.'

Trish reacted with a pout and a sigh of exasperation. She turned to the woman who owned the shop and asked: 'What else do you have in my size?'

The shop owner reacted swiftly and once again turned her attention to the racks of dresses in their clear covers. After a short search another dress was taken down and held up. 'How about this one? This is a really lovely dress and it would suit you, madam.'

Trish viewed it critically. 'I'll try it on,' she announced. She disappeared into the fitting room with the shop owner. Debbie was glad of the few minutes' break. She glanced at her watch. It was almost half past one. She was beginning to feel decidedly weary. She had lost count of the number of dresses that had been displayed for her approval.

The planning of the forthcoming wedding had not been without its ups and downs. Trish had kept her word, and several weeks after her initial announcement she had brought her fiancé round for Debbie's approval. Don had insisted on taking her and Trish out for an expensive meal. Debbie had got on well enough with him, but somehow she found it difficult to establish the same rapport with him as she had with Paul. Later in the day, Jan, Paul and Jamie had arrived for tea, and the conversation had been amicable but slightly strained. Only Jamie's activities had livened things up a bit. Debbie had been tempted to invite John over for the day, but in the end decided that perhaps it was best on the first meeting to confine things to the family.

It was after this that family relationships had started to be strained. Trish's announcement that she would not have Jamie as a pageboy had brought an immediate response from Jan that in that case she would not be matron of honour and might not even come to the wedding. Debbie had stepped in to mediate, but the atmosphere remained tense between her two daughters. Undeterred, Trish had continued to demonstrate her likes and dislikes. Debbie's suggestion that John be invited to give the bride away had met with a firm refusal and the explanation from Trish that she had already elected her boss for that role. As Debbie had offered to pay for the reception, she had exercised her wish that John be invited to the wedding in any case. The last hurdle on the bumpy path of preparation was the current expedition to purchase the wedding dress.

Debbie's musing was brought to a sudden halt by the parting of the fitting-room curtains and Trish's reappearance.

'What do you think, Mum?' Trish paraded in front of her.

Debbie was more enthusiastic this time. The dress, with its cleverly cut neckline, suited Trish. It also did a better cover-up job than the previous one. 'Trish, that really is perfect for you. You look lovely in it.'

Trish made no comment, but she strutted up and down looking at herself in the shop mirrors. 'It looks beautiful,' observed the shop owner approvingly.

Trish promptly made a decision. 'I'm going to settle on that one,' she announced.

Debbie breathed an inward sigh of relief. At last. Now perhaps they could have something to eat. Her optimism was short-lived.

'And the accessories, madam?' enquired the shop owner.

Debbie had to endure another half an hour while Trish viewed this and that and squeezed her feet into ridiculous shoes. At one point, eyeing the pair of white satin-covered shoes Trish was trying on, and concerned at the amount of money Trish was spending, she intervened to comment that she would be better off buying shoes she could wear after the wedding as well rather than something that would be worn only once. In the end, common sense prevailed. The bill was paid, which almost made Debbie wince, and the dress was left at the shop for Trish to collect nearer the day of the wedding.

At last Trish turned to her mother. 'Thanks a million, Mum. I'll buy you some lunch now.'

Debbie breathed a sigh of relief; the announcement was welcome.

'Well, how did it all go?'

Madge sat at Debbie's kitchen table and warmed her hands on her mug of coffee. She helped herself to another biscuit as she waited for Debbie's answer. It was Christmas Eve, and the morning after the wedding. Madge was making one of her quick visits to drop in a Christmas card and invite herself for coffee at the same time.

Debbie didn't answer immediately. The last few weeks had drained her energy and she hoped she didn't look as tired as she felt. It had been quite a stressful time, for despite Trish's screen of apparent self-confidence there had been last-minute nerves and she had made some frantic telephone calls to Debbie. At the same time, Debbie had been trying to deal with the strained atmosphere between her two daughters.

She had even offered to go up to London and help Trish get ready on the big day, but her offer had been turned down with the explanation that Don would be banished to his parents in North London and that one of Trish's girlfriends would stay overnight and help her.

Jan's attitude to her sister had softened a little as the wedding day approached, and in the end Jan had reluctantly decided that she would leave Jamie with Violet, and she and Paul would give Debbie a lift to the register office. Paul was used to driving in London and knew the area quite well. Debbie had been concerned that John would have to make his own way up to London by train and meet everybody at the wedding ceremony, but it hadn't bothered him at all.

The day had been cold and damp, and Debbie had shivered in the costume she had bought for the wedding. Lining up for photographs after the rather drab and brief ceremony had been particularly miserable, with light rain making an appearance.

The reception, at a rather upmarket hotel, had been dominated by people Debbie didn't know; most of them were Trish's friends and colleagues from the office, together with a host of people from Don's family. Debbie had been glad of John's company, though she felt sorry that he had been plunged into a crowd of strangers.

They had seen the bridal pair off to the hotel where they were going to stay overnight before departing on their honeymoon, and then made their way home. Jan had been anxious to get back to Jamie and she had kept a running commentary of what she thought had been wrong at the wedding all the way back.

After letting her thoughts wander to the previous day's events, Debbie returned to Madge. 'Oh, I think things went quite well, considering,' she answered thoughtfully.

Madge finished munching her biscuit. 'You don't sound very sure,' she said, scrutinising Debbie.

Debbie hadn't intended to open up to her, but suddenly her fears and doubts took over, and with somebody to talk to they bubbled to the surface. She elaborated on her previous remark. 'Well, you know, everything has been so quick. Trish has only known Don a few months. Then she said she didn't want any help, then at times she did and I got panic calls. On top of that there's been this friction between Jan and Trish over not having Jamie as a pageboy.'

Madge took a gulp of her coffee and put the mug down on the table. 'That's weddings – if there's no grief at the time, it comes later.'

This made Debbie laugh. 'It's not always like that,' she replied.

Madge shrugged. 'Tell me when it's not,' she said, taking another biscuit.

Debbie took a sip of her own coffee, holding the mug with both hands and looking at Madge over the rim. 'Did you never have an urge to get married?' she asked.

Madge shook her head. 'No. As far as I can see men are like children, needing attention all the time; either that or all they're interested in is their own pleasure – usually in bed with you.'

Debbie smiled at the answer. Madge's attitude to men had always intrigued her. It prompted her to ask another question. 'Did you never have any serious relationships?'

Madge gave what was almost a grunt. 'A few in my time, but mostly they fizzled out. Usually I had to ditch them. Men can be quite pathetic at times. One of them even wanted to dictate the type of underwear I wore.'

Debbie found the last remark amusing. She couldn't help wondering what sort of underwear Madge's partner had wanted to see on her muscular frame, but before she could make a suitable answer Madge changed the subject.

'Where are the happy couple going for their honeymoon?'

'Bali. They're flying out today.'

Madge sighed. 'Lucky them. I could do with being in Bali now and getting away from this miserable weather.'

'I don't envy them the long flight,' observed Debbie.

Madge gave her one of those 'poor you' looks. 'Nothing to it,' she announced. 'Anyway, all you have to do is sit back and enjoy it.'

'I suppose so,' Debbie replied, without any apparent enthusiasm.

Madge suddenly stood up. 'I'd better be on my way,' she announced. Debbie strolled to the door with her.

'What are you doing tomorrow?' Madge asked over her shoulder.

'Oh, I'm going to Jan's for the day. Jamie will want to show me all his Christmas presents,' Debbie replied. Then out of courtesy she enquired: 'How about you?'

Madge laughed. 'As little as possible. I intend to spend some time trying to sort out a holiday for myself – somewhere warm to go in the New Year. I'll have a look on the internet.'

'Well, enjoy your day.' Debbie didn't know what else to say. Madge always scorned the Christmas festivities.

'Cheerio. Don't eat too much.' Madge turned to walk to her 4x4.

'Bye, Madge,' Debbie called after her from the front door. She waved as Madge drove off, and went back into the house. Sometimes she felt sorry for Madge at this time of year, and even a little guilty that she didn't invite her to share some of the Christmas festivities, but she was only too aware of Madge's opinion about such events and knew an invitation would be refused. She returned to the kitchen and started to clear up the dirty mugs and replace the uneaten biscuits in their tin. As she was pottering, the kitchen was suddenly flooded with light as the sun burst through the clouds. It made her pause to look out into the garden, now sleeping for the winter. Her thoughts turned to Tom. Only a few weeks ago he had told her that he would not be available for much longer than the New Year. His announcement had started to cause her concern. He had been unable to find anybody from among his contacts who was willing to take on the job. Debbie knew that it was going to be hard to find anybody who would be as dedicated as Tom. He had often worked for longer than she had paid him for and refused any extra money, saying that he enjoyed himself and didn't do it for the money. After so many years working with him, the prospect of starting afresh with a stranger did not appeal to her.

In spite of her denials to both Jan and Trish on the subject, there had been times recently when she had started to wonder whether it was indeed sensible to go on living on her own in such a large house. It had been Tom's imminent departure that had stimulated this new way of thinking. But where would she go? She hated the thought of being cooped up in a flat somewhere, and that seemed to be what most people considered the only option. On top of everything else,

Jan had again hinted several times about buying her house. Debbie knew Jan and Paul wouldn't wait for ever for her to make up her mind. Making a decision about it seemed to be the last thing she could do at the moment. It cropped up in her thoughts from time to time, but she repeatedly dismissed it from serious consideration.

The sound of the front doorbell broke her train of thought. She wondered who it could be. She wasn't expecting a caller. She quickly dried her hands and went to answer the door.

Rosemary Bilton stood on the doorstep, an envelope and a sheaf of papers in her hand. 'Oh, Debbie, I thought perhaps you were out. I just wanted to drop in our Christmas card to you.'

Debbie took the envelope. 'That's really very nice of you. Would you like to come in?' She did not see much of the Biltons apart from their coming and going in their two cars.

'No, dear, I won't come in. I just wanted to see you for a minute. Oh, and before I forget, thank you very much for your beautiful card.' Debbie had done her round of delivering Christmas cards to the neighbours several days previously.

Rosemary fumbled with the papers she was carrying. Extracting the one she wanted, she gave Debbie her full attention again. 'Now. Patrick has been sorting out details for the Neighbourhood Watch scheme. You know there was another burglary down the road recently?'

Debbie hadn't heard. 'No. I never heard anything,' she replied. The news brought back her anguish of a few months ago.

Rosemary nodded as if to confirm what she was about to say. 'Yes. The Joneses at number 44. Mrs Jones lost a lot of jewellery and a laptop computer.' She studied the papers in her hand as she continued speaking, and then looked at Debbie. 'Can we put you down as an interested person for the Neighbourhood Watch scheme?'

'Yes, of course you can.' Debbie had almost forgotten that Rosemary had brought up the subject at the time of her own break-in.

'Excellent. We've had a really good take-up. Almost ninety per cent of people are interested.' Rosemary ticked the sheet of paper.

'Are you sure you won't come in?' Rosemary seemed to be struggling a little with her papers.

'No, I must go. I have more people to visit, and quite a few things to do for tomorrow yet. My son and his wife and three children are coming for the day. It's usually chaos when they arrive.'

Debbie laughed. 'I know the feeling – it's the same when my grandson comes.'

Rosemary gathered her papers together and turned to go. 'What will you be doing tomorrow?' she asked.

'I shall spend the day with my daughter and son-in-law, and of course my grandson. It's almost tradition that I go there for the day now.'

Rosemary beamed at her. 'Have a lovely day, Debbie.'

'And you too, Rosemary.'

'I will. We must get together for coffee sometime soon. But cheerio for now, and a Merry Christmas.'

'That would be nice. Bye.'

Debbie watched Rosemary for a few seconds, responded to her goodbye wave and then went back into the house. For some reason she wandered into the lounge. One of the Christmas tree decorations had fallen off and lay on the floor just where it might be trodden on. She picked it up and carefully put it back into place. Setting up the Christmas tree was one of the traditions she maintained in spite of being on her own most of the time. Each year when she took it down she vowed that she wouldn't bother to have one the following year, but each year as Christmas came round she would weaken and change her mind. Heaven knows what the girls would say if she didn't have a tree in place, and of course there was Jamie to think of.

She looked around the room. Everything else was in order. She went into the kitchen and made herself a drink and a snack and then carried them back into the lounge. Turning the standard lamp on cast a warm glow in the room, making it look cosy. As she sat there eating, an idea began to form. She felt concerned about John. The previous day, in spite of fitting in beautifully, he had spent a good deal of the time isolated from her. Plunged into a mass of strangers like that, he must have felt awful, yet he had coped extremely well. And the worst part for Debbie was that he had had to travel to and from the event entirely on his own. She was beginning to wish she had suggested that he stay the night before in her house so that they could travel to the wedding together, but it was too late now. However, she could do what she had in mind now. Why not invite him over for Boxing Day? She would be at Jan's tomorrow, but on Boxing Day she would be on her own, and she knew that Jan and Paul would be going to visit some friends who also had a young family.

Abruptly she put her tray aside, went over to her desk and picked up the phone. She could almost remember the telephone number now. It only rang a few times at the other end before it was answered.

'John Hammond.'

Debbie was overjoyed she had caught him in. 'John, it's Debbie. How are you? I felt so guilty abandoning you to return home alone – and for that matter neglecting you most of the day. I just had to give you a ring.'

There was a bit of a laugh at the other end of the phone. 'Well, you had your duties to perform. Besides, I got in the photograph.'

She felt a bit relieved. John was always so understanding. It had been Debbie who had insisted, with Trish, that he stand beside her in the wedding photograph.

'And you got home OK?'

'Fine, no problems. How about you?'

'Likewise – except that I had to put up with Jan grumbling about what was wrong all the way home. I hope you didn't notice the friction between my two daughters.'

'No. I thought everything went quite well, really. It was a pity the weather wasn't kinder. Of course, I didn't know many people there, but that didn't matter.' He gave his nervous laugh again.

Debbie was about to answer, but he got in first. 'Are you all ready for tomorrow?' he asked.

It was Debbie's turn to laugh. 'Oh yes, I think so. It's over to Jan's tomorrow and entertain Jamie with his presents while Jan finishes cooking the dinner. Roast turkey and Christmas pudding. I expect I'll eat too much, and then we'll listen to the Queen's speech at three o'clock. Tea, and back home in the evening.' She sighed as she finished. It all sounded so familiar.

John echoed her thoughts. 'It all sounds familiar,' he observed.

'And you're going to spend the day with Rob and Cathy?' Debbie asked. John had already indicated that such an event was on the cards. 'Oh yes. I can't miss Cathy's Christmas dinner,' he enthused.

Debbie couldn't wait any longer. 'What are you doing on Boxing Day?'

She waited. John took several seconds to answer. 'Nothing, really. Taking things easy, I suppose.'

'Would you like to come and spend the day here?' Debbie held her breath.

'I'd love to. What time would you like me to come?' He sounded quite enthusiastic.

Debbie could hardly contain her joy at his reply. She was already mentally planning the day as she replied. 'Come in time for lunch. I'll cook us something nice.'

And then another idea came to her, which she immediately voiced. 'And John, why don't you stay overnight? That way we can have the whole evening together and you can have a drink.' She waited for his reply. Perhaps he might think this was too much.

'OK. I'll do that.'

Debbie's sense of excitement poured into the telephone. 'Oh, that's super. I'm really going to look forward to the day after tomorrow. 'And…' She hesitated before saying her next bit. 'And, John, there are still no strings attached.' She felt she had to say it, but immediately she thought it sounded a bit corny. She heard a little laugh at the other end of the phone.

'OK,' he said, and then in almost the same breath: 'I've got a present for you.' His tone was positively tantalising.

Debbie played along. 'Hmm, that sounds both exciting and mysterious,' she joked. She couldn't hold herself back from asking: 'What is it?'

'I'm not going to tell you – but it's something you want.' John was enjoying the game.

'OK, let me think… It's a bit like the old twenty questions game. Can you wear it?'

'No.'

'Can you eat it?'

'No.'

'I give up. I'm going to wait, eaten up with curiosity,' Debbie responded breezily.

John laughed. 'I wasn't going to tell you anyway,' he said jokingly.

'Oh, John. You're horrible to me,' Debbie joked, in tune with him. Then she added: 'I don't mean that really. I'm going to enjoy Boxing Day. Anyway, I've got a present for you… and… I'm not going to tell you what it is!' She laughed flippantly.

John pretended to be disappointed. 'Oh, all right then. I suppose I'll just have to wait.'

It was Debbie who brought the conversation to a close. 'John, I'd better get to the shops to get one or two extras for us. Can we leave it there, and I'll expect you the day after tomorrow for lunch?'

John jerked into action. 'Yes, and I'd better make sure the car has petrol and oil in it, just in case my usual filling station is closed tomorrow. Can I bring anything?'

Debbie shook her head instinctively as she answered. 'No. Just yourself.'

'OK, then. See you soon.'

'OK, John. Bye for now.'

'Bye.'

Debbie replaced the receiver. The day had completely changed for her. She was feeling quite excited at the thought of John's company for a whole twenty-four hours. This time they could relax and enjoy themselves. Her brain was working overtime, making plans about all the little finishing touches she had in mind for the day. It would be Christmas all over again, but this time with John. She glanced at the clock on the wall. She had plenty of time to go to the shops.

And then panic set in. It was Christmas Eve: the shops might close early. She had to hurry.

It was almost dark when she returned, carrying two bags of shopping. She thought perhaps she had bought too much, considering the fact that she had already laid in extra stock for Christmas just in case any of the family turned up, but she was determined to make things nice for John and had added a few extras, including two bottles of wine, and two bottles of beer for John, items she didn't normally have in the house. She had been perplexed in the shop as to which wine to buy, and whether it should be red or white. In the end she had chosen one of each at random. It was all quite heavy to carry and she wished she had taken her car. On top of that a kind of snowy rain was beginning to fall. She was relieved when she reached her front door.

She put her purchases away and made herself a cup of tea. She felt good about everything now. She had got everything she wanted. Tomorrow she would spend with Jan and family, and then she had all day and evening with John the day after.

She carried her tea into the lounge and turned on the lights. It was warm and cosy, and as a special treat she turned on the Christmas tree lights.

As she sat there she idly picked up the newspaper, which she had abandoned earlier on the coffee table. She glanced through its pages. It was mostly full of last-minute ideas and suggestions for Christmas. She had almost finished scanning through it when she noticed a large advertisement, showing an elderly couple standing in front of a new house. 'DEVELOPMENTS FOR RETIREMENT' read the heading, and underneath were the words 'Exclusive sites nationwide'.

Debbie read the advertisement, taking in the contents. There was a form to send off for more details of the sites available. She looked up from the newspaper. The advertisement had captured her interest.

It was a concept she had never considered before, and she wanted to know more. Why not, she thought. Sending for a brochure didn't commit her to anything. She jumped up from her chair and took the newspaper to her desk. Carefully she filled in the form and sealed it in an envelope. After the holidays she would post it.

Chapter 15

'I think it's a fantastic idea.' Jan glanced up from the brochure on her lap and looked across at her mother.

They were sitting in Debbie's lounge. Debbie was amusing Jamie, who was playing with a toy on the carpet in front of her.

'I think you should go ahead,' Jan continued, without waiting for an answer.

Debbie took her time. The brochure from the company specialising in properties for retired people had arrived several days before and she had carelessly left it lying in full view on her desk. As soon as Jan walked in she spotted it and set about perusing its contents. Debbie was a bit put out: she hadn't intended the family to be in on her investigation for alternative living accommodation until she had found out more about the development herself. Now the cat was out of the bag.

'I haven't really looked at it in any detail yet,' she said, vainly hoping that her vague reply might put an end to the subject for now.

'There's one in Oxford, not so far away. Did you know?' Jan wasn't going to let the matter die down.

'Yes, I had noticed that.' Debbie continued concentrating on Jamie's activities.

'I think you should go for it. Then Paul and I can buy this house from you.'

'Yes, but they're flats and I don't want a flat,' Debbie replied.

Jan's response was quick. 'No, Mum. There are some houses as well. It says so at the bottom. They're going to build some.'

Debbie had been caught out. She had received another brochure about the houses being built on the site in the second phase of the small development. She had left it in her bedroom after reading it in bed the previous night. Her remark had been made to dampen Jan's enthusiasm, but now it put her on the spot. 'Yes, but not yet,' she retorted.

'I know, but you don't know how old the brochure is. They're probably built now. You don't want to waste any time. They'll be snapped up quickly.' Jan wasn't going to let go.

'I'll try and give them a ring sometime,' Debbie replied vaguely, wishing the subject would go away.

Jan returned to the attack. 'Mum, would you like me to take the brochure and let Paul have a look and see what he thinks?'

That was the last thing Debbie wanted. She needed time and she wanted to let John have a look at the brochure and see what he thought about it. She had begun to value his opinion and she knew she would get an honest answer from him. While she respected her son-in-law, in this particular case there was too much of a vested interest involved. She regretted very much leaving the brochure just where Jan could see it. She knew she had to take control now.

'Look, dear, you must give me time to look at things myself. I'll talk to you about it again when I've had a chance to study it a bit more.' She tried to make her words sound as final as possible.

Jan looked at her mother. She recognised the signs and the tone of voice. It reminded her of when she had been younger and had been scolded for some misdemeanour. She knew there was no point in trying to move things along at this stage. She knew what Paul would say. They had had many discussions on the subject of moving house, and Paul's patience was beginning to wear thin at the delay in persuading his mother-in-law to move out so that they could buy her house. There was also the matter of Jan's decision, as a result of Paul's recent promotion, to have another baby now instead of following her original intention of returning to work when Jamie started school. She wanted to be settled in a new house before the baby arrived. But she knew there was no point in pursuing the subject at the present.

'OK, Mum. I'm sorry. I didn't mean to pressure you. But if you want any help, you know where we are.'

'All right, dear. As soon as I decide to do anything, I'll let you know. I promise.' Debbie felt relieved that she had extracted herself from a difficult situation.

Jan glanced at the clock and then at her watch. She looked down at Jamie. 'Come on, Jamie, we'd better be going. Say bye-bye to Gran.'

Jamie's face puckered up. He was enjoying what he was doing. Deftly his mother distracted him. 'We've got to get back home and get you ready to go to Emma's birthday party,' she said gently.

The strategy worked. Jamie's thoughts wandered from his present focus. 'Party,' he repeated.

'Yes, this afternoon,' cooed Jan.

Debbie saw them off and then went back into the lounge and sat down again. She was glad she had managed to fend Jan off for a little while. In her own time she would contact the company and find out more information about the houses. She knew that moving would be a big decision for her, and the last thing she wanted was for her family to take over the whole process.

It was now just over two weeks since Christmas. The decorations had been put away and life had gradually returned to normal. The highlight of Debbie's Christmas had been on Boxing Day when John had turned up just before lunch. Debbie had made a big effort and had everything ready. She had bought a small chicken and cooked this with all the trimmings; she had even purchased a small Christmas pudding. She had been up early and had the dining table all laid ready, with candles in the centre to make everything look cosy. By the time John arrived she had just managed to change into a pretty dress and a pair of high-heeled shoes.

She had met him at the front door and he had greeted her with a kiss. These days they were more relaxed with each other. Debbie had suggested a pre-dinner drink, and John had liked the idea, particularly when she produced one of the beers she had purchased for him. They

151

had taken their time over the drink, catching up on each other's news, Debbie visiting the kitchen several times to check that their food was not being overcooked. Dinner had been a leisurely event, full of chatter. John had brought a bottle of wine, and this had made the atmosphere even more congenial. By the time they retired to the lounge for a cup of coffee and a mince pie, Debbie had lost all interest in doing any washing up. When John offered, she had tactfully suggested leaving it until later.

It was at this point that Debbie had produced her present for John from beneath the Christmas tree. She had noticed on previous occasions that the pullover he often wore was showing signs of wear. She had trusted that she would buy the correct size to fit his lean frame. John had been delighted, and she had been relieved that he liked her choice and that it fitted perfectly.

She hadn't been prepared for the next bit. John had gone to his bag and come back with a flat parcel, handing it to her with a grin. 'Merry Christmas. Careful – it's a bit heavy.'

Wide-eyed, she had taken it from him. It was heavier than it looked. 'Oh, John, how sweet of you!' She had been as excited as her grandson had been when opening his presents the day before.

'Open it, but be a bit careful,' John had urged, still smiling at her.

Debbie had sat with the package on her knee, carefully undoing the paper. It had been fairly simply wrapped and it had been an easy task, but her curiosity had been running high. It hadn't taken her long to reveal the flat object. She had recognised instantly what it was. A squeal of delight had burst from her lips. 'It's a computer, isn't it?'

John had nodded, smiling at her excitement. 'Open it.'

Debbie had fumbled for an instant to find how it opened.

'There's a catch just here.' John had shown her.

Debbie had gazed at the shiny piece of new technology for an instant, and then she had looked up at him. 'John, you spoil me. I never expected anything like this. It must have cost the earth.'

John had smiled again. 'I'll let you into a secret. It's actually second-hand, but there's a story attached to it.'

She had waited, keen to learn more.

'Rob bought it about twelve months ago and then decided he needed something more advanced, so he was going to dispose of it, and I immediately thought, that's just the thing for Debbie to play with.'

Debbie had turned her attention to the laptop on her knee, still feeling a bit overwhelmed. She had often considered learning how to use a computer, and now one had actually arrived. Just looking at it had made it seem even more mysterious. 'Do you think I'll be able to use it?' she had asked anxiously, adding hopefully: 'I used to be able to use a typewriter in my youth.'

'Of course you will,' John had assured her. 'I'll show you.'

Suddenly Debbie had felt a little bit concerned. She had come down to earth and her expression was more serious now. 'John, it's such a lovely present, but a very expensive one. I shouldn't really let you buy it for me.'

John had just laughed. He had expected this reaction from her once her surprise had died down. 'I have to say that it wasn't as expensive as you might think. It was surplus to requirements and I thought to myself, ah, that's waiting for Debbie.'

'When can you show me how to use it?' Debbie had resigned herself to accepting the gift.

'As soon as you like. Everybody needs to be able to know their way around computers these days. Anyway, we older generation shouldn't let the youngsters think they know it all. We need to keep up with them.'

What John was saying made good sense. Debbie had been thinking of going to classes to learn how to use a computer for ages now. Now she actually had one she could play with – if it wasn't too difficult. Suddenly she had put the computer down on the settee beside her, stood up and then faced John. Taking his hand, she had said: 'I must sound quite ungrateful. Thank you for having such a lovely idea, and thank you for such a marvellous present.'

Then she had leaned forward and kissed him. This time she had ignored his cheek and planted a kiss on his lips.

The rest of the day had been sheer contentment for Debbie. For the first time in years she was spending time at Christmas doing something she really enjoyed, entertaining John and sharing his company instead of being the dutiful mother and grandmother. It was a new role and she enjoyed playing it. John was so thoughtful and caring. Later in the day he had endeavoured to teach her the basics of operating a computer. He had displayed the same degree of patience and understanding that he had exhibited when he had taught her to use the digital camera. She had become reasonably proficient with that, thanks to his help. She could still see the looks of amazement on Jan and Paul's faces as she had demonstrated her new-found skill. Now she hoped to do the same with her latest toy.

The sound of the telephone ringing woke her with a start. For a few seconds she struggled to remember where she was. Then reality came back to her. Sitting in the chair and going over events, she must have dropped off.

The telephone trilled away. She got up to answer it. It might be John; she hadn't heard from him for almost a week. It might even be Trish. Debbie had spoken to her two days ago when she returned from her honeymoon. She had been feeling decidedly sorry for herself after catching some sort of tummy bug while she was away, and she was still experiencing the after-effects.

Debbie picked up the receiver. 'Hello.'

'Mrs Patterson?' It was a female voice.

'Yes.' Debbie was deliberately vague. She suspected it might be somebody trying to sell her something.

'I'm Nickie from Morgan Manton.'

'Yes?' Debbie struggled to recall what Morgan Manton was.

Nickie helped her out. 'I'm so sorry, Mrs Patterson. Morgan Manton Properties. You sent for our brochure. Did you receive it?

Debbie fell in. 'Oh yes, of course. I'm sorry. I didn't recognise the name at first.'

'That's quite all right, Mrs Patterson. Was our brochure of any interest to you?'

'Well, yes, in a way. But I haven't made my mind up what to do yet.'

'No, of course not. It's a big decision, isn't it?' Then Nickie added: 'Most people who do decide to move into one of our properties say afterwards that they wished they had done so earlier.'

'Yes, I'm sure.' Debbie didn't really know what to say.

'Which site were you interested in?' Nickie asked next.

'Well, the one near me. I don't want to move far away.' Debbie couldn't remember the name of it.

Nickie paused for an instant, obviously looking up something. 'Oh yes. You live in Oxford, don't you? Oh, we have a marvellous site there. It's just being completed. It's one of our prestige developments.'

Debbie hesitated, unwilling to commit to anything.

Nickie seemed to sense her reluctance. 'Would you like to view the site? It doesn't put you under any obligation. We don't force people to buy our properties.'

'Well, I don't really know at this stage.'

Nickie wasn't going to give up. 'Look, I'll tell you what I'll do. I'll get in touch with Trudi, our local representative, and ask her to give you a telephone call. You can have a chat with her, and if you want she can arrange a time to view the properties near you. She won't pressurise you into anything, I promise. Shall I do that?'

Debbie thought for an instant. Why not, she decided. After all, it didn't put her under any obligation to do anything. And it wasn't very far away. And Nickie did sound quite sincere and understanding.

'Perhaps it might not be a bad idea,' she replied, hoping that her reply didn't sound too vague.

'Good. I'll contact Trudi now and she will give you a ring and arrange a suitable time.' Debbie could sense Nickie's satisfaction.

'When will that be?' Debbie asked.

'Oh, it'll be quite soon. You can arrange everything with her.'

'I'll wait to hear from her.'

'Fine. Thank you for your time, Mrs Patterson. Goodbye for now.'

'Goodbye. Thank you.'

Debbie put the receiver down. Well, she thought, having a look didn't commit her to anything. One thing was certain, though: if she went to view the properties, she would go alone. If Jan or Paul were there, they would immediately start to put pressure on her.

It was a cold but bright and sunny January afternoon when Debbie drove to the site to view the properties. The day after speaking to Nickie she had received a telephone call from Trudi, who had sounded very nice and friendly. Now she was on her way, the pack she had received from Morgan Manton lying on the passenger's seat beside her. Trudi had given her detailed directions and she had no difficulty in finding the area; only a little concern that she might not find the right road at the end of the journey.

However, Trudi's directions had been very specific and Debbie found herself driving down a rather pleasant tree-lined suburban street. It reminded her of her own. At first she thought the road ended in a cul-de-sac, but then she saw that it had been extended onto a building site, where a small development of houses and flats had recently been constructed. Debbie liked what she saw from her first glance at the houses; they were built in blocks of two or three on either side of the road. She saw Trudi's car with the company's name on the side parked outside one of the blocks, and parked neatly behind it. As she got out of her car, Trudi was already walking towards her, a document case under her arm. She was a young woman of about Trish's age, immaculately dressed in a smart black business suit.

She greeted Debbie with a cheerful smile and offered her hand. 'Mrs Patterson, it's nice to see you.'

Debbie greeted her and shook her hand.

'I'll show you the apartments that are still available,' Trudi announced, starting to walk in the direction of one of the blocks.

Debbie stopped her. 'I'm really only interested in a house,' she said.

Trudi's confident sales ardour flagged for just an instant. She paused for a moment before replying. 'I'm afraid all the houses have an option on them,' she said. And then to justify the statement she added: 'This is a very popular site. Most of the properties were snapped up within days of being released.'

This was a blow to Debbie. After speaking to Nickie, she had carefully studied the brochure. She had been taken with the locality of the site and the fact that each small house had a tiny garden attached to it. Now castles in the air tumbled down. She could scarcely hide her disappointment. 'Oh, I'm sorry to hear that. It was really a house I wanted...'

Trudi could tell that Debbie was saddened, but she was not going to miss even the smallest sales opportunity. 'I'm sorry, Mrs Patterson. I can see you're quite disappointed. But may I make a suggestion? I'll show you one of the houses while you're here. You never know – sales can fall through. People can change their minds.' She looked at Debbie sympathetically and with optimism.

Debbie felt she couldn't refuse, even though there appeared to be little point in looking. 'I would like to see one,' she replied, forcing a smile.

'Good.' Trudi was beaming again.

Trudi started to walk in the direction of two of the houses, choosing her path carefully in her stiletto heels. The road was as yet unmade and was a mass of rough uneven ground, potholes filled with water and large stones.

'This road will be made up as soon as the site is completely finished,' she explained as they walked.

Debbie liked the house. It was just as she had envisaged. And the small garden the lounge looked out upon was the topping on the dessert. Trudi carefully showed her round the house, bringing her attention to this and that. Debbie tried to show an interest, but she was still disappointed. As a result their pace round the house to view its attractions was quicker than it might have been. When they were outside again and Trudi had closed the front door, she turned to Debbie again. 'While you're here, do have a look at one of the apartments. They really are superb. You will be quite surprised.'

Debbie hesitated. She really wasn't interested in an apartment.

'Please,' Trudi urged.

Debbie gave in. Having a look wouldn't cost her anything.

The apartments were indeed spacious. They were built in blocks of six and were well laid out. Each one had a small balcony with ornamental iron railings. Debbie liked them, but they did not compare with the houses. She said little as she walked around with Trudi, listening to her sales patter.

They made their way back to their vehicles. Debbie was thinking about what might have been and Trudi was still trying her best to keep all her options open. As they stood again beside Debbie's car, Trudi made one last attempt. 'I can see you're quite disappointed that all the houses are spoken for, Mrs Patterson, but do give some thought to the apartments. Let me give you my card, just in case you want to contact me.' She extracted a card from her document case and handed it to Debbie. 'You can get me on this number, and if I am not there leave a message and I'll ring you back.'

Debbie thanked her and took the card.

Trudi held out her hand and smiled cheerfully at Debbie. 'It's been nice meeting you, Mrs. Patterson. I hope we meet again. Do keep in touch with us and if you have any queries please don't hesitate to contact us. Remember we're here to help.'

'Thank you very much.' Debbie shook Trudi's hand and then, noticing that she was shivering, she exclaimed: 'Oh, do get back in your car, or you'll catch a cold.'

'Yes, it is cold isn't it?' Trudi released Debbie's hand and turned to totter back to her car, giving a wave of her hand as she did so.

Debbie climbed into her own car. She couldn't help smiling to herself. In spite of her warm overcoat, she had felt cold. How Trudi in her thin business suit had coped she could not imagine, and on top of that she had been barelegged. She must have been freezing. Again Trudi reminded her of Trish in her pursuit of business fashion and the discomfort that went with it.

Debbie drove home feeling disappointed. It was something she wouldn't have thought possible a few months ago. But gradually, in spite of her protests to Jan and the rest of the family, during the last few weeks she had been giving more and more thought to making a move. As she studied the brochure, the idea of moving had begun to take up more of her thinking. She had always known that one day the house would become too much of a burden for her to cope with and that then she would have to make the decision to move somewhere smaller; and Tom's leaving, the difficult task of getting a replacement for him, and the arrival of Morgan Manton's brochure had begun to push her in this direction. Now it turned out to have all been a waste of effort. She had never considered the fact that the houses in the brochure might not be available.

Tonight, she decided, she would give John a ring and ask his advice. He had been supportive when she had told him about her plan to visit the site. These days he always seemed to be able to give her wise counsel, and she respected his opinion. He might even come over to see her; he had already made several visits since Christmas to help her out with problems she had encountered playing with the computer he had given her as a Christmas present.

As she swung the car into her forecourt in the now rapidly advancing twilight of the winter afternoon, the thought cheered her up a little. It was something to look forward to.

Chapter 16

Over a month had gone by. February was now drawing to an end and the darkness of winter was just beginning to give way to longer hours of daylight.

Debbie had spent the weeks since her brief house-hunting afternoon immersed in her normal routine. There was the house to attend to, shopping to do and her regular visits to the Women's Institute and her yoga class. Several times since Christmas she had looked after Jamie, who was becoming more demanding. When she told Jan about her visit to the new houses, at first Jan listened eagerly and intently, but as Debbie expressed her disappointment, her daughter's enthusiasm was replaced by critical observation. She couldn't see why her mother didn't opt for one of the apartments, and said so in no uncertain terms. Debbie did her best to try and put forward her point of view, but in the end a kind of beg-to-differ situation existed. It made Debbie glad she had made the visit to the site on her own without her family at her elbow. At the same time she felt a bit sorry for Jan, because she knew she was under pressure from Paul to make a decision about their housing status.

Trish showed only mild interest when Debbie told her of her intention to move house. These days Trish seemed to be kept busy between her job and looking after her husband. Debbie had only seen her once since the wedding, when she had called in briefly on her way back to London from a business trip. On that occasion Trish had casually dropped in some wedding photographs for Debbie and Jan and then disappeared quickly without looking at them with her mother. Debbie had expressed a desire to get to know her new son-in-law a little better, pointing out that she had only met him twice. Trish had shown little concern and had casually replied that she and Don would drop in 'sometime'. The remark had once again raised the concerns Debbie had felt when Trish had announced her sudden and imminent marriage.

Only John seemed to be supportive of Debbie and her decision regarding alternative housing. When she related her experience meeting Trudi and her disappointment at none of the houses being available, he simply remarked in his quiet way that there was no point in buying a property she wasn't happy with. Something else would turn up, he said. Debbie hoped so too. Now that she had decided to change her mode of living, she felt that she wanted to move as soon as possible, though these were thoughts she did not share with her family. Her decision had been spurred on when Tom turned up at the end of January, smartly dressed, to announce that he and Ada had arranged to move and that he had come to say goodbye. Debbie had felt quite sad afterwards. She had grown used to his visits every week. Finding a replacement was not going too well. Tom's efforts had failed and Debbie had asked friends and neighbours if they knew anybody, all to no avail. The situation was beginning to worry her, because she knew that very soon the garden would need more attention and stamina than she was able to give it on her own.

However, it was an eventful day at the end of the month that really brought things to a head. Debbie got up early, intending to go shopping before Mrs Hudson arrived. As she was eating her breakfast, it started to rain heavily and steadily with no sign of stopping. She decided to put off her visit to the shops until things improved. This was still the situation when Mrs Hudson arrived in her battered old car, grumbling about the weather. Debbie was not prepared for the bombshell that arrived with her. Mrs Hudson immediately announced that this would be her last visit. She had obtained a job with a firm of industrial cleaners; the hours suited her and the pay was better. Debbie was flabbergasted. She had had no inclination of Mrs Hudson's intentions and it was apparent that the situation was not up for discussion.

Mrs Hudson had been with Debbie for over three years, coming each week to do the routine cleaning for her. They had got on well together, or so Debbie thought. Over a cup of tea, Mrs Hudson would chat about her family or do quite a lot of grumbling about this and that. Not once had she mentioned money or asked Debbie for any more. Debbie accepted her decision with as much grace as she could. There was no point in parting on bad terms, she thought, even if she was annoyed at Mrs Hudson's sudden announcement.

It was after Mrs Hudson had left that the difficulties began to sink in. Now she would have to find a new cleaner as well as a gardener.

The rain was still falling steadily. Debbie made herself a coffee and spent ten minutes looking at the newspaper while she waited in the vain hope that the weather might improve. In the end she decided to drive the car to the shops instead of walking. She just had to do some shopping today. She had put on her macintosh and had the car keys in her hand when the phone rang.

'Oh no. Not now.' Her exclamation was accompanied with a deep sigh. She put the keys down and hurried to the phone.

'Hello.'

'Hello, Mum. It's Jan. I just thought I'd give you a ring to see how you were getting on.'

Debbie smothered her thoughts with a silent sigh. Sometimes her daughters chose the most inconvenient moments to call her. 'Oh, hello dear. That's nice of you. You just caught me. I was about to go out.'

'Oh, where were you going?' Jan asked.

'Oh, just shopping. It was raining earlier when I planned to go and then I had to wait until Mrs Hudson went. I was going to take the car.'

Jan's solution was quite simple. 'Go tomorrow.'

Debbie did not respond. At times the younger generation didn't always quite understand that even in retirement people had a certain routine. Instead she changed the subject. 'How is everybody? Has Jamie got over his cold?'

'Oh, he's fine now, driving me mad. I'll be glad when he starts school.'

Debbie was about to remark that her daughter's problems would not end when Jamie went to school, but before she could say anything Jan spoke again.

'Mum, I wanted to ask you something.' Jan hesitated.

'Yes, dear. What did you want to ask?'

'Well, it's just that Paul and I have been talking again. We do need to move house soon, especially if I have another baby. We want to be in a new place before that.' She hesitated again, only this time Debbie did not help her out. Debbie could guess what was coming. Jan continued. 'Have you decided what you want to do, Mum? We do really need to know.'

Debbie took a deep breath. She had dreaded a return to this subject, but it was something that had to be dealt with.

'I don't really know what to say, dear. If the right place came up I would probably move now, but I told you that the houses I visited, which I did like, have all been spoken for.' Debbie knew the subject would not end with her statement.

'Have you looked anywhere else?' Jan asked. Her voice had an interrogating tone to it.

'No, not yet.' Debbie wished she could end the conversation.

There was a pause at the other end of the phone. Then Jan spoke again. 'Paul's got an idea.'

Debbie wondered what was coming. 'Oh, that sounds intriguing. What is it?' She tried to sound interested.

'Paul and I thought that if we bought your house, we could build an extension, a granny flat for you. What do you think?'

Debbie took another deep breath. It was more than she could cope with at the moment.

'I don't really think that would be a good idea.' Debbie knew that she might as well eliminate the suggestion from the start. The thought of living in cramped quarters so close to her daughter was really too much to even consider.

'Mum, why not? We thought it was a super idea.'

Debbie struggled to find the right words to reply. She didn't want to upset Jan, but this suggestion did not appeal to her at all.

'I just don't think it would be a good idea. You as a family need to be on your own. You don't want me living virtually on your doorstep.'

'But you would be on your own.' Jan was not going to give up easily.

Yes, just a wall away, thought Debbie. 'Perhaps,' she replied, 'but I don't really consider that I'm ready for a granny flat at the moment. I'm not old and decrepit, you know.' I might as well say it, she thought.

'Oh, Mum, we didn't mean it that way. We just thought it was a good idea, that's all.'

'I know, dear,' Debbie replied. She didn't know what else to say.

'Mum, we haven't upset you, have we?' asked Jan anxiously.

Debbie smiled to herself. She knew her Jan of old. 'Darling, of course you haven't. It was a lovely idea, but I just know it wouldn't work, living in such close proximity.'

There was a pause. Debbie could almost hear the sigh as Jan responded to her words. 'In that case we may have to start looking somewhere else. Paul's getting a bit impatient. Will you mind if we do that?' Jan's tone had altered slightly.

Debbie jumped in immediately to make amends. 'Darling, of course I don't mind. I understand perfectly. At the same time, please try and understand how I feel. I don't want to embark on something I know I won't be happy with.' At least I've said it, she thought.

'I know what you mean, Mum.' Jan's reply was hardly convincing.

Debbie tried to elaborate. 'It's just that feeling that as you get older people try to sell you the idea that you're getting past it — that you can't cope on your own any longer.'

'I don't think that, Mum. I think you're fantastic,' Jan butted in quickly.

Debbie laughed. 'I'm glad of that,' she chipped in. Then, as there was no response from Jan, she continued: 'I can manage the house perfectly. It's just the garden that's a bit too big. It was all right until Tom announced he was going.'

'Have you found anybody else?' Jan asked, almost casually.

'No. No luck so far. And with the better weather round the corner, very soon I really will start to need somebody. And on top of that, Mrs Hudson announced today that she was going. No notice, nothing. Just like that.'

'Why was that?'

'She's going to a cleaning company somewhere. I wish she'd said what was on her mind, not just sprung it on me like that.'

'You always got on OK with her, didn't you?'

'Absolutely. We got on very well together. Now I have to find somebody else.' Debbie hesitated for an instant. Talking about her loss brought back the reality of the situation starkly.

Jan changed the subject. 'Have you heard from Trish recently?'

Debbie gave a little laugh. 'No. Not since she brought the wedding photographs, and then that was quick quick.'

'I haven't seen or heard anything of her since the wedding,' Jan replied rather gloomily.

'I know,' Debbie sympathised. Her two daughters had never been close and since they had become adults the situation had not improved a great deal. The disagreement between the two of them at the time of Trish's wedding had not improved matters.

There was a commotion at the other end of the phone. Debbie could hear Jan calling out: 'No, Jamie!' The next second, Jan spoke again. 'Mum, I've got to go. Jamie's up to something.'

'OK, dear. I'll speak to you soon.'

'You're sure I haven't upset you over the house?'

'No, of course not.'

'OK then. Bye for now.'

'Bye-bye, dear.'

Debbie put the phone down. She gave a slight sigh. She hadn't liked speaking so forcibly to Jan, yet at the same time she had felt it necessary. She wondered what would happen now. Clearly Jan was under pressure from Paul to make a move. It was odd, she thought, that sometimes children felt you were obliged to carry out their wishes. Even thinking about a granny flat made her shudder. She wouldn't go down that street, even if it meant losing the chance of letting Jan and Paul buy her house.

The sight of her keys lying on the nearby chair where she had abandoned them reminded her that she had been on her way to the shops when the telephone rang. The rain was still pouring down, but undeterred she drove to the local parade. The only problem was that parking was limited. She was lucky on this occasion: a car was just pulling out as she arrived. As the two cars passed, she recognised the driver of the other car. It was Freddie Foster. She quickly waved but was unsure whether he recognised her. It was odd to see him at this time of day; she had never bumped into him before on her shopping trips. She wished she had arrived a few minutes earlier, when she might have had the opportunity to talk to him. She hadn't actually seen him in person since the day of Jill's funeral. It had been a sad occasion, with many members of the WI group there. Freddie had been surrounded by what appeared to be a large family, and Debbie's conversation with him had been brief. When she had recovered from the trauma of the burglary, she had phoned him, but he had appeared to be positive and in control and it had left her with the feeling that there was little more she could do, in spite of her good intentions. Since the funeral she had only seen him driving his car, and according to some members of the WI who were closer to him, he appeared to be coping well with his loss.

Debbie went into the tiny supermarket and made her purchases. Then it was a quick visit to the Post Office next door to buy some stamps. She had used her last stamp the previous day.

It was almost an hour after leaving home that she pulled into her drive. Immediately she spotted Trish's car in front of the garage. She parked alongside it; she would have to put the car in the garage later when Trish had moved hers. The rain had eased off a little, which made unloading her purchases from the boot a little easier. She let herself into the house and called out: 'Hi! I'm back!'

Trish appeared from the kitchen, a steaming mug in her hand. 'Hello, Mum. I just called in. I didn't think you'd be out.' As Debbie walked towards her, she condescended to give her mother a peck on the cheek.

'I had to go to the shops. Have you been here long?'

'No, not all that long. I've just made myself some coffee. Do you want one?'

'Yes, please.' Debbie jumped at the offer. It was rare for her daughter to make a drink for her.

Trish led the way into the kitchen. She busied herself with a mug and the kettle while Debbie took the opportunity to put away her shopping.

'You managed the alarm OK?' enquired Debbie.

Trish made a face. 'The damn thing nearly went off before I managed to remember the code.'

'Oh, thank goodness you did remember it. It's quite a problem if it does go off like that. Would you like something to eat with your coffee?'

'It wouldn't be a bad idea. I didn't have any lunch. I'm on my way back to London. I want to get to the office before they finish.'

Debbie glanced at the clock as she placed some eggs in the fridge. 'Goodness, you'll have to hurry. It's turned three now.'

'Oh, I'll make it all right.' Trish put her mother's mug of coffee on the table and slumped into a chair.

'What would you like to eat?' Debbie enquired, holding the fridge door open and looking first inside and then at Trish.

'Just a biscuit will do. We're going out to dinner tonight and I've got to watch the calories.'

'That's not very substantial. What about a cream cracker with something on it?'

Trish looked at her mother over the top of the mug, her hands clasped round it. 'Got any cheese?' she asked hopefully.

'Yes, of course.' Debbie reached into the fridge. She had forgotten Trish's childhood passion for that delicacy on biscuits. 'Two biscuits or three?' she asked, busy with the biscuits and cheese. She realised that she hadn't had any lunch herself and was preparing a snack for herself as well as Trish.

167

'Two,' Trish replied, kicking off her shoes and rubbing a foot. 'These shoes are killing me,' she remarked.

'Why don't you wear flat shoes for driving?'

'Not likely,' Trish retorted, almost indignantly.

Debbie smiled to herself. Neither of her daughters related fashion to comfort. She carried the plate of biscuits and cheese to the table and sat in a chair opposite her daughter. 'You could always change when you got out of the car,' she suggested tactfully, glancing first at the shoes Trish had removed and then at Trish.

'Oh, it's only because they're new,' Trish responded quickly.

For a few minutes there was silence between them, Trish busy munching and Debbie wondering whether she should tell her about her conversation with Jan. Trish also seemed deep in thought as she ate her biscuits and sipped her coffee. Suddenly she looked up at her mother. 'Mum, Don and I have had our first row.'

'Darling, no! What was it about?'

Trish looked a bit glum. 'Oh, he doesn't like it when I have to stay away somewhere. He wants me around all the time.' She was quite matter-of-fact about her explanation.

Debbie thought for an instant, choosing her words carefully. 'But he knew what your job entailed before you married. Did he object then?' she asked tactfully.

'He was all right then,' replied Trish gloomily. 'Since we got married he's started to get stroppy about it.'

Debbie tried to take a practical view. 'Perhaps it's just the newness of marriage that is the problem for him. He'll accept the situation after a while,' she suggested hopefully.

Trish shrugged her shoulders but said nothing.

Debbie decided to bring up another aspect of Trish's marriage that concerned her. 'You know, darling, I hardly know Don. I've only met him twice. Why don't you both come and stay for a weekend sometime?'

Trish's reaction was swift. 'That's another thing. Nearly every Sunday we have to go to his parents for lunch. I'm getting sick of it.' She was fairly bristling.

Debbie looked at her in silence. The revelations she had just heard raised once again the concerns she had felt before Trish's marriage. Things did not bode well for future harmony. But she knew that she had to tread carefully. She had never quite had the rapport with Trish that she had with Jan. Trish was the more headstrong of the two. She thought carefully for a few seconds before responding to Trish's outburst.

'You know, dear, you will have to have a talk together if you are going to resolve your differences,' she replied gently.

'I suppose so.' Trish's reply was hardly enthusiastic.

'What about interests? Do you have common ground there?'

'Oh, he's mad about football. I can't stand it,' Trish responded with a disgusted tone, adding for good measure: 'He supports Chelsea.'

'What about friends? Do you have many together?' Debbie asked hopefully.

Trish took a sip of coffee and nodded. 'They're all right,' she replied. Then as an afterthought she added: 'Except if any other male looks at me he gets a bit hot under the collar.' She grinned ruefully.

Perhaps, thought Debbie, that was the key to the problem. Don suffered from jealousy. It explained why he didn't like Trish staying away for her job. 'Darling, you'll have to have a chat with him about things,' she repeated.

'I suppose so.'

Debbie was about to say something else by way of encouragement, but her thoughts were interrupted by Trish, who suddenly looked at her watch and then at the clock. 'Gosh, I'd better go!' she exclaimed, hastily putting on her shoes again.

'Darling, do take care,' urged Debbie, observing the rush in which Trish was gathering her things together.

Trish ignored her remark, but as she made for the door she asked: 'Have you heard from Jan recently?'

'Yes, as a matter of fact she phoned today.'

'I'll have to give her a ring sometime.'

'Yes. Do make a point of that. She'll appreciate it.'

Debbie was still conscious of the rift between her two daughters. She didn't feel like talking to Trish about the details of her conversation with Jan. Besides, there was no time now.

Trish opened the front door and turned to her mother. 'Bye, Mum.'

'Bye-bye, dear. Drive carefully.'

Trish made a face.

'I hope you manage to have that talk with Don,' Debbie said as Trish walked towards her car.

'Oh, it'll be all right in the end,' Trish called back.

Debbie waved as she drove away. She watched until the car disappeared from view and then went back into the house. She returned to the kitchen and started to tidy up the dirty dishes, deep in thought as she did so. What a day it had been: first Mrs Hudson, then Jan to deal with and lastly Trish with what looked like the start of marriage problems. It was funny how things so often all came at the same time. It was hard to know how to deal with each problem. She hoped Mrs Hudson would not be as difficult to replace as Tom. She decided to ask some of the other women at the WI if they could think of anyone. That would be a good start. Above all, she was apprehensive of just engaging a stranger to come into her house and work. She would be much happier to have somebody who came recommended. As to Jan's episode, there was nothing more she could do there. She had said how she felt and there was little more she could add. Secretly she hoped that Jan and Paul would delay moving, but somehow she doubted it, and that was something she would have to accept. It was a missed opportunity, but it had to be. As for Trish's problem, Debbie felt uneasy about the situation. Trish had always been a bit of a worry for her, in particular in her relationships with men. Even as a teenager she had caused concern to both her parents with her free and easy attitude to boys. Debbie had always had her doubts about the marriage and now she just hoped things were not as bad as she feared. At the moment it was a case of 'wait and see' and be as supportive to Trish as she could be.

She was still thinking things over as she went into the lounge. Perhaps she could play on her laptop for half an hour or so before preparing a meal. She was gradually getting used to it and was beginning to absorb some of its mysteries, though on more than one occasion she had been forced to ring John and ask him to help her out of some situation or other she had got herself in.

Thinking of the laptop brought her thinking round to John. She hadn't spoken to him for several days. Perhaps she would ring him this evening. She had just taken the laptop out of its case and put it on her desk, when the telephone rang. Somehow she had a hunch it might be John. She picked it up and answered.

It was a female voice. 'Mrs Patterson?'

Debbie was disappointed. 'Yes.'

'Mrs Patterson, good afternoon. It's Trudi from Morgan Manton. Have you a few minutes?'

Debbie could have groaned. What now, she thought. A follow-up call to see if I want one of the apartments, I expect. She stifled her irritation. 'Yes, of course. Go ahead.'

'Are you still interested in a property?'

Debbie was cautious in her reply. 'Well, yes, if I can find the right one.'

Trudi responded immediately. 'I think I may have something of interest to you. We have a property available on the site you vis—'

Debbie stopped her. 'I'm not interested in one of the apartments,' she stressed.

Trudi was in full control. 'Of course not. No, this is one of the houses.'

Debbie was still not completely on the same wavelength. 'But I thought all the houses were sold.'

'Yes, that was the case when you viewed the properties, but one of the people who was going to buy one has decided to take an apartment instead. As you showed an interest, I'm giving you the first option.'

'Oh, I see.' Debbie's enthusiasm was beginning to emerge.

'Would you like to view the property?' Trudi enquired cheerfully.

Debbie could hardly believe what she had just heard. She knew she had to jump at the chance now. 'Yes, I would.'

'I'm on-site tomorrow. Would that be convenient for you? Unfortunately, I shall be on a week's leave after that, but I can get a colleague to step in for me if tomorrow is not convenient for you.'

'I can come tomorrow. What time?' Debbie couldn't wait now.

Trudi must have sensed her excitement. 'Would half past one in the afternoon suit you?' she asked.

'Yes, that would be fine.' Debbie did not hesitate. There was a WI meeting, but so what?

'Good. I'll look forward to seeing you again, Mrs Patterson.'

'Thank you very much. I'll see you tomorrow.' Debbie was beginning to feel good.

'Goodbye for now, then.'

'Goodbye.'

Debbie put the phone down. It wasn't such a bad day after all. All thought of playing with the computer disappeared. She couldn't remember the last time she had felt so excited. Yes, she could: it was when she met John on holiday last year. Thinking of him made her pick up the phone again. She just had to share the news with him.

Chapter 17

John stifled a yawn as he filled the kettle. He had been out late the previous night. It had been the annual prize-giving of the camera club and one of his photographs had come top in the 'landscape' section. It was the first time he had won the award and he felt justly proud of the fact. After the meeting, one of the other club members had invited him round to his house and it had been close to midnight when he had gone to bed.

The sun was already streaming in through the kitchen window. It was unusual for him to get up so late, but he felt the previous night's event justified it. He made himself a mug of tea and wandered into the lounge. The winning photograph was now perched in the centre of his settee, in full view. He picked it up and studied it as he sipped his tea. It was one of the photographs he had taken on holiday and he couldn't help feeling pleased with the result. It was a picture of the seashore he had taken close to Brillport. He had entered it in the competition without thinking it might win. He made a mental note to tell Debbie about his success as soon as possible.

Debbie had been in his thoughts quite a lot recently. Over the months since their meeting on holiday he had steadily grown fond of her. So often when you meet somebody on holiday and then see them afterwards in their own environment it is impossible to recapture the magic of the holiday, but he had not found that with Debbie. Each time he had seen her during the last few months, the sparkle of those days in Dorset had returned. In between their meetings it was the little reminders that popped into his thoughts from time to time: her infectious laugh, her smile… and her shyness, which swamped her strengths. Under his guidance, despite her reservations, she had taken to the digital camera with comparative ease, and she was doing remarkably well with the computer considering that she had no previous experience. He would be glad when the better weather came. Then perhaps they could spend more time together. That was what he enjoyed most: her company. He was thinking of all these things as he drank his tea and gazed out of the window. People were going off to work now. He watched several leave his block of flats. Thank goodness he was done with all that. His tea finished, he wandered back into the kitchen. He had idled long enough. It was time to start the day proper.

He was shaving when the telephone rang. Its shrill sound penetrated even the noise of his electric razor. Who could be ringing so early in the day? He wasn't expecting any calls. It wouldn't be Rob so early: he would ring from work later if necessary. Perhaps it was someone from the camera club offering congratulations, but it was an odd time to ring. He switched off his razor and picked up the receiver.

'Hello, John Hammond.'

'John, it's Debbie. Have I got you up?'

'Good Lord, no. But I was just shaving. Bit behind this morning.' He laughed.

'Oh, I'm so sorry for disturbing you. I just wanted to catch you before you went out or something.'

He could detect the slight embarrassment in her voice. 'It's all right, really. It's great to hear from you. I was going to give you a ring later today. I've had a bit of good news.'

'It's always nice to hear from you, John.'

John could detect a trace of emotion in her voice. His voice echoed concern now. 'Are you OK, Debbie? Is everything all right?'

There was that little nervous laugh before she replied. 'Oh, I'm fine. I had one of those days yesterday, but I also have some news. In fact, I really wanted to talk to you about it.'

John knew he had been correct. She was worried about something big. It explained the early telephone call. She wanted his help.

'What's the problem? You sound a bit worried. How can I help?' He tried to make his voice sound as sympathetic as possible.

Debbie answered quickly. This time her voice sounded just a degree lighter. 'Oh, I expect I'm worrying over nothing.' She hesitated.

'What's happened?'

'Well, you remember the houses I looked at and they were all sold?'

'Sure.'

'Well, one of the houses has become available again. The woman rang me yesterday. I've arranged to look at it this afternoon.'

'Gosh, that's fantastic news! How do you feel about it?'

'When I put the phone down afterwards, I was quite excited. Now in the light of a new day I feel a bit panicky and nervous.'

He was about to say something, but she spoke again. 'I tried to ring you yesterday.'

'I was out all afternoon and then I went straight to the camera club,' John replied. His news could wait. He asked: 'Would you like me to come with you to view the house?' He prayed she would want him to.

Her response was instantaneous. 'Oh, John, would you? I'd be ever so grateful if you could. You know what I'm like at doing these things on my own.'

'What time is your appointment?'

'Half past one.' There was still a trace of anxiety in her voice.

'I'll be there.'

Debbie sounded happier now. 'When can you get here?'

John glanced at his watch. It was nearly half past eight. 'I'll come over as soon as I get myself in gear,' he said.

'Come to lunch if you can.'

John leapt at the idea. 'How about if I get to you for half past eleven?'

'That would be fantastic. I'll have everything ready.'

'What else happened yesterday?'

'It can wait until later. I'll tell you all about it over lunch.'

'OK. I'd better get ready now. I'll see you later on.' He was pleased that Debbie had now lost the anxious tone to her voice.

'Super. Until then, John. And thank you so much for helping me out.'

'It's no problem. I'll see you later.'

'OK. Bye for now.'

'Bye.' He put the phone down.

He paused for a moment. Poor old Debbie, he thought. She did get herself in a state over things. He guessed she hadn't told her daughters about the new offer and had turned to him immediately for support. He was pleased she had. He would do whatever he could to help.

It was almost half past one when they pulled into the entrance road to the housing site. John drove carefully over the unmade road and parked where Debbie suggested. There was no sign of Trudi.

'She said she'd be here,' Debbie remarked, a little anxiously.

'She'll be here,' John replied in his best laid-back style.

As if to give substance to his words, at the next instant a car pulled into the road and parked behind them. Debbie glanced round and recognised Trudi.

They quickly got out of the car and walked over to meet her just as she was locking her car. She turned to greet them.

'Hello again, Mrs Patterson.' She turned to John and held out her hand. 'Hello. I'm Trudi Meadows.'

'This is a friend of mine, John Hammond,' explained Debbie.

'Pleased to meet you,' said Trudi. They shook hands.

Trudi led the way to one of the nearby houses. Debbie was pleased to see that it was one of the slightly larger end properties.

'You're very lucky,' Trudi explained as they neared the house. I know you enjoy gardening, and this house has one of the larger gardens, as well as a garage.'

'Oh, that would be nice,' Debbie said. She guessed this would all make the purchase price higher. She couldn't remember telling Trudi she liked gardening, but she realised she must have done so.

176

Trudi took a set of keys from her briefcase and opened the front door. She stood aside to allow Debbie and John to enter. Next she took them round the house, extolling all the good points. For the most part, they just listened.

When they were downstairs again after the tour, Trudi stopped and faced them. 'Well, what do you think?' she asked, addressing Debbie.

Before Debbie had a chance to answer she spoke again. 'This really is one of the prestige houses on the site. There are lots of extras with this one and for anybody who likes gardening it is ideal. It won't be on the market very long.' She looked knowingly at Debbie.

The feeling of panic came over Debbie once again. 'I'd like to have another look,' she ventured. What she really wanted was to just wander round the house with John, without Trudi near.

Perhaps Trudi read her thoughts, or perhaps she had dealt with clients similar to Debbie before, because she immediately said: 'Look, I've got to go over to the apartments for ten minutes. Why don't you stay here and look around as much as you like and then ask me any questions afterwards? Would that be all right?' She looked enquiringly at both Debbie and John.

It was John who replied. 'That would be fine. Please carry on,' he replied cheerfully.

'All right. I won't be long.' Trudi picked up her briefcase and with a smile departed.

They heard the front door click shut. John turned to Debbie and grinned. 'Let's look round again while it's peaceful,' he suggested.

Debbie just smiled in agreement. She was trying to imagine herself living in the house.

It didn't take them long to explore on their own. The house was quite well designed. A small hall gave way to a good-sized lounge, the kitchen and a smaller room.

'Make an ideal room for the computer,' John remarked as they looked into it again. 'Bookshelves along the wall,' he added as an afterthought.

They looked into the tiny cloakroom that cleverly utilised the space under the stairs. 'It's certainly compact,' Debbie remarked.

They went upstairs again. Three bedrooms and a bathroom occupied that level. 'At least it's a good-sized master bedroom,' observed John.

Debbie had gone very quiet. She was still struggling to imagine living in this house. She knew it had all the facilities she needed, yet for some reason she couldn't summon up immense enthusiasm for the idea. She knew she would have to make a decision that day, but instead of feeling euphoric she was almost miserable. John hadn't noticed her dilemma, and she trailed after him in silence as he explored every nook and cranny of the house making encouraging comments.

They returned to the lounge and looked out into the garden. A patio door opened onto a small paved area. 'I say, you could have a table and chairs here and have breakfast out here in the summer!' John exclaimed.

'Under an umbrella,' Debbie added with a fleeting smile.

'It needs a lawn beyond the paving and perhaps a bird bath in the centre, then a path down the side – and there's even room for a small shed or greenhouse in the corner at the bottom,' John observed enthusiastically.

Debbie listened to him but said nothing. John continued to look out into the garden and plan its development. He had his back to her and did not notice her wander through the nearby door into the small kitchen. She had intended to look again at its facilities, but instead she stood and gazed unseeing out of the window, deep in thought.

She hardly noticed John come into the kitchen. 'I quite like this place. I don't think you'll find anything better,' he announced cheerfully as he entered.

Debbie turned to him, her face serious. 'Share it with me, John.'

John stopped in his tracks. At first his face took on a more serious expression, and then it faded. 'You mean come to live here with you?' He seemed almost amused.

'Yes. I don't want to live here on my own.' Debbie was still serious. Her face looked strained. She spoke in little more than a whisper.

John smiled and shook his head. 'Couldn't do it. Wouldn't think of it,' he replied cheerfully.

Debbie turned away from him. It was all so useless. She didn't want to hear his explanation. She felt miserable and alone.

John walked over to her. He put his arm round her and instinctively she turned to face him. She looked up into his face.

He held her, still smiling as he spoke. 'But I tell you what. I'll willingly carry you over the threshold as Mrs Hammond.'

He continued to look at her with a quizzical smile. Debbie gazed at him, unbelieving. She tried to assimilate what he had just said. When she did speak, she found it difficult to summon up the right words. 'You… you mean—?'

John interrupted her. He still had his arms round her. He spoke softly. 'Debbie, I'm asking you to be my wife.' The smile had gone.

Suddenly Debbie sprang to life. She flung her arms round him. 'Oh, John, I never dreamed you would ask me. I just don't know what to say. I think I'm going to cry.' She buried her face in his jacket.

John held her close. His hand stroked her back. 'We'll get married right away. I'll sell my place and we'll move in here.' Then he added: 'That's if it is a yes.'

Debbie eased away from him slightly and looked at him. Her eyes were full of tears, but they were tears of joy. 'Of course it's a yes. I feel so silly crying like this.'

She fumbled in her pocket, but before she could find a handkerchief he handed her one.

Debbie dabbed at her face for a second, then as she saw John smiling at her she once again threw her arms around him and their lips met. The kiss was long and lingering.

John held her in his arms. When their lips parted, Debbie whispered: 'John, you don't know how happy you've made me.'

He continued to hold her close. Their lips met again.

'Oh, I'm sorry.'

Neither of them had heard Trudi return. She stood in the doorway of the kitchen, clearly slightly embarrassed.

Instinctively they sprang apart. Debbie immediately tried to dry her eyes on the handkerchief to hide her embarrassment. John took control and saved the situation. 'It's all right. Come in,' he urged Trudi, and then, as if it were an everyday event, he announced quite calmly: 'We've just decided to get married.'

Trudi's look of embarrassment changed to one of admiration. 'But that's splendid! Congratulations to you both.' She sounded as if she really meant it.

'And we're going to have the house – that's if my future wife agrees,' said John jovially. He looked at Debbie, but words were still difficult for her. She just smiled and nodded.

'That's marvellous,' responded Trudi.

Debbie never really remembered what happened next. John and Trudi did most of the talking as Trudi gently ushered them into the lounge to discuss the business side of things. She wanted to know who to contact in future, and John told her to continue to contact Debbie. Trudi would have liked to go into matters in a bit more detail, but John diplomatically asked her to give them a few days to talk things through. She readily agreed. Then, with a glance at her watch, she said she had to go. After shaking hands and saying goodbye, she walked towards her car.

'Don't forget to invite me to the wedding,' she called out as she closed the car door.

They watched her drive away and then returned to John's car. Debbie slipped into the seat beside John. Suddenly everything had changed. Not half an hour ago she had been miserably walking round the house trying to imagine herself living there on her own, and then in a few seconds her world had erupted into something completely different. A strange feeling was coming over her, one that she had not experienced for a long time.

As she settled in her seat, a worry crept into her thinking. She turned to John. 'You did mean, it didn't you?' she asked, clutching his arm.

John put his arm round her and drew her close. He spoke softly. 'Of course I did. Every word. I've thought about it for a long time, but never plucked up courage to ask you.' He kissed her lips.

Debbie tried to smile, but for some reason she still felt tearful. 'Oh, you big silly. Why didn't you say something? I thought you liked being a bachelor. I think I've been in love with you since we first met. And now you've asked me, I'm acting like a silly little girl.'

John kissed her again. His cheek touched hers and he felt the wetness of her tears.

A sound outside forced them apart abruptly. Two workmen from the site were walking past, grinning at them.

'Oh no...' Debbie almost wailed softly.

John laughed. 'They're just jealous,' he remarked, clicking his seat belt closed.

Debbie fumbled for hers. 'Let's go, quickly. First Trudi and now those two...'

'Next time it'll be someone you know,' John quipped, starting the engine.

'Oh, heaven forbid. That would be too awful.'

John laughed again. He put the car in gear and they moved off. Debbie pulled down the passenger visor and looked at herself in the mirror. 'I must look a mess.' She studied her reflection critically.

'You look beautiful.'

Debbie made a face at him, but John did not see. He was concentrating on his driving. It was Debbie who spoke again first. 'So silly to cry like that, but you know I can't remember the last time I cried with happiness.'

'I can't remember when I felt as happy as I do at the moment,' John replied.

Debbie had a sudden desire to touch his arm, but she resisted the urge. After all, he was driving. 'I don't know what the girls will say.' More practical aspects were now beginning to creep into Debbie's thinking.

'Most likely they'll be glad to think they've got rid of the responsibility of Mum,' John replied, chuckling to himself. 'I don't envisage any problems with Rob,' he added.

Debbie thought for a minute. 'Well, I know Jan will be pleased. It will solve one of her problems. She and Paul will be able to buy my house at last.'

The thought prompted her next question. 'John, when do you think we'll get married?'

'As soon as possible – tomorrow if you like.'

Debbie glanced at him. Sometimes she could never tell whether he was joking or not. In this case she joined in his humour. Quickly she chirped: 'We can't do it that quickly. I've got to buy a trousseau yet.'

John gave her a quick glance. 'OK, Mrs Hammond-to-be, if there must be a delay.'

'Gosh, that's another thing. I'll have to get used to a new name.'

Debbie was still coming up with practicalities, with John a patient listener, as they completed the short drive home. John parked the car neatly in front of her garage. 'Home again, Mrs Hammond-to-be,' he announced.

Debbie made a face at him, but she leaned over and gave him a peck on the cheek. 'First thing is a cup of tea,' she announced as she swung her legs out of the car.

'Best idea you've had all afternoon,' John observed drily.

Chapter 18

Several days had passed since John's proposal of marriage. Debbie was gradually adjusting to the idea that her whole life was shortly going to change dramatically. She was to be a bride again. If anybody had suggested to her a few months previously that such a thing would happen, she would have considered the notion quite ridiculous, but when John had proposed to her, somehow it had released within her the pent-up emotions of the past few months. She had been quite aware for a long time now that she had developed a strong attachment to him, but their relationship had always been kept within the bounds of just being good friends. True, there had been moments when she had allowed her dreams to develop the situation into something more, but always they had ended with the realisation that John was happy in his bachelorhood and wanted nothing more from her than her occasional companionship; and this concept of their relationship had always brought her down to earth with a bump. That realisation had not stopped her from being aware that John, underneath his veneer of a casual and often humorous approach to things, was a kind and caring person.

She had had no hesitation in saying yes to his proposal, even though at first she had not been sure if he was joking or not. Just walking round the new, empty house that afternoon had made her realise how drab and monotonous her life had become. The only highlights over the last few months had been the occasional meetings with John – her soulmate. Her suggestion that he share the house with her had been a desperate, out-of-character cry for help. She had not for one moment thought that he would agree to her proposal, but his response had been beyond all her expectations.

When she had returned home with John that afternoon, over a cup of tea they had both chatted like teenagers, making plans and exploring their new status. With that had come the practicalities of their situation and the various aspects of their current lives that would have to be dealt with before they embarked on a new life together. It had been late when John departed. Now they telephoned each other nearly every day to discuss something or other that was important.

For two whole days after John proposed to her, Debbie had not told anybody her news. It was her secret and just for a short time she wanted to keep it to herself and enjoy the experience.

It had been a telephone call from Jan that had broken the spell.

'Mum, how are you? We haven't heard from you for several days.' Jan's voice had an air of concern.

'Oh, I'm fine – on top of the world. How are you all?' Debbie tried hard to keep the excitement she still felt out of her reply.

'We're all OK, except I think Paul's caught Jamie's cold. He was moaning a bit last night.'

'Oh dear.' Debbie commiserated for a second, and then she could not contain herself any longer.

'I've got some news for you.'

'Oh, what's that?'

'How would you like to have my house?' Debbie was still trying not to let the excitement show in her voice.

'You mean you've found somewhere?' exclaimed Jan. 'Where is it? You never said you were looking anywhere.'

Debbie restrained her own enthusiasm. 'Well, it all happened in a bit of a hurry, but one of the houses on the site I told you about came up unexpectedly, so I went and had a look and decided to buy it.'

'Hmm... You should have let me or Paul come with you. Are you sure everything is OK?' Jan was sounding a bit more cautious now.

Debbie hesitated for a second. Now for it, she thought. 'Well, you see, I have another bit of news.' She paused again, choosing her words carefully. 'How would you feel if I got married again?'

'Mum, that would be fantastic! Who's it going to be? Anybody we know? Is it John?' Jan's voice had risen to quite a high pitch.

Debbie was quite composed now. Her brief anxiety had disappeared. 'Yes, it's John. He asked me to marry him and I said yes.'

'That's marvellous. He's really sweet. You'll get on fine with him. When's the wedding going to be?' Jan sounded really excited.

'Perhaps May or June. It will be a quiet event – just family. And of course it all depends on when everything is settled regarding houses. We want to move straight into the new one.' She and John had only briefly talked about a possible date.

'Oh, Mum, I'm so pleased for you! I feel quite excited about it. How many other people have you told?'

Debbie laughed. 'You're the only one who knows at the moment. I must ring Trish as well today.'

Jan's reply was more sober. 'I haven't spoken to her for a long time now. If I ring she's always out and if I leave a message she never calls me back.'

'Oh well, you know what Trish is like. She does the same to me sometimes.' Debbie always tried to heal the differences between her two daughters as diplomatically as she could. Briefly she wondered whether she should say anything to Jan about Trish's marriage problems, and then decided against it. It was a confidence.

Jan returned to the subject of the wedding. 'Will you get married in church this time, Mum?'

'No, I don't think so. John isn't keen and I don't think I am now.'

'I'm glad we got married in church now,' Jan pondered. 'I mean it's all right in a register office the second time, but it's nice to do it properly the first time. It seems so drab otherwise.'

Debbie gave a little laugh. 'I know what you mean. But it's so long since my first time that I've almost forgotten all about it. I can remember it was a freezing cold day in March.'

'Did you have a honeymoon?'

Debbie laughed again. 'In Brighton, and the weather was awful. Going abroad wasn't as popular then as it is today.'

Debbie was quite unprepared for Jan's next question: 'Did you and Daddy have sex before you were married?'

Debbie was a bit taken back, but at the same time she was glad her daughter felt enough at ease with her to ask such a question. She decided to treat the question as if it were quite ordinary.

'No, we didn't. It was before the permissive society.' Then she added, for Jan's benefit: 'But it's a miracle we didn't. Daddy was quite amorous. And he was considered quite a catch by all the girls.'

'Gosh,' Jan exclaimed. Then she remarked: 'We've never talked about this, have we, Mum? You don't mind me asking, do you?'

'Of course not, dear. It's not really a secret.'

'You and Daddy met at work, didn't you?'

'That's right. He worked at the same company as I did – only he was further up the ladder than I was. I was only a shorthand typist and he was at management level. I got quite a shock when he asked me out.'

'But you were very pretty. I've seen your photographs.'

Debbie chuckled to herself. 'Yes, I was in those days.' Her reply contained some degree of lament.

'Mum! You're still quite attractive,' admonished Jan.

'Well, maybe I am, but in those days I was more so,' Debbie replied wistfully.

'And now you're going to get married to John. Mum, I'm so excited for you! I'm going to ring Paul straight away and tell him – and about the house.' Jan exploded into enthusiasm once again.

They chatted for a few more minutes and then Jan decided she had to finish the call. 'I'll be in touch, Mum,' she almost shouted down the phone as she rang off.

Debbie smiled to herself as she replaced the handset. You could always trust Jan to become excited about something.

She did not have quite the same response from her younger daughter. When she tried to contact Trish at work, she was not available, but the receptionist said she would let her know that Debbie had rung. It was late in the afternoon of the same day that Trish returned the call.

'Hello, Mum. Did you want me for something?' Trish often dispensed with formalities.

'Hello, dear. I just wanted to tell you something, but it can wait if you're busy.'

'No, it's all right. I can speak to you. I'm on my mobile, anyway.'

Debbie decided to take things slowly with her news. Her youngest daughter could be difficult to handle. 'Well, first of all, how are you and how is Don?'

There was a quick response. 'Oh, we're all right. How are you?'

Debbie could sense that Trish was being evasive. She decided to try a different tack. 'I'm fine,' she answered, then immediately followed it with: 'But how are you and Don getting on? Are things settling down now?'

'Oh, so-so. You know.'

Debbie recognised the signs. Trish didn't want to talk about it. Her thoughts were interrupted by Trish. 'Did you want me for anything special, Mum?' she asked.

Debbie decided to plunge in. 'Well, yes. I've got some special news and I want to let you into a secret.'

'Umm, that's sounds mysterious. What's it all about?'

Debbie took a deep breath. 'Well, first of all I'm selling this house to Jan and Paul and moving to a smaller one, and the other thing is, how would you feel if I got married again?'

Trish's reply was immediate. 'OK, I suppose. It's a bit hard to imagine you married again. Who are you getting married to? Anybody I know?'

'John proposed to me a few days ago and I've said yes.'

'John? Oh yes, I know. I met him once at the house and he was at our wedding. He's a bit quiet, isn't he?'

'Not when you get to know him. I'm sure you'll like him.'

Debbie was treading on slippery ground, and she knew it. Trish's next remark confirmed it. 'I can't really see why you want to get married again at your age.'

Debbie took another deep breath. 'Why? Do you think the

younger generation have exclusive rights on marriage?' She gave a little laugh as she spoke, in an attempt to inject a bit of humour into the conversation.

'Oh, I don't know. It just seems a bit weird to me older people getting married and having sex and things.'

Trish's reply made Debbie smile. Her daughter's down-to-earth approach was sometimes misguided. Debbie chose her next words carefully. 'Darling, it's not like that. Really, it's not. John and I just happen to like the same things, we're both a bit lonely and we think it might be a good idea to team up. You wouldn't want me to live in sin with him, would you?'

Her words seemed to have an effect on Trish. 'No, I suppose not.' Trish paused for a second. 'Anyway, I hope everything works out for you both.'

Debbie seized the ground she had gained. 'I'm sure it will,' she replied quickly.

'But what about Daddy?' Trish enquired suddenly.

Debbie recognised her daughter's concern immediately. Trish had been particularly close to her father. She moved in quickly to stem the flow of thought in that direction.

'Darling, that's not a problem. You mustn't worry about it. Daddy and I often talked about this and we always agreed that if one of us passed on, the other should feel free to remarry if they met anybody.'

Her words appeared to have the desired effect. Trish's next remark indicated that her explanation had been accepted. 'When's it going to be? The wedding, I mean.'

'Perhaps May or June. Just a quiet affair with the family. And there is quite a lot to do before then. Jan and Paul have to buy this house first.'

'Why are they buying it?'

'Well, because they want a larger house and this one will be for sale. I might as well sell it to them rather than to a stranger. It's rather nice that the house stays in the family, don't you think?' Debbie hoped she sounded convincing.

'I suppose so.' Trish hardly sounded convinced.

Debbie moved in again. 'Darling, I'm not going to leave you out of things. I'll make sure you're both treated the same. And this new house will be your home as well. There will be a room for you to use.'

Trish seemed to accept things at last. 'I'm being a bit stuffy, aren't I?'

Debbie laughed. 'Darling, of course you aren't. It's only right that you should ask questions.'

She was about to say a bit more, but Trish butted in. 'Mum, I'm sorry, but I must go. Somebody wants me. I'll give you a ring this evening.'

'All right, dear. Give my love to Don.'

'Will do. Bye for now, Mum. Thanks for the news.'

'Bye.'

Debbie put down the phone and breathed a sigh of relief. At least in the end, with a bit of diplomacy on her part, breaking the news to Trish appeared to have gone reasonably well. That was the problem with Trish: you never knew just how she would take things. She was a completely different kettle of fish from Jan.

Informing her two daughters was the start of Debbie's spreading the information about her intended marriage to a wider circle. At the next WI meeting she casually made a remark about it. The result was that she became embroiled in a barrage of questions ranging from who the bridegroom was to what she was going to wear – something she hadn't given any thought to. There were too many other pressing things to attend to. Moving from the house where she had brought up her family and which had been her home for over thirty years would have been an overwhelming task on her own, but fortunately John was now at her elbow to render his support.

Madge dropped in on one of her impromptu visits. This time it was in the middle of the afternoon.

'A cup of tea?' Debbie enquired after the brief formalities of greeting were over.

'Prefer a mug of coffee,' was Madge's reply as she selected an armchair to sit in without waiting for an invitation. Debbie had been sat at her desk in the sitting room when Madge's 4x4 had pulled up on her driveway, and she had ushered her unexpected guest into the same room.

Debbie disappeared into the kitchen, leaving Madge to scrutinise the newspaper, which lay as yet unread on a nearby coffee table. When she returned with two mugs of coffee and a plate of biscuits, Madge was deeply engrossed, but she put the paper down at the sight of the coffee.

'So, what have you been up to?' Debbie asked when they were settled.

Madge bit into a biscuit. 'Not a lot. I just had to go to the solicitor again. Peter's affairs are still not settled.'

Debbie sympathised. 'Yes, it does take a long time to get everything sorted out. I remember when Ron died it took ages.'

'I don't know why it has to,' Madge replied. Then she asked: 'What have you been up to?'

Debbie gave a little laugh. 'Oh, lots of things. But I have some big news to tell you.'

'Go on.' Madge took another biscuit.

Debbie paused. Suddenly she had to choose her words carefully. 'Well, first of all I'm going to sell this house and move.' She paused again. 'And the other big news is that I'm going to get married again.'

Quickly she studied Madge's face for a reaction. There was none. Madge bit into her biscuit. 'Must be mad,' she replied casually, as if she were commenting on something she had read in the newspaper.

Debbie repeated her little laugh, partly to comfort herself. She had not expected enthusiasm from Madge, but her comment was quite amusing really.

She was concocting a suitable reply when Madge calmly asked another question. 'Who's the feller?'

Debbie responded to the glimmer of interest. 'John. You remember, I met him when we were on holiday and stayed on my own for the week.'

'That's only a few months ago,' Madge retorted, as if the time period were significant.

'Yes, but I've seen quite a lot of him since,' Debbie replied as a kind of defence.

'Anyway, when's the wedding going to be?' Madge asked, quite casually.

'Perhaps May or June. I'm going to sell this house to Jan and Paul and then John and I are going to buy another one. We're in the process of doing that now. It's a brand new house, not so far away.' Debbie stopped at that point to allow Madge to digest what she had said.

Madge made no reply. Instead she just took another drink of her coffee.

Sometimes Debbie found her a bit irritating. However, she tried to adopt a light-hearted response to her visitor's lack of enthusiasm. 'You'll come to my wedding won't you?' she asked.

'Of course, but don't expect me to wear a dress.' Madge grinned at her.

Debbie studied Madge. She was quite serious now. 'Did you never want to get married?' she asked.

Madge shook her head. 'Not really,' she replied, adding for good measure: 'As far as I'm concerned, men come with a label attached marked trouble.'

Debbie laughed at her description. 'They're not all like that.' She gave Madge one of her coy looks.

'Find me one who isn't.'

Debbie gave up. Sometimes you just couldn't get through to Madge. There really didn't seem to be much point in continuing this line of conversation.

It was Madge who returned to the theme of Debbie's marriage. 'Tell me about this John, then.' She helped herself to another biscuit.

Debbie hesitated, wondering just how much to tell her. In the end she kept her reply as brief a possible. 'Well, he lives in Reading. He lost his first wife some years ago. He lives on his own in a flat and he has a married son.' And she added for good measure: 'And he likes the same things as I do.'

There was not much of a reaction from Madge. 'How's he off financially?' she asked.

Debbie laughed. 'I've never asked him. But I think he's quite well off.'

Madge was unimpressed. 'Keep your bank account locked,' was her reply.

Debbie was about to answer, but at that moment the phone rang. It was Renee, one of the WI members, who wanted to ask Debbie how she felt about something coming up on the agenda. Debbie was forced to listen while Renee went into great detail before asking her opinion. Debbie was as noncommittal as possible, which was just as well because Renee appeared to have already made up her mind and only wanted confirmation. She would have continued to chat, but, wanting to end the conversation, Debbie said she had a guest waiting.

Not long afterwards, Madge said she had to go. Debbie accompanied her to the front door. As she was about to walk to her car, Madge turned to her one last time. 'Well, I hope everything works out for you, with all your plans. Let me know when the wedding is,' she added with a grin.

'Oh everything will go just fine,' Debbie replied confidently, 'and I'll be in touch as soon as a date is fixed.'

'Great. See you then.' Madge moved towards her vehicle.

'Bye,' Debbie called after her and then with a wave went back into the house.

The next day, John came over. Debbie met him at the door. 'Darling, it's so good to have you here.' She embraced him. Now she did this automatically without embarrassment.

John held her for a few seconds. He could just about smell her perfume, faint but there somewhere.

'It's three whole days since we were together,' Debbie whispered into his jacket.

'Three days, five hours, ten minutes and three seconds,' was his reply. Then as they parted he continued to hold her by the shoulders and look at her.

'Hi,' he said simply, grinning. 'How's Mrs Hammond-to-be?'

Debbie planted a kiss on his lips before breaking free. 'Marvellous, darling, now you're here.' Then she turned to move towards the sitting room. 'Coffee's ready. And I've got lots of news to share with you,' she said breezily over her shoulder.

John closed the front door and followed her. She was already pouring coffee into the cups. 'I made it in a percolator as a special treat,' she announced proudly as she put the cup down in front of John, who had slid into one of the armchairs.

'And apple cake.' John's eyes had already settled on his favourite.

'Again, just as a treat. I don't want you to put on weight.' Debbie placed a plate in front of him. 'I can't stand men with big bellies,' she added, cutting a small piece of cake for herself.

'Or women.' John grinned at her and glanced at the meagre portion on Debbie's plate and then at her trim figure.

'Don't worry, darling. When we're married I intend to keep myself trim especially for you.' She gave him one of her coy little looks. 'Do you want to hear my news now?' She was eager to talk about things.

'I'm all ears.' He grinned at her again.

Debbie finished her mouthful of cake. 'Well, first of all I've started to tell everybody I'm getting married. I've told the girls.'

'How did it go?'

'Jan was quite excited, especially when I told her about the house. Trish was a bit iffy. But that's just Trish. She'll be fine. And I've told the women at the WI.'

'Any comments?' John asked as he took a sip of coffee and looked at Debbie.

'Oh, all sorts of bits of advice – you know the kind of thing… Oh, and I must tell you this. It's quite funny.' She looked at him to ensure she had his full attention before continuing. 'There was one elderly lady who took me aside and whispered to me to make sure I had a thick and horrible nightdress on the wedding night, to make myself as unattractive as possible, in case you wanted sex with me, because she knew a woman of eighty who got married again and her new husband wanted to have sex with her.'

She looked at John, waiting for him to share her frivolity. John, however, merely chuckled politely. Debbie reacted immediately. Intimacy between them had not so far been discussed and she suddenly realised that her comment had been badly timed. She quickly changed the subject. 'But the best bit of news is that Jan and Paul think they have a buyer already for their house. It's somebody they know and there won't be any chain to slow things up.'

'That's great news,' John agreed.

'And I've had a letter from Morgan Manton. They want to have a meeting with us and also have details of our solicitors etc.'

She paused. 'And there's something else. I've found out...' She looked at John. This was one of her best bits of information. She was determined to build up his anticipation. John looked at her, grinning, playing the game.

Then she continued: 'I've found out there are some allotments close to our new house.'

'What? How did you do that?'

'Well, I went over there one day, just to have a look again. And I thought I'd explore the roads around there, and that's how I came across them. It's quite a secluded site.'

John was immediately enthusiastic. 'I'll check it out,' he said.

'But there's more to it.' Debbie jumped up and hurried to her desk. She returned with a slip of paper in her hand. 'I saw somebody working on the site so I went in and asked him about availability of plots and he gave me the telephone number to enquire.' She handed him the slip of paper.

John looked at it and carefully put it in his pocket. 'I'll follow it up. Thank you for your efforts.' He beamed at her.

'The man I spoke to seemed to think there were some plots available. But he was a bit guarded. I didn't look much like a gardener when I went there.' Debbie recalled with amusement her encounter with the man. She had been dressed up in one of her suits and when he had eyed her up, she had known what he was thinking. 'Didn't I do well?' she asked.

John looked at her. She was laughing at him. 'Fantastic. In fact I might just take you on permanently,' he replied, pretending to be serious.

'I might consider your offer.' Debbie sipped her coffee.

'I've told Rob now,' John announced suddenly.

'Oh, what did he say?'

'Go for it, Dad.' He grinned.

'I'm so glad he said that. You must let me meet him soon.' She looked at him a little anxiously.

John nodded. 'We'll arrange it.'

It was Debbie who changed the pattern of conversation. 'So if everything goes on as smoothly as it started, it looks as if June might be a good time for the wedding.' She looked at him enquiringly.

'I think so,' said John. 'What shall we do for a honeymoon?'

Debbie hadn't given the matter any thought until now. 'Any suggestions?' she asked, beginning to ponder.

John considered for a moment. 'Go on a cruise... or visit the south of France... or what about Jersey?' His ideas ran out, and he looked at Debbie.

Debbie had come up with an idea. 'You know what I'd really like to do?' She looked at John with a smile. Seeing that he waited for her suggestion, she continued, voicing her thoughts as she spoke. 'A cruise would be lovely later on. But there is something I'd like to do immediately after we're married.' Again she stopped to study his reaction.

'Command, and it shall be done.' He grinned at her.

'What I'd really like to do is to go to Brillport again for a few days. Stop at the Grand Hotel and sit in the window seat again at dinner. We could walk on the cliffs and on the beach again.'

'I'll make sure I take my first aid kit along, then,' John joked.

Debbie feigned indignation. She made a face at him. 'Don't be like that! If it hadn't been for me treading on that glass, we would never have met. I thought what a nice, kind man. Now I'm not so sure.'

John just laughed. 'Now then Mrs Hammond-to-be, let's look at dates,' he said, draining the last of his coffee.

Chapter 19

Debbie lay back in bed and let her eyes wander round the room. This was the day she and John were to get married. Then they would be together instead of just seeing each other occasionally and having to keep parting.

Her gaze fell on the two-piece suit that hung on the back of her bedroom door, its clear polythene cover bearing the name of the boutique where weeks ago she had purchased it. In a few hours John would see it for the first time. Close by, on the seat of a chair, was the box containing the shoes to go with the outfit. It had been a struggle to obtain a pair to match the pale lilac of the suit and in the end it had meant a trip to London. Tired out after trying unsuccessfully in numerous shops, she had at last been successful, but even now she shuddered at the price she had had to pay to secure just what she wanted.

The last few weeks had been hectic, with so many things happening all at once. The purchase of the new house had gone smoothly enough, but the sale of her house to Jan and Paul had stalled several times and on one occasion it had looked as if she and John might have to change their wedding date. Then there had been the mammoth task of dealing with all the items in the house and sorting through more than thirty years of accumulated possessions. John had been a tower of strength, tackling such jobs as clearing the loft and helping her dispose of many unwanted items. At one point he had been with her nearly every day. Fortunately both Jan and Paul had displayed a very laid-back approach to the whole business and appeared almost to be content to move into the house as it stood and allow her to walk out with just a suitcase. They were happy to accept nearly all the furniture and fittings, and this suited her and John as they had decided to furnish the new house almost from scratch.

Trish's room had been a problem. When Debbie had suggested that she might come over and spend a day going through and clearing out her room, Trish had replied: 'But Mum, I just haven't got the time at the moment.' She had left it a few days and then tried again. This time the reply had changed to 'Mum, what am I going to do with everything?' She had tactfully suggested that Trish sort out the things she wanted and leave the rest for John and her to dispose of. The strategy had worked, because a few days later Trish had announced that she was coming to sort things out the next day.

She had arrived at half-past eight in the morning, dressed in her business suit and an alarming pair of high heels.

'Hi,' was her greeting. Debbie read the signs. Trish was in one of her moods.

'Hello, dear. Have you had any breakfast?' Debbie asked tactfully.

Trish shook her head. 'No. I wanted to come early. I've got to go into the office on the way back.' Trish glanced at her suit. Clearly she did not intend to stay long.

'What about a cup of coffee and something to eat?' asked Debbie.

'Fine. Toast would be nice.'

Debbie moved towards the kitchen, followed by Trish, who immediately slipped into one of the chairs.

'How's Don?' Debbie asked over her shoulder as she prepared some refreshment for them both.

'He's OK. He's gone to Zurich for something or other,' Trish replied casually.

'How are things between you now?'

'Much the same,' said Trish, scrutinising her fingernails closely. Debbie was about to try and get her to elaborate, but Trish changed the subject. 'Mum, I don't know what I'm going to do with all the stuff in my room,' she complained. 'Our flat is so poky.'

Debbie took a deep breath. 'I know. But what about just sorting out the items you really need and you intend to use? I mean, that old computer you have up there doesn't work, does it?'

'I suppose I could,' Trish replied without any enthusiasm.

'John's coming over soon and he'll help,' Debbie suggested tactfully.

'OK.'

Debbie had made the coffee and was about to finish the toast for Trish when there was the noise of a key in the front door.

'Oh, this is John now,' Debbie exclaimed. She had given him a key weeks ago.

Two seconds later John appeared in the kitchen. 'Hello there. Ah, do I smell coffee?' was his cheery greeting.

'Hello, darling.' Debbie jumped up and gave him a kiss on the cheek.

John turned to Trish and grinned. 'Hello Trish.'

'Hi,' was her response.

The three sat at the kitchen table, John and Trish munching toast. Debbie sat drinking her coffee and tried to initiate a three-way conversation. For the most part Trish remained uncooperative. At last she jumped up and announced that she was going to start work on her room. She left the kitchen, taking her coffee with her.

As soon as she was out of sight and hearing, Debbie looked at John and made a face. 'We're not in a very good mood,' she whispered.

John grinned. 'I'll sort her out,' he whispered in return.

Debbie didn't know how, but she was optimistic. At times her daughter could be quite difficult to deal with. She knew underneath it all the main problem with Trish was her own forthcoming marriage to John. She could sense that from the first announcement, Trish had been opposed to the idea, in spite of appearing to accept her explanations. It was a situation that worried Debbie, but one she felt she could do little about.

She and John sat together and finished their coffee. Overhead, from time to time, they could hear Trish in her room opening cupboard doors and turning things out. Then John announced that he was going to make himself useful and disappeared and Debbie busied herself doing the washing up. About twenty minutes later she heard the sound of Trish's laugh. Intrigued by her apparent change of mood, Debbie decided to investigate. In the hall she was met by John coming down the stairs carrying Trish's old computer.

'Just in the right place, at the right time. Can you open the front door, please?' he called out.

Debbie opened the door and stood back to let him pass. The next moment there was a thud as he deposited his load in the skip that was now rapidly filling up on the driveway.

'That's got rid of that,' he announced cheerfully as he came back into the house, rubbing his hands.

'I've wanted her to throw it out for years,' replied Debbie. She followed him upstairs. Was he really helping Trish?

The scene that met her gaze as she stood in the doorway of Trish's room amazed her. Trish had changed out of her business suit into a pair of jeans and an old shirt. Her heels were abandoned in a corner. Cupboards and drawers were all open and the contents strewn about. Trish was busy sorting through everything and throwing unwanted items in John's direction by the door. The most striking thing Debbie observed was the congenial atmosphere between the two of them. Trish was actually giggling and making jokes.

Debbie left them to it. When John came downstairs with more items for the skip, she grabbed his attention. 'What on earth did you do? Trish is actually cooperative,' she observed, intrigued but relieved that Trish's manner had improved.

John just gave her one of his grins. 'Charm,' he said simply.

Debbie made lunch for them all. In direct contrast to breakfast, it was quite an agreeable meal. Trish and John chatted like old friends, much to Debbie's relief.

In the early afternoon Trish loaded her car up with the items she was going to take with her and after a quick cup of tea was off, leaving Debbie and John to clear up the mess in her room.

It was a relieved Debbie who finished the day. Trish's attitude to her wedding had been worrying her. Unlike Jan, who had immediately latched onto the prospect, albeit with a slightly vested interest, Trish had only given reluctant acceptance to the whole idea. What had actually triggered the change, Debbie never really found out. When she chatted to John about it afterwards, he explained that he had only offered to help Trish by carrying away the items she was discarding and in addition transporting the items she wanted to keep to their new house. Perhaps that had been the key: his offer had indicated to Trish that she was still part of the family even after Debbie moved into the new house with John. Certainly his easygoing approach helped, as the two of them now seemed to get on like a house on fire, a situation for which Debbie was truly thankful.

Trish had telephoned her several times since then and now appeared to be quite content with everything. It made Debbie realise once again how sensitive her younger daughter was. It had always been that way. As a child, Trish had required a great deal more attention than Jan. As she grew up, she had developed a kind of impulsiveness that was at times worrying to Debbie, such as her impromptu marriage, which did not appear to be going too well. But as in all the situations Trish got herself into, any advice from Debbie fell on deaf ears. Debbie had long since realised that her best role was to be a good listener and offer a shoulder for her daughter to cry on when required. But even that did not stop her from worrying about her.

It was the sound of the newspaper arriving through the letter box that brought Debbie back to the present and halted her recollections. She really must get up, she told herself. She did not normally dally in bed in the mornings, but it had been nice to just take a few minutes to go over all the events of the past few weeks and clear her mind for the day ahead. There was another reason for her 'laziness'. She had been up the previous night until well past midnight sorting out her clothes. It was a job she had consistently let slide down to the bottom of her list of things to do. Yesterday it had become urgent. She had selected all the items she wanted to keep and transported them to the new house in the evening, together with a carefully packed suitcase for her honeymoon. Then on her return she had sorted out everything else that needed attention, like the pile of clothes designated for the charity shop. In contrast, the events for the day ahead should go smoothly enough. At half past eleven, she and John were to be married at the register office, with just a few family members and friends present. Then the whole party would retire to a local hotel for lunch. Afterwards, those who wanted to would follow the newly-weds to their new home, which would be open house for the rest of the afternoon and evening for her other friends to call in if they wished. The next day she and John would drive down to Brillport and the Grand Hotel for a few days' relaxation before returning to sort out the rest of the contents of her house and John's apartment. With all the arrangements now in hand, she felt surprisingly relaxed. All she had to do was get ready for when John came to collect her to drive the short distance to the wedding ceremony, and after that everything was taken care of for the next few days.

The thought of getting ready alerted her to the time. A quick glance at her watch and then at the bedside clock indicated that it was almost eight o'clock. Normally she would never still be in bed at this late hour. A slight feeling of panic that she would not be ready in time made her throw back the duvet and get out of bed. She snuggled into her old dressing gown – she had purchased a new one for life with John – and went downstairs. After quickly filling the kettle and setting it to boil, she went to pick up the paper. Suddenly it struck her that the paper needed to be cancelled. She would have to do that this morning.

As she was walking back to the kitchen she was startled by the shrill ringing of the telephone. She stopped in the hall and answered it.

'How's Mrs Hammond-to-be this morning?' There was no mistaking who it was.

'John, darling. I thought it would be Jan or somebody. I'm fine, except that I've been completely lazy this morning. I've only just got up. How are you?'

'Terrific. Can't wait! I'll aim to arrive at about half past ten.' He sounded cool, calm and collected.

'John, try and get over a little earlier, just in case of traffic problems or something. Then we can have a coffee together to steady my nerves before we go.' There was just a slight hint of anxiety in her reply.

'That sounds a good idea. I wish I'd thought of it.'

Debbie glanced at her watch. Panic was on the horizon. 'Darling, it's lovely to talk to you, but if I'm to be ready on time, I'd better get started.'

'OK. I'll let you get on, and I'll see you soon. I'm picking up the bouquets for everybody on the way.'

'Oh, that's marvellous.' She had almost forgotten that John had volunteered for this task.

'See you soon. I'm counting the minutes.'

'Me too,' said Debbie. 'Bye for now.'

'Bye, darling.' John clicked out.

Debbie replaced the handset. What a pleasant surprise John's call had been. It spurred her on to start the day in earnest.

John arrived early, his car full of flowers. He was dressed in a new suit, a deep blue, which suited him. Debbie just about managed to be ready when he arrived. Changing into the lilac suit had triggered a few moments of excitement. Today, her life would change dramatically. She would be a married woman again, looking after a husband. She and John would be together permanently. She could not help making comparisons with her first marriage. On that occasion she had changed into her white wedding dress, her mother had been fussing over her, and she had not had any contact with Ron until she entered the church and walked down the aisle; this time she got ready on her own, and she and John would drive to the register office together.

The ceremony was brief, like many register office marriages. John, Debbie and their guests waited in an anteroom for another wedding to finish. They had deliberately kept the event small. Jan and Paul came without Jamie, who had suddenly developed a cold, Trish had brought

Don, which was a pleasant surprise for Debbie, and John's son Rob was there with his wife, Cathy. A few close friends completed the party. After waiting for about five minutes they were ushered into the room where the marriage would take place. Debbie was pleased to see that it was bright and airy, with plants around. The registrar was a cheerful, middle-aged woman, who beamed at them from behind glasses.

As she stood beside John, Debbie was surprised how calm she felt. Compared to her first wedding, she was quite relaxed about the whole thing. Only when John slipped the ring on her finger did a quiver of excitement run through her. She was now Mrs Hammond. From then on things moved at quite at rapid pace and it seemed only a matter of seconds before she was smiling next to John for the photographs. Sam, a close friend of John who was also an ardent photographer, had offered to take the wedding snaps.

Next, everybody departed for the hotel for lunch. As she slipped into the car beside John, Debbie stole a glance at the new band of gold on her finger. She hadn't seen it before the wedding: it had been one of John's secrets. John noticed her looking.

'Too late now to take it off,' he joked.

'Oh, John, don't say that! I don't want to take it off. It's beautiful.' Debbie pretended to frown at him. Then she kissed him on the cheek.

'I'm glad it fits OK. Just imagine if it hadn't gone on your finger.' He looked at her and grinned.

'How DID you know what size to buy?'

John just grinned again. 'Ah, that's a secret,' was all he said.

It was no more than five minutes' drive to the hotel. They were the first to arrive and in the traditional manner greeted everybody as they entered. The pre-lunch reception was a relaxed affair. John and Debbie circulated among their guests, a glass of sherry in hand. Debbie felt a glow all over. It was good to have John at her side and to be surrounded by her family and friends. Even Madge had turned up – and in a dress, for once. In spite of the few problems along the way, things could not have gone better. Debbie was now John's wife.

At one point she excused herself to the ladies' room to freshen up. She was surprised to find that the only other occupant was Trish. She greeted her with a cheery smile. 'Well, fancy meeting you here!'

Trish turned to face her mother. She was sombre-faced. 'Mum... ' No more words came.

Debbie was quick to take in her daughter's worried look. 'Darling, what's wrong?'

Trish hesitated. Then she spoke. 'Mum, I'm really sorry I was so stuffy about you getting married again. John is a really nice guy. You deserve him.'

Debbie suddenly hugged her daughter. 'Darling, that's the nicest thing you could have said, and today of all days. Thank you.' She held Trish for a few seconds. Then she looked at her. 'Darling, how is your marriage now? Are things any better between you and Don?'

Trish shook her head. 'I think I made a mistake, Mum. But I don't want to talk about it today and spoil things for you.'

Debbie squeezed Trish's hand. 'Why don't you phone me or come and stop over for the night when we come back from our honeymoon?'

Trish nodded. 'I might do that,' she said.

They left the room together. Debbie was glad Trish had spoken to her. Things would be better now, but she was concerned about Trish and her marriage. But just for today she was not going to think about it.

It was a long day. Lunch was a simple affair. There were no speeches, an innovation they had both decided on beforehand. Afterwards, only a few of their guests took up the invitation to come round to their new house. Madge excused herself immediately after the meal, and shortly after they arrived at the house Trish and Don announced that they had to return to London. Jan had been fretting over Jamie all the time and it was not long before she and Paul decided to leave. After that, there was a steady stream of guests, mainly Debbie's friends and neighbours, who dropped in with good wishes.

The invitation had been for between three and eight, but it was after half-past ten when John and Debbie stood in the doorway seeing the last guest off. As they went into the house and closed the door, they turned towards each other and kissed. They were alone at last, for the first time as man and wife.

Almost two hours later they lay side by side in bed. Debbie's head was on John's shoulder and his arm encircled her. The only light in the room came from the waxing moon.

'I'm damn sorry about this.' John gently stroked Debbie's back as he spoke.

Debbie stirred. She used both hands to draw his lips towards hers. 'It doesn't matter, John, it really doesn't,' she whispered softly.

'My darling, it's the last thing I wanted to happen. I feel quite bad about it.' John's voice reflected his anguish.

Debbie raised herself a little higher to look at him. 'Darling John, you must stop worrying about it. It's not important. Just being here with you lying like this is heavenly to me. It's all I want, really.'

She was doing her best to reassure him. John knew that, but his failure weighed heavily on him now. He felt a mixture of embarrassment and irritation with himself. 'It's never happened before,' he answered gloomily.

Debbie used her free hand to play gently on his face as she spoke. 'Darling, don't be so hard on yourself.' She paused for a response, but when none came she continued. 'Yes, it would be nice if it happened, but just being here with you is the most important thing to me.' As she spoke, she allowed two fingers to linger on his face, tracing the outline of his lips and cheek.

John stared at the dark ceiling. 'I feel such a fraud, letting you down, as well as myself.' His words came almost as if he were thinking aloud.

Debbie suddenly raised herself up further and bent her head close to his. She spoke softly and with feeling. 'John, you mustn't feel bad. Everything is fine just as it is.' She hesitated for a second then continued, this time more assertive. 'Besides, look at everything logically. We've been tearing around all day, we had more alcohol than normal and then we try to act like seventeen-year-olds.' She ended up laughing.

John gave a little sigh. 'I suppose you're right,' he remarked.

'Of course I am,' Debbie responded. She was pleased with her handling of the situation and even in the dim light of the bedroom she had not failed to notice the grin return to John's face as he uttered his last remark.

Suddenly she sat bolt upright. 'Do you know what I'd like to do?' she asked, looking down at him. Without waiting for an answer, she continued. 'I'd like to go downstairs, make a cup of tea and have a piece of wedding cake.'

John laughed for the first time since they had gone to bed. 'I'll join you,' he replied. She was already reaching for her dressing gown.

Ten minutes later they were in their newly furnished sitting room. Debbie snuggled up to John on the sofa. He had one arm round her and managed his mug of tea with the other.

When they had both finished their tea, she lay full length on the sofa with her head on his lap. He clasped her hand and kissed her. 'Happy, darling?' he asked gently.

'It's marvellous. I'd forgotten how it felt to be so contented,' she replied, pressing her bare toes into the arm of the sofa.

'In spite of me making a mess of things,' he whispered.

Debbie clasped his hand tighter. 'Don't,' she said.

There was a few moments' silence between them as they rested there lost in each other's company. It was Debbie who broke the spell. 'Things can only get better,' she said.

John leaned down and kissed her. 'Of course,' he replied.

Chapter 20

After their late night, Debbie and John slept in. It was the sound of the telephone ringing that woke Debbie. At first she was unable to relate to the sound. Everything seemed strange: the bed she was in, the room she had just slept in. Then she remembered. She was in the new house, and John was sleeping peacefully beside her. She crept out of bed and tiptoed down the stairs to the hall. She picked up the phone.

'Mum, it's Jan. I just wanted to see how you are and wish you both a nice honeymoon.'

'Oh, that's sweet of you, dear.' Debbie stifled a yawn. 'We've not got up yet.'

'Gosh, Mum, it's nearly half past eight.'

Alarm bells sounded for Debbie. 'Good gracious! So late! I'd no idea.'

'I thought you were planning to leave early for Brillport. That's why I rang now.'

Debbie gave a little laugh. 'We did plan to, but we were so late last night.'

'Anyway, have a lovely time.'

'It really is nice of you, dear. How's Jamie this morning?'

'Grizzling a bit. I'd better go and see to him.'

'OK, dear. Thank you for the call. Love to Paul and Jamie.'

'Thanks, Mum. Bye for now. Love to John.'

'Bye, Jan. Bye.'

Debbie put the phone down. It was one of the first calls they had received in their new house. Suddenly she shivered in her nightgown and bare feet. She hurried back up the carpeted stairs to the bedroom. John was standing in the doorway, stifling a yawn.

'Good morning, Mrs Hammond.' He kissed her.

'Good morning, John,' she responded breezily. 'That was Jan, ringing to wish us a happy honeymoon.'

'Good girl. I thought it might be.' He yawned again. 'Sorry. These late nights…' he apologised with a grimace.

Debbie laughed. 'Do you know what the time is? It's turned half past eight. I haven't been so late getting up for years. You're encouraging me into bad habits already.'

He kissed her again. 'Sorry about that,' he said, grinning. Then he asked. 'Who's going in the bathroom first?'

Debbie quickly responded. 'Oh, let me have five minutes and then I can go and get our breakfast ready.' She was already making a move in the direction of the bathroom.

'Good idea,' John called after her, watching her go.

Just before she closed the bathroom door, Debbie remembered something and called over to him. 'John, we need to get a telephone for the bedroom.'

'It will be done,' he called back, smiling.

It was after eleven o'clock when they left for Dorset. Debbie had treated herself to a brand new dress for the trip and this was the first time John had seen it. On the journey they stopped at a roadside hotel and spent an hour or so over a leisurely lunch. They reached the end of their journey late in the afternoon.

Renewing their acquaintance with Brillport and particularly the Grand Hotel was a magical experience for both of them. They sat at the same table in the dining room where they had sat together twelve months previously and were served by the same waitress, but now they were man and wife and not two strangers getting to know each other.

The few days seemed to fly by as they indulged in each other's company. They took to simple pleasures like walking hand in hand on the beach or cliff paths. They spent hours chatting over the odd coffee, talking together, revelling in the pleasure of their new lifestyle.

Only one thing caused Debbie some concern, and that was their failure to consummate the marriage. She was not worried for herself, but she felt for John. She had not given a great deal of thought to the sexual side of her second marriage. She had naturally assumed that at their age any physical contact would be limited or non-existent. Of course she did know that some couples continued sexual activity well into old age, but they had no doubt kept the practice up over the years. On the other hand, she was aware that a lot of couples abandoned their interest earlier as their families grew up and they grew older. There seemed to be quite a lot of personal choice in it all. Even her and Ron's activities in that field had been reduced in the last years they were together. Then widowhood had changed everything.

When John had attempted to make their marriage physical, she had been ready to respond and rekindle the feeling that had been put to sleep all those years ago. The failure had brought forth all her compassion and sympathy for him. She knew that for a man it was the ultimate embarrassment, and these thoughts had been with her in the first few days of their honeymoon.

She need not have worried. On the third day of their stay the situation changed. It happened early in the morning before breakfast. Debbie was up first and spent some time in the bathroom. She emerged wearing her dressing gown over her bra and panties. John was still in bed, but his pyjama top was open, revealing his muscular frame. Debbie went over to him and, leaning over, kissed him on the lips, intending it as a good-morning gesture. John held her close for a minute, and things developed from there.

A little while later they lay peacefully in each other's arms. Debbie's head was resting on John's chest. One of his arms encircled her; the other played with her hair gently.

'I'm so glad it's happened, John,' Debbie murmured. She waited for a second expecting John to reply. When he said nothing, she continued. 'I didn't mind for myself, but I really felt awful for you the other night.'

'Well at least you really are Mrs Hammond now.' John followed his remark with a chuckle and Debbie knew that it was his way of relieving his embarrassment.

Suddenly she raised herself slightly and made a face. 'I don't know what the girls would say about their mother. Jan would probably be surprised and raise her eyebrows, and Trish would be disgusted with me.' She laughed.

'We won't tell them,' John said emphatically, and chuckled again.

'I'm a bit out of practice.' She returned her head to the comfort of his shoulder.

'Me too,' he replied softly, adding: 'Out of steam as well.'

Debbie raised her head again and gently kissed him. 'It was all right, John, really it was. I was just pleased that it was a success this time. Remember we aren't sixteen.' She continued to look at him.

John smiled briefly. 'I'm sure it wasn't as good as on my first honeymoon, or yours,' he commented drily.

Debbie continued looking at him. Now her face was serious. 'My first honeymoon was a mess,' she said.

John was tempted to ask why, but he knew he had to wait for her to elaborate.

She hesitated. Somehow that comment had slipped out. She hadn't intended to relate the secret she had held close for so many years, but now suddenly she wanted to tell John about it. She laid her head on his chest for comfort before continuing. 'I was a virgin when I got married. We had the classic honeymoon, four-poster bed and all the trimmings. On the first night, Ron could not break my hymen and penetrate me. It would not break. We tried again and again. I felt awful about it.'

'But it was all right in the end?'

She shook her head. 'In the end I had to go and confide in my mother. She took me to a clinic and they had to do it surgically. I was so upset and embarrassed.'

'Oh, poor you. How awful.' He held her close.

After a few moments Debbie continued. 'I've never talked to anybody about it. The only people who ever knew were Ron, my mother and the doctor and nurse involved. Even the girls don't know.'

John kissed her head. 'Thank you for telling me.'

Debbie raised herself up again. She was smiling slightly now. 'So you see, John, you needn't have worried. I've had my share of embarrassment over my sex life as well.'

He held her close again. Neither of them said anything for several minutes. It was Debbie who broke the spell. Suddenly she released herself from John's embrace and sat upright. 'Hey, just look at the time! We'd better make ourselves respectable and go for breakfast, or everybody will guess what we've been up to.'

'Pensioners don't do that sort of thing.' John laughed as he said it, but he was already following Debbie's example and making a move.

It was on their return home that the full impact of their new lifestyle took hold. In the first few months of their marriage there seemed to be so many things to attend to. There was the task of finally clearing the last remaining unwanted and surplus items at Debbie's house, and then they helped Jan and Paul move in. After that there was the minor job of sorting out John's flat and disposing of the contents. On top of all that there was the more pleasurable job of adding all the little extra touches to turn their new house into a home. They had both done some work in the small garden. There was a new lawn, complete with a bird table, and the patio outside the French windows was now a pleasant area where they could sit and relax over a cup of tea or just enjoy the outlook. The trappings of their sought-after idyllic lifestyle were beginning to emerge. John had even found time to sort out an allotment. Debbie was overjoyed that he included her in the planning, because one of the things she had regretted was losing her garden and the hours of pleasure she had spent there. They had begun to meet and get to know their neighbours. They liked the couple next door, who were in similar circumstances to them. Bill and Jean Meadows were three years into their second marriage. Both were retired teachers and, like John and Debbie, had met and married for a second time after losing their partners. They were madly enthusiastic about holidays and seemed to spend a great deal of time travelling round the world to various places. Bill was a rather quiet individual, but Jean made up for that with her naturally chatty personality. Both Debbie and John found the atmosphere of their new environment pleasant. The development their house was part of consisted of only twelve apartments and ten small houses. It was so compact that all the residents got to know each other quite quickly, and the fact that they were all retired or of retiring age meant that they had a kind of common interest and outlook. Once all the properties were occupied, a sense of community started to emerge. Everybody seemed to find the site a congenial place to live.

Somehow, in the rediscovered pleasure of married life and the activity their change of lifestyle had produced for Debbie and John, the summer months slipped by into autumn. They were both blissfully happy and revelled in the pleasure of discovering new things about each other. Only occasionally was their lifestyle marred by something, usually an outside event. They were made abruptly aware of this one afternoon when the telephone rang while they were taking a break from gardening with a well-earned cup of tea. John answered the telephone and the length of time he was away made Debbie guess that the call was for him.

When he came back he was looking glum. His change of mood concerned Debbie. 'John, is something wrong?' she asked.

'Sam's just died.' John sank into his chair again.

'Sam? Do I know him, darling?' Debbie enquired, racking her brains to remember a Sam.

'Sam Collier. He took the photographs at our wedding.' John glanced at her, waiting for recollection to return to Debbie.

'Oh yes, I remember. Quite a jolly sort of person.' She recalled the nimble and energetic man who had darted here and there on their wedding day, taking photographs.

John continued. 'That was Angus Bellamy on the phone; he's the chairman of our photography club. Apparently Sam died yesterday in hospital of a heart attack.'

Debbie looked at him. She could see he was upset at the news. 'But he looked so young and fit at our wedding, and that was only a few months ago,' she replied.

'He was only fifty-eight.' John took another drink of his tea. He appeared deep in thought, even though he continued the conversation.

'Oh, how awful. Was he married?' Debbie asked.

John shook his head. 'Divorced, I think, some years ago. He lived on his own. He and I have been members of the photography club for years. In fact it was Sam who encouraged me to join.'

'What about family? Did he have any children?'

John thought for an instant. 'I think he mentioned a daughter somewhere, but I don't think he was very close to his family.'

'That's sad.'

John nodded. 'Yes. And when it happens like this, it's the suddenness of everything that really gets to you. He was as fit as a fiddle at our wedding and now he's dead. It really makes you stop and think.'

'More tea?' asked Debbie. As she took his cup and poured, she continued the conversation. 'Yes, I know. And I suppose as we get older these things have a greater effect on us.' She paused as she handed John his cup. 'I'm sure I never noticed quite as much when I was younger. You never think of death and dying.'

Their conversation was brought to an abrupt halt as the telephone rang again.

'I'll answer it, darling. You sit still.' Debbie had already got up from her chair. As she headed for the telephone, she commented: 'I don't know who that can be. I spoke to Jan this morning.'

Debbie picked up the receiver. 'Hello.'

'Mum, it's Trish.'

'Trish! Darling, it's lovely to hear from you. I've tried to ring you a few times recently, but I never get you.' It was true. Secretly Debbie had become worried about Trish. She had not seen her since the wedding, and a few brief telephone conversations had been the only contact. Trish's remoteness made her recall the attitude she had

214

displayed when Debbie announced she was getting married to John. Were the negative feelings still lurking in the background? Debbie had talked about her concern to John and he had suggested she have it out with her daughter. But putting the suggestion into practice had proved difficult.

'Oh, I've been busy. Anyway, how are you, Mum?'

'We're fine. But how are you? And how's Don? We hardly ever see either of you.'

'I'm OK, except that I've been pretty busy the last few weeks. Sorry I haven't been in touch, Mum.'

Debbie sighed to herself. She knew it would be no good protesting. Instead she repeated her previous question. 'And how's Don?'

'He's OK.' The tone of Trish's answer concerned Debbie, but before she could respond Trish blurted out: 'I'm starting a new job, Mum.'

Debbie was surprised by the news. 'But I thought you liked your job,' she replied.

'It was all right, but the new job is more money and less travelling, so I decided to make a change. Besides, I've been with the other one for four years.'

'That's really not that long. Your dad stayed at his last company for fifteen years.'

Debbie's comment was more an observation than a condemnation, but Trish was immediately on the defensive. 'I know, Mum. But that was years ago and now if you stop too long in a job they think you are an old stick-in-the-mud with no ambition.'

Debbie laughed. 'That's all new to me. It wasn't at all like that in my day.'

'Well, it's different now.'

Debbie recognised indignation in Trish's voice. She decided to change direction. 'What does Don think about it?' she asked.

'I haven't discussed it with him.'

The brief answer told Debbie what she wanted to know, but she ventured another question. 'How are things between you now?'

'About the same.'

The briefness of Trish's answers could be infuriating at times, but Debbie let this one pass, instead suggesting: 'Darling, why don't you come and spend the weekend with us sometime – you and Don?'

'He wouldn't come, but I might sometime.'

'Darling, when? We'd love to have you and you haven't visited us since we got married.'

'I really am sorry about that, Mum. I have intended to drop in, but I always seem to be somewhere else.'

Having gained what she thought was a slight advantage, Debbie decided to press for more positive results. 'Why don't we make a date now? It's Jamie's birthday soon. Why don't you come for that? I don't think he even realises he's got an auntie. He sees you so rarely.'

'I know. I'm not doing very well, am I?' The remark was a bit reflective.

Debbie persisted. 'What about it, then? When can you come?'

'Gosh, Mum, I can't make a date just like that, but I will come – I promise.'

Debbie admitted defeat. 'All right, dear, but don't make it so long.'

'I won't, I promise.'

'Have you spoken to Jan recently?' Debbie already knew the answer, but she asked anyway.

'No. But I'll give her a ring sometime. Anyway, she never rings me.'

Debbie smiled to herself. Trish's accusation did not appear to have much foundation, but she did not respond. Instead she suggested tactfully: 'Perhaps she hasn't managed to get through to you. Like me.' She laughed.

Trish did not take the bait. Instead she abruptly interjected: 'Mum, I've got to go. I'm wanted. Somebody's breathing down my neck.'

'OK, dear, I'll say goodbye then. Thanks for ringing. Don't forget about the weekend with us. Oh, and give my greetings to Don.'

'I won't forget, and I will tell Don. I've got to go. Bye, Mum.'

'Bye, darling. Look after yourself.'

'And you, Mum. Bye.'

Debbie replaced the handset and sighed again to herself. It had been quite an afternoon. First the sad news about Sam, and now Trish being her usual evasive self. She went back into the lounge to join John and tell him about her conversation with her daughter.

Chapter 21

Trish did not come to Jamie's birthday as Debbie had hoped. The event passed without any communication from her.

It was almost a month after their telephone conversation that Debbie received the long-awaited announcement of Trish's arrival. She was busy in the kitchen one Thursday morning in early November when the telephone rang. When she picked up the receiver and put it to her ear, Trish's voice piped up immediately. 'Mum, It's Trish. I've got to be quick – I'm on my mobile and I think the battery's down.'

'Hello, darling. How are you?'

'Fine, Mum. Can I come and stay this weekend?'

Debbie thought quickly. She and John had agreed that they would go out for a meal on Saturday night and include Jan and Paul, but that could be put on hold, or Trish could come as well.

'Of course you can, dear. When and what time?'

'Umm, tomorrow afternoon, lateish.'

'OK. Looking forward to it.' Then another thought struck Debbie. 'Is Don coming with you?' She had two reasons for asking. First of all, she wanted to know how Trish's marriage was going, and secondly, if Trish was coming on her own she could sleep in the small bedroom, which had been earmarked for her, but if Don was coming as well, she would have to do a bit of work to get the bedroom ready.

Trish's answer told her all she wanted to know. 'He's going away for the weekend.'

Debbie was just about to make a tactful reply when Trish said: 'I'll see you tomorrow then.'

'All right, darling. Until tomorrow.'

'Bye then, Mum.'

'Bye-bye, dear.'

Trish rang off immediately. Debbie was just about to return to the kitchen, when John came through the front door. He had been shopping. 'Hi. Mission accomplished,' was his greeting.

Debbie went to meet him and took the bag from him. She planted a kiss on his cheek. 'I've just had Trish on the telephone. In a hurry as usual. She's coming for the weekend.'

'Great,' replied John. 'Don as well?'

Debbie made a face. 'No. On her own.'

John immediately fell in. 'Oh well, we'll take her out for a meal as well.'

'That's what I thought.' Debbie was on her way to the kitchen with the bag of shopping. 'We might learn a bit more about the marriage problems,' she remarked casually over her shoulder.

Friday's preparations did not go completely to plan. Debbie and John had been to the shops early to buy in extra food. John normally took Debbie, because she had sold her car and did not like driving his. They had planned to sell John's car eventually and buy a smaller one that Debbie would be happy with as well, but so far they had not had the time to investigate new cars.

When they returned from shopping, John decided that as it was a nice day he would spend a few hours on the allotment. Debbie busied herself getting things nice for Trish's visit. She was pottering in the kitchen when the front doorbell rang. Puzzled, she hurried to the door.

Madge stood on the doorstep. 'Hiya,' she said.

'Madge, I didn't expect to see you. Do come in.' Debbie threw open the door. Madge was a visitor she could have done without on that particular morning, but she hid her feelings.

'Any coffee going?' Madge was already in the hall.

'Yes, of course. I'll put the kettle on.' Debbie closed the door and led her visitor to the kitchen.

Once there, Madge immediately selected one of the kitchen chairs to sit down on. 'Where's that feller of yours?' she asked.

Debbie clicked the switch down on the kettle. 'John's having a few hours on the allotment to tidy it up a bit and take advantage of the dry spell.' Then she added: 'Trish is coming for the weekend.'

'Great,' Madge replied, almost disinterested, her eyes wandering round the kitchen.

'We haven't seen you since the wedding. What have you been up to?' Debbie asked, putting a spoonful of coffee in each mug.

'I've been away on holiday several times,' Madge replied, watching her intently. 'I'm going away again on Sunday,' she volunteered next.

'What are you doing this time?' Debbie asked, placing a plate of biscuits on the table in front of Madge.

'Mediterranean cruise. Had to come and buy some gear today. That's how I'm here. I thought I'd drop in and see you guys at the same time,' replied Madge, helping herself to one of the chocolate biscuits.

'A cruise? That's exciting. John and I talked about going on one, but I'm a bit worried about being seasick.' Debbie came to the table with the two mugs of coffee and sat down opposite Madge.

Madge laughed. 'That's what everybody who has never done one thinks.'

Debbie was about to ask more questions about cruises, but Madge piped up before she had time. 'How are you two lovebirds getting on?' she asked, grinning.

Madge's terminology slightly irritated Debbie, but she made an effort not to show it. 'Fine,' she answered, hoping the brief reply would be sufficient.

Madge seemed intent on continuing on the same tack. 'How's married life again?' She bit into her biscuit.

'Fine,' Debbie repeated. And then, because she thought the answer to be a bit brief, she added: 'It does need a bit of adjustment to have a man around again all the time.'

'In what way?' Madge asked, not inclined, it seemed, to let the subject drop.

Debbie hesitated. Talking to Madge about such things made her feel awkward and vulnerable. She chose her words carefully. 'Oh well… You know. Remembering the little things that men like. Keeping oneself smart, putting lipstick on, adding a dab of perfume – things like that.'

Immediately Debbie knew this had been the wrong thing to say. Instead of closing the matter, her answer opened up the opportunity for fresh questioning. 'Is it worth it?' Madge asked, scrutinising her.

'Of course it is,' Debbie replied, adding a little smile for good measure and taking a sip of her coffee.

Madge was quick with a reply. 'Well, in my opinion it only encourages men to pursue their selfish interests. Get you in bed and have two seconds' pleasure with their miserable little penises.' She casually bit into another biscuit as she finished speaking.

'Madge!' Debbie's exclamation was partly a reprimand and partly an expression of surprise. She had been taken aback by Madge's comment. 'It's not like that,' she went on, feigning a half-smile. 'I don't keep myself attractive just to stimulate a sex interest in men,' she added, as forcefully as she could.

Madge looked at her over her mug. 'No? I bet that feller of yours couldn't wait to get you into bed.' She took a swig of coffee and then added casually, as if it were an afterthought: 'Still, I expect you're both too old for sex.'

This was too much for Debbie. Really, Madge was the limit at times. She fought back her irritation, conscious that Madge was watching for her reaction, but she took her time and formulated her reply with dignity and an air of superiority. 'Well, as a matter of fact you're wrong. We aren't.' She felt obliged to amplify her confession. 'OK, we're not at it hammer and tongs every night, but it has happened.'

It was completely out of character for her to discuss such delicate matters, but Madge had got her hot under the collar and her confession had slipped out after Madge's remarks about her age and being past it. Anyway, she thought, what does it matter if she does know? Madge always came over as a complete man-hater.

Madge was uncompromising. 'Oh well, everybody to their own thing.' Her statement was accompanied with a slight shrug of her shoulders, as if that was the end of the matter.

Debbie felt she had been violated and exposed, and this added to her irritation. The feelings prompted her into a bit of retaliation. 'Did you never have any serious relationships with men, Madge?' she asked. She took another sip of her coffee and watched Madge's reaction.

Madge's reply was casual and matter-of-fact. 'I've had a few in my time, but none of them have changed my opinion. Selfish and demanding – that about sums men up.'

Debbie burst out laughing. 'They're not all like that,' she replied, trying to be as objective as she could.

'Show me one who's not,' Madge responded, helping herself to another chocolate biscuit.

Debbie could see that it was useless to continue this discussion. She decided to change the subject. 'Tell me about your cruise,' she suggested cheerfully. 'Tell me where you're going.'

The strategy worked. Madge entered into a detailed description of her forthcoming holiday, where she would go and what she would see. It was a good half-hour before she departed. Debbie returned to the kitchen. A sizeable chunk of the morning had been taken up by Madge's unexpected visit. She was washing up the dirty mugs when she heard John's key in the front door. He entered the kitchen. 'I'm back,' he announced, coming over to the sink.

Debbie turned her face for a kiss. 'Have you had a good morning, darling?' she asked.

'Quite productive, in fact.' John's enthusiasm came out. 'How about you?' he asked, grinning.

Debbie pulled off her washing-up gloves. She made a face and shook her head. 'Not really. I've had Madge here for ages.'

'Oh, I see the problem,' commiserated John.

Debbie's feathers were still a bit ruffled from Madge's visit. She turned to John. 'She was in one of her opinionated moods. Do you know, I think that woman is a born man-hater?'

John burst out laughing. 'I know what you mean, but Madge isn't really feminine, is she?' he observed reflectively.

Debbie continued. 'It's just that her attitude rubs me up the wrong way. She's always got this thing about men. Today she was trying to imply that if a woman puts on a dab of scent, it's done to attract men.'

'What sort of job did she do?'

'Military. She was in the army for years and years. Perhaps that accounts for her masculine appearance,' she added thoughtfully.

John smiled at Debbie's suggestion. 'More likely she had a bad first experience with a man and let it cloud her future relationships,' he offered. Suddenly he leaned forward and kissed Debbie on the cheek again. 'I'm glad that didn't happen to you, my darling.'

Debbie responded by kissing him on the lips. She felt better now. Suddenly she glanced at the clock on the wall and broke free from his embrace. 'Just look at the time! We've got a guest coming and no preparation done yet.' She laughed as she gave him a final peck on the cheek.

It was early evening by the time Trish arrived. Debbie was in the lounge when she heard her car pull up outside. She hurried to the door, calling out to John, who was in the kitchen, to let him know.

Trish had already got out of her car and opened the boot. She looked up and smiled as Debbie appeared. 'Hello, Mum.' She turned to give her mother a kiss on the cheek.

'Hello, darling. It's lovely to have you here at last.' Debbie gave her a hug.

John appeared at the door. 'Hello, Trish,' he announced cheerfully. Trish responded with a shake of his offered hand, a brief kiss on the cheek and 'Hi, John,' accompanied by a quick smile.

John led the way into the house, carrying her bag.

Debbie had noticed that Trish was still in her business suit, complete with outrageous heels. 'Have you come straight from work, dear?' she asked.

Trish made a face and nodded. 'It was my last day at that place. I start my new job on Monday.'

'Are you looking forward to it?' asked Debbie, as cheerfully as she could.

Trish shrugged. 'It should be all right,' she replied without any apparent enthusiasm.

Debbie said nothing. She could tell the kind of mood her daughter was in. She was hoping things would improve over the weekend. Once in the hall she turned to her. 'Here we are. John will take your bag upstairs. Yours is the small room at the back. We've put your things from the old house in there.' She tried to be as bright and breezy as she could.

'Fine,' said Trish, looking around.

'I thought we'd eat in tonight. Tomorrow John's going to treat us all to a meal out. Jan and Paul are coming as well. Is that all right?' She looked at Trish for approval.

'Fine. I think I'll clean up and get out of these clothes,' Trish responded.

'OK, dear. Our meal is a cold one, so take your time.'

John reappeared a few moments later. Trish disappeared without any further conversation.

Once Debbie was alone with John, she confided to him in a whisper: 'Oh dear. I don't think we're very happy.' She nodded in the direction of Trish's room.

He grinned. 'We'll sort her out.'

It was half an hour before Trish reappeared. She had changed her formal dark business suit for a faded and tatty pair of jeans and a top that left a good deal of her midriff exposed. Bare feet had replaced the stilettos. Debbie glanced at her daughter's appearance but said nothing. She knew she was most likely expected to say something, but she decided to let the incident pass. Ever since she was a teenager, Trish had dressed to shock from time to time.

The meal was a sombre affair, with Debbie and John keeping the conversation going by asking questions and receiving only the vaguest answers from Trish. Debbie could sense that Trish's concentration was only partly on the conversation. She thought she knew what was on her daughter's mind, and she hoped that over the weekend she might learn more. After the meal Trish announced that she was going upstairs for a while and John hurried to the lounge to catch up on a sports programme he wanted to watch on the television. Debbie busied herself clearing away the dishes. She pottered in the kitchen for a while and was surprised to see, on looking at the wall clock, that almost an hour had flown by. John was still in the lounge; she could hear the television.

There had been no sign of Trish since she left the table. Debbie left John to it and went up into their bedroom to fetch something. As she did so she noticed that the door of Trish's room was pulled to but not completely closed. A light showed through the wide crack left. On the way back downstairs, she hesitated outside the door. She called out 'Trish' and tapped at the door. There was a faint response from inside the room. Debbie pushed open the door. Trish was curled up on the bed in a foetal position. She had taken off her jeans and was just in her top and minuscule panties. Her face was turned away from the door.

Debbie entered the room, pushed the door closed and spoke softly. 'Darling, are you all right? You've been so quiet.'

Trish turned to face her mother. Her face was a picture of misery.

'Darling, is something troubling you? Is it about Don?' Debbie asked as gently as she could. She just hoped Trish would respond to her. She could be absolutely stubborn at times.

Suddenly the tears that were close to the surface burst forth. 'Oh, Mum,' wailed Trish, 'I feel so miserable.'

Debbie sat on the bed beside her. She placed her hand on Trish's. 'Darling, is it Don?' she asked gently.

Trish gave a bit of a nod. 'Mum, I've made such a mess of things,' she sobbed.

Debbie reached for a tissue from the bedside box and handed it to her. 'Do you feel like telling me about it?' she enquired, adopting the soothing tone of voice she had used when Trish as a child had run home in tears after some incident at school.

Trish wiped her tears with the tissue and blew her nose. She was silent for a minute, her hands clasped round her ankles, gazing at her feet. When she eventually looked up at her mother, she hesitated. Then she spoke as if she was thinking aloud. 'I feel so awful about everything,' she sobbed. 'I should never have married him.'

Debbie knew that Trish would tell her more in good time. She recognised that Trish had a need to talk to her. Gone was the high-flying businesswoman. Trish had become for a time the little girl who had sought her mother to pour out all her troubles. Debbie moved so that she could put an arm round her, just as she had all those years ago. 'Darling, would you like to tell me all about it?' she asked.

Trish wiped her eyes again and sniffed. 'It's all gone wrong,' she said miserably.

'In what way?'

Trish waited a few moments before answering, and then she replied quietly: 'We just don't get on.'

'Can you tell me more?' prompted Debbie gently.

Trish blew her nose. 'All he thinks about is football and sex,' she replied, 'and he's got this mother thing. She dotes on him.'

'Have you tried talking to him?'

Trish nodded. 'It's a waste of time. We just end up shouting at each other. Then he runs home to his mother.'

'Has he always been like that? I mean, before you got married?'

'He seemed all right then,' Trish replied miserably.

Debbie thought for an instant, and then she asked: 'Darling, which one of you wanted to get married?

'I did.'

'Were you in love with him?'

'Of course I was.'

Trish's reply was defensive. Debbie knew that if she was to be of any help to her daughter and continue the current confidences, she had to tread carefully. 'And then it all went wrong after you were married?' she suggested gently.

Trish nodded. 'He's so demanding,' she murmured.

'In what way?' Debbie asked again.

Trish was silent for a minute or so. Debbie feared that she was not feeling inclined to confide any further, but suddenly she spoke again. 'He expects me to wait on him like his mother does, and...' Trish paused for a second, and then she continued. 'He wants to have sex all the time, whenever he feels like it. It doesn't matter how I feel.'

Debbie absorbed her daughter's confession, and then she replied sympathetically: 'That doesn't sound very good. Have you talked about it?'

'I've told you, we just end up rowing.'

Debbie was about to respond, but suddenly Trish said: 'Mum, I've got to get away from him. I can't stand it any more.'

'Does he know this?' Debbie asked.

'I think so.' Trish wiped away a stray tear.

Debbie hadn't realised that things had gone that far. She knew so little about her son-in-law that it made forming any conclusions difficult. She was fully aware that Trish had an impulsive nature, and the collapse of a marriage after such a short period seemed to emphasise that very quality, but it sounded as if Trish had already made up her mind. Debbie decided that the best and only strategy for the present was to be as supportive to her daughter as she could.

'Has it really gone that far?' she asked.

Trish blew her nose. 'I just can't take things any more, Mum.'

'What will you do? Move out?' Debbie asked.

'Not likely. It's my flat.' Debbie could have smiled. There were signs of the normal Trish in the tone of voice.

'And then what? Divorce?' Debbie enquired gently.

Trish nodded slightly, without looking up. 'If I can raise the money. It costs an arm and a leg these days.' She seemed to be thinking things out as she spoke.

Debbie thought for a few seconds. It was at times like this that

227

children needed their parents, in spite of their pretensions of independence. She held Trish a bit tighter. 'Darling, if things are really that bad and there is no other way, I'll help you with the money.'

For the first time, Trish looked directly at her mother. There were still traces of tears in her eyes. 'Will you really, Mum?' she asked.

Debbie smiled at her. 'Darling, of course I will. That's what parents are for,' she replied, trying to sound as cheerful as she could.

'Oh, Mum, I don't know how to thank you.' Impulsively, Trish hugged her mother. Her face suddenly looked a bit more cheerful. Then she asked anxiously: 'But what will people think – Jan and my friends?'

Debbie came to the rescue. 'I think you'll find that they're a lot more supportive than you expect,' she replied with conviction.

'Do you really think so?' Trish's face was beginning to cloud over again.

'Of course I do.' Debbie had come to the conclusion that she needed to take control of the evening. She gave her daughter another hug and a kiss. 'Do you feel a bit better now, darling?' she asked.

Trish nodded and reached for another tissue. 'Thanks, Mum.'

Debbie glanced at her watch. 'Gosh, just look at the time! I think we'd better go downstairs now, don't you? John will wonder where we've got to.'

The ploy worked. Trish made a move to get off the bed. Debbie stood up and Trish eased herself into a sitting position, her feet on the floor. 'I must look a mess,' she said miserably.

Debbie came to the rescue again. 'Just put some clothes on and clean up your face,' she urged. 'You'll be fine.'

Trish started to take off her top. As she did so Debbie noticed the tattoo on her shoulder: it was a heart with 'Don' written on it. Debbie touched it. 'Darling, I never noticed that before.'

Trish's reaction was one of startled awareness. She groaned. 'Oh, Mum, I'd forgotten about that. I had it done on our honeymoon. I was best part drunk at the time. Don's got one as well.' She attempted to look over her shoulder at the mark on her skin. 'Can you get tattoos removed?' she asked, turning to look at her mother.

Debbie was a bit shocked that Trish should have had her beautiful skin spoilt by such a crude mark, without considering how a few minutes' impulsive thinking might produce a problem for the future. All she could muster was: 'I expect you can.'

Trish retrieved a white blouse from her overnight bag and pulled on her jeans again. She glanced at her feet and then reached into the bag again and slipped on a pair of tatty flip-flops that had seen better days.

Debbie watched her preparations, and as Trish started to work on her hair she made a move. 'I'll see you downstairs, darling,' she said, with a smile.

'OK, Mum.' Trish's voice did have a lighter tone to it now.

Debbie made her way downstairs. It had been quite a day.

Chapter 22

'Do you know, I think I've actually done it?' Debbie paused in the doorway of the lounge. There was excitement in her voice.

John roused himself from his nap, in the process letting the newspaper he had been reading slide onto the floor.

'Gosh, I dropped off for a few moments.' He jerked himself into more alertness.

Debbie could not contain her excitement. 'I'm sure I've actually done it. I've sent an email to my sister. Aren't I clever?'

John resumed a more upright position. He grinned at her. 'I told you it was easy,' he said, retrieving the newspaper from the floor.

Debbie bent over him and planted a kiss on his forehead. 'Yes, I know. But I still consider it a major step forward for me. Gwen will get a bit of a shock.'

John looked at her and smiled. He had instructed Debbie in the mysteries of emails a few weeks previously, but she had not been too happy with her progress. Now he could see she was overjoyed with her success.

He took hold of her arm, drew her towards him and kissed her on the lips. 'Well done, darling.'

Debbie responded and then gently drew herself away. She glanced towards the window. 'Just look. It's almost dark and it's only just turned four.' She walked over to the light switch and plunged the room into a brilliant glow. She went over to the window and drew the curtains, shutting out the gloom.

'December 21st – the shortest day,' John reminded her.

Debbie came back over to him. She smiled. 'Another three days, and it'll be Christmas.' She sat down and looked at him. 'So much has happened since last year. We got married, moved house and now we're back to Christmas again.' She paused for a second and then commented breezily: 'And I've learnt to use a computer.'

John smiled again. 'Are you glad it all happened?' he asked.

Debbie pretended to frown at him. 'Of course I am.' She paused for an instant and then, reflecting as she spoke, said: 'When I look back, I realise how dull life had become – just a routine of housework and playing grandma at odd times.'

John looked at her. 'I know what you mean,' he said.

Debbie changed the subject. 'You know, Gwen keeps asking me when we're going to visit them. I wouldn't mind going, but the long flight puts me off.'

John thought for a moment. 'If she asks again, why don't we give it a go?' he suggested, adding for good measure: 'We'd have each other for company, it would all be a new experience and – who knows? – perhaps we could break the journey somewhere or something like that.'

Debbie digested this. You could always rely on John to bring a practical element to anything. And his idea was catching on with her. She started to look at the details. When she replied, she was almost thinking aloud. 'I suppose we should give it a try. After all, thousands of other people do it every year, and my fears are based on no experience of long flights… And perhaps we could arrange it round Jan.' Only the previous weekend, Jan had announced that she was pregnant again.

John nodded enthusiastically. 'Of course we could.' He thought for a moment. 'I'll look into it.'

Debbie was definitely warming to the idea. 'That would be nice,' she said. Then another thought struck her. She glanced anxiously at John as she voiced her concern. 'But what about the cruise? You were looking forward to that.' They had been talking about a cruise for months now. She knew he was keen to go, and her enthusiasm had been steadily rising.

'We'll do both,' announced John. 'First a visit to your sister, and then a cruise when everything has settled down with Jan.'

Debbie jumped up. 'Oh, John, you're marvellous! Do you think we can?'

John just grinned at her. 'Of course. Why not?' he replied.

She was going to say something, but John spoke first. 'How about a cup of tea?' he asked.

'I'll make one for us.' Debbie got up, but her intention was interrupted by the telephone shrilling.

'I'll get it.' She was already heading in the direction of the hall.

'I'll make the tea then,' called John, making for the kitchen.

Debbie picked up the phone. 'Hello.'

'Mum, it's Trish.'

'Darling, how are you?'

'I'm fine.'

'And how's Don?' She almost hesitated to ask. Since her visit in November, Trish had volunteered very little information on her circumstances, a situation that worried Debbie.

'He's all right. Mum, would it be OK if I came for Christmas?'

Debbie was overwhelmed with surprise, but excited at the prospect. It was several years since Trish had spent Christmas with her. 'Darling, of course it would be. Will Don be coming as well?'

She was to be disappointed.

'No. Just me.' Trish was being irritatingly vague.

Debbie decided to be direct. 'Trish, how are things between you? You know I'm concerned about you.'

'Sorry, Mum. I'll talk about it when I see you.'

Debbie could see that she wasn't going to get anywhere at this point. She decided to change tack. 'Any idea when you'll be arriving?' she asked.

'Christmas Eve. I'll come down late afternoon. Is that all right?'

Darling, of course it is. We'll have a nice cosy evening, just the three of us. On Christmas Day we'll be going to Jan and Paul and then on Boxing Day they'll come to us. Will that be all right?'

'Fine.'

'Oh, that will be nice. I'll ring Jan and tell her. Jamie will be excited.' Debbie suddenly thought about the bit of news she had. 'Oh, by the way, Jan is expecting another baby. She told us a few days ago. I expect she'll give you all the details.'

'I expect so. I'll see you Christmas Eve, then.' Trish sounded a bit vague and it was clear that was going to be the extent of the conversation.

'OK. We'll look forward to seeing you.'

'OK, Mum. See you then.'

'Bye-bye, darling. Drive carefully on the way down.'

'Bye, Mum.'

There was a click as Trish put the phone down.

Debbie replaced the receiver and went into the kitchen, where John was making a pot of tea. He turned to face her with an enquiring look.

Debbie could hardly contain her surprise and excitement. 'You'll never guess! Trish has just announced she's coming for Christmas.'

John took the news in his stride. 'Great!' he exclaimed, reaching for the teapot.

'You don't mind, do you? After all, this is the first Christmas you and I will spend together.'

He beamed at her. He could see she was thrilled at the prospect of having all her family around her.

'Of course not!' he exclaimed. 'The more, the merrier.'

Debbie thought for a second. 'Do you know this will be the first time for three years that Trish has spent a Christmas at home?'

'How are things with Don?'

Debbie sighed. 'Not a word. When I asked Trish, she told me she would update us when she saw us. Things can't be that good if she's coming on her own.'

John looked at her. He knew she was worried about her daughter, but there was not much he could do except render support when needed. 'When is she arriving?' he asked.

Debbie gave a little sigh. 'Christmas Eve afternoon, she told me, but just in case it's later, I'll make us a cold meal so that nothing will spoil.'

John finished making the tea. For a few seconds Debbie was quiet. Suddenly she said: 'John, I've just been thinking. We really must invite Rob and Cathy for a weekend. We seem to do so much with my family. I don't want to appear to hog things with my tribe.' She looked enquiringly at him.

John smiled at her. 'I think they understand, and anyway they're both pretty busy people.' Then he added: 'But I tell you what, we'll invite them for a weekend in the New Year. They'll enjoy that.'

Debbie was enthusiastic. 'Yes, why not? Let's do that. We can take them out somewhere.'

John picked up the tea tray. 'I'll arrange it,' he said, making for the lounge.

Debbie followed him. Her thoughts turned to Trish again. She smiled as she sat down.

'Knowing Trish, I bet it'll be early evening before she gets here.'

Debbie was wrong. She and John were just relaxing after lunch on Christmas Eve, having spent most of the morning last-minute shopping, when she heard a car outside. She went to the window to investigate.

'It's Trish — she's here already,' she announced excitedly, turning to John, who had already risen from his chair. She rushed to the front door, followed by John at a more leisurely pace.

By the time Debbie opened the front door, Trish had already stopped the engine and flung open wide the door of the sports car and was in the process of swinging her legs out, exhibiting a wide expanse of tights. Debbie was surprised to see her daughter wearing a skirt instead of her business suit or jeans. Trish looked up towards the front door, where Debbie was standing sheltering from the rain that was now falling steadily. 'Hi,' she called out with a wave of her hand.

'Hi,' Debbie called back. By this time John had joined her.

Debbie was slightly amused by the next bit. She watched Trish change the flat pumps she had been wearing in the car for a pair of high-heeled shoes. Only a few months previously, Trish had ridiculed her suggestion that she wear sensible shoes for driving. Now she appeared to have adopted the idea. A suitcase was flung out of the car and John went to retrieve it. Debbie watched as Trish gave him a kiss on the cheek. One of the highlights of her marriage was that both her daughters had taken to him.

Trish arrived in front of Debbie, her hands full of bags. She planted a kiss on her mother's cheek. 'Hello, Mum. I'm not too early, am I?'

'Of course not, darling. Come in out of the wet.'

Once they were inside, Trish dumped her bags on the floor and kicked off her shoes. John had already disappeared upstairs with her suitcase. Trish glanced around and looked as if she was going to say something, but it was Debbie who spoke first. 'Have you had any lunch?'

Trish shook her head. 'I came straight here.' Then she pointed to the bags on the floor. 'They're Christmas presents. That big one is for Jamie.'

Debbie reached down to pick up the bags. 'I'll put them under the Christmas tree, if that's all right.' Then she asked: 'What about something to eat? Have you had anything since breakfast?'

Trish shook her head. 'Only a cup of coffee. I wouldn't mind something to eat.'

'Will a cheese sandwich do? Or do you want something more substantial?'

'A sandwich'll be fine. And can I have a cup of coffee?'

'Of course you can. You take the presents into the lounge and I'll get it for you. You can keep John company.' John had returned from his mission and retreated to the lounge.

Five minutes later Debbie appeared, carrying a tray. Trish was sitting on the settee with her feet tucked under her. She and John appeared to be having a discussion about cars. Trish was looking at one of the brochures John had collected. He and Debbie had promised themselves a new model in the New Year, one that Debbie could drive.

'Thanks, Mum.' Trish looked up as Debbie placed the tray close to her on the coffee table. 'I'm going to change that thing of mine,' she remarked, biting into a sandwich and still looking at the brochure.

'But you haven't had it long,' volunteered Debbie.

'I know, but I'm fed up with it and it's too expensive to run.' Trish continued to browse through the brochure while she ate.

The conversation about cars continued, mostly between Trish and John, with Debbie making a comment now and then. She was anxious to know more about Trish's marriage, but she knew she had to wait until the right time.

The opportunity came a little later when John politely and diplomatically excused himself, explaining that he had some paperwork to do. Debbie looked at her daughter, who was curled up on the settee and still looking at one of the brochures with mild interest. She voiced the question that was uppermost in her mind.

'So how are things between you and Don now?' she asked, as casually as she could muster.

Trish looked at her for an instant and then drew up her legs and clasped her hands round her knees. She replied slowly, her voice tinged with sadness. 'We've separated. I'm going to get a divorce. I've been to see a solicitor this morning. I took the day off work.' The information was brief and straight to the point.

Despite her slight shock, Debbie responded immediately. 'Oh, darling, I'm so sorry. Was there no other way?'

Trish shook her head. 'No, Mum. He got violent with me.'

This startled Debbie. 'Trish, I had no idea things were that bad. Why didn't you tell me?'

Trish glanced at her mother, and then lowered her eyes again. Her voice became tinged with emotion. 'It happened just after I came here in November. We had a blazing row and he hit me several times. I had bruises.'

'Darling, you should have said something. Where is he now?'

'I threw him out. He's gone back to his parents. I'm the bad wife.' Trish tried to smile as she looked at her mother, but it didn't really work.

Debbie was suddenly overwhelmed with compassion for her daughter. Poor Trish. She had blundered into this marriage, but Debbie knew that she and John must support her in any way they could. When she replied, her words echoed her feelings. 'Trish, you mustn't start blaming yourself. From what you tell me, it seems that you made the only decision you could. What did the solicitor say?'

'He seems to think it will be fairly straightforward as long as Don doesn't try to be too difficult.'

'Is that likely?'

'I don't know,' replied Trish gloomily.

Debbie tried to be of comfort. 'It will work out fine, you'll see.'

'I hope so.' Trish had fixed her gaze on the carpet, but suddenly she looked up at her mother, her face miserable. 'I've made a real mess of things, haven't I?'

Debbie responded quickly with as much support as she could muster. 'Of course not, darling. You weren't to know what would happen. Things will be sorted out. You'll see.'

The words seemed to comfort Trish and cheer her up a little. She gave an imitation of a smile. But it was short-lived. She addressed her mother again. 'I must look a real idiot to everybody.'

Debbie rose to the challenge. 'No, darling, you don't. You'll most likely find that people have a lot of sympathy.'

Trish gave what appeared to be a little sigh. 'Thanks for being so understanding, Mum.'

The conversation came to a halt as John reappeared. It was a cue for Debbie to resume the preparations for Christmas that had been stalled by Trish's arrival. 'Why don't you go upstairs now, unpack and perhaps get changed?' she suggested tactfully.

This appeared to be received with at least some enthusiasm. With 'OK, I need to get out of these clothes,' Trish swung her feet to the floor and jumped up from the settee. She looked around. 'I left my shoes somewhere…'

'They're in the hall,' said Debbie.

Trish departed, and Debbie gave John a knowing smile.

The rest of Christmas Eve went off a great deal better than Debbie had envisaged. After the rather gloomy start, the atmosphere cheered up considerably. It was some time before Trish reappeared, and this gave Debbie the chance to do a few of the remaining jobs she had planned.

As she was putting the finishing touches to the evening meal, Trish suddenly appeared in the kitchen. 'Can I give you a hand, Mum?'

Debbie glanced up. An offer of help from her youngest daughter was unusual. She observed that Trish had changed into slacks and a blouse, which suited her.

'Not really – it's nearly all done,' she said, drying her hands. 'I'm just going to freshen up myself now. You go and keep John company.' She scrutinised Trish's clothes. 'Darling, you look very smart. That outfit suits you.'

Trish glanced down at her clothes. 'I bought the blouse this morning. Christmas present to myself. And the shoes.' She exhibited a foot for Debbie to view more clearly.

Debbie issued the required approval. After a few more pleasantries on the subject, Trish went into the lounge and Debbie disappeared upstairs.

The rest of the evening was quite congenial. Debbie was amazed at how cheerful Trish had become. She chatted and joked with John and gave no sign of the gloominess Debbie had experienced on her arrival.

It was a pattern that continued all over Christmas. After the coolness that had existed between Trish and Jan ever since Trish's wedding, Debbie had been concerned how things would turn out when the three of them went to see Jan and Paul on Christmas Day.

She need not have worried. The day turned out to be one of surprises, starting shortly before the three of them left the house. Trish, who had been out of sight for an hour or so, had to be prompted by Debbie from the hall: 'We're ready, Trish.'

Trish appeared at the top of the stairs. Her usual home garb of slacks had been abandoned and replaced with a smart dress and matching shoes, albeit with the usual alarming heels.

The day continued to deviate from the expected. Trish surprised Debbie by having presents for everybody. She seemed to be going out of her way to be happy and cheerful, and she spent some time playing with Jamie. Debbie, who had been worrying how her two daughters would get along, was in for another shock. At one point she ventured into the kitchen to see if she could help with the food preparation only to discover, much to her surprise and delight, Trish with an apron on helping Jan. There was every indication that her two daughters were now getting along like a house on fire.

Only when the three of them returned home in the evening did Debbie realise how much of an effort Trish had had to make to remain cheerful all day. When they were sitting in the lounge after their return, Debbie noticed that she was rather subdued, barely joining in with the conversation. When Debbie went to make a drink for the three of them, after a minute or two Trish followed her into the kitchen. Debbie looked up as she entered.

'Mum, it was all right, wasn't it? I wasn't too gloomy, was I?'

Debbie stopped what she was doing. She gave her daughter a quick hug. 'Darling, you were marvellous. Thank you for making such a big effort.'

Her words seemed to pacify Trish.

'I told Jan about getting divorced, and she was quite supportive,' Trish volunteered.

'Oh, I am glad.' Debbie really meant it. The coolness between her daughters had been worrying her. She couldn't help adding for good measure: 'I told you she would be.'

'I promised I'd phone her a bit more often,' Trish remarked, picking up the tray with the drinks Debbie had prepared.

'Oh, that would be good for both of you. And you appear to have made a real hit with Jamie.' Debbie gave a little laugh as she followed Trish out of the kitchen.

'He's really quite sweet,' Trish replied over her shoulder.

Debbie breathed a sigh of relief. In spite of all her fears, the day had gone well, just as John had told her it would. She just hoped the events would herald a new era in family harmony.

Chapter 23

'Just look at the rain!' exclaimed Debbie. The taxi carrying her and John from Heathrow encountered the rainstorm as they neared Oxford. After a journey under an overcast and grey sky, suddenly the heavens opened and heavy rain bounced on the road and threatened to overload the windscreen wipers as they struggled to keep the screen clear.

'April showers in May,' responded John with a smile. 'Short and sharp. Look, there's blue sky appearing already.' He pointed to the horizon ahead, where the clouds were just breaking to reveal a glint of blue.

'It's supposed to be a good day, anyway.' The comment came from their driver.

'What's the weather been like the last couple of weeks?' asked John.

'Pretty awful for May,' replied the driver. 'Yesterday was all right, but there's been a lot of rain recently.'

He and John chatted as he steered the taxi through the early-morning commuter traffic. Debbie remained silent for the most part. For one thing, she was feeling tired. On the overnight flight she had hardly slept and now that all the excitement of the past two weeks was subsiding, the lack of sleep was beginning to overtake her.

The months since Christmas had not been without anxieties. First had been the worry over Trish. Once the process of divorce had commenced, things had not gone as smoothly as Debbie had prayed they would. It seemed that Don was not being as cooperative as Trish would have liked, and at one point she had been on the phone to

Debbie every day, complaining about the situation and leaning on her for support, which Debbie had willingly given.

Alarm had swept over Debbie when Jan's pregnancy started to develop complications. For a period there had been some concern in medical quarters, and Jan's additional visits to the clinic had meant that Debbie had been called in to look after Jamie whenever an appointment fell on a non-school day.

With all this, doubt had hung over Debbie and John's plans to visit Debbie's sister in Vancouver. Even just a few weeks before their departure they had been talking of the possibility of having to cancel the trip.

Fortunately they had managed to get away, and now the holiday was over and they were returning home. It had been an exciting but tiring fortnight. Gwen and Bobby had insisted on showing them all the sights, finding a new one each day. On top of that, the long evenings of chatter followed by the inevitable shorter nights had taken their toll of Debbie's energy, and while she had enjoyed every minute of the visit, now they were drawing near to home she welcomed the prospect of being back.

'Here we are. Home again.' John's announcement roused her from her musing. The taxi pulled up outside their house. It was still raining, but not the downpour of earlier, and blue sky was increasing.

'You go into the house and I'll bring the suitcases,' suggested John.

Debbie was glad to accept the offer. She collected her hand luggage, alighted from the taxi and accepted with her free hand the keys John held out.

By the time she had opened the door, deposited her bag in the hall and looked around, John had arrived with the suitcases. She threw open the door to the kitchen. Two neat piles of post were deposited on the table, together with a loaf of bread and a carrier bag. 'Oh, look, John!' exclaimed Debbie. 'Isn't she sweet? Jan must have been shopping for us. And I'll bet...' She opened the fridge door. 'Yes, I thought so — she bought us some milk as well.'

John grinned. 'Good girl. We can have a cup of tea.'

'Coffee is what I need. I nearly fell asleep in the taxi.'

John smiled. 'I know,' he replied. 'I could have dropped off myself.'

Debbie took control. 'Look. It's still quite early. You take the things upstairs and I'll make us some breakfast and then we can have a rest.'

'Best idea you've had all morning,' said John, jokingly.

'And then I must ring Jan and tell her we're back,' Debbie almost had to call out, as John was already halfway upstairs.

Things did not quite work out as Debbie had planned. The telephone on the bedside table woke her from a muddled dream in which she had been desperately searching for her suitcase somewhere. In a daze, she groped around, almost dropping the handset in the process.

'Hi, Mum. Welcome back. Did you have a nice time?' It was Jan.

'Darling, how nice of you to ring. Yes, we had a marvellous time. Aunt Gwen really spoiled us. We got back early this morning.'

'Yes, I know. I checked when your plane landed.'

'How have you been?' asked Debbie.

'Fine. Everything seems to be under control now. I have to go back and see the doctor next week.'

'Do you want me to look after Jamie that day?' It was half-term at his school the following week.

'Oh, please – could you, Mum?'

'Of course. I'll have recovered by then.'

'Did you get caught in the rain this morning?' asked Jan.

'We saw it from the taxi. And before I forget, it was so thoughtful of you to get us some supplies in. Thank you.'

'Oh, that's OK. I came round yesterday afternoon.'

'Well, it was very much appreciated. We were able to have some breakfast. I'll go shopping later.' The thought made Debbie glance at the bedside clock. 'Goodness!' she exclaimed. 'It's nearly one o'clock. I thought we'd only rested for about an hour.'

Jan laughed. 'Good for you, Mum.' Then she added: 'I'd better go now. I just wanted to hear how you got on. Did John enjoy the trip?'

'Absolutely,' Debbie replied. 'But it's back to routine now.'

'OK, Mum. I'll let you get on with it. I'll pop by tomorrow if you like.'

'That would be lovely. We've such a lot to tell you.'

'Bye, Mum. Till then.'

'Bye, darling. Love to Paul and Jamie.'

Debbie replaced the handset. She turned to John, who was now propped up on an elbow observing her. 'As you must have guessed, that was Jan. She's coming round tomorrow.'

'How is she now?'

'Things seem to be OK. She's going to the clinic again next week. I volunteered to look after Jamie.'

John lay back in bed and stretched. Debbie prodded him. 'Hey! Do you know what time it is? It's turned one and we'd better do some shopping, or we'll starve.'

John made a face at her. 'Slave driver,' he joked.

'I can't understand why you never did it before.' Madge munched the last of a biscuit.

Debbie picked up her mug of coffee from the worktop and joined her at the kitchen table. She glanced down at the brochure Madge was looking at.

'You mean go on a cruise?' she asked.

Madge finally put the brochure down. 'Sure. It's the ideal way for a single person to go on holiday,' she replied casually, helping herself to another biscuit.

Debbie nibbled a biscuit, more to keep Marge company than anything else. She considered for a moment. 'I never really gave it any thought,' she commented vaguely. 'But now we're a team, John would like to go and I'm getting quite keen on the idea.'

Three weeks had passed since she and John had returned from Canada. A few days previously John had returned home with cruise brochures for them to look at. These had been lying on the kitchen table when Madge arrived unannounced.

'Where are you going?' asked Madge.

'We haven't really decided yet,' Debbie replied, beginning to wish Madge hadn't seen the brochures.

'I might go again this year,' was Madge's next remark, as she took a swig of her coffee, retaining a fleeting glance at the brochure she had just put down. Suddenly she looked straight at Debbie. 'You know what? I've just had a thought. Why don't I come with you? I could show you the ropes.' She continued to gaze at Debbie, clearly enthralled by her idea.

For a second Debbie was in a panic. Anything but that, she thought. The idea of being on another holiday with Madge did not even bear thinking about, and as to Madge tagging onto John and her... She struggled to get out of the difficult situation.

'Well, as things are at the present with Jan, we've not made a definite decision,' she replied as casually as she could, thankful that the answer had come into her head. It was true: Jan was again experiencing problems with her pregnancy.

Madge looked as if she was going to reply, but the conversation was brought to a halt with John's arrival in the kitchen. He greeted Madge.

'Coffee, darling?' asked Debbie, already getting up from her chair.

'Great,' he replied, sliding into a chair opposite Madge.

'Been to your allotment?' asked Madge.

'Yes, just been sorting things out,' John replied. 'It could do with a bit more sunshine,' he added, nodding in the direction of the window and indicating the grey sky.

'How many hours a week do you spend on it?' quizzed Madge.

He thought a few seconds. 'It depends. This week I've done two mornings, about two hours each time.'

'Isn't it more convenient and more efficient to go and buy your bits of vegetables at the supermarket?'

John laughed and shook his head. 'Not a bit,' he replied, chuckling. 'Besides,' he added, 'it tastes nicer straight from the soil.'

'And there's exercise in the fresh air to take into account,' Debbie chipped in, bringing John's mug of coffee to the table.

Madge sniffed in disbelief. 'I can think of better ways of getting exercise,' she retorted, effectively ending the conversation on that topic.

Debbie was going to reply, but it was Madge who spoke again. 'I hear you guys have bought a new car.' The comment was directed at John. Debbie had already told her that they had purchased a new model before their trip to Canada.

John nodded. 'Yes, that's right. We decided to make a change and just have one smaller car.'

'What make is it?' Madge wanted to know.

'Another Ford. We don't really need a large car and I wanted to get one Debbie was happy with.'

'And one that would use less petrol,' Debbie piped up.

Madge ignored the remark. She made a face. 'Give me a big car any time,' she replied.

'Like the tank you've got,' observed Debbie, laughing.

'You can't beat a 4x4,' Madge replied, as if that was the last word on the subject.

The conversation continued for another ten minutes, mostly about trivial matters, with Debbie greatly relieved that Madge didn't get round to the subject of cruises again. At last Madge looked at her watch and said she would have to go. Debbie saw her to the door and waved her off.

When she returned to the kitchen, John was washing up the mugs and plates. He glanced round briefly as she entered the door. 'Everything OK with Madge?' he asked, smiling at her.

His question sparked a strong reaction. 'That woman is impossible at times,' she announced.

'What's she been up to now?' John grinned. He knew how Madge had a habit of ruffling Debbie's feathers.

'Of course she had to see those cruise brochures, and that was it. She actually suggested that she come on a cruise with us!'

John shook his head. 'No, thank you,' he said.

'But the cheek of it!' insisted Debbie. For good measure she added: 'If I go on a cruise, I want to enjoy it without Madge around.'

'I guess she gets a bit lonely at times,' suggested John.

'I know,' replied Debbie, grabbing a tea towel. Look what she's missed,' she added breezily, giving him a peck on the cheek.

'You know, I've been thinking.' Debbie reappeared in the lounge carrying two mugs of cocoa, their late evening nightcap.

John looked up from his book enquiringly.

She put the mugs down on the coffee table and sat down on the settee opposite him. 'We really ought to invite Rob and Cathy again for the weekend soon. We haven't seen them since Rob's birthday.'

John picked up his mug. 'You're right. I'll give Rob a ring tomorrow and arrange something.'

'If they came Friday evening, we could take them out for a meal and then we could all go out for the day on Saturday,' Debbie suggested, taking a sip of her cocoa.

'Good idea,' John responded, and then he had another thought. 'What about taking the whole family out for a meal on Sunday, before they go back home?'

Debbie jumped at the idea. 'Oh, that would be lovely!' She made a face. 'I'll get out of doing any cooking.'

Their planning was interrupted by the telephone ringing. Debbie looked at her watch. 'Nearly half past ten. Who on earth can that be?' Then a thought struck her. 'Oh, I know. It'll be Trish. I'll get it.'

She picked up the telephone.

'Mum. It's me, Trish.'

'Hello, darling. How are things?'

'Fine. Am I too late for you?'

Debbie laughed. 'Another ten minutes, and you might have been. We were just having a mug of cocoa before going to bed.'

'Mum, I'm dreadfully sorry. I didn't realise it was so late.'

'It's OK, darling. How are things going now? With the divorce, I mean.'

'Great. Don's caved in at last. The solicitor seems to think it'll be quite straightforward now.'

'Oh, darling, that is good news. I really am pleased.' Debbie allowed the relief to filter into her reply. She had been worried about this divorce and the way it had been going, with Don demanding more than his fair share.

'So am I.' Trish gave a little laugh. Then she continued. 'Mum...' She hesitated. 'Mum, do you remember you said you might be able to help...?' she paused again. 'With the money, I mean.'

Debbie rose to the occasion. 'Of course, dear. Let me know when you want it.'

'Mum, you're an angel. The only other way for me would have been to get a bank loan.' Trish was ecstatic. For good measure she added: 'Or sell this flat.'

'No. Don't do that. I'll help you.'

'That would be fantastic.' Trish was clearly relieved. Before Debbie could say anything else, she spoke again. 'Mum, it's getting late. How would it be if I came and spent a weekend again soon?' There was optimism in her voice.

'Darling, of course you can. Just let us know when.' Debbie suddenly had visions of Trish wanting to come on the same weekend as Rob and Cathy.

'I will. I'll let you go to bed now, Mum.'

'OK, dear. Remember to let us know when.'

'Bye, Mum. Thanks a million.'

'Bye-bye, dear.'

Debbie put down the phone. 'That was Trish,' she said.

John smiled. 'I guessed that,' he replied.

Debbie took another sip of cocoa. 'She was worried about money for the divorce. You remember I promised to help her? I think she just wanted reassurance that I would still do that.'

John smiled again. 'That's what mums are for, aren't they?'

Debbie sighed. 'I suppose so.' Then she remembered the other bit of news. 'She's going to come for the weekend again soon.'

'Great!'

Debbie sighed again. 'You know, John, once Jan has had this baby and Trish has got through this divorce, we can go on that cruise. Just the two of us, and I'm going to enjoy it.'

Unfortunately, things did not work out as she hoped.

Chapter 24

The warm night air brushed Debbie's cheek as they walked the length of the ship's deck, watching the twinkling lights of the distant shore. They ambled along slowly, silent in each other's company, enjoying a midnight stroll before turning in for the night. John's arm encircled Debbie's waist. He was in his evening dress suit, and she wore her pale blue cocktail dress. She carried her sandals in her hand, enjoying the feel of the ship's deck beneath her feet.

Instinctively, they paused at the rail of the ship and savoured their surroundings. Debbie placed a hand on the rail. She could just feel the vibration of the ship's engines as it ploughed almost silently through the Mediterranean waters; it was a unique and not unpleasant sensation.

John turned to her, smiling. 'Happy, darling?'

Debbie looked up at him. Her face was radiant. She nodded. 'I'd forgotten how it felt to be so happy,' she replied softly. Then she added heartily: 'I feel sixteen again.'

'Sixteen, with sixty years' experience, I hope,' John joked.

Debbie gazed up at the stars in the night sky. 'I feel so contented and so romantic. I wish it could go on for ever,' she murmured.

Almost twelve months had slipped past since their return from Vancouver. Their plans to go on a cruise the previous year had come to nought. First there had been Jan's pregnancy and Debbie's duties as mother and grandmother following the birth of Emma, her first granddaughter. Then there had been the trauma of Trish's divorce, which had lingered on. Debbie's counselling skills had been required at times, together with the financial support she had promised. Then autumn had gradually turned into winter and they had abandoned the idea for that year.

When in the new year Debbie had caught a bout of flu, which had laid her low for almost two weeks, John had insisted that they book a cruise as something to look forward to, and Debbie had been more than willing to agree. The past few months had taxed her energy and she felt she needed a break to get away from the demands of being both mother and grandmother. The thought of being far away somewhere with just John for company appealed to her greatly.

The sixteen-night cruise was in its fifth day. Already they had visited Madeira and hurtled down the hillside on a wooden sledge, sliding over the cobblestones. They had visited Gibraltar, explored the Rock and seen the apes. They had wandered through the small town and enjoyed a lingering coffee in the warm sunshine outside one of the cafés, watching the world go by. Now they were heading for Casablanca.

'Where do you think those lights are?' Debbie asked.

'Somewhere on the coast of Africa, I guess,' replied John. He added: 'I was bottom of the class at geography.'

'Oh, John, I bet you weren't! I was,' laughed Debbie.

They stood there for a while longer, enjoying the peace and tranquillity of the night. They had the deck to themselves. Most of the passengers were either already in bed or still lingering in the ship's lounges or bars.

A sound behind them disturbed their solitude. A couple of about their own age were bearing down on them. 'Here come the Bawley-Smiths,' Debbie whispered.

The Bawley-Smiths shared a table with them. Albert was a retired civil servant and sported a very handsome handlebar moustache. He had an extremely military appearance and John had immediately nicknamed him 'The Colonel', explaining to Debbie that Albert reminded him of an officer he had encountered during his National Service. Melanie Bawley-Smith appeared to have plenty to say on most subjects. She had a rather loud, artificially cultured voice, which was monotonous at times. John and Debbie had early on in the cruise decided to make a point of avoiding sharing any more of the couple's company than they were forced to.

The Bawley-Smiths walked slowly up to them. Melanie clutched her husband's arm and beamed at them.

'Marvellous evening, what?' said Albert.

John smiled and nodded in agreement, but before he could answer, Melanie piped up. 'Enjoying an evening stroll before bedtime?' She smiled condescendingly at Debbie.

'It's so heavenly out here,' Debbie replied.

'Oh, but it's not like the Caribbean, is it, Albert?' Melanie cooed.

Albert ignored his wife's prompting and addressed John again. 'Been playing bridge,' he announced. 'Do you play?'

John shook his head. 'I'm afraid not. I've never learnt.'

Albert grunted. 'Damn pity.'

His wife took over. She smiled at Debbie again. 'What a shame. We could have got together. We couldn't live without our bridge, could we, Albert?'

Albert said nothing, and before Debbie or John could come up with a reply, Melanie glanced down at Debbie's shoeless feet and the sandals she carried in her hand. 'Having problems with your feet, dear?' she asked, adding for good measure: 'We saw you dancing.'

'No, it just feels nice to walk without shoes,' Debbie replied truthfully.

Melanie was undeterred. 'You really shouldn't dance in high heels at your age. You could have a nasty accident, particularly at sea,' she advised.

'Yes, I know. But I am careful,' Debbie answered. But something made her slip a sandal first on one foot and then on the other.

Melanie beamed at them. 'Well, we're going to turn in now. Don't forget the ship's in port again tomorrow and it will be a long day. We girls have to get our beauty sleep.' She gave Debbie a knowing look.

After the Bawley-Smiths had departed and were out of hearing range, John turned to Debbie and grinned. 'Thank goodness we don't play bridge,' he observed.

Debbie was indignant. 'What cheek! Talking to me about wearing high heels like that!'

John laughed. 'You sound like Trish,' he remarked.

'Hey, whose side are you on?' Debbie exclaimed and then laughed.

John kissed her. 'Yours, of course.'

She gave a gentle sigh and once again looked up at the starlit sky. 'It really is heavenly out here, feeling the ship glide through the water and watching the land drift past... And the stars seem to be brighter than at home.'

'That's because there's no distraction from other lights like there is in a town,' he replied, joining her gaze at the stars overhead.

'John, you are so knowledgeable about everything,' Debbie said softly, her eyes still distant.

He chuckled. 'Master of useless information,' he replied.

Debbie shook her head in disagreement. Her next remark was completely unrelated. She continued to look into the distance as she spoke. 'You know, if anybody had told me a few years ago that I would be doing all this now, I would have told them they were completely mad.'

John put his arm round her shoulders. 'Glad now you cut your foot on the beach at Brillport?' he asked.

Debbie turned to look at him. He was smiling at her. 'It was worth it a thousand times over.' She paused and then continued slowly. 'I was walking along, feeling lonely and sorry for myself and suddenly I felt a stab of pain. And then you appeared. My saviour.'

John grinned at her. 'Cinderella on the beach.'

Debbie placed her arm on his. She looked up at him again. 'Isn't life strange? Just a few minutes, or even seconds sometimes, can completely change your life. If I hadn't cut my foot that day, we would probably never have met, or perhaps we would have passed each other on the beach and just said a polite good morning to each other.'

John was more serious now. 'I watched you walk away. You looked so lonely. I thought about you a few times that day. I wondered if you were married, but somehow I thought you weren't.' He took Debbie's free hand and gently squeezed it.

Debbie gave him a coy little look and smiled again. 'I thought about you all day. I think I was attracted to you immediately I saw you. You seemed so kind and considerate. Quite different from some men I know. I just hoped I'd see you again, and then next day I did.'

'Thanks to the rain,' he interjected.

'And the Beach Café,' she added.

For a few minutes there was silence between them as they stood and watched the night. It was Debbie who broke it by glancing at her watch and exclaiming: 'Gosh, look at the time! It's turned midnight – already a new day and we haven't been to bed yet.'

John laughed. 'Life at sea,' he said. 'Still, Melanie is right about one thing – we have a long day ahead and I guess we should get some sleep.'

Debbie sighed. 'You're absolutely right. In spite of the romantic night, I'm beginning to feel tired.'

They took one last look at the scene around them and then walked slowly hand in hand towards the door leading to the interior of the ship. They paused just once, as he gently kissed her.

Chapter 25

The beginning of the day followed the pattern of many others. Debbie woke up to the distinctive sound of the newspaper being delivered through the letter box and landing on the hall carpet. John still slept peacefully beside her. Minor noises rarely disturbed him.

She slipped out of bed and made her way quietly to the bathroom. It was their usual routine. John would take his time getting up and then spending time in the bathroom while Debbie made the breakfast.

Today she was keen to get downstairs as soon as possible and get everything under way without any delay, as they planned to go out early and do their weekly food shopping in Wickton, a small town about twelve miles away. Wickton had been one of the additional pleasures they had discovered since buying a new car. Initially they had done a run there to let Debbie get used to the controls, and one of the finds had been the quiet supermarket in the centre. They also liked the interesting shops, and an added bonus had been finding a pleasant little coffee shop aptly named The Coffee Pot in the main street. A break for coffee after doing their shopping turned a weekly task into a pleasant interlude.

Almost a month had slipped by since they returned invigorated from their cruise. It had taken them several days to get back into their normal routine. Life on the ocean wave agreed with the two of them and, as Debbie put it, they both felt ten years younger. There was even the thought of doing it again sometime.

It was close to eight o'clock when Debbie arrived in the kitchen. She set the kettle to boil and then went into the hall to fetch the newspaper. She glanced at the headlines on the way back to the kitchen, but they did not inspire her. As she put the newspaper down on the worktop, she looked out of the window at the tiny garden, which was already illuminated by the June sunshine. The weather forecast was for a bright sunny day; it would be a pleasant drive over to Wickton.

She had the breakfast ready when John appeared. He had collected the post on the way through the hall and held a bundle of letters in his hand. He planted a kiss on Debbie's cheek. 'Good morning, Mrs Hammond,' he said.

'Good morning, darling.' Debbie hugged him briefly.

Formalities over, John sat down at the table and studied the post as he sorted it out.

'Anything interesting?' Debbie enquired, bringing their bowls of muesli to the table and sitting down.

John responded by pushing several letters across the table to her. 'Two for you, a couple of bills, and a circular asking us if we want to sell our house.'

Debbie laughed. 'No, thank you.' She paused for a second and then, looking at John, voiced her thoughts. 'You know, John, I've really got quite fond of this house.'

John nodded, his mouth full of muesli. He took a few seconds to acknowledge verbally. 'I know what you mean,' he said eventually. 'I don't miss my flat one bit.'

Debbie was more reflective. 'I used to think when I lived at the other house, this is it. I'll finish my days here. I never even dreamed I would one day get married again. And then I met you.'

John looked at her, a smile of amusement on his face. 'And then found an old widower.'

Debbie made a face at him. 'More tea?' she asked, teapot already in her hand.

John pushed his cup towards her. 'Please,' he replied.

Debbie filled his cup and replenished her own. She set the teapot down on its stand again. She glanced up, suddenly remembering something. 'Oh, I forgot to tell you. When you were out on the allotment yesterday Trish rang.'

'Oh, how is she getting on?'

'She seems to be much happier now the divorce is behind her. I'm just hoping she'll find somebody nice and settle down.'

'Is she still coming for the weekend?' A provisional arrangement had been made the previous week.

Debbie nodded. 'That was partly the reason for her call – to confirm that we were still expecting her.' She thought for an instant. 'Perhaps over the weekend we'll learn more about what she's up to now.'

John could tell from the tone of her voice that she was still worried. 'I expect it'll all work out in the end,' he replied encouragingly.

Debbie nodded. 'I hope so.' She got up and picked up a pen and a scrap of paper from the worktop. Scrutinising it she returned to the table. 'You know, there was something I was going to add to our shopping list and I didn't put it down at the time. Now I can't remember what it was.' She looked at John for inspiration.

He grinned at her. 'Baking powder,' he replied.

Debbie gave a little sigh. 'Oh, of course. How on earth did I forget that?' She scribbled the evasive item on her list. She looked up at John enquiringly. 'How did you know that?'

John grinned again. 'You mentioned it when you were baking yesterday.'

Debbie sighed again, this time with more amusement. 'Oh well, thank goodness you have a good memory. It'll teach me to put it on the list straight away next time.'

Two hours later, their shopping over, they walked back to the car, each carrying a bag.

'Do we need to go anywhere else?' Debbie asked.

'I just want to nip into the camera shop,' John replied, glancing at his watch, though there was no urgency in their excursion that day.

Debbie quickly turned to him. 'Look, you go there. I can put the shopping in the car.' She attempted to relieve him of the bag he was carrying.

He hesitated for a second, but Debbie insisted. She knew he liked chatting to the owner of the small camera shop in Wickton about matters that were way over her head, and after all it wasn't very far to the car. She took control by grasping the handles of John's bag. 'It's quite all right,'she said cheerily. 'I can manage, and we'll meet up in the coffee shop.'

John relented. He reluctantly relinquished the bag. 'OK, if you're sure. First one at The Coffee Pot does the ordering,' he added.

'See you later.' Debbie continued on her own, vaguely aware of John disappearing back down the alleyway that led to the main street. She walked slowly on towards the nearby car park. It was a beautiful sunny morning and it was pleasant just to absorb the sights and sounds around her. It only took a few minutes to reach the small, secluded car park, which was for the most part surrounded by a high wall overlooked by trees. When they first discovered it, John had remarked: 'You might be miles from anywhere, not close to the centre of a small town.' As she walked further into the parking area, Debbie was surprised to discover that in spite of it being mid-morning she appeared to be the only human being amid the parked cars. Only the singing of the birds close by interacted with the sound of the traffic in the distance.

But the tranquil atmosphere was suddenly broken by the noise of an object striking metal. Debbie's eyes traced the direction of the sound. The sight that met her gaze was disturbing. Two boys of perhaps ten or eleven had suddenly appeared and were idly strolling among the cars. One of them had a stick with which he was hitting the bonnets. Debbie's reaction was immediate; the boy was moving dangerously close to their car. In spite of the load she was carrying, she hurried over to the two boys. They looked as surprised to see her as she had been to hear and see them.

'Stop it! Stop it this minute! You'll damage the cars.' Her voice was raised in the hope that her tone would deter the two from their escapade.

The smaller boy, who was brandishing the stick, merely grinned at her and recommenced his activity. Bang. The stick resounded on another car.

'Stop it! I'll call a policeman if you don't stop.' Debbie suddenly felt a bit helpless. The boy gave her a 'stop me if you can' look. His companion, who looked a bit older, simply scowled at her.

Debbie moved slightly nearer to the boy with the stick. It was the wrong thing to do. He turned and made as if to poke her with it. Debbie instinctively tried to grab it. She managed to catch hold of the end, and for a full two seconds there was a tug of war between them. Then suddenly the boy let go of the stick. With Debbie firmly holding it, it tapped him smartly on the arm. He gave a roar of shock and disapproval.

'Leave him alone.' The other boy joined in for the first time.

'Look, I'm dreadfully sorry. I didn't mean to hit you.' Debbie attempted to make amends by taking hold of the boy's arm to inspect it, but he pulled away and swore at her. She was thankful that the damage appeared to be negligible, and was trying desperately to think of a way to rectify the situation, when a fourth person joined them.

'What's going on here? You leave my kid alone.'

Debbie turned to see a rather unsavoury-looking young man standing glowering at her. 'Are these your sons?' she asked him.

'Yeah. What of it?' The reply was hardly encouraging, but Debbie persevered. She took a deep breath. 'Well, you know you should keep an eye on what they're doing. They've been damaging cars in this car park.'

'Yeah? Who says they have?'

Debbie's cheeks began to flush with anger, but she was determined to try and remain calm and keep the situation under control. 'I do. I saw them.' She strove to keep the emotion out of her voice.

Her words seemed only to increase the man's aggression. Suddenly he pushed his face into hers. His breath smelt of beer. 'Yeah? You stupid old woman. You should be put away. The law should do something about people like you.' The words were accompanied by a kind of leer. The two boys looked at Debbie with a 'that'll teach you' smirk on their faces.

Debbie fought her rising anger and feeling of frustration. The man was impossible to talk to. Now her only wish was to try and retreat from the confrontation without further incident. She only hoped she would be able to do that. Desperately she wished someone else was around.

The smaller boy complained to his father. 'She hit me.'

'Yeah? Where?' The father looked at his son and then glowered at Debbie.

'It was an accident. I'm sorry.'

The man turned the full force of his anger on her. 'You b—' he swore at her. 'I'll have the law on you. You're not safe to be out on the streets.'

Debbie's heart was thumping, but she tried to keep calm. 'Look. I'm dreadfully sorry, but it was an accident. I have apologised and I don't think there is any serious injury. It was only a light tap.'

'Yeah? Who says?'

'It really was an accident – and it was your son's fault entirely,' she protested.

'Clear off, before I get really mad.' The man swore at her again.

It was an impossible situation. Debbie knew she couldn't make any headway with the man. Mustering as much dignity as possible, she picked up her bags and retreated from the scene of the conflict. It was only a few steps to her car, and she desperately hoped the trio would not follow her or try and interfere with her any further. Tremors of fear were running through her body now. She couldn't remember ever having such a conflict with anybody like that before. It made the whole morning seem unreal.

She placed the bags of shopping in the car boot and shut the lid. The habit of many years made her attempt to unlock the driver's door, completely forgetting that the car had remote-control locking. Her hand was shaking as recollection dawned and she corrected her mistake. The man and the two boys were still hanging around watching her. She felt uneasy. She didn't like them being able to identify her car, but there was nothing she could do about it. John would be waiting for her in the coffee shop. She wished he were there to support her. She heard the boy still complaining to his father.

She left the car park, not daring to look round to see if the three were still watching her. The incident had affected her badly, partly because it had all happened suddenly, quite out of the blue, and her inability to sort out the situation had left her feeling vulnerable. She was still shaky when she arrived at The Coffee Pot a few minutes later. John was already there when she entered its cosy, olde worlde interior. It was a popular place and by mid-morning it was already crowded, but John had found an unoccupied table in a corner.

'Hello there. What kept you so long?'

Debbie said nothing. She sat down quietly.

'I'll get the coffee,' John announced, seeming not to notice her distress.

Debbie nodded and feigned a faint smile. John disappeared to the counter, leaving her to ponder over the events in the car park.

She was sitting glumly staring down at the table when John came back with the coffee. He placed the cups on the table and sat down.

He glanced at Debbie, conscious that she had said nothing since joining him. He had been watching her from the counter. She looked miserable.

He leaned over to her. 'You're very quiet. Anything wrong?'

Debbie continued to gaze down for an instant. Then she looked straight at him. When she spoke her voice was shaky.

'John, I've had the most awful experience.'

'What happened?' John was anxious now. He had never seen her looking so disturbed.

Debbie was now eager to unload. 'Well, it was in the car park, just after you left for the camera shop...'

John listened intently, asking a question here and there as she related her experience. When she had finished, she looked at him again. 'John, it was so awful. I've never had anything like that happen to me before.'

He nodded. 'Sign of the times, I suppose,' he replied. Then, seeing that she was clearly still concerned, his thoughts turned to practical matters. 'Perhaps we should try and find this guy. Get the police involved or something.' He looked anxiously at Debbie.

She immediately shook her head. 'No. Let it go. I just want to forget it all now that I've told you.'

'I guess that's the best thing to do.'

Chapter 26

Debbie tried hard to forget the incident, but it wasn't easy. Throughout the rest of the day, while she did her best to make things appear quite normal, the conflict with the young father and his sons kept coming back to trouble her. Quite out of the blue when she was busy doing something else, the episode in the car park would suddenly appear in her thoughts. She would go through the sequence of events over and over again and wonder if she could have handled things any better. John was as supportive as usual, but for his sake she tried hard not to appear to dwell on the subject, and for the most part she kept her stress to herself.

The next day she woke up, tired and with a headache, after a troubled sleep in which she had been plagued with dreams that did not seem to make sense. It was raining and John's plans to go to the allotment were thrown into disarray. Debbie had been intending to visit Jan and baby Emma while he was out, but John's decision to stay at home made her hesitate to do her own thing. In the end John retreated to the den, as they called the small room with the computer and the desk. Once he had settled, Debbie made up her mind, and with his blessing she departed for Jan's house.

The hour she spent with Jan and Emma took Debbie's thoughts away from the previous day's unpleasant encounter for a short while. It was several weeks since she had seen them, and as usual Jan had plenty of news to relate. Jamie was at school and Emma was now more alert and demanded a watchful pair of eyes every waking minute. Debbie had already decided not to tell her family about the incident in the car park. She knew that to do so would spark off a discussion and bring back the events just when she was trying to forget them.

It was after midday when she returned home. The rain had now cleared and a bright sunny afternoon had appeared. John, who had spent the morning doing paperwork, decided over lunch that as it was now fine he would go to the allotment after all. He suggested that Debbie join him, but she said she would prefer to have a restful afternoon at home, perhaps reading or listening to music – a rare opportunity to do either.

It was well past two when John finally departed. Debbie washed up the few dishes and then retreated to the lounge and took up *The Daily Telegraph*. Perhaps today she might get to read a little more of it rather than just scanning the pages as she usually did. She settled down quietly in the armchair. At one point she got up to make a mug of tea for herself and then returned to her solitude.

It was the sound of the doorbell that alerted her to everyday life. She felt irritated by the interruption. It had to happen just when she was enjoying a bit of relaxation. She wondered if it might be Madge; she was due to make one of her intermittent visits, though Debbie's instinct made her think it was more likely to be somebody ever hopeful that they could sell her something she didn't want. She and John had a house rule about not buying anything at the door. With a sigh she made her way to the front door. Before she got there the bell rang again, this time long and urgently.

As soon as she opened the door, she knew something was wrong. Two police officers, one male and one female, stood on the doorstep, and parked on the road behind them she could see a police car.

Before she could say anything, the male officer addressed her. 'Mrs Deborah May Hammond?' he asked.

Debbie was surprised to hear her full name. It made the question formal and alarming. 'Yes,' she replied simply.

The officer glanced at a notebook he had produced from his pocket and then gave her his full attention again, scrutinising her as he spoke. 'We're making some enquiries about an incident that took place in the High Street car park in Wickton yesterday morning at approximately eleven o'clock. Can you confirm that you were there at that time?'

Panic and alarm suddenly enveloped Debbie. The police were asking about her encounter with the two boys. Her desire that it would all be forgotten was not going to be satisfied. She managed a reply. 'Yes, I was there about that time.'

'It's been alleged that you were directly involved in the incident. Is that correct?'

Debbie felt sick. Somebody must have informed the police. But who? And why? She knew she would have to explain her involvement with great care, but for the moment she was completely devastated. How could something so trivial involve the police? She wished John were there. Desperately she tried to appear calm and answer the question. The two police officers studied her intently as she strove to find a suitable answer.

'I had an argument with two young boys and their father.' She tried to keep her answer simple.

'Can you tell us what the argument was about?' The female officer spoke for the first time.

Debbie felt panicky. What could she say? Clearly the police had information from somewhere. Now she was being asked to justify herself. Her brain raced. What could she say? How did you explain such an incident effectively? She took a deep breath to try and steady her nerves. 'I caught the two boys hitting cars with a stick. I told them to stop and then their father seemed to appear from nowhere. He really was most unpleasant.'

'The father wasn't there when you first spoke to the boys?' asked the male officer.

Debbie shook her head. 'No. He came later.'

The man looked at her intently, as if he was trying to read her thoughts. He spoke again. 'It has been alleged that you struck one of the boys on the arm, with a stick or some other object. Is that correct?'

The question threw Debbie completely off balance. Up until then she had assumed that the police had called to ask her to be a witness. Now the realisation of what was happening struck her. Tremors of fear and intimidation raced through her body. She was being accused over such a small incident. It was almost ludicrous, but the police officers in front of her clearly thought otherwise. What could she say?

To Debbie it seemed like minutes before she replied, but in reality she knew it was merely seconds. All the time the two officers watched her impassively and waited for her to answer. When she did, it was in a concerned and worried tone. 'Well, yes. But it was an accident. I was trying to take the stick away from the boy and he suddenly let go of it and it hit him on the arm. It really was an accident.'

The officer appeared unmoved by her anguish. His eyes studied her. 'But you admit striking the boy on the arm?' he asked.

Flustered now, Debbie tried desperately to improve on her previous reply. 'Yes, but he let go of the stick suddenly,' she pleaded. Then as an afterthought she added: 'If he hadn't let go of the stick, it wouldn't have happened.' She looked at the officer, desperately hoping that he might understand.

Instead he asked: 'Were there any other witnesses to the incident that you were aware of?'

Debbie shook her head. 'I didn't see any,' she replied.

It was the female officer who spoke next. She turned to Debbie. 'Do you have any children, Mrs Hammond?' she asked.

Debbie was puzzled by the question. She couldn't see what it had to do with the current situation. Surprised, she answered: 'Yes, I have two girls. They are grown up now.'

'Did you smack them when they were small?'

Debbie was on the edge of becoming flustered. 'Well… yes… I might have given them a tap when they were small if they were naughty.'

'Did you do that on a regular basis?'

'Of course not. It was a rare occurrence.' Debbie felt upset by the question.

The young male officer looked at her indifferently. His next words sent a sense of panic through her. 'We shall have to ask you to accompany us to the station to answer a few more questions and make a statement.'

His request threw Debbie into a panic. 'Can't you do that here?' she asked hopefully.

'I'm afraid not, Mrs Hammond,' replied the female officer.

Debbie was completely flustered and showed it. The woman recognised her distress and addressed her now in a more caring manner. 'Do you want to take your handbag or anything? And perhaps you'd like to tell your family where you are.'

Disorientated, Debbie tried desperately to regain control. 'I should tell my husband where I'm going,' she replied miserably.

The officers watched as she collected her handbag and retrieved her mobile phone from its interior. With trembling hands she called John's number. There was no answer. 'I can't get through,' she appealed to the two officers.

'You can try again later,' the female officer replied reassuringly.

Like a zombie Debbie allowed herself to be ushered from the house. The two police officers led her to their car and installed her in the back seat. A final humiliation for Debbie was that one of the neighbours saw all that was happening. She wondered how many more were aware of what was going on in the normally quiet street. She hoped nobody would tell John what they had seen before she could speak to him herself. She wished he was with her now. Never had she needed his calm support and strength so much.

Her escorts settled themselves into the front seats. The male officer drove. The female officer turned round and instructed Debbie to fasten her seat belt, which in her fluster she had forgotten to do. She meekly complied with the request, angry with herself for the oversight. They must think I'm a complete idiot, she thought.

She could remember little of the drive: how long it took or where she was taken. The only sounds in the car were the occasional word or two between the two police officers and the constant interruptions from their radio. She sat alone with her thoughts. She could scarcely comprehend the change that had taken place in such a short time. Not more than an hour ago she had been quietly sitting, relaxing and enjoying a few minutes to herself. Now she was being driven in a police car to answer questions about an incident she had been trying to forget.

Suddenly the journey came to an end. She just had time to see the illuminated sign outside the police station before the car turned down a passageway leading to the rear of the building and stopped in a yard where several other police cars and vans were parked. The police officers got out and the man opened her door. 'Will you get out, please?' The request was curt.

Debbie complied and the three of them walked into the building, the woman leading Debbie by the arm. It made her feel uncomfortable, almost as if she were a prisoner.

They walked down a corridor into what was clearly the main entrance to the station. There was the usual counter and beyond it a wide area with a few seats, where several people were already sitting or standing. The two officers ushered Debbie into this area and asked her to wait. They then retreated behind the counter and talked to another officer. Debbie did not catch all of the conversation but she did hear the third officer say that the interview room was in use. Then her two escorts disappeared.

She did not have to wait long. Within a few minutes the officer who had driven the car appeared again and instructed her to accompany him. They walked through a door and along a corridor and then a door was thrown open.

'Will you wait in here, please?' The request was firm but polite.

As Debbie obediently stepped through the open door, she realised with a shock that she was being put in a cell, just like a prisoner. She was barely conscious of the door being closed behind her and the departure of her escort. When asked afterwards, she could not remember whether the cell door was locked or not. The trauma of her situation seeped into her. She tried to answer the questions that racked her confused brain. Why was she being treated this way for such a trivial encounter? The police officers had told her they just wanted her to answer some more questions and make a statement, yet now she found herself in a cell. For the second time in the last hour or so she found herself shaking. She tried desperately to keep calm. She took in her surroundings. The cell had bare walls and a solid floor. A small barred window almost at ceiling level let in daylight. There was no furnishing except a fitted bed with a black shiny mattress against one wall. A toilet pan without a seat was the only other item.

For what seemed a long time Debbie stood in the centre of the cell, traumatised and disorientated. Then, as there was nowhere else to sit, she perched on the edge of the bed. Seeing the toilet made her realise that she could do with its facilities, but she was worried the police officer might come back suddenly. She could hear sounds of activity outside the cell. She wished John were there, and thinking of him made her take out her mobile phone and try his number again. Once again there was no answer. It made her all the more miserable. Oh, why didn't he have his mobile turned on? There was nothing she could do except wait.

Chapter 27

Alone with her thoughts, Debbie had no idea how long she spent in the cell. It might have only been five minutes; it might have been longer. The situation she was in seemed to dispense with time. Suddenly the door of the cell was flung open and the young police officer stood there again.

'Will you come this way, please?'

They were words Debbie welcomed. She immediately jumped up and walked past the police officer as he held open the door for her. He led her along what seemed to her to be a maze of corridors and then threw open a door with the sign 'Interview Room' on it. Debbie caught a glimpse of a much brighter room with a table and chairs. The officer indicated that this was where she was to go, but the sign on the door opposite reminded Debbie of her need. 'May I use the toilet?' she asked.

Her escort nodded assent and Debbie disappeared into the little room. A few minutes later she reappeared, greatly relieved. She was ushered into the interview room, and at the same time two more officers appeared, a slightly older man and a young woman. Her escort closed the door and disappeared.

'Please sit down.' It was the man who spoke.

Debbie obediently complied. She was trying hard to remain calm and composed, but the apprehension and stress of her predicament were only just below the surface.

The officer glanced at his papers and then looked straight at her. 'Mrs Hammond, do you understand why you are here? You have been brought in to answer some questions and complete a statement regarding the incident yesterday in Wickton High Street car park.'

'Yes. The officers who brought me here explained that.' Debbie surprised herself by giving such a calm reply.

The policeman addressed her again. 'I'd like to make it clear to you that at this stage you are not under arrest. A complaint has been made and we are duty bound to investigate.'

His words were of small comfort to Debbie. The very word 'arrest' threw her into a panic and for an instant she could not comprehend what was happening to her. Everything seemed so unreal. To be here in a police station answering questions over such a trivial incident…

Something made her speak. 'But it was only an accident. I apologised at the time for what had happened.' She looked appealingly at the two police officers.

Her interrogator glanced at his papers again. 'It is alleged that you had a confrontation with two boys and their father and that during the argument you struck one of the boys on the arm with a stick.'

His words alarmed Debbie. She desperately tried to explain. 'But it wasn't like that,' she pleaded. 'The boy had a stick and he was going to poke me with it. I grabbed one end and then he suddenly let go of his end. It tapped him on the arm. It was a complete accident.' Stress was beginning to overtake her. It showed in her expression and her voice.

The officer remained unmoved. He looked up from the notes he was making and spoke again. 'The boy has claimed to have a bruise on his arm as a result of the blow.'

'But it was an accident,' Debbie pleaded again. She didn't know what else to say.

'You admit that the boy was struck on the arm by a stick held by you?' The question was intimidating.

'Yes. But it was an accident,' Debbie repeated desperately. She felt trapped and helpless. It was becoming clear that the boy's father had made a good job of complaining about her. Fear of what might happen next clouded over her. The whole thing seemed to be blown out of proportion. Frantically she added to her reply. 'I don't understand why everything has been blown up and distorted. It was just a simple argument. I tried to be a good citizen and stop the boys damaging cars and now I find myself here answering all these questions.'

'It is always best to call the police in these cases and let them sort it out.' said the second officer.

Debbie felt even more vulnerable and miserable. 'But there was no time. Another second, and the boy would have been hitting my car with the stick,' she insisted.

The first officer sorted out the papers in front of him. He picked up his pen. 'I'd like to take down a few more details,' he said, looking straight at Debbie.

Debbie made no reply. There didn't seem to be any point. What could she say, other than repeat again what had happened in the car park?

She would never forget the questioning she had to endure. Starting from her personal details, name, address and age, they stretched on to questions such as whether she had ever had any problems involving the police and whether her children had ever been involved in anything requiring police intervention. The questions dragged on and on, seemingly endless. She felt as if she were in a dream. How could all this be happening to her over such a trivial incident? She felt drained and devastated by the whole process. Never in her worst nightmares had she imagined this would happen to her.

At last a statement was produced for her to sign. It was read out to her and then she was asked to read it herself and sign her name. As far as she could ascertain, it was an accurate enough account of the encounter. She obediently signed the document.

The policeman who had interviewed her picked up the statement and glanced at it. Then he looked at Debbie, who was sitting looking dejected. 'That's all for now. You are free to go.'

Debbie looked up. 'What will happen now?' she asked.

'Further enquiries will be made. If it is considered that there is sufficient evidence to support a charge of assault, you will be arrested and placed on bail to appear in court.'

Again the word 'arrested' made Debbie shudder. What did it all mean?

'What will happen to me then? I mean if I have to appear in court?' She could hardly say the words.

'You could go to prison.' The answer was quite matter of fact. But seeing the look on Debbie's face, the officer added: 'But as it's a first offence you will most likely be let off with a fine or put on probation to keep the peace.'

His words were of little consolation to her. The thought of having to attend a court hearing and fearing the result were too much for her to comprehend. What she had thought at first was just a case of answering a few questions now seem to have turned her into a criminal. She felt devastated and helpless. She hardly noticed that the woman police officer was leading her back to the front of the station. The seating area was empty.

Before she left, the officer turned to Debbie and gave a half-smile, the first glimpse of any compassion Debbie had seen since entering the building.

'I know how you feel, Mrs Hammond, but I'm afraid that in this day and age when a complaint is made we have to follow it up and ask questions.'

Witnessing this glimmer of sympathy prompted Debbie to speak. 'But it seemed such a trivial incident. And the boy's father was so horrible to me. Now I seem to be the guilty party.'

'The individual concerned is known to us,' said the officer. Then she asked: 'Have you anybody who will pick you up?'

Debbie nodded. 'I'll ring my husband. That is, if I get an answer. I tried before and couldn't get through.'

'If you have a problem let us know and we'll see what we can do,' replied the officer more briskly, and with 'Goodbye, Mrs Hammond,' she was gone.

Debbie collapsed onto one of the chairs. She took out her mobile and with trembling hands keyed in her home number. 'Oh, please, PLEASE answer,' she prayed. It seemed an age before the telephone was picked up.

'John Hammmond.'

Relief swept through her. She found herself almost in tears. 'Oh, John, it's Debbie. Please pick me up.' Her words were almost frantic.

'Where are you? I was worried.'

'Wickton police station. Please come and get me.'

'What happened?'

Debbie tried to be more coherent. 'It's about yesterday, the problem I had in the car park. But can you pick me up?'

'I'll be right over.' John could detect that she was in distress. There was no point in trying to ascertain what had happed at this stage.

'Please hurry, John,' she pleaded.

'OK, I'll be as quick as I can. See you shortly. Bye for now.'

'Bye,' Debbie whispered and switched off her mobile. How long would it take for him to get there? Her fuddled brain ceased to try and answer the question. In the meantime she had to endure this awful place. Dejected, she sat and waited. There was little activity going on around her, for which she was glad. The counter was unmanned most of the time. A middle-aged couple came in to leave a wallet they had found. They looked at her but made no comment. She was alone with her thoughts for most of the time.

How long she was there she had no idea. Suddenly John was there in front of her. He looked worried. 'What's happened?' was his first remark.

Debbie looked up at him. There was a trace of tears in her eyes. 'Take me home, John,' she almost whispered, on the verge of breaking down.

John put his arm around her and led her away. A young police officer who had just appeared at the counter watched them depart through the swing doors. They walked in silence. Debbie could not talk and John knew it was not the right time to press her for answers to the questions to which he desperately needed answers.

It only took them a few minutes to reach the car park – the very car park that had been the scene of Debbie's ordeal. John helped Debbie into the car and closed the door. When he was seated behind the wheel, Debbie made an effort to talk. 'It was those boys yesterday.

Their father must have gone to the police. The police arrived at our house soon after you left. They insisted that I come over here with them and answer questions.' The words came out fragmented as she tried to recount the events of the previous few hours.

John turned to her. He could see how stressed she was. He did his best to reassure her. 'OK. When we get home you can tell me all the details. For now, just lean back and try and relax a little.'

His words were a small degree of comfort. Debbie settled back in her seat and he started the engine. Thank goodness she had him to be close to her and support her.

She said little on the drive home. She was too preoccupied with her thoughts, going through again every detail of the last few traumatic hours. From time to time she leaned back and closed her eyes. Eventually she was conscious that they had arrived home. John stopped the car in front of the garage. Automatically she got out and walked towards the front door. At least she was home again.

They entered the house and John closed the door behind them. Suddenly he put his arms round her. 'Shall I make us a cup of tea?' he asked. 'Then you can tell me everything.'

Debbie did her best to try and be normal. 'Oh, thank you, John. That would be lovely.'

'You go and sit down. I'll make it.' He was already hurrying to the kitchen.

As if in a dream Debbie kicked off her shoes. She couldn't remember where she had left her house shoes, but suddenly it didn't matter. She wandered into the lounge shoeless. She sank into a chair, the same chair she had been sitting in when the two police officers had arrived. The newspaper she had been reading still lay abandoned on the floor. So much had happened in the few hours since she had hurriedly dropped it. Her life seemed to have been turned upside down. A few hours ago she had been just a wife, mother and senior citizen. Now she was on police files, perhaps soon to be arrested for assault.

John reappeared with the tea. He handed Debbie a mug and then sat down opposite her. 'Do you feel like talking now?' he asked gently.

Debbie clasped the mug. She nodded slowly. She tried to formulate her thoughts so that she could recall her experience with a degree of accuracy. She sat looking down, still dejected, but slowly she began to talk.

'It was just after you left me this afternoon. I thought I would have ten minutes with the newspaper and then the doorbell rang… ' Slowly she related the events of the past few hours. When she had finished she paused and looked at John. 'Oh John, it was awful. I…' Her voice filled with emotion. 'I feel like a criminal.' Tears started to form in her eyes. But before John could react, another trauma flooded into her thoughts. Her tears started to flow freely. 'John, I may have to go to court… I may even go to prison.' She looked appealingly at him.

He sprang to her side and put his arm round her. 'It's not going to come to that,' he said firmly.

'But suppose it did?' The idea haunted her. Then something else clouded into her thinking. She turned to look at John. 'John, if that did happen, we'd have to move away. I couldn't go on living here. Everybody would be looking at me and pointing the finger.'

'It's not going to happen.' He tried to make his reply as gentle but firm as he could.

Another wild thought struck her. 'John, what am I going to tell the girls?' she asked miserably.

'They'll understand. They'll be quite supportive. You'll see. They're big girls now.'

Debbie did not reply. The thought of telling everybody about her experience was daunting, but somehow it would have to be done. She pulled a tissue from the nearby box and wiped the remains of the tears from her face. Then another thought occurred to her. She looked up at John. 'Trish is coming this weekend.'

'Shall we ring her and ask her to postpone?' he asked gently.

Debbie clutched the tissue and thought for a moment. It was tempting to just shut herself away until something happened, but she couldn't do that. That would be admitting defeat. No. Somehow with

John's help she would cope with the next few days. She had to. She became conscious that he was waiting for her answer.

'I could give her a ring. She will understand,' he said.

Debbie shook her head. 'No. I'll manage somehow,' she replied. Then for good measure she added: 'That is, unless they come and arrest me before then.'

Chapter 28

Sleep did not come easily to Debbie that night. She lay awake going over in her mind the events of the day. She asked herself whether she could have answered the police questions any better, and always there was the underlying thought of what might happen next. Would the police come to arrest her? What would happen then? Would she be put in that cell again and locked in? How long would she be there? She knew she would most likely have to appear in court. The police had told her so. But what would happen then? Surely they wouldn't send her to prison for such a small offence. And if they did, what would happen to her there? Again and again the same questions raced through her brain.

It was close to dawn when she eventually dozed off into a fretful sleep troubled by dreams. The sound of John moving about in the bathroom eventually woke her. She glanced at the bedside clock. They were already later than usual – just when they had a busy day ahead of them. She had intended to do a little local shopping and then some cooking to get everything nice for Trish's visit. Now her plans for an early start were in disarray. On top of that was the constant thought that the police might appear at any time.

It was ten minutes before John appeared. 'Good morning, darling. I thought I'd let you sleep on.' He gave her his customary kiss.

'I'm so glad you did, darling. I've had the most awful night.' Debbie sighed. 'And with Trish coming I intended to be up early and do so many things.'

'Don't worry. It will all sort itself out.'

Dear John, she thought. He was always so positive and supportive. And heaven knew she was going to need that support in the days ahead.

After breakfast John had to take the car to the garage to have something or other checked. Debbie hated the thought of being left on her own with the prospect of the police making another unexpected call on her. She considered going with him, but the thought of everything she had to do made her drop that idea. She could not face the thought of going shopping, so in the end she threw herself into cleaning the house and getting Trish's room ready. In spite of keeping busy, whenever the opportunity presented itself she would find her gaze directed to the road outside the house with the dread of seeing a police car standing there.

By the time John returned, she had finished the housework and felt up to doing the shopping. She was glad John did not offer to drive her there, or offer to go there instead of her. Somehow she felt that she wanted to just have a quiet walk on her own.

Even that strategy was not without its dose of stress and a reminder of her current predicament. Hardly had she ventured a few steps from the house than she was greeted by one of their neighbours. Mrs Browne, a retired civil servant who lived across the road with her husband, called out to her. Debbie paused and the neighbour came over to her.

'Good morning, Mrs Hammond,' she said. Debbie and John did not know these neighbours very well and were not on first-name terms.

'Good morning, Mrs Browne.' Debbie braced herself for what she knew was coming.

Mrs Browne lowered her voice. 'Mrs Hammond, I noticed you going off in a police car yesterday. Is anything wrong?'

For an instant Debbie almost panicked. Then she regained control. People would know sooner or later, particularly if the police came back to arrest her. The best option was to be truthful and relate what happened, even if it was painful for her. She took a deep breath. 'Oh, the police wanted to interview me over an incident in Wickton the other day. I stopped two boys damaging cars with a stick in the car park and in the process appear to have become the aggressor.'

'But how?'

Debbie hesitated. She was loath to go into detail, but there didn't seem to be much of an alternative. She gave a brief account of the incident. She was unprepared for the response.

'But that's dreadful. How can such a thing happen? What are the police thinking about? They should be thanking you for helping to keep the peace.' Mrs Browne was highly indignant.

Debbie was too weary to do any philosophising. She replied simply: 'When a complaint is made they have to follow it up.'

'What will happen now?'

'I'm waiting to find out,' Debbie replied glumly.

'Well if there is any way in which I can be of assistance to you, do let me know.' Mrs Browne was most emphatic.

Debbie thanked her and, keen to end the encounter, made the excuse that she was in a bit of a hurry. Right now she did not seem to have a great deal of energy for conversation, particularly with almost complete strangers.

She continued to the shops. Even there she was not her normal organised self. She had not made the usual list of what she needed and was relying on her memory. It was not a good strategy. She walked home slowly, tense with the horrible thought that she might find a police car waiting on the drive.

It was a relief, when she could see their house, to discover that the space in front of the garage was empty. Perhaps the police had already been. Perhaps they intended to return, she pondered; but then her logical thinking took over. No: they would have waited for her. She let herself into the house. John heard the key in the lock and was standing in the kitchen doorway as she entered.

'Ah, just in time for a cuppa.' His greeting was cheerful. It didn't sound as if her fears had been justified.

'Oh, lovely. I'll just put these things away.' Debbie felt relieved.

'Jan rang,' John announced casually. 'She wants to give you something or other.'

Debbie's heart sank a little. Jan was another person she would have to tell about her ordeal.

They had hardly finished their tea when a noise on the doorstep announced the arrival of Jan and the children. John went to let them in and give Jan a hand.

'Here we are. We've come to see you,' Debbie heard Jan announce, her voice backed by Jamie's chatter.

Debbie went to meet them, greeted by an excited Jamie who was waving a drawing he had done at school and desperately wanted to show her.

'Hello, Mum.' Jan came in with a fretful Emma in her carrycot. 'I had to keep Jamie off school yesterday and today. He had that tummy bug. It's been going round the school. But he's all right now.' The news update was made almost in one breath.

Debbie and John managed to get the trio ushered into the sitting room. For a full five minutes pandemonium reigned: Jan was trying to talk, Jamie was demanding attention, and Emma was grizzling. Eventually, Debbie managed to get Jan a cup of coffee, John took Jamie into the garden to play, and Debbie took Emma from Jan to see if she could settle her down.

At last Jan had imparted all her news. She turned her attention to her mother. 'Mum, you're looking a bit down. Is everything OK?'

The time had come. Once again yesterday's events had to be gone over yet again. It all came over a bit disjointed, because Jan kept interrupting her mother to ask something or make a shocked exclamation. At last Debbie finished.

Jan immediately said: 'But Mum, they just can't do that.'

'It looks as if they have,' remarked Debbie, forcing herself to fake a slight smile.

'But we have to do something,' insisted Jan. 'Get a solicitor or contact somebody.'

'I expect that will come,' replied Debbie as she returned her sleeping granddaughter to the carrycot. Jan got up to help her and for a few minutes the discussion of Debbie's ordeal was interrupted; only when Emma was settled did Jan return to the subject. 'Mum, we can't just sit here and do nothing.' Her voice was now full of concern and worry.

Debbie tried to put on a calm front for her daughter's sake. Jan was usually quite relaxed and logical, but she was clearly alarmed by her mother's news. 'All we can do at the moment is just wait and see what happens.' Debbie tried to sound confident, but for the hundredth time that day she glanced out of the window, dreading what she might see.

'But suppose they do come and arrest you. What then?' Jan was quite agitated now.

Their conversation was interrupted by the reappearance of John and Jamie. Jan immediately turned her attention to John.

'John, what do you make of all this?'

His reply was brief and to the point. 'Political correctness gone mad.'

This did not satisfy her. 'Yes, but I mean what do you think will happen?' she asked.

'It's extremely hard to say. We'll just have to wait and hope common sense prevails. It really is a crazy situation.'

'But shouldn't we get a solicitor or something?'

John shook his head. 'Not at this stage.'

She was still not satisfied. 'But there have been cases in the newspapers like this – innocent people arrested over misunderstandings. We don't want to let that happen. I think we should get some advice or something.' She turned to Debbie. 'I'm worried about you, Mum.'

Debbie was keen to end the discussion. She said: 'I think I would rather wait and see what happens at this stage.' She tried to make the statement as firm and conclusive as she could.

Her words seemed to have some effect. 'I'll talk to Paul about it,' was Jan's final comment on the matter.

It was John who managed to change the tone of the conversation. 'Everybody all set for the meal tomorrow?' he asked. It had been his idea. As soon as he had learnt that Trish was coming for the weekend, he had suggested that they all go out to eat, and Debbie had phoned Jan. It was all arranged. Jan would get a babysitter for a few hours and she and Paul would join them at the restaurant. John had already reserved a table.

'But should we go now?' Jan asked, attending to Emma who had woken up and started to grizzle again.

'Of course we're going,' replied Debbie. Though her response was quite firm, a horrible thought had crossed her mind. Suppose they came and arrested her before then? Would they keep her in custody? She thought not.

Jan left soon afterwards, remembering to give her mother the pile of magazines she had accumulated and had made the excuse for the visit.

After goodbyes and a final wave, John and Debbie returned to their now tranquil lounge. Debbie collapsed into a chair and let out a big sigh. 'Whew. I've never seen Jan quite so over the top before. She really was quite concerned about me.'

'Understandable, I suppose,' replied John.

Another thought struck Debbie. 'If Jan was like that, what's Trish's reaction going to be?' she asked. 'You know what she's like.'

John laughed. 'We'll sort her out,' he said.

Debbie was glad of John's approach to things. During the last twenty-four hours she had been conscious of his quiet but firm support. It was good to have someone like that around at this time. She wondered how she would have coped with everything without him being there as her tower of strength.

Talking about Trish brought other matters into focus for Debbie. She glanced at her watch. 'Goodness, just look at the time! I'd better get on or there will be no meal tonight.'

'What time is she coming?' asked John. He looked at the clock. It was already after three.

Debbie was on her way to the kitchen, collecting Jan's dirty coffee cup as she went. 'She said after work. That could mean any time up till seven.' She laughed. It was the first time humour had entered her conversation in the last twenty-four hours.

She had just finished putting the finishing touches to the salad for their evening meal and wandered back into the lounge when once again she glanced out of the window. It wasn't a police car that stood on the drive, but Trish's. Still in her business suit, Trish was busy pulling things out of the boot.

'She's here!' exclaimed Debbie, looking at the clock. It was only five o'clock. She hadn't expected Trish for at least an hour. John looked up from the newspaper he was reading. He abandoned it on the floor as he rose to follow Debbie to the front door.

'A good job I got everything ready in time,' observed Debbie over her shoulder.

By the time she reached the front door and opened it, Trish was on the doorstep, a bag in each hand. 'Hi, Mum.' She planted a kiss on Debbie's cheek.

'Hello, dear,' said Debbie. 'You're nice and early.'

'I left work early and missed all the traffic. Hi, John. There's a couple of bottles of wine in here. I've got another bag in the car.' Trish thrust one of the bags into John's hand, gave the second one to Debbie and hurried back to her car.

It took a few minutes for things to settle down, but eventually the three of them ended up in the lounge. Trish seemed quite happy to chat for a while. Debbie tried her best to appear relaxed and normal, but she found it difficult. Every so often she found her eyes wandering to the window, dreading what she might see. Fortunately Trish and John made up for her subdued feeling and reluctant conversation. After a while Trish announced that she was going to get changed and Debbie retreated to the kitchen to put the finishing touches to the evening meal, leaving John to the newspaper.

She had everything ready by the time Trish reappeared. She was surprised to see that her daughter had abandoned her jeans for once and was dressed in a pretty skirt and blouse. 'That's a nice outfit, dear,' she remarked.

Trish glanced down at her clothes. 'I bought them last week.'

'They suit you.'

'The shoes are brand new. I only bought them at dinner time.' Trish looked at her mother and then down at the high-heeled sandals she was wearing. 'Do they look OK?' she asked a bit anxiously.

Debbie approved the choice. 'They go really well with the skirt and blouse,' she said.

Over supper they opened one of the bottles of wine Trish had brought and lingered a long time at the table. At the end of the meal John insisted on doing the washing up and clearing away, ushering the two women into the lounge. Debbie knew instinctively that this was a ploy to give her the opportunity to talk privately with Trish.

At first Trish chatted and Debbie said very little, only adding a word or two here and there. After a while Trish looked at her curiously. 'Mum, you're very quiet this evening. Is anything wrong?'

Debbie tried to give a bit of a smile, which did not work. She knew she had to tell Trish her worrying news now. 'I'm all right. It's just that...' And she began her account of the previous day's ordeal at the police station.

Trish listened, asking the occasional question. Surprisingly, unlike her sister she remained calm and composed. When Debbie had completed her story, Trish took a deep breath. 'Mum, that's an awful thing to happen. Really quite ridiculous.'

Debbie nodded. 'That's what everybody says,' she said.

'But isn't there anything we can do?'

'I've talked it over with John. At the moment it seems that the best thing is to wait and see what happens.'

Trish seemed to be deep in thought for a few seconds. Then she said: 'The whole thing seems a bit fragile to me. I can't quite see how they can prosecute you. You were only trying to prevent damage to the cars, and in any case what happened with the stick afterwards was an accident.'

Debbie nodded in agreement. 'I hope you're right.'

Suddenly Trish slipped out of her seat. She came over to Debbie and sat down beside her. Then she put her arm round her. 'It'll be all right, Mum. You'll see. I just know everything is going to be all right.'

Debbie could almost have cried. Here was her daughter, who

had always needed so much comfort and support, now displaying so much strength and caring towards her. She did her best to smile.

Trish spoke again softly. 'I know it will be OK. I bet you'll hear no more about the whole thing.'

But she was wrong.

Chapter 29

In spite of her current anguish, Debbie enjoyed the weekend. On the Saturday evening, she and John ate in the restaurant with Trish, Jan and Paul and for a few hours she relaxed just a little. On the Sunday Jan invited them all over for lunch. It was a pleasant distraction for Debbie to have all her family around her, and she did her best to put on a brave front and appear relaxed.

One of the surprises of the weekend was the amount of care Trish showed for her mother. Several times she had taken her on one side and quietly talked to her, offering little bits of advice and doing her best to be supportive. It was a side of Trish that had suddenly made an appearance, and for Debbie it was a complete reversal of roles. It reminded her of the hundreds of times she had had to put her arms round her younger daughter and comfort her. Now her daughter was doing the same for her and to Debbie it appeared that Trish had suddenly grown up.

It was on the Sunday morning, when she and Trish were having a leisurely few minutes at the end of breakfast, that Trish made an announcement. In a lull in their conversation she appeared to be deep in thought, and then she suddenly said: 'Mum, I have something to tell you.' She paused as if to ensure that she had her mother's full attention, then she came out with her news. 'I've got a new boyfriend.'

Debbie concealed her apprehension and instead responded with enthusiasm. 'Oh, darling, that's marvellous! Tell me more.'

Trish took her time as she replied, choosing each titbit of information carefully. 'Well, he's a year older than me. He's got his own business and he's rather sweet.'

'Has he been married?'

Trish nodded. 'For three or four years. He got divorced just before I did.'

Debbie absorbed the information she had just gleaned. Perhaps some concern showed briefly in her features, but before she could say anything Trish butted in quickly. 'It's all right, Mum. I'm not going to do anything silly this time. I've learnt my lesson.'

Debbie smiled at the revelation. She would have been the first to admit that Trish's excursions into relationships had worried her in the past. However, after Trish's admission of her failings, she was determined not to express any signs of alarm on this occasion. Instead she asked: 'What's his name?'

'Alan. His family are quite well off and his parents live near Southampton.'

'When are we going to meet him?'

'I'll bring him down sometime.'

Debbie couldn't resist asking the question that was on her mind. 'Are you living together?'

Trish shook her head. 'No, Mum. It's early days yet.'

Debbie felt relieved. She was about to ask more questions when John reappeared. Trish immediately grabbed his attention. 'John, there's something wrong with the screen washer in my car. It doesn't work. Can you have a look at it?'

John grinned. 'Perhaps it needs filling up,' he suggested.

Trish made a face at him and replied with mock indignation: 'As a matter of a fact, I do know how to fill it up. I did it the other day, but it still doesn't work.'

'Most likely a blocked nozzle,' John replied. 'Want me to have a look at it now?'

'Yes, please.' Trish had already jumped up from her chair.

Debbie watched them depart. One of the bonuses of her marriage to John had been how well he and Trish had taken to each other. Debbie sometimes felt that in Trish John had discovered the daughter he had never had.

She washed up the breakfast dishes and then wandered into the lounge. In the last few days it had become a habit. Always she had her eye on the drive of their house, half expecting to see a police car standing there. For a brief interlude, while Trish had been talking about her new boyfriend, she had forgotten about her own problems. Now everything flooded back to her. She gazed out of the window for a few minutes, deep in thought, as John and Trish bent under the bonnet of Trish's car.

To take her mind off things, she picked up the Sunday newspaper and sat down in her favourite chair. But she could not even get interested in the headlines, let alone delve any deeper into the content. She was still sitting there when John and Trish came back into the house. She heard Trish bound upstairs, and then John popped his head round the door.

'Blocked nozzle,' he announced.

'Did you fix it for her?' Debbie asked, a bit disinterested.

'Yep, all working again.' John held up his dirty hands and gave her a wide grin.

That evening, when Trish had gone and they were enjoying a few minutes together before bedtime, Debbie told John about the chat she had had with her younger daughter. 'Trish told me she's got a new boyfriend,' she announced.

John digested the news. 'I hope he's more suited to her than that guy she married,' he observed.

Debbie gave a little sigh. 'So do I, but from the sound of it this one seems OK. I do hope so. I just want her to settle down and be happy with someone.'

'She deserves it. She's a good kid.'

Debbie looked at him. 'You get on really well with her, don't you?'

John smiled. 'She's a nice girl.'

'I really appreciate your interest in her. She can be difficult at times.'

John nodded. Before he could say anything else, Debbie spoke again. 'You know, John, one of the things that has surprised me this weekend is Trish's reaction to my problem. When I told her about having to go to the police station and the possibility of being arrested for assault, she really was quite supportive and caring. She even came and put her arm round me. I've never seen that side of her before.'

John smiled slightly. 'Hidden talents – like her mother,' he observed.

'Oh, John.' Debbie burst out laughing, but her mirth was short-lived. Memories of her recent experience quickly returned.

John looked at her anxiously. 'Still thinking about everything?' he asked.

Debbie nodded. She was serious again. 'All the time. I just can't forget what happened on Thursday. And the worst bit is the uncertainty of what's going to happen to me.'

John's reply was optimistic as usual. 'I know. You can't even contact the police and ask what's happening. All you can do is wait. The only consolation is that the longer the delay without any contact, the greater the chance of it all coming to nothing.'

'Do you really think that?' Debbie asked, hope in her voice.

John nodded. 'Yes, I do.'

Debbie said nothing. John could see that she was still eaten up with worry. He had noticed over the weekend that being with her family had taken her mind off things for a while. He guessed that now things had quietened down, all her fears had come back. He did his best to reassure her. 'Look, we're in this together and we'll face the outcome together. You know that.'

Debbie looked at him and nodded. 'I know, John. I don't know how I'd have coped if you hadn't been here.'

'You see – a use for the old dog yet,' he quipped, in the hope of lessening the tension.

It worked. Debbie jumped up, smiling. 'Well, as long as you don't mind visiting me in prison.' Then she added: 'I'm going to make us a drink.'

She bent over and gave him a kiss as she passed his chair. 'Cocoa all right?' she called over her shoulder as she headed for the kitchen.

'Great,' he called back. He was pleased that at least for the present his strategy had worked.

The following day was wet and gloomy. Debbie plunged into housework and John decided to fix one or two things about the house that he thought needed attention. Debbie's more optimistic outlook of the previous evening had dispersed overnight and her old concerns had returned. She found herself again making a point of glancing out of the window every so often, dreading what she might see. Even so, the doorbell took her by surprise. She could hardly bring herself to answer it, vaguely hoping that perhaps John might do so; but when it sounded again she walked slowly to the front door with a heavy heart.

She threw open the door, wondering what to expect, but it was Madge who stood on the doorstep. 'Hiya. Thought I'd drop in to see you guys,' was her greeting.

Debbie was almost relieved. 'Oh, come in, Madge. How are you?'

Madge needed no urging. She was already on her way in.

Debbie led the way into the kitchen. 'John,' she called out, 'Madge is here.'

Once in the kitchen Madge eased herself into a chair. 'Coffee?' Debbie asked.

'Great.' Madge never waited to be asked twice.

John appeared in the kitchen. 'Hello, Madge,' he said, and sat down opposite her.

'How's life with you guys?' Madge asked.

Debbie turned round from filling the kettle and clicking its switch to boil. Should she tell Madge what had happened? It was John who decided for her. 'We've got a bit of a problem at the moment,' he announced.

'What's that?' Madge queried.

Debbie looked at John and John looked at Debbie, each contemplating who was to answer. In the end Debbie plucked up courage to briefly tell Madge what had happened.

When she had finished, Madge launched into a lengthy discourse about how she felt about political correctness and what she thought should be done about the legal system.

Debbie had brewed the coffee and placed the mugs in front of everybody before Madge finished. Only then did Madge show any concern about Debbie's situation. Helping herself to a biscuit she asked: 'So what's going to happen now?'

'That's what we'd like to know,' replied Debbie, taking a sip of her coffee. For once she was too concerned about her own problems to be irritated by Madge's attitude.

'Most likely nothing,' Madge responded, in the middle of munching the biscuit.

'That's what we'd like to happen,' Debbie observed quietly, almost as if she were thinking aloud.

The thought of such an outcome was short-lived. In her next sentence Madge came out with 'Mind you, they do some crazy things now. Only last week I read in the newspaper about a woman in similar circumstances to you who was shoved in prison for a week for a quite trivial offence.'

'Charming! I wonder which prison they'll send me to.' Madge's remark had irritated Debbie.

Madge could see that she had overstepped the mark. 'Sorry. I guess I shouldn't have said that.'

'No,' replied Debbie curtly.

John, ever the peacemaker, butted in. 'The problem is the waiting. The whole thing has been blown up out of proportion. Twenty years ago the incident would have been dismissed without a thought. Now it seems everybody has their rights, even if it's to the disadvantage to some other poor individual. We just hope in Debbie's case common sense prevails and no action is taken.'

'Well, if you need a good solicitor I know an excellent guy,' Madge offered.

'I hope I don't,' chipped in Debbie.

Madge decided to change the subject, much to Debbie's relief.

From then on she related in detail her plans for her next holiday, which was imminent. Most of the conversation took place between Madge and John, with Debbie just adding a vague comment here and there. Half an hour later Madge stood up and said she must go.

Debbie went to the front door and saw her off. Just before she left, perhaps conscious of her earlier indiscretion, Madge turned to Debbie and took her hand. 'Sorry if I appeared a bit flippant. I do really care and I hope everything turns out all right for you.'

Debbie gave her a hug. 'It's all right, Madge. Really it is.'

'OK. Keep in touch. Let me know what happens.' And with that Madge departed.

Debbie shut the door and went back into the house. John had returned to his DIY and she busied herself washing up the dirty coffee cups. Somehow Madge's visit had revised her own thinking just a little. Almost four days had gone past since her police interview. Surely the police would not wait much longer if they were going to take further action. Each day that passed with no contact raised her hopes just a little. Perhaps things would blow over as some people suggested. However, as subsequent events were to show, she was to be proved wrong.

Chapter 30

The next day was fine and sunny. John decided to spend some time on the allotment and Debbie threw herself into doing some washing. She was about to put a load into the machine when the telephone rang. Dumping the basket on a chair, she hurried to answer it, fearful that its shrill ringing would end before she reached it. She picked up the receiver.

'Mum, have you had any more news?' It was Jan.

'Hello, dear. No, not so far. I suppose you could say that no news is good news.' Debbie tried to sound as casual as possible. Jan's reaction when she had first told her of her encounter in the car park and subsequent questioning by the police had concerned her a little.

When Jan replied there was clear anxiety in her voice. 'Mum, Paul and I have been talking about things. We really think you should see a solicitor.'

Debbie took a deep breath. The last thing she wanted was a worried and impulsive Jan to deal with matters. This needed a careful answer. 'Oh, that's ever so nice of you both, but I think I'll wait and see for a few days before doing anything. You know, except for being interviewed by the police, nothing else has happened.'

'But you could be charged with assault, even sent to prison. Surely you realise that. We need to get you help.' There was almost panic in Jan's voice.

Debbie realised that she had to take control of the conversation. 'Darling, I have thought about that. I think about it most of the time. But I really don't want to go over the top at this stage. If the police contact me again, I'll have to do something and then I'll appreciate your help.'

Jan was clearly not convinced. 'Well, we think you should do something now.'

'Just give it a couple of days.' Debbie tried to sound as firm as possible.

'Umm. Well…'

Before Jan could pile on more pressure Debbie changed the subject. 'How are the children?'

'Emma's a bit grizzly today. I think she's got a bit of a cold. But I must tell you this: Jamie came home from school and announced that he was going to drive a fire engine when he grows up. Goodness knows where he got that idea from.'

Debbie laughed. 'Perhaps he saw one somewhere.'

'I don't know. Perhaps.'

Debbie kept the conversation going, mainly talking about her grandchildren and Jan's activities. Anything, she thought, to keep the topic away from herself. In the main she was successful, but eventually Jan returned to the subject of the police investigation.

'Mum, are you sure you don't want me and Paul to get hold of a solicitor for you?'

Debbie sighed. Sometimes Jan could be as hard to handle as Trish. She knew she had to be firm. 'No, dear. Not at this stage. Give it a few more days to see what happens.'

Jan was clearly not impressed with her decision. 'All right then, but both Paul and I think you are taking this all too lightly.'

Debbie did her best to smooth things over. 'Darling, I know you're worried about me and I appreciate your concern. I really do. But just give it a couple more days.'

She thought she could hear a resigned sigh at the other end of the phone. 'OK then. I guess I'd better get back to Emma and go and do some shopping.'

'All right, dear. Keep in touch and thank you for your concern.'

'Bye, Mum. I'll ring tomorrow or come round. Will you be in?'

'We should be. Nothing planned.'

'I'll ring first. Bye for now.'

'Bye-bye, dear. Love to Jamie and Emma… and Paul.'

Debbie replaced the handset. She gave a little sigh. Sometimes it was hard to handle her daughter's caring concerns. She glanced at the wall clock. Gosh, she thought, nearly half past ten and I've not done the washing. She returned to the task, deep in thought.

Despite the casual and relaxed front she tried to present, she was worried. The weekend with the family around her had been a happy distraction, but even then her thoughts had returned from time to time to her predicament. Now the situation she was in occupied a greater part of her thinking. What would happen? There were times when she wished the police would contact her again. At least then she would know her fate.

She worked steadily on, but eventually came to the conclusion that she was not going to finish the washing and ironing before lunch. John would be back shortly. In the end she decided to make herself some coffee and take a break. She would just have to finish after lunch. She wandered into the lounge, mug in hand. She had just sat down when the telephone rang again. She got up to answer it.

'Mrs Hammond? It's Mary Browne. I haven't had a chance to see you, but has anything more happened? I just had to ring you and find out.'

Debbie adjusted her thinking. She had expected the call to be from John. 'Hello, Mrs Browne. No, nothing's happened yet. Still waiting.'

'Oh dear. That's not very good. It's all so uncertain, isn't it?' Her neighbour was clearly trying to be as sympathetic as she could.

'Yes, extremely.' Debbie didn't know what else to say. Then she added: 'Sometimes I just wish something would happen, instead of this endless waiting.'

Mrs Browne started to say something in reply. 'I was wondering—' She broke off suddenly. When she continued, her voice was one of alarm and concern. 'Goodness. There's a police car outside your house now.'

Debbie was speechless. She moved so that she could see out of the window. Her eyes confirmed Mrs Browne's statement. She could see a police officer emerging from the police car that stood on the drive.

She was conscious of Mrs Browne speaking again, but she did not take in the words. 'I've got to go,' she whispered into the telephone.

She heard Mrs Browne say something like 'Let me know what happens,' but she was already putting the phone down. She stood rooted to the floor, her heart thumping. The doorbell rang. She would have to answer it, yet it was as if her legs had turned to jelly. The police must be coming to arrest her. She glanced at her feet. She was in her house shoes. Would they give her time to change? What should she take with her? The doorbell rang again, this time long and hard.

Debbie dragged herself to the door. She wished John or even Jan were there, but there was no time to phone either of them. Again she would have to face the ordeal ahead of her all alone. With a heavy heart she opened the front door. An older police officer she had not seen before stood on the doorstep. Another officer was with him. Debbie recognised her as the one who had been present on the first visit.

The officer on the doorstep studied Debbie briefly. Without a trace of a smile he asked: 'Mrs Hammond?'

'Yes,' replied Debbie.

The second officer said: 'Good morning, Mrs Hammond.' Her expression was equally serious.

Debbie could never remember whether she replied. The situation was too tense. Her eyes glanced at the handcuffs at the officers' belts. They looked menacing and intimidating. Surely they wouldn't use those on her?

Every second felt like an hour to her. She seemed suspended in time, with everything moving so slowly. She saw the officer glance at the clipboard he was carrying, and then at her. This was it. She waited for the words that would announce that she was under arrest. Then the officer spoke. 'We're calling in connection with the incident in Wickton car park last Thursday morning.'

He paused for a second, perhaps to ensure that she had his full attention. She said nothing. She had a sick feeling in the pit of her stomach and dreaded what would come next. Then she was conscious that the officer was speaking to her again. This time a slight smile accompanied his words. 'You will be pleased to know that there will be no case for you to answer. No charges will be made.'

Debbie was astounded. 'You mean… You mean nothing will happen…?' she stammered.

The officer smiled at her again. 'Absolutely nothing,' he replied.

Debbie did not reply. She felt weak at the knees again. She wished she had a chair nearby to collapse into.

'Are you all right, Mrs Hammond?' asked the other officer.

Debbie struggled to regain control. 'Yes… Yes, of course… It's just the relief, I suppose.'

'It must have been a very stressful time for you. I'm sorry we had to put you through it all.' The officer smiled at her as she spoke.

Debbie was slowly regaining her composure. 'Can you tell me why nothing more will happen?' she asked.

The older officer, who she now saw had rather a kind face, replied: 'The complaint against you was withdrawn. It could be something to do with the fact that the person who made the complaint was arrested for burglary last Saturday evening.'

'The person concerned was known to us from previous incidents,' added his companion.

'Thank you for coming to tell me.' It was all Debbie could think of saying.

The two police officers seemed to understand how she was feeling. They appeared to be almost sympathetic towards her. The older of the two spoke again. 'I'm sorry you've had to go through all this, Mrs Hammond. Unfortunately, when a complaint is made we have to follow it up.' He paused for a moment, looking at Debbie, and then continued. 'When I started out as a police officer, I doubt it would have happened the way you have experienced. We would have talked to both parties and most likely that would have been it – but now everything has changed.'

'You mean all the political correctness,' Debbie could not help saying.

He nodded. 'You could call it that,' he replied with a smile.

'Anyway, you can forget all about it now, Mrs Hammond,' said his colleague.

For the first time since they called, Debbie smiled. 'I'll try,' she remarked, and then, remembering her ordeal at the police station she added: 'But it won't be easy.'

'If you want any further assistance from us, you can always contact me at the station,' the man continued. 'I'm PC Brayne.'

'Thank you.'

The police officers said goodbye and departed. Debbie watched them get into their car and then closed the front door. Once again her whole life had changed in the space of just a few minutes. She had been certain the police had come to arrest her, but that had not happened. It was all over, but the effect on her was not quite as she had anticipated. She felt as if she were suspended in mid-air. She now had to readjust to the situation. The anxiety of the last few days had been lifted, but now she had to return to ordinary life.

She went back into the lounge and flopped into the same chair she had been sitting in when Mrs Browne had phoned. Her mug of coffee was still resting on the table where she had abandoned it. She picked it up and took a sip. It was still warm. She noticed that her hands were shaking. She had to sort herself out. She had to telephone John and Jan – and Mrs Browne – and tell them her good news.

She rang John's mobile. She hoped he had it switched on and somewhere handy. It was not unknown for her not to get an answer when he was on the allotment. This time she was in luck. John answered almost immediately. 'Hello, Debbie.'

The reality of her new situation was gradually sinking in. When she responded, excitement was beginning to filter into her voice. 'John, I've got some marvellous news. The police have been again, and guess what? Nothing is going to happen. The complaint has been dropped.'

'What? That's splendid news! Couldn't be better. I'm coming back straight away.' Even John was excited.

'I'll put the kettle on.'

'Great — see you soon.'

'I'm going to ring Jan and Trish now.'

Debbie immediately telephoned Mrs Browne and briefly told her what had happened. She was still on the phone to Jan when John arrived. Jan seemed to want to go on and on and in the end Debbie had a job to get away.

John was standing waiting. As soon as Debbie had finished talking to Jan, he put his arms round her and kissed her. 'Congratulations, darling. That's the best news yet.'

Debbie nestled in his embrace. She was almost tearful now. 'Oh, John, I feel so relieved. It's just as if a huge weight has been lifted off me.'

'I want to hear all about it.'

'I'll make us a cup of coffee and then I'll tell you what happened. I intended to be all ready for you, but I just couldn't get off the phone from Jan — and I haven't finished the washing.'

She made as if to walk to the kitchen, but John grabbed her arm and stopped her. 'Hang on. We've got something to celebrate. Leave the washing. Go and get changed. We're going to have a meal out.'

'You're on.' Debbie broke free and headed for the door. Then she paused, as a thought struck her. 'I'd better just give Trish a ring before we go.'

Chapter 31

Over the next few days, Debbie did her best to return life to normal. At first she found it quite difficult. Always there lurked in her mind the thought of what might have happened. Jan had been ecstatic when she told her what the police had said. She had almost squealed with delight. 'But that's fantastic!' had been her immediate response. Then: 'We've got to celebrate.'

It had taken Debbie a few minutes to talk down her daughter's excitement. Oddly, she had no desire for a big celebration. She and John went out for a pub meal immediately after the last visit from the police, but as far as she was concerned that was it. She now wanted to just try and forget the incident and get on with her life. She had evaded Jan's invitation by simply replying: 'Perhaps, but not right now. A bit later on, when I've got back to normality, we'll all get together again.' Jan had seemed to accept her decision and Debbie was glad of that.

Her vague suggestion of a family get-together was nearer being realised than she expected. When she rang Trish to tell her the news, she was surprised at her calm reaction. 'Oh, Mum, I'm so pleased for you. I really felt for you when you told me what had happened.'

'It's so nice to hear you say that, Trish. I really appreciate it.' Throughout the ordeal Trish had shown previously unrevealed depths of compassion. Debbie was seeing a part of her younger daughter she had been unaware of before. Trish's reply rather spoilt the effect. 'Oh, that's all right.'

Debbie decided to move the conversation away from herself by asking a question she was longing to know the answer to. 'How are you and Alan getting on?'

'Great. I'm thinking of buying a new flat and he's going to help me.'

'That's nice. Where are you moving to?'

'Oh, not very far. I've got my eye on a place.'

'That sounds quite exciting.'

'Not really. But I've been thinking about it for some time. I need more room. This place is so cramped.'

'Yes, I understand that.' Debbie had only visited Trish's flat a few times, but she recalled that it was extremely small. Vaguely she wondered whether Trish and Alan were moving in together, but she did not like to pry. However, Trish's next remark half-answered her.

'Mum, Alan would like to meet you.'

Debbie was delighted. 'Why don't you bring him here one weekend?'

'We thought we might come down on a Saturday sometime and stop over until the Sunday. Would that be all right?' There was a degree of uncertainty in Trish's voice.

Debbie jumped at the opportunity. 'Of course you can, darling. Just let me know when.'

'How about the weekend after next?'

'Smashing. I'll look forward to it.' Debbie really meant it.

'Mum, there's just one thing… Well, actually…' Trish hesitated. 'It's just that… Alan and I sleep together.'

Debbie smiled to herself. The reason for Trish's hesitation was clear. She rose to the challenge. 'Oh, that's all right. You can both sleep in the back bedroom instead of your room.'

Trish was clearly relieved. 'OK, Mum. Then we'll see you Saturday after next.'

'That will be splendid.'

Both Debbie and John looked forward to Trish and Alan's visit with pleasure tinged with a slight degree of anxiety, Debbie more so than John. When Debbie had announced the news of Trish's intended visit and they were mulling over the prospect, she expressed her concerns.

'You know, John, I hope this new relationship of Trish's works out. She worries me sometimes. I do wish she would settle down.'

John was as usual completely logical in his reply. 'It takes some people a long time to find a suitable partner,' he observed thoughtfully.

Debbie was more critical. 'Yes, I know, but Trish has had so many boyfriends – quite unlike Jan. I'm sure Jan only had two or three before she settled down, but Trish seems to have had dozens.'

'Sign of the times,' John murmured, almost to himself, but he followed it with a grin at Debbie.

Debbie was not convinced. 'I'm not so sure it's such a good thing for young people. They never really get a chance to get to know each other. It seems that as soon as they meet they're in bed together.'

John nodded. 'I know what you mean,' he said. 'But you have to admit Trish isn't like a great many young people these days. She didn't get married too young.'

The remark stimulated a brief sigh from Debbie before she replied. 'But then look what happened. She married Don in haste and it was a dreadful mistake. I know for a fact that they were living together only a few weeks after they met.'

'Certainly a mismatch there.'

'I do hope Alan turns out to be all right for her.'

'Well, she seems quite keen to bring him here to meet us, and that's a good sign,' observed John.

His remark prompted a brief spontaneous laugh from Debbie. She followed it with an explanation. 'You know, John, I think Trish felt a bit awkward about telling me they slept together.'

He grinned. 'A bit like her mother. Chip off the old block there.'

'John!' Debbie admonished, but she was smiling as she said it. The next moment he ducked as she hurled a cushion at this head.

Debbie worked hard to have everything ready for Trish and Alan's visit. She cleaned the house from top to bottom, went shopping and stocked up with food and by the Saturday morning everything was ready. She had prepared lunch and the table was laid ready. Jan had insisted that they all go round to her house in the afternoon, and John had suggested taking everybody out for a meal in the evening, an idea that appealed to Debbie, who was pleased that she would not have to prepare a second meal that day.

By ten-thirty, everything was complete, and Debbie retreated upstairs to freshen up and change. She chose a pretty, deep blue dress she had bought recently, and enhanced it with the special necklace John had bought her to go with it. To suit the occasion she even suffered the higher-heeled shoes that matched the outfit.

By the time she returned to the lounge, a full half-hour had elapsed. John glanced up from the newspaper as she entered the room.

'I say, Mrs Hammond, you're looking rather glamorous,' he said.

Debbie took careful steps over to him and placed a kiss on his cheek.

'Well, I want to make a good impression as a prospective mother-in-law,' she replied gaily.

'Careful he doesn't fall for you instead of Trish,' John quipped.

Debbie was about to make a suitable reply, but something made her glance out of the window.

'John, they're here!' she exclaimed. She glanced at him. 'Go and change quickly. No, there's no time. Do it later.'

As she spoke, she was making for the front door as fast as her restrictive footwear would permit. John followed, grinning. He knew she was quite excited.

Debbie had the front door open and was waiting on the step. Trish was getting out of the car, which Debbie didn't recognise and guessed was Alan's. Trish looked at her and waved. 'Hi, Mum,' she called out.

Debbie waited. She was surprised to see that Trish had abandoned her usual weekend jeans and was dressed in a smart two-piece suit, complete with heels. Then she got her first glimpse of Alan as he extracted himself from the car. Her first impression was of a tall, attractive man, dressed smartly but casually.

The next few minutes were a confusion of mixed conversation and greetings. Trish placed a kiss on her mother's cheek. 'Mum, this is Alan. Hello, John. Meet Alan.'

Alan grasped Debbie's hand and she offered him a cheek to kiss. She was aware of his fair hair and pleasant smile. 'Hello, Alan.'

'Really pleased to meet you, Mrs Hammond,' he said.

Debbie took charge. 'Right, everybody inside. Trish, you know where your room is. I'm going to make us a drink. Alan, would you like coffee?'

'Yes please, Mrs Hammond, that would be great. I'll just get the bags from the car.'

'I'll give you a hand,' said John, pleased to be able to do something.

The two of them went over to the car. Trish followed her mother into the kitchen. Once the men were out of earshot, she confronted her mother and almost whispered: 'Mum, Alan's really anxious. He was quite worried about meeting you.'

Debbie gave her daughter a hug. 'Darling, I understand. It'll be all right.'

As they pulled apart, Trish whispered: 'Thanks, Mum.'

To lighten the conversation, Debbie looked at Trish's outfit and remarked: 'Darling, you look very smart.'

Trish gave a tiny smile. 'I dress up a bit to please Alan. He likes to see me looking nice.'

Debbie was going to say something positive in reply, but the two men reappeared with the bags. Trish and Alan disappeared upstairs and Debbie busied herself making the coffee. John watched her. 'Seems quite a pleasant fellow,' was his comment.

Debbie turned to face him, kettle in hand. She nodded. 'He appears to be very nice,' she agreed, talking in a lowered voice so as not to be overheard.

John and Debbie's impressions were confirmed over the next few hours. Trish and Alan's stay proved to be an enjoyable experience for them all. Once he had got over his initial shyness, Alan proved to be an amiable guest. He chatted freely and helped John with a problem on his computer, and when they visited Jan and her family he even played for a while with Jamie. For Debbie the big thing was that he and Trish appeared to get along splendidly together. There was clearly chemistry between them, and Debbie hoped their relationship would blossom.

When Sunday evening came and their guests had departed, Debbie and John sank gratefully onto the settee. Debbie voiced her thoughts. 'I really do hope Trish and Alan make it together.'

John looked up from the newspaper. 'All the signs look good,' he replied thoughtfully.

'I like the way Alan seemed to be at ease with us all. Did you see the way he played with Jamie? I was quite impressed.'

'Yep, I did. Bit of a dad in the making.' He suddenly thought of something else. 'Quite a whiz-kid with computers as well. He fixed that problem we had with the email program. It's fine now.'

Debbie was still philosophising. 'You know, John, Trish seems to have matured quite a lot lately. I don't know if it's Alan's influence, but a lot of her rebellious attitude seems to have disappeared.' She laughed suddenly. 'Did you see her take her high heels off to run down the stairs? I've been on to her for years about that.'

John smiled and nodded. 'I did,' he replied. Then he added thoughtfully: 'She's a good kid really.'

Debbie was being reflective. 'Isn't it strange how your children can be so different in character? Jan and Trish are so unalike. I think Jan has a little of me in her, but I don't know about Trish.'

'Oh, she takes after her mother, absolutely.' John was emphatic but smiling.

Debbie was not so sure. 'Do you really think so? Perhaps just a bit.'

John tossed his newspaper aside. 'Anyway, Alan seems a nice guy. I hope things work out well for them. How about a cup of something before bed?'

'Oh, that would be nice. I'll make us some cocoa.'

'No, I'll do it.' He was already getting up.

As he disappeared, she kicked off her shoes and stretched her legs out on the settee. It was just nice to relax for a few minutes and ponder over the last twenty-four hours. She suddenly realised that for the last day or so she had forgotten the recent trauma in her life. She hoped that would continue. Now her thoughts were concentrated on Trish. If she and Alan got married, everything would be really good.

Debbie was not to know that this prospect would soon be eclipsed by other events in her life with John.

Chapter 32

Debbie concentrated on the small screen in front of her, busy sending an email to her sister Gwen in Canada. She had gradually mastered the basics on the computer, and one of the bonuses was that she could now handle emails, though it still required some concentration on her part.

She clicked the send button and breathed a sigh of relief as she watched the message disappear from the screen. It was still a minor miracle to her each time she realised that her efforts had been successful.

She carefully shut down the computer and eased herself out of her chair. Her attention was attracted to the window and the view of the tiny garden; now in December it looked cold and uninviting, unlike the blissful days of summer when she had spent time pottering about, or enjoying her coffee with John on the tiny patio. As she watched, a few flakes of snow started to fall from the leaden sky and were whisked around by the wind.

She glanced at her watch. It was already mid-morning. John should be back soon from his shopping expedition. Almost time for elevenses, she decided. She made her way to the kitchen and filled the kettle ready to click the switch when John returned. She wandered into the lounge, thinking about having a few minutes with the newspaper, but a glance at the window put a stop to that idea. Jan's car was outside.

She hastened to the front door and opened it. Jan was already out of the car and was looking anxiously at the house. Her face broke into a smile as Debbie appeared. She called out: 'Oh, you're at home. I just wanted to check before getting Emma out of the car.'

Debbie hurried over to them. 'Why didn't you give me a ring?' she asked.

'We were almost passing the door and we thought it would be a good idea to call and see Gran. Didn't we, Emma?' Jan started to lift her daughter from the car seat.

Debbie could see that this meant an end to her plans for the rest of the morning, but she kept that thought to herself and feigned joy at seeing her visitors. 'Come on inside, quickly,' she exclaimed. A bitterly cold wind was blowing.

Jan had now extracted Emma from the car. 'Here we are. Here's Gran.' With that, Debbie was presented with her granddaughter. She hurried into the house, leaving Jan to deal with her bags.

It was a good five minutes before a semblance of calm prevailed; Debbie sat on one of the kitchen chairs trying amuse a beaming Emma, and Jan sat opposite her, apparently exhausted.

'Would you like a coffee?' Debbie asked.

'That would be marvellous, Mum.' Jan gave a sigh. 'I just had to get out and do some shopping this morning.'

Debbie handed Emma back and turned her attention to the kettle. 'I just can't believe it's only a week to Christmas,' she said over her shoulder.

There was a groan from Jan. 'Don't mention Christmas.' She paused as if to emphasise the statement, then continued, assured that she had her mother's full attention. 'You'll never guess what's happened now.'

Debbie was spooning coffee into the mugs. She stopped and looked at her. 'What?' she asked, becoming concerned.

'Paul's mother is coming for Christmas.' Jan's indignation showed to the full.

'Oh, I see.' Debbie had only met Mabel, Jan's mother-in-law, a few times, but she knew she had strong opinions about most things and that she had a reputation for wanting to be waited on during her rare visits to her son's house. Pouring water into the mugs, she asked: 'How did that happen?'

Jan was clearly still irritated. 'I don't know. Paul talked to her the other night on the phone and this is the result. I was furious with him. We nearly had a row about it.'

Debbie tried to tread carefully. 'Did he invite her?'

Jan made a face. 'I don't really know,' she replied. After a few seconds she added: 'I suspect so, but he won't admit to it. Anyway, she's arriving on Christmas Eve.'

Debbie brought the mugs to the table. She voiced her thoughts. 'But that's going to mean a lot of extra work. Perhaps John and I shouldn't come over on Christmas Day.'

Jan was horrified. 'Absolutely not! You must come. The children expect you to be there and you know how Jamie likes to play with John.'

Debbie laughed. It was a fact. Jamie seemed to have taken to John and they were like buddies when they met up. But something else was concerning her. 'But will you be able to manage? That's going to be a lot of extra work. Shall I come over early on Christmas Day and give you a hand with the dinner?'

'Oh, would you, Mum? That would be such a help.' Jan was clearly relieved.

Their conversation was interrupted by John's arrival in the doorway. 'I say,' he said, 'just in time for coffee. Hello, Jan.'

Debbie got up to greet him. 'Hello, darling. Did you have a successful trip?'

John smiled. 'Mission completed,' he replied.

Jan spent another twenty minutes chatting and then indicated that she had to go. 'School's breaking up today and I've got masses to do before I pick up Jamie. I don't know how I'm going to get everything done in time for Christmas with two children under my feet.'

'We could look after Jamie one day, if that would help,' said Debbie.

'Oh, that would be great! What about Thursday?' Jan could not hide her enthusiasm.

'That would be all right with us, wouldn't it, John?' Debbie was anxious to include him in the decision.

'No problem at all,' said John.

'That's great.' With that, Jan got up to leave.

Debbie saw her off and then returned to the kitchen. 'She's in a bit of a state because Mabel has decided to come for Christmas.'

'Poor Jan.'

Debbie busied herself washing up the dirty mugs. There was an unusual silence as she did so. She turned to John, who was still sitting at the table. He was stroking his chin, a habit he had when pondering some problem. Debbie immediately recognised the signs and sensed that all was not well.

'Darling, are you all right? You're very quiet.' She tried to keep concern out of her voice.

John looked at her and gave her one of his grins. 'Fine. That is…' He stopped and then continued as if he was just starting the sentence. 'You know, I think I'll trot down to see Dr Wilson one of these mornings for a check-up.'

Debbie immediately stopped what she was doing and slipped into a chair beside him. It was unusual for John to talk of not being well. She looked at him anxiously. 'But what's the problem?'

John smiled at her again before he answered. 'Oh, not a lot. It's just that I seem to be having a bit of a problem with the old waterworks at the moment.'

Debbie decided to take control. 'You must go and see the doctor. Look, let me go and make an appointment for you now.' She got up from her chair before she had finished speaking.

John hesitated for a few seconds as if he was going to object, but then he just gave an 'OK' and accompanied it with a nod of consent. Without saying another word Debbie disappeared to the telephone. In less than three minutes she was back.

'I say, that was quick,' observed John.

'11.30, the day after tomorrow,' Debbie replied. She was about to say something else when the telephone rang. 'I'll get it,' she said.

She picked up the phone. 'Hello.'

'Hello, Mum.'

'Trish! Darling, how are you?'

'Fine. What about you and John?'

'Oh, we're fine. How's the new flat?' Debbie decided to change the subject quickly. In any case she had hardly spoken to Trish since she had moved into her new flat almost a month before.

'Super. I can hardly believe how much space I've got now.'

Debbie laughed. 'You'll fill it up.'

'That's what worries me.' Debbie could detect a chuckle at the other end of the phone.

'How's Alan?'

'Oh, he's fine. He was super helping me move. I don't know how I'd have done it on my own.'

Debbie was about to ask another question, but Trish spoke again first.

'Mum, would it be all right if I came for Christmas?'

'Of course it would. We'd love to see you and hear all about the new flat.'

'OK, I'll come down on Christmas Eve. Can I bring anything?'

'No. Don't bother to do any shopping, just turn up. Will Alan be coming as well?'

'No, Mum. He's already arranged to go to his parents.'

'Oh, that's a pity.' Debbie tried to sound convincing, but she was relieved at Trish's answer. She did not relish the thought of entertaining a relative stranger in the house over Christmas, even though Alan was quite amiable.

Trish made no response to her mother's reply. Instead she suddenly announced: 'Mum, I'll have to go. Somebody wants me on the phone. If that's all right I'll see you on Christmas Eve.'

'Fine. What time?'

'Afternoon. I must go. Bye for now, Mum.'

'Bye-bye, darling,' Debbie just had time to say, and with that Trish was gone.

Debbie returned to the kitchen. John was still sitting at the table. 'That was Trish. She's coming for Christmas.'

'Alan as well?'

Debbie shook her head. 'No. Apparently he's going to his parents. I wanted to find out more, but Trish was in a tearing hurry.'

John smiled. 'I expect we'll hear all about it,' he concluded.

Debbie returned to their previous conversation. 'John, it's so unusual for you to be unwell. What's the real problem?'

John rubbed his chin with his fingers. It gave him time to give an appropriate answer. 'Oh, I don't think it's a big deal. It's just that I seem to be having to go for a pee more often during the night. A pill or something like that will probably put it right.'

'Dr Wilson is very good. I'm sure he'll sort the problem out.' Debbie could tell that John was unwilling to talk about his problem in detail. She thought there was perhaps more to it than he was letting on, but she decided that pressing him was not going to achieve anything. Better to wait until he had seen the doctor. In the meantime she would keep her concerns to herself.

The day of John's appointment with the doctor was also the day Debbie had agreed to look after Jamie, who was dumped unceremoniously at their house at just after ten in the morning, with the agreement that Jan would pick him up 'sometime in the afternoon'. From then on Debbie was kept busy amusing him. John disappeared for his appointment and she waited anxiously for his return, one side of her thoughts on Jamie and the other on him.

It seemed an age before he returned. She heard the front door close and the next minute he appeared in the doorway. He gave her one of his grins.

Debbie looked up from Jamie and his drawing. 'What happened?' she asked.

'I had to have some blood tests. Dr Wilson thinks it's a prostate problem,' John announced, almost casually.

'And when do you get the results?'

'Christmas Eve. I've got another appointment.' John was quite matter of fact in his reply. The next second he had turned his attention to Jamie. 'Now, young fellow, what's this drawing all about?'

'I'm going to do a few jobs in the kitchen,' Debbie said, and left them to it. She would talk to John later when Jamie had gone. She reasoned that there was probably little else to relate at this stage anyway. Besides, very shortly she would have two hungry men wanting lunch.

The next few days flew past and suddenly it was Christmas Eve. Immediately after breakfast Debbie set about trying to finish getting everything ready before Trish arrived. She packed John off with a last-minute shopping list and then concentrated on preparing a cold supper for the three of them.

John had only been gone about ten minutes when the telephone rang. Debbie had her hands in water at the time and she had a bit of a rush to reach it before the answerphone cut in. A bit breathless, she picked up the handset. 'Hello.'

'Hello, Mum. It's Trish. Can I come a bit earlier?'

'Hello, dear. Yes, of course you can. What time is earlier?'

'I've a bit of shopping to do. Say, about lunchtime?'

'That's fine. We'll wait to eat with you.'

'Great.'

'Are you coming straight from work?'

'No. I've taken the day off. It's only the office party, anyway.'

'Oh, you'll miss all the fun.' Debbie laughed.

'Not really. Everyone drinks too much and some guys just want to get you drunk enough to get your panties off and exercise their manly skill.'

Debbie could not help laughing at Trish's description. 'It's not always like that, is it?'

Trish was still philosophical. 'You'd be surprised,' she replied, but there was humour in her voice. 'Anyway, I couldn't go drinking and then drive to you.'

'Of course not.' One of the rules Debbie had drummed into both her daughters when as teenagers they had started to drive was that drinking and driving together were out.

It was Trish who ended the conversation. 'OK, Mum. I'm going shopping now and I'll see you later.'

'OK, dear. See you later. Bye for now.'

'Bye, Mum.'

Debbie replaced the handset. She glanced at her watch. Gone were her plans for the rest of the day. She now had no more than perhaps two or three hours before Trish arrived. She had carefully planned that as soon as John returned she would set to and prepare some of the vegetables for Christmas dinner at Jan's. It had turned out in the end that she would not only help with the preparation and cooking, but also supply some of the extras.

She plodded on in the kitchen. She had already got Trish's room ready, so now it was just a case of finishing preparing supper. Lunch would have to be soup with a sandwich. Several times she glanced at the clock. John was taking his time, but she knew that he often found somebody to talk to on these expeditions. There was also his appointment with the doctor that morning. She hoped he hadn't forgotten about it.

After a brief discussion following John's previous visit to the doctor, neither of them had referred to the matter again, preferring to 'see what happens', as John put it. Debbie knew that in spite of his casual approach he was a bit concerned, as she was herself. On one occasion she had found him looking up prostate problems on the internet; but there was no point at this stage in making something larger than it perhaps was. After all, she reasoned to herself, it might well be something that was quickly and easily treatable.

The slam of the front door announced his return. A few seconds later he appeared in the kitchen doorway, his hands full of bags.

Debbie looked up from the sink. 'Did you get everything, darling?' she asked.

'Mission completed. Had a bit of a job to get the parsnips though – ended up going to three shops.' Debbie had planned to roast them the next day.

That's good. I'll tackle those right away and save time tomorrow.'

She took the bag from him. She suddenly remembered: 'Trish rang. She's coming early, in time for lunch. I thought I'd have the afternoon to start preparing things for tomorrow. I'll have to get up early and do the vegetables.'

'I'll peel the spuds,' John offered.

'Darling, that would be a great help if you will.' As she said it she glanced at the clock on the wall.

'John, your appointment with Dr Wilson. Don't be late.'

John looked at the clock. 'No problem. It's only four minutes down the road,' he said. 'I've still got over half an hour.'

'Would you like a drink before you go?' Debbie asked, again looking at the clock.

'I'll settle for a coffee, but I'll make one,' he replied.

'No. You sit down. I'll make it.' Debbie had already grabbed the kettle.

The coffee was quickly made and they sat at the kitchen table savouring the refreshment. Debbie related the content of Trish's telephone call and they both laughed over her description of office parties. Then John announced that he had to go.

Left on her own, Debbie set to work again. She was surprised how much she got through and was just about to take a break when the sound of the post being put through the letter box alerted her. She was just about to retrieve the letters from the mat when she noticed something just visible through the glass. She opened the front door to see Trish's car parked in front of the garage.

Trish was half in and half out of the car. She looked up. 'Hi, Mum!' she called.

'Hello, darling. You're nice and early.'

Trish arrived at the doorstep laden with bags. 'I got everything done quite quickly. There was a queue at the petrol station though.'

'Everybody filling up for the holiday,' Debbie suggested, picking up some of the bags Trish had deposited on the doorstep.

It was a good three or four minutes before Trish finally made it into the house. The small hallway was now filled with a suitcase and numerous plastic bags. Trish surveyed everything for a few seconds and then kicked off her shoes, at the same time making a face and remarking: 'These shoes are a bit tight.'

'Haven't you got any comfortable house shoes? Debbie asked, looking down at her daughter's bare feet. She was about to comment on Trish seemingly always buying shoes that were too tight for her, but thought better of it.

'Somewhere…' muttered Trish, rummaging in one of the bags. The search produced a pair of soft white pumps, which she squeezed her feet into. At the same time she asked: 'Where's John?'

'Oh, he won't be long. He had an appointment.' At this stage Debbie did not want to elaborate. There did not seem to be any point. She was glad Trish accepted her explanation without query and almost immediately turned her attention to the various bags she had arrived with.

'That one's got Christmas presents in it for Jamie and Emma. This one's got some goodies for us, and I got a couple of bottles of wine for John.'

'Oh, you're spoiling everybody,' Debbie replied, laughing. Then she asked: 'Would you like a drink of something? Coffee or tea?'

'Yes please, Mum. A coffee would be super. I haven't had anything since about seven this morning.'

'Fine. We'll be having lunch as soon as John comes back, but why don't you take your things upstairs while I make your drink?'

'OK.' And with that Trish grabbed her suitcase and a couple of bags and made for the stairs.

Debbie headed for the kitchen and set the kettle to boil. She was just about to make a mug of coffee for Trish when she heard the key in the front door. John was back.

A few seconds later he stood in the doorway. He looked quite solemn.

Debbie rushed towards him. 'Darling, what's happened?'

John did his best to smile. 'Well, it seems the PSA level is high and apparently that's not a good sign. Dr Wilson is going to get me an appointment with a consultant immediately after Christmas.'

It was a blow. It had been Debbie's hope that everything would be normal and that John would return with better news.

'So what will happen now – I mean when you see the consultant?'

John thought for a few seconds. 'Some sort of internal examination, I believe.'

Debbie put her arms round him and gave him a hug. 'I'm sure everything will turn out all right.' She tried to sound as encouraging as possible.

John smiled reassuringly. 'Got to be positive,' he replied, adding for good measure: 'Nothing is certain yet.'

Steps sounded on the stairs. Trish was returning.

'Don't say anything.' Debbie whispered, as she broke free.

John nodded. The next instance he was greeting Trish. 'Hi there, Trish. Move your car a minute and let me into the garage.'

Debbie heard them disappear and finished making Trish's coffee. She felt a bit subdued at John's news, but she was determined to appear positive, for his sake and hers.

After Christmas they would face together whatever needed to be faced.

Chapter 33

On Christmas Day Debbie woke from a muddled dream and lay there a few minutes trying to remember it, but failed completely. The luminous hands of her bedside clock showed that it was coming up to six o'clock. Quite early, but she still had to get some of the vegetables ready for dinner. She had prepared some the previous day, but time was going to be limited, particularly with John and Trish around. She decided to get up and make a start. She remembered John's offer of help, but he was sleeping peacefully beside her and there did not seem to be any point in disturbing him.

She slipped out of bed and tiptoed to the bathroom. It was tricky trying not to make a noise. Ten minutes later she was creeping downstairs in her dressing gown and slippers. Once in the security of the kitchen she closed the door and flipped a switch, flooding the room with welcoming light. She felt quite good about being up early. With luck she would have everything done before John and Trish appeared.

She had been working away methodically for about twenty minutes when she was conscious of a slight sound in the hall. The next moment the door opened and Trish stood there in her pyjamas, with tousled hair.

'Mum, what are you doing?' Trish spoke almost in a whisper.

'Darling, I'm so sorry. Did I wake you up?' Debbie was concerned that her 'keep quiet' strategy had not worked. She kept her voice deliberately low.

Trish shook her head. 'I was awake. But why are you up so early?'

Debbie beckoned her into the kitchen. 'Come in and shut the door.' When Trish had complied, she explained. 'Jan's mother-in-law has arrived for Christmas and Jan's in a bit of a state. I told her I would help with the dinner. I was awake, so I thought I'd make a start.'

'I'll give you a hand.'

Debbie did not refuse. For one thing she welcomed the opportunity to chat to her daughter. 'Oh, that would be marvellous,' she replied, at the same time glancing at Trish's apparel. 'You'd better put on something warmer, though. Slip your dressing gown on.'

Trish made a face. 'I didn't bring one, but I'll put some clothes on.' And with that she disappeared. In no more than three minutes she reappeared, wearing jeans and a woolly pullover. 'What can I do?' she asked.

'You can finish off these potatoes and I'll start on the Brussels sprouts. John grew them on the allotment.'

Trish moved to take her mother's place at the sink. 'OK.'

'Shall I make us a drink?' Debbie asked.

'Oh, let me do it. I could do with a coffee to wake me up properly,' was Trish's quick response.

Debbie was amazed. She could almost count on one hand the number of times Trish had offered to make a drink for her. She accepted gracefully. 'Perhaps I'd better have a coffee to keep me awake.' She gave a little laugh.

Debbie concentrated on the vegetables while Trish made the coffee. When the coffee was ready Trish put both mugs on the kitchen table and sat down. It was clear she considered that having a coffee meant sitting down to drink it. Debbie joined her. They would still get the jobs done, and this was an opportunity to have a rare face-to-face chat with her daughter. 'So are you happy in your new flat?' she asked.

Trish sipped her coffee. 'Oh yes. It's great.' She thought for a second, then continued. 'The thing is, I might not be there long.' She hesitated again and then announced: 'Mum, Alan has asked me to marry him.' She looked at Debbie for a response.

It was news that Debbie had somehow expected, but she was a bit surprised at the suddenness of it after her last chat with Trish on the subject. She decided to play for time before being exuberant over Trish's announcement. 'And have you said yes?'

Trish shook her head. 'I've told him I want a little time to think about it.'

Debbie smiled. 'And what did he say to that?'

Trish gave a little smile. 'He's very sweet about it. He says he'll wait, but he'll keep on asking me until I say yes.'

'And how do you feel about it?'

Trish was quite philosophical. 'I like him a lot. We get on well together. He's very caring and considerate. Quite different from Don. In a way he's good for me, because he keeps my feet on the ground.'

There was silence for a few seconds, but before Debbie could answer Trish spoke again. 'I mean, I want to get married again sometime, but I don't want to mess things up like last time.'

Debbie smiled at her daughter. She thought for a few seconds and then contributed a few words of reassurance. 'I think what you've done is sensible. It's best not to rush into things, but from what you've just said it would seem that there are the basic ingredients for a happy marriage.'

'How do you mean?' Trish asked, looking directly at her.

It was a tricky question. Debbie constructed her reply carefully. 'Well, the basis of a happy and long-lasting marriage is not about being madly attracted to someone and jumping into bed with them. It's about having respect and admiration for each other and wanting to spend time in each other's company. Then of course you have to be able to work together sorting out life's problems.'

'But you and Daddy made it,' Trish interjected.

'Yes, but it wasn't plain sailing all the way. We had our ups and downs, but we always managed to sort things out together.'

'What about you and John?'

Debbie gave a soft laugh. 'Well, one hopes that the second time around one's learnt from the mistakes of the first time.'

'Hmm... I see what you mean.'

Debbie wondered whether she had said too much. It prompted her to add: 'I hope what I've said doesn't make a decision difficult for you.'

Trish gave a grin. 'No, it's all right – really, Mum.'

Debbie could detect that that was the end of the conversation on the subject. No doubt Trish would make up her mind in due course. She drank the last of her coffee and glanced at the clock. 'Gosh, we'd better get going with these veggies.'

With the two of them working it did not take long to complete the job. All the vegetables for Christmas dinner were now ready for cooking. Debbie was pleased with their efforts. It would be a tremendous boost later on when she was helping the harassed Jan with the dinner.

She and Trish had just about finished when the kitchen door opened and John stood there in his dressing gown. 'Morning all,' was his greeting.

'Good morning, darling. Happy Christmas.' Debbie gave him a kiss on the cheek. Trish greeted him with a 'hi'.

John glanced around the kitchen. 'Now, what about those spuds? Let's get cracking.'

Debbie laughed. 'Too late! Everything's done. Trish helped me.'

'By Jove, I timed that well,' observed John, looking round and grinning.

He and Trish seemed inclined to linger in the kitchen a while. Debbie took control. 'Right, everything's done here. I'm going to get breakfast going and you two can fight over the bathroom, then I'll have a quickie clean-up when you've finished.'

'OK. I know when I'm not wanted,' retorted John, getting up from his chair.

'Ten minutes' more sleep might be a good idea,' observed Trish, obediently making for the door and yawning.

The day went better than Debbie had expected, even though she spent the better part of the morning in the kitchen. With two children and her mother-in-law around, all demanding attention, Jan was clearly finding it difficult to cope. Debbie could see the problem. Donning an apron to protect her dress, she automatically assumed the role of head cook, much to Jan's relief. She was helped from time to time by John and Trish, both eager to escape for a few minutes from Mabel's criticism and grumbling.

Trish was the first to be under fire from Mabel. A glance at her stilettos prompted the remark: 'How on earth do you young girls walk in shoes like that? You'll ruin your feet.'

Trish pouted a bit, and then replied: 'I don't see it as a problem.'

Mabel was about to respond, but Debbie hurriedly butted in and asked her if she had had a good journey up from Bristol the previous day.

When Trish came into the kitchen later to help her mother, her first remark was: 'Did you hear what that old bat said about my shoes?'

This prompted Debbie to wonder what sort of comment she would receive when she put on a pair of heeled shoes later on for dinner. She had kept a pair of flats on for working.

When Jan joined them a few minutes later, Debbie realised the stress she was going through with her mother-in-law around. 'She's been sitting on that settee whingeing and criticising ever since she arrived yesterday afternoon,' Jan almost whispered to them.

'Does she live on her own?' Debbie asked.

Jan shook her head. 'Her younger sister lives with her. From what I can glean she's little more than a servant.' She lowered her voice. 'The trouble is, Mabel's the one with the money.'

The brief conversation was halted by the appearance of Paul carrying a tearful Emma. 'I think she wants changing,' he said to Jan.

'Darling, can you do it? I was just going to help Mum with the dinner,' Jan pleaded.

'Paul! PAUL!' Mabel's voice sounded from the lounge.

'Coming, Mother!' Paul looked desperately at Jan.

'Oh here, let me do it. Give her to me.' Jan took Emma from Paul, who immediately disappeared in the direction of the lounge.

A frustrated Jan turned to her mother and Trish. 'You can see my problem, can't you?' Making a face, she left the kitchen carrying her daughter.

As soon as she had gone, Debbie whispered: 'Poor Jan. She's really got her hands full. I guess I'll have to do most of the cooking today.'

'I'll give you a hand. It's good practice for me.' Trish chuckled.

'Well, thank goodness I'm in a kitchen I'm familiar with,' observed Debbie.

In spite of all the time she ended up spending in the kitchen, Debbie enjoyed Christmas Day. Trish was with her for quite a lot of the time and it gave them the opportunity to chat about a wide range of subjects, albeit with frequent interruptions from Jan trying to help and John intending to help but usually being dragged away almost immediately by a demanding Jamie.

It was not until Christmas was over and Trish had gone back to London that Debbie returned to thoughts of John's health problem. Over the holiday she had put it to the back of her mind. Once the initial shock had dispersed a little, she had adopted a more optimistic attitude. After all, she reasoned, nothing was proven yet, and until John had further tests they didn't know anything for certain. This had been reinforced by John himself, who had maintained a low-key approach to the situation. They had both agreed from the start that there was no point in mentioning it to the family until they had more information. As John had remarked, the whole thing could be a storm in a teacup.

A few days after Christmas, John was playing on the computer while Debbie pottered in the kitchen. It was one of those cold, wet days when neither of them felt inclined to venture forth. Debbie heard the plop of the post on the mat and went into the hall to collect it. There were two letters: one for her and one for John. She recognised at once the hospital logo on the envelope addressed to John. She called out: 'John, there's a letter for you from the hospital.'

John appeared almost immediately. He said nothing but took the envelope from her and tore it open. It only took him a few seconds to scrutinise the contents. He looked at her. '9am next Wednesday,' he announced.

'That's the third of January.'

'Dr Wilson said it would be quick.'

'Will they be able to tell you what the problem is then?'

John answered vaguely: 'I'm not sure. If they think it's cancer, they may want to do more tests.'

Alarm bells sounded for Debbie. This was the first time John had mentioned cancer. It seemed to make everything more sinister. She had worried from the start that it might be cancer, but she had kept her thoughts to herself in order not to worry John more than necessary. Now that he had spoken the word, it was up to her to show a strong front.

'It's not going to be cancer. I'm sure of it,' she announced firmly.

John nodded. 'I expect you're right.'

Debbie made a move in the direction of the kitchen, 'Come on,' she called over her shoulder, 'It's time for elevenses. I've baked an apple cake.'

'You're on,' enthused John, hurrying after her.

The weather turned decidedly bad over the next couple of days. Snow fell and then froze on the roads, making driving difficult. John and Debbie had been invited to spend New Year with Rob and Cathy. The idea had been to drive down on New Year's Eve, stay overnight and then drive back the following day. Debbie had been looking forward to their visit for two reasons. After her catering stint at Christmas, she welcomed the thought of somebody else doing the cooking; and she always worried a little that she was very involved with her own family, but they saw so little of John's relatives. She did not like the idea of driving on icy roads, though, and it looked as if they might have to cancel the trip. It was John who came up with a solution. The trains were still running. Why not go by train, he suggested.

It turned out to be an enjoyable respite for both of them. Cathy spoiled them and Debbie welcomed the opportunity of being entertained by her and Rob in their own home and getting to know them a bit better. It was when they returned home after the interlude that the nearness of John's hospital appointment started to make its impact on them. John still maintained his jovial and rather casual approach to things and Debbie did her best to remain cheerful and positive for his sake, but she was worried and she knew he felt the same.

Wednesday came round swiftly. John departed soon after breakfast and Debbie amused herself as best she could, finding odd jobs to keep her mind off things. At one point Jan rang and was on the phone a long time giving a detailed account of her mother-in-law's visit over Christmas. Debbie listened, offering a word of sympathy here and there.

When Jan had at last ended her call, Debbie wandered back into the kitchen. It was difficult to concentrate. She made herself a drink and carried it into the lounge. The newspaper lay on the side table where John had abandoned it earlier. She picked it up and glanced through the contents, but when she came to an article on cancer and survival rates she lost interest. It was the last thing she wanted to read about this morning.

It was close to midday when John returned. Debbie heard the garage door close and hurried into the hall to meet him. He gave her what she thought was a reassuring smile.

'Darling, what happened? Is it good news?'

John shook his head. 'I have to go back next week to find out for certain.'

'Oh no...' Debbie could have wept. 'I was so sure we would know today,' she said.

'So was I.'

Debbie struggled to come to terms with the new development. 'But why the wait?' she asked.

John put his arms round her. 'I think to be certain about the results of the tests, etc.' He gave her one of his grins. 'It'll be all right. You'll see.'

His calm approach nudged Debbie into a calmer appraisal of the situation. It was no good going over the top. It was her job to support him in a calm and dignified way. She gave him a peck on the cheek and forced a smile. 'Did they say when next week?' she asked in as positive voice as she could muster.

'Wednesday.'

So it was to be another week of waiting. Well, if John could cope with it, so would she. She turned her attention to other matters. 'Let's have lunch,' she suggested. 'It'll only take a few minutes to warm up some soup.'

She turned and headed for the kitchen, followed by John. It was a blow still not knowing what his problem was. But there was really nothing either of them could do except wait until the following Wednesday and hope for good news.

Chapter 34

Debbie offered to drive John to the hospital but he refused, making the excuse that it would mean a lot of waiting around for her. Debbie accepted his reasoning. She guessed that he wanted to be alone for his appointment, without an anxious wife around.

He left with his usual parting kiss and this time they lingered longer than usual over the exchange. Debbie watched him get into the car and then with a wave he was gone.

While he was away, time seemed to pass very slowly. Debbie pottered about in the kitchen, not really concentrating on any job. Her thoughts were with John and the information he would receive. She prayed that it would not turn out to be cancer, but deep down she knew he would not have been given a second appointment if there had been no area of concern. If it was cancer, she knew that it would affect their lives considerably. How many men survived prostate cancer? She had read somewhere that the odds were against survival if the cancer was not found in the early stages. Perhaps the odds were in John's favour. He had gone to the doctor as soon as he realised there was a problem. She had seen to that. The most dreaded thought that gripped her from time to time was what she would do if she lost John. Since she had met him, her life had taken on a new vibrancy; it was almost as if she had woken up from a dream. She had started to live again. If that were to end...? She could not face the thought.

It was the telephone that dragged her out of her melancholy. Who could it be? It was too early for John to be ringing her. She went into the lounge to answer it.

'Mum, it's Trish.'

'Hello, darling. I didn't expect it to be you.'

'Mum, I've got some news for you. I've accepted Alan's proposal of marriage.'

'Darling, that's marvellous! When's it going to be?'

'We thought May or June. What do you think?'

'That's a lovely time to get married.' A thought flashed through Debbie's head. How would John be? But she dismissed it immediately. Instead she asked: 'Where will it be?'

'We've not quite decided yet. Neither of us likes the idea of London. It could be somewhere near Alan's parents or perhaps in Oxford. Where you got married to John looked good.'

'Oh, that would be nice.' Memories flooded back to Debbie. So much had happened since that day. She went quiet for a few seconds.

'Mum, you are glad, aren't you?'

Debbie rallied to the challenge. 'Darling, of course I am. You've just caught me a bit on the hop. I think it's a splendid idea and Alan comes over as a very nice person. I'm sure you'll be very happy with him.'

'I've thought a lot about it and also about what you said to me at Christmas. I'm sure he's the man for me.'

'Have you told Jan?'

'Not yet, but I'm going to.' Suddenly she piped up: 'Mum, can you get married in church if you're divorced?'

Debbie thought for a moment. 'I'm not sure. It probably depends on the church. Why? Were you contemplating a church wedding?' Such a suggestion from her unconventional daughter surprised her.

Trish's next comment enlightened her. 'It's just Alan's mum. She thinks it would be nice. They have a lovely old church in their village.'

'Oh, I see. You'd have to go and see the vicar,' Debbie answered, but her thoughts were already straying back to John.

Debbie could hear a chuckle at the other end of the line before Trish spoke. 'It's only an idea. Alan and I are the ones who are getting married. We'll make our own minds up about where it will be.'

It was perhaps the best way, Debbie thought, but before she could answer Trish chipped in: 'If I did get married in church, do you think John would give me away?'

The suggestion caused Debbie to panic. Surely she should tell Trish about John, in spite of the fact that they had agreed not to say anything to either family until they knew for sure what was happening. What would the situation be in six months' time? It was something she didn't want to contemplate. Suddenly she found herself replying: 'Oh, I'm sure he'd love to.' It did not help her state of mind.

It was Trish who ended the call. 'Mum, I'd better get some work done. I'm at my desk on my mobile. I just had to tell you the news.'

'Darling, it was lovely of you to do that. Why don't you and Alan come and see us again soon?' As soon as she realised what she had said, guilt attacked Debbie yet again. Surely she should say something... What was going to happen to John?

'Will do. Bye, Mum.' Trish's quick reply made a decision for her.

'Bye-bye, darling.'

Debbie replaced the handset. She felt miserable for not telling Trish about John, but somehow she hadn't been able to bring herself to do so. It was ironic that Trish should ring with her news on the very day that John was to find out if he had cancer. Why did things happen like that? She felt that she should have responded in a more positive way, but she had let her feelings influence her reaction. Perhaps Trish hadn't noticed...

She wandered back to the kitchen, but she knew there was nothing to do there. It was too soon after breakfast to make a drink. She stood looking out of the window at the tiny garden. It looked cold and uninviting in the January light. She had spent many hours pottering out there since they had moved into the house. After John had done the heavy work of digging the beds over, it had mainly fallen to her to do the rest, though recently she had been joining him on the allotment more often, enjoying the open-air environment and the sociability there. During the summer, she had even been persuaded at the last minute to help run the annual barbecue.

She turned from the window and looked around the kitchen. No jobs inspired her, though eventually she would have to prepare some lunch, but it was a bit early for that and she didn't know when John would return. He had promised to text her and let her know, but her mobile phone lay silent on the kitchen table. Something made her pick it up and put it in her skirt pocket.

A noise at the front door jerked her into action. Someone seemed to be having difficulty in getting something through the letter box. The sound made her rush to the door. She reached it just as the bell rang, and opened it to find a postman on the doorstep holding a package. 'Got something for you,' he announced, smiling at her. She knew at once what it was: it was a gardening book John had ordered.

'Oh. Thank you.' She relieved him of the package. It was certainly too big to go through the letter box.

'Thanks. Bye.' And with that the postman was on his way again.

'Bye,' Debbie called after him as he walked back down the drive.

She was about to close the door when a 4x4 turned into the driveway. She recognised it immediately. It was Madge.

Debbie's heart sank. Oh no, she thought. Not Madge, today of all days. The thought was unbearable. Desperately she tried to think of some excuse not to entertain her. Could she say she was just going out? But dressed the way she was it hardly looked like it. Madge was already getting out of the car. 'Hiya!' she called out.

'Hello, Madge.' Debbie felt that her greeting was hardly inviting.

Madge moved towards her. 'Thought it was time I dropped in to see you guys.' Clearly she had the usual coffee and biscuits in mind.

'Come in.' Debbie stepped aside to let Madge enter the hall. She felt trapped but somehow could not bring herself to turn Madge away. She closed the front door. 'I expect you'd like a coffee,' she said.

'You bet.' Madge was already heading for the kitchen.

Debbie filled the kettle and clicked it on to boil. Entertaining was the last thing she wanted to do at present; certainly not Madge. But she was at a loss as to how she could have avoided letting her into the house, short of bolting the door.

'Where's John?' Madge asked.

'He had to go out for something.' Debbie tried to be as vague as possible. Madge was the last person she wanted to discuss John's problem with. She blocked any further questions on the subject by asking one of her own. 'Did you have a good Christmas?'

Madge nodded, her eyes already on the plate of biscuits Debbie had put on the table. 'I went on a cruise,' she said in a matter-of-fact tone of voice.

'Was it good?' Debbie asked, trying to maintain an interest.

'Better than sticking around here,' Madge replied, helping herself to a biscuit as Debbie placed a mug of coffee in front of her.

'Has your problem blown over?' Madge asked, scrutinising the biscuit.

'My problem?' Debbie was puzzled for a moment. For a few seconds she could not grasp what Madge was referring to. Her mind was occupied with John.

Madge bit into the biscuit. 'That problem you had with that guy in the car park,' she replied, taking a drink from her mug.

'Oh, I'd almost forgotten about that.' It was true. For Debbie, the unpleasant encounter in the summer had gradually merged into the past, occasionally to be recalled when some reported incident brought it to light again. Now with John's problem foremost in their minds, the episode had lost its intensity. It was odd how you went through a bad patch and thought it was the worst you could experience, then another one loomed up and made the previous one seem insignificant.

Madge picked up on Debbie's less than breezy manner. 'You're a bit down in the dumps this morning. What's wrong?'

Debbie responded quickly. 'Oh, I'm fine. Just January blues, I expect.' She tried to smile.

Madge was about to reply, but Debbie took evasive action. 'Tell me about your cruise,' she said. She wasn't interested, but at least it would change the subject. She didn't really want to talk to anybody. She was willing John to return and she wanted Madge to go. Why, today of all days did she have to have a dental appointment and drop in to see them?

Madge droned on, talking about her holiday, and then went on to

332

cruising in general. Debbie listened, occasionally asking a question, but mostly just sitting there pretending to be interested and wishing she would leave.

The minutes seemed to drag. Debbie's eyes frequently focused on the clock on the wall behind Madge, but the hands seemed to move so slowly. Almost half the plate of biscuits had disappeared, and still Madge showed no sign of departing.

It was the bleep of Debbie's mobile phone that broke the pattern. She took it out of her pocket and pressed the button. The text message was brief: 'Be home soon.' She clicked the phone off and put it down on the table. One thought ran through her mind. How much longer would Madge stay? The thought of her being around when John returned was really too much to bear.

'Was that your man?' Madge enquired.

'Yes. He's on his way back.' Debbie hoped this comment might urge Madge to go. It was to no avail. Madge continued to talk, while Debbie sat opposite and fumed.

It seemed to be only a short while before there was the sound of a key in the front door. Debbie's heart sank. She had so desperately wanted to be on her own when John returned.

He appeared in the doorway. 'I'm back,' he announced and then, spying the visitor, he added: 'Hello Madge.'

'Hi there,' she replied.

'Hello, darling. Would you like a coffee?' Debbie did her best to behave as normal.

'Please.'

John sat down at the table in the chair Debbie had vacated. Madge seemed inclined to chat, but Debbie could detect that John's brief answers indicated that his thoughts were elsewhere. Something had happened; she knew it. Oh, when would Madge go?

Debbie made a mug of coffee for John and placed it on the table in front of him. For the next ten minutes the conversation was between him and Madge. Debbie remained almost silent. All she wanted to do now was talk to him and find out what had happened.

At last Madge got up from the table. Debbie accompanied her to the front door. Goodbyes were brief and Debbie did not wait for Madge to drive off. She returned to the kitchen where John was still sitting at the table. As she entered, the pent-up feelings burst out. 'Why of all days did that woman have to call this morning?'

John looked up at her, but he did not speak. His face was clouded in deep thought.

Debbie recovered her composure quickly. This was not the time to give vent to her personal feelings. She could see that he had not had good news from the hospital.

She slipped into a seat next to him, placed her hand on his arm and asked the question that was uppermost in her mind. 'What happened at the hospital?'

John looked at her as he spoke. 'Not good news, I'm afraid.' He tried to give the imitation of a smile.

'Tell me.'

He continued to look at her. 'Darling, it means an operation.' He spoke calmly.

She tried to assimilate the news. It was information she had hoped would not appear. But now it had, she had to appear strong and positive for John's sake.

'So it is cancer?' She hated saying the word, but it had to be talked about.

John nodded. 'It would appear so,' he replied glumly.

'When did they say the operation would be?' Debbie asked gently.

'As soon as possible,' he replied. 'Whatever that means.'

Debbie guessed the news had hit him harder than he had anticipated. She had no doubt that once he had accepted the situation he would return to his usual calm and logical self. In the meantime it was up to her to support him as much as possible. 'What else did they say?' she asked.

'They think the cancer is in the early stages.' He sipped his coffee.

'Well, that's good news, isn't it?' Debbie tried to accompany the suggestion with a reassuring smile.

'That's what the surgeon said,' replied John, with a glimpse of one of his grins. Then, after another mouthful of coffee, he added: 'He's a really nice chap.'

'Well that's a good thing as well.' Debbie was determined to remain positive. While John finished drinking his coffee she continued to ask questions, drawing out from him the details of the morning's ordeal.

After ten minutes or so, she had a good idea of what had taken place, but best of all she could detect that by talking with her, John was very slowly getting over the initial shock of the news he had been given. It was a good sign. At one point he said: 'Gosh, I'd better give old Rob a ring later and tell him the good news.' There was now a trace of humour in his voice.

John's remark triggered a thought in Debbie. 'I'll have to tell the girls as well, if that's all right with you.' She looked at him for confirmation.

'Of course.' He changed the subject. 'What did Madge want?'

'Oh, the usual thing, coffee and a chat.' Debbie was feeling a bit more kindly towards Madge by now. But she had to add: 'Sometimes that woman really gets under my skin, particularly today when I was waiting for you.'

John smiled, but said nothing.

Debbie got up from her chair. 'I'm going to make lunch,' she announced.

'Best idea you've had all morning,' quipped John, with just a sign of his old self.

Debbie was about to deliver an appropriate retort, when she suddenly remembered something. She talked over her shoulder. 'Trish rang while you were out. She and Alan are going to get married, May or June time.'

John responded cheerfully. 'That's great. Trish deserves a guy like Alan.'

Debbie thought of something else. 'She's talking of getting married in church. She's planning to ask you to give her away.'

John thought for a minute, and then broke his silence. 'Got to be there for that,' he said.

Lunch was a quiet affair. Both of them tried to maintain a normal atmosphere and chat about general matters, but Debbie knew that both of their thoughts were on John's problem. She deliberately did not press John for more information; she knew it would come in time when he had come to terms with everything.

After lunch John said he had a few things to do on the computer and Debbie guessed that he wanted to be on his own for a while or perhaps find out more on the internet. She readily complied and told him she would call him for a cup of tea later in the afternoon.

'More tea?' Debbie asked, teapot in hand.

'Please.' John held out his cup. The last remains of daylight filtered into the room. They had gravitated into the lounge as usual and it became the time for them to talk over what lay ahead of them. Debbie wanted to know more about John's visit to the hospital and now with the dust settling he was more inclined to go into detail. She was pleased to see that he was taking a much more philosophical view of things, though at times it was obvious that he was feeling despondent. She was determined to put on a cheerful and positive front, not only for John's sake but also for her own, and she concentrated on the more positive aspects of their changed situation.

At one point John remarked: 'I just had a thought — being unfit for duties is going to make a bit of a mess of the start of the allotment season.'

'I can plant things,' she announced firmly. 'You can supervise.'

John gave an impression of a smile before replying. 'As long as you plant the onion sets the right way up.'

She was about to respond with mock indignation, but he spoke again. 'Might have to give up the allotment,' he remarked glumly.

Debbie was aghast. 'Of course you won't. You'll just miss the first bit of the year.'

'I suppose you're right.' He did not seem convinced.

Debbie could see that he was lapsing into despondency. Strong action was needed on her part.

She moved to sit beside him on the settee. She looked at him for a few seconds, then said quietly: 'John, it's going to be all right. I just know it is.'

He nodded. 'It's just all the uncertainty,' he replied thoughtfully.

Debbie placed her hand on his arm. Gently she said: 'John, there are thousands of men walking around who have had prostate cancer, all of them just fine. You know, having cancer these days is not an automatic death sentence.'

John looked at her and smiled reassuringly. 'Yes, that's quite true. Having cancer is not a death sentence.'

They sat together side by side holding hands, silent in the gathering dusk of the afternoon.

Chapter 35

'Mum, I'll never be able to wear these shoes.' The statement was preceded by a wail of anguish.

Debbie sighed under her breath. The tone of Trish's voice demanded her immediate attention. She stopped what she was doing and walked from her bedroom into the one occupied by Trish. It was the day before Trish's wedding to Alan and so far the morning had been one of last-minute nerves and unexpected problems that usually required Debbie's calming input.

Trish was standing in her underwear next to the bed, which was strewn with various items of clothing. She was scrutinising scornfully the pair of shoes on the floor beside her. She glanced up as Debbie appeared in the doorway.

'I can't wear these tomorrow – they're just too tight.' Trish looked anxiously at her mother and then at the shoes again.

'Haven't you tried them on before?' Debbie asked, curious as to how the situation had occurred.

'I tried them on in the shop. They seemed to be all right then,' Trish replied with a pout.

'Perhaps we can stretch them a little. I've got a pair of those things you put inside shoes to make them more comfortable.'

Trish shrugged. 'I doubt if it will work.'

'Shall we try?' Debbie asked, anxious to remedy the situation.

Trish thought for a moment. Then she snapped into action. 'I'm going into Oxford to buy another pair.' She grabbed her jeans from where they lay abandoned on the floor.

Debbie was about to intervene but changed her mind. Sometimes it was just better to let things happen.

'I'm going to have a job to find any,' Trish grumbled as she struggled into her jeans. 'It took me ages to find those,' she added, glancing at the offending objects.

Debbie said nothing, but handed Trish her shirt, which was draped over the back of a chair. As she did so she noticed a slight discoloration on Trish's shoulder. 'You've got rid of the tattoo,' she observed.

Trish glanced briefly at her shoulder. 'I had to, for Alan's sake,' she replied glumly, continuing dressing.

'Was it difficult?'

Trish made a face. 'The price was. It cost £500.'

'But it's left a mark,' Debbie observed, thinking £500 was a large sum of money to rectify a few minutes' madness and then leave a mark.

'They told me that will disappear. I hope so. I wish I'd never had the wretched thing done.' Trish grabbed her car keys and shoulder bag from the dressing table, as if to end the subject.

Debbie hoped so, too. She could never quite understand the popularity amongst young girls of disfiguring their bodies with tattoos.

'I'm going,' announced Trish, glancing round the room and then making for the door.

'OK, dear. Do you want a coffee before you go?' Debbie asked, partly because she fancied one herself.

'No time, Mum.' And with that Trish was off.

For some reason Debbie lingered in the bedroom. She heard Trish scamper down the stairs and stop for a minute to put on some shoes, and then there was the slam of the front door. The next minute she heard Trish's car starting up.

She looked around the room. Behind the door hung Trish's dress, an attractive one with a deep vee neck. This time, much to Debbie's relief, Trish had done her own shopping for a wedding outfit. Her two suitcases for the honeymoon were neatly packed and stood outside on the landing.

Debbie went to leave the room, but something made her stop and pick up the shoes that had been the reason for Trish's sudden departure. They were a pretty court style with a tiny bow on the front. The leather did not feel as hard as Debbie had imagined it would. She felt sure that with a bit of perseverance and stretching the shoes could have been serviceable. But it was too late now. She regretted not insisting before Trish's rapid departure that her solution might work.

She left the shambles of the room and wandered back to her own bedroom. Her outfit for the wedding was hanging up with John's suit. Everything was ready except for a few last-minute jobs. She found she could not concentrate on what she had been doing prior to Trish's interruption. Her thoughts were elsewhere. In the end she gave up and went downstairs to the kitchen. She made herself a cup of coffee and sat down at the table. Alone in the house, she began to think about the events of the previous six months.

John's operation had taken place in January. It had gone better than they both expected and Debbie had been surprised how quickly John had recovered. The doctors emphasised that they thought they had caught the problem in its infancy. Once he had got over the initial shock of the diagnosis, John had remained remarkably cheerful and optimistic and Debbie had been concerned at the start of the season when he announced that he was fit to tackle working on the allotment. She had immediately offered to help him, tactfully explaining that she was keen to get over there and assist him as there would be a lot to do after the long winter. While they were both now satisfied that things had gone well, uncertainty always lurked at the back of their minds.

When John received an appointment to learn the result of follow-up tests, Debbie had been horrified. 'But that's the day before Trish's wedding!' she had exclaimed. She knew that neither event could be altered easily, but the thought of bad news on the eve of her daughter's big day tormented her.

Planning for the wedding had not been without its difficulties, most of which fell to Debbie to sort out. Trish had stuck with her intention of a June wedding but had dithered about where it should be held. In the end she and Alan had chosen the register office Debbie and John had used. This had caused some concern from Alan's parents, who would have liked the couple to marry in their village. Oxford had been chosen because it was easy for most of Alan's relatives to reach from Birmingham. Only his parents and his married sister lived in Hampshire. Compromise was eventually reached when it was agreed that Alan's parents would travel up by car with his sister and brother-in-law for the wedding and travel back the same day. Trish had handled most of the arrangements for the reception, but as it was to be held in a hotel close by, John and Debbie had found themselves doing many of the routine jobs such as booking taxis, ordering the bouquets and checking on things to pacify an anxious Trish.

Trish had arrived the previous evening and from then on things had been hectic. She had kept thinking of other things that needed her mother's attention. All the time, at the back of her mind Debbie had been concerned for John. As usual he had remained calm, supporting Debbie and often acting as a father figure to Trish.

Debbie sipped her coffee, enjoying for a few minutes looking at the tiny garden bathed in sunshine. Just for once it was pleasant to sit there by herself and think about things. She was looking forward to seeing Trish get married again, but she was also conscious that the events of the year so far and the increased activity of the previous few days had left her feeling drained of energy. John had suggested that once things calmed down, they could fix a holiday, but first life had to return to normal. For Debbie to really enjoy a break, good news about John's health was essential.

Thinking of his return prompted a return of her concerns. She glanced at the kitchen clock. Nearly eleven o'clock; John should have been back ages ago. Suppose he had had bad news? Perhaps there was something the doctors hadn't told him. Perhaps he had to have more tests. The thoughts raced through her brain.

The sound of a key in the front door jerked her out of her

melancholy. She immediately jumped up from her chair. It could only be John or Trish. She rushed into the hall. John was changing his shoes. 'John, what's happened?'

He turned to look at her. He was smiling. He gave a thumbs-up sign. 'All clear,' he announced, still smiling.

Debbie rushed towards him and threw her arms about him. 'Oh John, when you were so long I was sure it must be bad news.' She pressed her face into his shoulder. She could not say any more. Tears of relief were close to the surface.

John held her close for a second. 'Hey, steady on. There's life in the old dog yet.'

She eased herself away from him and wiped a tear from her eye. 'I'm sorry for acting so silly. It was just that I was getting worried sitting waiting on my own.'

He was about to reply, but she chipped in, determined to regain control. 'Tell me what happened.'

John gave her one of his grins. 'Not a lot to it. Everything's fine. I've just got to go back for a check-up in six months.'

'Come and tell me about it. I'll make you a drink.' Debbie was already on her way to the kitchen.

John followed her and slipped into one of the chairs. 'Where's Trish?' he asked.

Debbie stopped in the middle of filling the kettle. She gave a little sigh. 'She went out to buy some shoes.'

'What?'

Debbie explained. 'She complained that the ones she bought for tomorrow were too tight, so she dashed off to buy another pair. Heaven knows what time she'll be back.'

John laughed. 'Good old Trish,' he exclaimed.

'She nearly drove me mad while you were out. Every few minutes she seemed to find some problem that needed sorting out,' Debbie remarked glumly, returning to filling the kettle.

John was still amused. 'Well, let's face it, she doesn't get married every day.'

Debbie looked at him and smiled. 'A good job. I don't think I'd survive if that happened. I don't know how you keep so calm.'

'You're doing just fine. By this time tomorrow everything will be in full swing.' John gave her a wink as he spoke.

Debbie was about to respond, but he continued before she could say anything. 'Oh, by the way, just as I came back, Jean next door called me over. She offered to let us park Trish's car on their forecourt. They're going away for a fortnight.'

'Oh, that was very sweet of her,' Debbie exclaimed. She added enthusiastically: 'And it solves another problem.' There was only room for one car in front of their garage. If there was a car standing there, it always had to be moved to get John's car in or out of the garage. Both John and Debbie had foreseen that it could be a problem while Trish was on her honeymoon.

Before either of them could speak again the telephone rang.

'I'll get it.' Debbie was already halfway out of the kitchen. She hurried to the phone and picked it up. 'Hello.'

'Hello, Mum.' It was the familiar voice of Jan.

'Hello, dear. I didn't expect you to ring. Everything all right?'

'Mum, I don't think we'll be able to come tomorrow. I think Jamie is sickening for something.'

'Oh no! What's the problem? Trish will be so disappointed.' Debbie tried to hide her own disappointment.

'He's a bit feverish and says he feels sick. He was all right yesterday.'

Debbie thought quickly. 'Why don't you see if you can get an appointment with Dr Wilson?' she suggested.

Jan seemed to be luke-warm to the idea. 'I suppose I could. But it's a bit late for today.'

'Well, try.'

Jan's tone changed. 'OK, I will as soon as I've rung off.' Then she asked: 'Is Trish with you?'

'Yes,' replied Debbie. 'She got here last night. Alan's coming tomorrow morning.'

'Can I speak to her?'

'She's not in at the moment. I'll get her to call you if you like.'

'OK. Where's she gone?'

'She went to buy a pair of shoes for tomorrow.'

'What, for the wedding? Ridiculous. She should have sorted that out ages ago.'

Debbie was about to explain, but Jan spoke again immediately. 'I'd better go, Mum. I'll ring the surgery now.'

'Let me know what happens,' Debbie insisted.

'Will do. Bye.' And with that Jan rang off.

Debbie sighed as she made her way back to the kitchen. It would be the last straw if Jan and her family couldn't make the wedding.

John looked up questioningly as she entered the kitchen.

'That was Jan. She thinks they might not be able to come tomorrow. Jamie isn't well.'

'I say, that's a bit of a disappointment for Trish.' John was clearly concerned. Then he added thoughtfully: 'Perhaps he will make a miraculous recovery.'

Debbie tried to be optimistic. 'I really hope so.'

It was late in the evening on Trish's wedding day. John and Debbie were relaxing on the patio in the last of the day's sunshine. John had taken off his tie with an exclamation of relief and Debbie had at long last thankfully removed her shoes.

John looked up from the newspaper he was casually glancing through and smiled across at Debbie. 'It didn't go so badly after all, did it?'

Debbie was more thoughtful in her reply. 'I don't think it could have been bettered in any way, in spite of all the minor problems beforehand.'

'And the hard work,' added John.

Debbie did not respond immediately. She was in a reflective mood. For all the anxious incidents beforehand, she knew the day had gone well and had been enjoyed by everybody, but the previous two days had been hectic and not without anxious moments. Trish had returned from her shoe-hunting expedition empty-handed. 'I couldn't get anything,' she had wailed on arrival. It had taken tact and persuasion for Debbie to assume control and stretch the offending objects overnight so that Trish could wear them. Fortunately her strategy had worked.

Alan had surprised everybody by turning up earlier than expected, much to Trish's dismay. She was in the bathroom when he arrived. It was John who came up with a solution for him to be out of sight while Trish got ready. He and Alan drove over to the hotel where the reception was to be held, to have a final check on arrangements and deliver Trish's going-away outfit and the honeymoon luggage. After the reception the happy couple were to fly up to Scotland for a week's holiday.

One early highlight had been when Jan had telephoned and announced that the family would be coming after all. Jamie's symptoms had been of short duration and he appeared to have made an overnight recovery, much to Debbie's relief.

In glorious sunshine everybody had departed in hired cars for the wedding venue. Trish and Alan had insisted on a vintage car, and John had arranged it for them. Everybody else had arrived in more modern transport.

Sitting in the pleasant register office surrounded by her family, Debbie had remembered with happiness her wedding to John, and the things that had happened subsequently. Seeing her youngest daughter getting married again had prompted a new peak of emotion.

The recollection of all this as she sat with John that evening prompted her to say: 'You know, John, I really think Trish has got it right this time. I've never seen her looking so happy.'

John nodded in agreement. 'Alan is a great guy. Trish really deserves somebody like him.'

'I thought she looked very pretty,' observed Debbie.

'Like her mother.' He winked at her.

Debbie was still in a reflective mood. 'When we were in the register office today I kept thinking about our own wedding there. So much has happened since then…' She hesitated a few seconds before adding: 'Good and bad.'

'But you're still glad you did it?' John was smiling at her, still in a light-hearted mood.

Debbie did not reply immediately. Instead she jumped up from her chair, gently leaned over him and kissed his forehead. 'Of course I am,' she murmured, before settling down beside him and resting her head on his arm. He placed his arm gently round her shoulders.

She was conscious of him picking up the newspaper again. Then he said: 'We need a holiday ourselves after all the recent events.'

'When and where?' Debbie responded softly, not moving.

John continued. 'I've been reading in this paper. How about touring Ireland? We could go almost straight away.'

Debbie's reaction was swift. She raised her head and looked at him. Her eyes sparkled with enthusiasm. 'That's a fantastic idea!'

'The Ring of Kerry?' he suggested. 'I've always wanted to go there.'

'The Blarney Stone as well.' She was excited now.

They sat in the last rays of the setting sun, chatting and planning. As the light faded and a gentle breeze made the air cooler, they retreated indoors for a hot drink before bed. Then, as dusk gathered around them, they sat together side by side, a happy exhaustion bringing silence between them. Debbie clutched John's hand; her head was on his shoulder. His other arm encircled her, holding her close to him.

'Happy, darling?' he enquired softly.

'Absolutely,' she murmured.

THE END